CLOSE CONTACT

AN ALIEN AFFAIRS NOVEL
Book 2

KATHERINE ALLRED

An Imprint of HarperCollins*Publishers*

This is a work of fiction. Names, characters, places, and incidents are products of the author's imagination or are used fictitiously and are not to be construed as real. Any resemblance to actual events, locales, organizations, or persons, living or dead, is entirely coincidental.

EOS
An Imprint of HarperCollins*Publishers*
10 East 53rd Street
New York, New York 10022-5299

Copyright © 2010 by Kathy Allred
Cover art by Don Sipley
ISBN 978-0-06-167243-9
www.eosbooks.com

First Eos paperback printing: June 2010

HarperCollins® and Eos® are registered trademarks of HarperCollins Publishers.

Printed in the U.S.A.

10 9 8 7 6 5 4 3 2 1

"YOU ARE A PRETTY ONE," HE MURMURED. THEN HIS VOICE HARDENED. "TOO PRETTY TO BE SUCH A GOOD LIAR."

Before I could blink twice, he had my skirt up and my knife in his hand, the tip pressed against my throat. "Helpless females such as you're pretending to be do not carry such weapons. Now I'll have the truth."

Alien Affairs instructors teach us to react to a threat first and think about it later. With no conscious decision on my part, my training took over and I was moving before he finished speaking. My left hand went over his arm and slammed it downward. The move shifted the knife from my throat and numbed his muscles so he loosened his grip. I caught the knife with my right hand and swung it up in an underhand arc.

Both Reynard and I stood frozen in place, staring down at the knife pressed to his stomach, him in surprise, me in horror. It's one thing to theoretically practice killing a human during training. It's another thing entirely to realize you'd almost done it for real, and involuntarily at that.

Especially when the human in question was one I'd been lusting after not a second before.

By Katherine Allred

Alien Affairs
CLOSE CONTACT
CLOSE ENCOUNTERS

For Heather Massey, owner of The Galaxy Express blog, for her enthusiastic support of the science fiction romance genre, and for all the fans who took the time to email and tell me how much they loved *Close Encounters*. You guys are great!

And for Larry, always.

ACKNOWLEDGMENTS

I'd like to give a rousing thanks to my editor, Emily Krump. She always knows how to make my stories better than I can make them on my own. Don't know what I'd do without her.

Thanks also to my agent, Laura Bradford, who is wise and supportive beyond reason, even when I'm in a bad mood because of life situations I can't control.

When I need an answer fast, Wikipedia is my site of choice, so thanks to them for being such a great resource.

And I could spend hours (and have) on the Hubblesite.org, just looking at the fantastic images. They are truly amazing.

CLOSE
CONTACT

<u>CHAPTER 1</u>

Kiera Smith should eat worms and die.

    Yeah, yeah, I know it's not the most politic thing for someone in my position to say. But then, I wouldn't be in this position if not for her, now would I?

Just because she saved the Buri from extinction, killed the bad guys, and gave the world Orpheus crystals is no reason for her to ruin my life.

Being a GEP, someone genetically created to do a particular job, just wasn't enough to make me stand out from the crowd of Naturals I worked with. Neither, apparently, was my name, Echo Adams, which was randomly generated by a computer, as all Genetically Engineered Person monikers are, so none of us accidentally end up with the same name. Zin forbid the Naturals should get us confused. We look so much alike, after all.

That was sarcasm, in case you're wondering. I look absolutely nothing like Kiera Smith. My hair is dark brown, my eyes are this weird greenish-gray color with a peculiar black ring around the pupil, and I'm average height. In other words, about as far from bombshell material as you can get. Most Naturals use the phrase "cute as a button" to describe me. Personally, I've never seen a button I was that enamored of, so I simply clench my teeth and keep smiling.

Unfortunately, the computer that named me had a penchant for Greek mythology from Old Earth. Curiosity being what it is, I'd looked the name up and discovered that according to some Natural named Ovid, Echo was a nymph, a great singer and dancer. That I could live with. But she also scorned the love of men which angered a pervert god named Pan, who tore her to pieces and then scattered her all over creation.

As I walked through the halls of Alien Affairs headquarters, I knew exactly how that felt.

But I digress.

I'm a party girl. No, that doesn't mean I was created to be a pleasure GEP, only that I spent a lot of time at parties. My creation was commissioned by the Galactic Federation's Department of Protocol. I was responsible for planning, hosting, and officiating at ceremonial events for visiting Federation dignitaries and heads of government, as well as coordinating logistics for the visits, making sure they were on time and had everything they needed.

And I was extremely good at what I did.

I loved my job. I loved the hustle and bustle of living in a city that encompassed an entire planet the way Centaurius did, loved being at the center of major universal events and in the know about the latest political intrigue. I loved rubbing elbows with bigwigs from all over the Galactic Federation.

My idea of a good time is three hours at a spa, getting groomed, pampered and massaged, followed by a night of dancing and barhopping with the leader of an obscure planet. Or a planet that wasn't so obscure. And I had no reason to believe that life as I knew it would ever end.

But then, thirty-two months ago—insert ominous music here—Kiera Smith's journal was released to the public.

Suddenly there was a mass stampede to the GEP archives, as Naturals the Federation over dug into the origins of every GEP created. And of course, I won the schite-kickers' lottery. My creator was none other than the infamous Dr. Gertz himself. Simon Gertz, the geneticist with a God complex who also created Kiera Smith, and did Zin knows what to the GEPs he designed, up to and including built-in psi abilities that no one had ever heard of before.

None of that woo-woo stuff from me, I assured my employer. I'm just your average, run-of-the-mill GEP.

But they didn't believe me. They dragged me into the big boss's office, sat me down, and explained they couldn't have a mind reader on staff. Made the hotshot politicians nervous, etc., etc., and yada-yada. Didn't matter one iota that I'd never exhibited a trace of psi talent.

Long story short, they sold my indenture to the Bureau of Alien Affairs.

I mean, come on. Me? Visiting newly discovered planets, hobnobbing with primitive aliens and eating Zin knows what, trudging through uncharted wilderness?

I am not a nature girl by any stretch of the imagination. I hate being dirty and hate animals. The thought of tramping through undisciplined flora where bugs abound makes me nauseous.

And yet, here I was, after completing months of grueling physical retraining—that I was amazingly good at, to my surprise—on my way to a meeting with Dr. Daniels, head of the Bureau of Alien Affairs, to receive my first assignment as their newest and best-groomed agent.

Yes, life sucks, and it's all Kiera Smith's fault. My only consolation is that I now know fifty-six ways to kill with one finger if someone pisses me off. Believe me; in my current mood, I'm not only dangerous, I could do it without batting an eyelash.

With a sigh, I stopped outside an ornately carved door of real wood bearing a discreet gold plaque engraved with Dr. Daniels's name, and rapped sharply three times.

"Come in," a voice called, muffled by the door's thickness.

Grasping the handle, I shoved the door open and stalked inside. I'd expected to work myself through at least three layers of secretaries before actually reaching Dr. Daniels, and then being made to wait for at least thirty minutes, all of which was standard procedure for the Department of Protocol. Instead, I entered a homey, comfortable, medium-sized office with plush, well-used furniture in muted colors. But I didn't let on like I was surprised. Instead I focused on the person who rose to his feet at my entry.

Dr. Jordan Daniels was an imposing man, tall and lean and nice-looking, despite his advanced cycles and silvered hair. There was a twinkle in his blue eyes that made me wary, like he knew something the rest of us mortals weren't privy to.

I'd seen him before, although never up close and personal. About a month after my retraining started, I noticed he occasionally showed up and watched whenever I was working on my new and improved bloodletting skills. And it always unnerved me. Which made me even more upset than I already was.

Why was I being singled out, and why did I care?

Since none of the other newly acquired Gertz GEPs got an audience with the boss, I suspected I was about to find out the answer to the first part of that question.

He gestured to a chair across the desk. "Agent Adams. Please, have a seat. I'm glad we have this opportunity to chat."

I sat and fussily smoothed the lines of the vegan silk business suit I'd chosen for this meeting. Not only did the brilliant red color complement my dark hair, but it also made me feel powerful.

When I was as comfortable as possible, I looked up and arched a brow at him. "I was ordered to this meeting. Don't try to make it sound like an afternoon tea with someone's great-aunt."

With a chuckle, he resumed his own seat. "Quite right, Agent Adams. You were ordered here. So, shall we get on with it?"

He shuffled through a stack of electronic papers that were in front of him and pulled one from the pile. "Here we are." Leaning back in his chair, he studied the data and then peered at me over the top of the sheet.

"Did you know that you tested higher for psi ability than anyone we've recruited since Kiera Smith was first tested?"

Shock ran through me, tinged with fear. Instantly I shook my head. "Your machine must be broken. I don't have any psi ability."

"You were tested three times just to be sure, and a different machine was used each time. They can't all be broken."

"Then someone fudged the results," I snapped. "Don't you think I'd have noticed if I could read minds, or move objects without touching them, or see the future? I can't even pick up emotions like your precious Kiera Smith does. It isn't happening and it's not going to ever happen."

He arched a brow at my vehemence as he replaced the data sheet on the desk. "Yes, I'm well aware of your supposed deficiencies in the psi area, as well as your aversion to having an ability. But we don't always get what we want, and what's intriguing in your case is that the testing devices couldn't pinpoint where your psi talent lies. Apparently, they've never encountered anything like it before, and so have no way of extrapolating what it might be."

"Well, there you go," I harrumphed. "If we don't know what it is and I can't use it, then for all intents, I don't have one and we can forget the whole thing."

"Not quite. I'm hoping we can get a clue about your talent today." He stood and pushed his chair back. "If you'll follow me, we'll get started."

I rose gracefully and trailed him to the door, taking the opportunity while his back was turned to run my fingers through my long, thick hair, assuring myself that every strand was in its correct position. After all, I'd spent a whole five minutes in the styler this morning, taming the unruly locks into their current sleek shape and I didn't want them reverting to form at the wrong time. "Where are we going?"

"Just down the hall."

Unlike his office, the room we walked to was heavily fortified and required a prolonged scan of his biochip before the heavy metal plating swung inward to allow us entry.

Biochips are the height of technology when it comes to identification. DNA can be faked, retinal patterns copied, and fingerprints altered, but the microprocessors that are implanted at birth on Centaurius, for both Naturals and GEPs, are unique to the individual. They record every physical aspect of our lives so no two are alike, and if a person dies or the chip is removed, it self-destructs and therefore can't be stolen. They can't be replicated because there's no way to make a fake chip match the real one. Our entire lives, including medical records, buying history, and available credits are on those tiny pieces of silicone. Only agents lack the chip, for security reasons. The Federation can't have potential spies running around with their ID showing after all.

I surreptitiously rubbed my arm where the chip had once been, feeling naked and alone without it, then forced myself to concentrate on the here and now. Stepping aside, Dr. Daniels waved me through ahead of him.

"I don't understand," I said, uneasily eyeing the rows and

rows of display cases filled with quartz of every imaginable shape and hue. "I mean, I know they're Orpheus crystals, but how are they going to tell you what my psi talent is?"

Dr. Daniels closed the door behind him before he answered. "We've come to realize that certain colors attract certain types of psi abilities. If you've read Kiera's journal, you'll know that Claudia Karle chose a green stone, even though she was never very fond of the color. Since then we've learned that particular shade of green is linked to a spatial psi talent. Which makes sense when you consider Claudia's chosen profession was mapping."

I looked dubiously at the rocks spread around the room. "What am I supposed to do? Whistle and hope one of them comes running?"

His lips twitched once before he schooled his expression and folded his arms across his chest. "Why don't you walk slowly down the rows and see if you feel drawn to one?"

"Can I touch them?"

"If you wish."

Okay, I could do this. Maybe when nothing happened, he'd accept the fact that there had been some kind of mistake on my psi test and leave me alone.

I started down the first row, trying my best to concentrate on the stones. Unfortunately, a low-pitched vibration coming from an ugly metal box standing alone in the corner made that hard to do. Why couldn't they turn the fragging thing off for a second?

A quick glance at Dr. Daniels showed me he was paying no attention to the annoying buzz. Well, if he could stand it, so could I.

Pausing halfway down the first aisle, I picked up a royal-blue stone and turned it in my fingers. The color was fantastic and would set off my lightly tanned skin, but I felt no urge to keep it. I put it back and clenched my jaw at the noise coming from the box. Was it my imagination, or was the damn thing getting louder?

I strolled to the end of the aisle, my Lista Bergen pumps clicking on the marble floor, and then stopped. This was ridiculous. How could anyone expect me to concentrate under these conditions? Why, that sound was actually making my teeth hurt!

"Look," I called to Dr. Daniels, my voice echoing in the big room. "I'm not trying to tell you your business, but you really might want to get a mech in here to check that machine. It's obviously broken."

He stiffened. It was such a slight move most GEPs would have missed it. But having spent my entire life working with Naturals, I'm real good at noticing the minutest change in body language.

"What machine?" he asked.

"The metal one, over in the corner." I pointed. "If it keeps making that Zin-awful noise it could shatter all the crystals in this room."

He stared at me for a second, and then lifted a hand to wearily rub his forehead. "I was afraid of this."

"Afraid of what? Don't tell me it's about to blow up or something." I glanced down at my suit. If it got ruined I'd never forgive him. Even on sale it had cost me an arm and a leg.

Ignoring me, he went to a wall-mounted comm unit and pushed a button. "My dear, could you join me? I'm next door in the crystal room. It appears my suspicions were correct. We've found the one we were looking for."

Who? Me? "They" were looking for me? It wasn't like I'd been hiding, or anything. Dr. Daniels had certainly known where I was located when he ordered me to this meeting. I checked the rest of the room to see if there was someone I hadn't noticed hiding behind a display case.

Nope, we were alone.

Across the room a recessed door slid open and the most gorgeous creature I'd ever seen stepped through. She was long, lean, and lush, with tanned skin and a thick blonde braid that hung to her waist. And she was half naked.

I didn't blame her. If I looked like that, I'd run around naked, too.

Deep emerald eyes swept over me, and I instantly felt dowdy and uncomfortable. The second I got back to my quarters, I was going to burn this scritching suit.

Apparently dismissing me as unworthy, she turned her attention to Dr. Daniels. "You don't mind if I leave the door open, do you? Thor is in a meeting, and Crigo is useless when it comes to corralling Teeah."

A movement from the other room drew my gaze while she spoke, and my jaw dropped. Inside was the biggest fragging rock cat I'd ever seen. He was sprawled languidly in the middle of the floor with a black-haired toddler crawling all over him.

Did I mention that children aren't high on my list of favorite things, either? And neither are rock cats that could swallow me in one bite and still be hungry.

Involuntarily, I took a fast step back and bumped into a display case, which caused both Dr. Daniels and the woman to turn and stare at me.

Wait a second. Abruptly, her words sank in. Thor. And Crigo.

Standing before me was Kiera Smith. My nemesis.

Instantly, all fifty-six of those ways to kill flashed through my mind.

She shot me a smile that was all teeth. "I don't think I'd try it if I were you."

Oh, yeah. I'd forgotten she was an empath, not to mention that overdrive thing she had going on.

"My apologies," Dr. Daniels interjected rather hurriedly. "Kiera, this is Echo Adams, our newest agent."

"The one you were telling me about from the Department of Protocol?"

"Yes, unfortunately." He sighed. "She certainly wouldn't have been my first choice for this assignment. According to her psych reports, she harbors a deep resentment toward you and the Bureau."

"Hey." I waved one hand. "Still in the room, here. And you're damn right I have a lot of resentment. I lost my job, my very way of life because of you two. Did you even once consider the ramifications for the rest of us Gertz GEPs when you released that journal?"

"She does have a point," the blonde goddess commented.

"Maybe." Dr. Daniels shrugged. "But it would have become common knowledge as soon as the scientists combed through Max's Orpheus archives, anyway. At least with your journal available, any wild speculations were squelched before they gained traction. And we *did* make provisions for any GEP affected."

In my peripheral vision, I caught a flash of movement and looked up just as a small iridescent purple creature zipped right at me.

"Eek!" I threw up one arm to protect myself, stumbled, and sent the display case behind me crashing to the floor.

"Peri, no!" Smith's voice snapped above the din of dozens of crystals skittering across the floor.

I peeked through my fingers in time to see the creature settle to another case in front of me, all four of its tiny feet gripping the metal rim.

"Sorry about that," Smith said. "Periwinkle is the only one we have left of Gem and Rayda's latest clutch. She hasn't decided on a companion yet. Her mother is the same color as your suit."

Okay, it was official. The suit, in flames, first chance I got. The thing was obviously cursed. Maybe I could get a refund.

Gingerly I lowered my arm, the better to keep an eye on what could only be a dragon bird. It was strutting along the edge of the case, moving ever closer to me, head cocked to one side as it looked me up and down. An oddly musical chuckling sound issued almost continuously from its small body.

"Shoo." I waved my hands at it, but it paid about as much attention to me as everyone else in this place did.

"Just ignore her," Smith said.

Yeah, easy for her to say. The woman had a giant rock cat for a pet.

And why didn't they turn that dratted machine off? It was driving me to distraction. If they weren't going to do it, I'd simply have to take matters into my own hands.

Warily, I edged around the dragon bird and marched to the box, stepping over the crystals that littered my path. "Where's the off button on this thing?" I asked, running my hands over its smooth surface. "I can't think while it's making that horrible noise."

"See what I mean?" Dr. Daniels commented.

"Yes, as usual, you were absolutely right," Smith replied.

She moved over next to me and did something I missed to the box. There was a whirring sound and a pedestal rose from the top. On it rested a teardrop-shaped black crystal twice the size of my thumb, attached to a silver chain.

My reaction was instantaneous and gut level. Moving so fast that even Smith blinked in surprise, I grabbed the stone and clutched it to my breast. The noise stopped and a warm, contented feeling flowed over me.

Until I saw the way they were watching me. "It's mine," I said fiercely, "and you're not taking it away. So just back off."

"No need to scream." Smith held up both hands, palms out. "Wouldn't dream of taking it from you. It was created for someone here at the training center, we just didn't know who. Looks like you're the one."

Still grasping the stone, I turned to Dr. Daniels. "Does this tell you what my supposed psi talent is?"

"Regrettably, no. It only tells me what your first assignment will be."

"What will it be? And before you answer let me make one thing clear. *I don't do swamps.*"

"Why don't we go into my quarters and get comfortable," Smith interrupted. "This is going to require some explanation."

While they moved toward the still open door, I paused long enough to fasten the chain around my neck and tuck the stone out of sight under my top. It took on the warmth of my skin, and seemed to pulse slightly in time with my heartbeat.

I'd just stepped over the threshold when it dawned on me that I was entering a room containing a toddler, a rock cat, and the dragon bird, which seemed bent on following me.

I came to a screeching halt, staring intently at the rock cat. When he ignored me, I crept along the edge of the room on tiptoes in order to give him as much space as possible.

Smith's quarters looked even more comfortable than Dr. Daniels's office, except all the furniture was over-sized. I chose a chair as far from the cat as possible and sat down.

"Anyone want a drink before we start?" Smith asked.

"Cafftea for me, my dear," Dr. Daniels told her, taking the chair angled near mine.

"I'll have wine. White, please. Maybe a Sirius '45?"

She arched a brow at my exotic choice, but then moved to the food prep unit. "Coming right up."

I turned to check on the cat and came eyeball to eyeball with the dark-haired toddler. We ogled each other in silence, then she reached out and touched my scarlet clad knee.

"Pittie," she said.

"You like it? It's yours. I'll have it sent over as soon as I get back to my quarters. It'll save a lot of smoke damage."

"I don't think it would fit her," Smith chuckled. "But thanks for the offer. Echo, meet Teeah, my daughter."

"Let me guess," sarcasm dripped from my voice. "She's a super GEP, too."

"Not exactly." She scooped the child up and deposited her at a table with a plate of snacks on the surface. "Since she was conceived and birthed the old-fashioned way, she's a Natural. On the other hand, Gertz ensured that our talents would be passed on to the next generation, so she has all my abilities."

"Wonderful. We really need a hundred or so like you around to mess up our lives."

"I think I like you, Agent Adams." She smiled as she handed over the drinks and then took a seat. "You say exactly what you feel, and it's rather refreshing."

"I live for your approval," I told her, taking a small sip of wine. Excellent. "Now, can we get this over with?"

"You know what the Limantti is?" She stretched out those mile-long legs and propped her feet on the cat's back. The animal turned his intense amber gaze on me and my palms broke out in a nervous sweat.

"Large black quartz crystal infested with an alien life form that has enormous psi abilities," I said, trying hard to ignore the cat. "Everyone in the Federation read your journal."

I almost spilled my wine as the dragon bird jumped to the arm of my chair and started making that weird chuckling noise again.

"Well, I discovered after I wrote the journal that the Limantti reproduces through a process called mitosis."

"Cell division," I commented, trying to keep one eye on her and the other on the dragon bird and the rock cat. "It produces a perfect replica of the parent cell."

"Exactly." She beamed approval. "A few weeks after I finished my journal, the Limantti began the process of dividing. It started with a small bump on her surface. When the division was complete, the Sumantti, or Daughter Stone, was totally separate from the Limantti."

"Great. So it gave birth." I lifted a finger and pointed at the dragon bird. "Not to interrupt or anything, but what is this creature doing?"

It had stealthily moved up the chair arm until it was level with my head. Now its wings were half unfurled and it was sticking its chest out, ruffling its feathers proudly while bobbing its head.

"She's displaying. That means she likes you."

"Well, tell it to stop," I snapped. "It's making me nervous."

"Sorry." Smith grinned. "Apparently she's decided you're her kind of people. I'm afraid you're stuck with her now."

"Oh, no." I scooted to the far edge of the chair. "I don't even like animals. She can just go find someone else."

"I've never known one to change its mind once it's picked a partner. Have you, my dear?" Dr. Daniels questioned Smith.

"No. They're very persistent. And I should tell you, they have rudimentary telepathy skills. After a week or so of bonding, she'll know what you're thinking, and broadcast her feelings to you."

"Nope, not happening." I turned sideways on the seat so my back was to the dragon bird. "Now, you were saying?"

She hid her grin by taking a drink from her cup before answering. "Yes, the Sumantti is currently smaller than the Mother Stone, and still very immature. Under normal circumstances, it would be cast into space to search until it found a quartz-rich world with a species advanced enough that it could choose one member to form a symbiosis with.

The search would give it the time and experience needed to mature."

Putting the cup down, she straightened, her expression serious. "However, it took the Limantti so long to find a suitable world that she nearly despaired. She didn't want her daughter to go through what she'd suffered. Instead, knowing how vast our resources are, she asked us to study the problem and find the perfect place for her daughter. Once there, the Sumantti would do the rest. So the Daughter Stone was placed on a ship heading here, to Centaurius, so we could do as the Limantti wished."

"Unfortunately, the Daughter Stone never arrived," Dr. Daniels inserted. "At this point, we don't know if the stone was stolen or if it took matters into its own hands and fled. Normally, the Limantti could find her daughter by herself, but she says the crystal simply vanished from her awareness in the space of a single instant. Now, it's imperative that we locate the Sumantti before its power falls into the wrong hands."

"So how do I fit into this plan?" I was doing my damnedest to ignore the dragon bird. No mean feat, since it had moved to the back of my chair and was now crooning in my ear.

"After the Sumantti vanished," Smith said, "the Mother Stone created that black quartz you're wearing. It's kind of a cross between the Rellanti, the stone used to form the mind bond for the Buri, and the Limantti. She says that once it's activated, it will help the wearer find her daughter. And she insisted that the person designated to wear it would be found here at the training center. Since today was the first time it's reacted to anyone, you're nominated."

My hand went protectively to the crystal lying under my silk top. "But I don't have any idea how to activate it. Or use it, for that matter."

"Honestly, neither do we. The Limantti has never made anything like it before. Auntie Em, the Buri elder, thinks it may be rather like this." She held up her hand so I could see the black lines etched on the palm. "The Limantti gave me this so I could communicate with her no matter where I am."

I gripped the stone a little harder, my mind reeling. "So, I'm supposed to be—what? A priestess to this Sumantti? I've read your journal. Isn't that what a Shushanna really is?"

"No, we don't believe that's the case. A priestess implies there's a religion involved, and there's not. A Shushanna is more of an interpreter and power focus. But that's not what you're going to be. I need you to understand this, Echo. If you try to form a symbiosis with the Sumantti without first being prepared by the crystals, you'll die. That's part of what your black stone is for. It should allow you to communicate with the Sumantti without actually forming the symbiosis. In other words, it will act as a buffer to protect your mind."

"And you know this because . . . ?" I waved one hand in the air.

"The Limantti told me. Just think of yours as a mini-Mother Stone."

"Does it have a name?"

She nodded. "The Buri call it *Imadei*, or 'Little Sister.'"

"This should help get you started on your search." Dr. Daniels reached into his pocket and pulled out another sheet of electronic data. "It's a list of all the quartz-bearing planets that were in the vicinity of where the stone went missing. There are six of them, and we hope that when you get close, the crystal you're wearing will let you know if the Sumantti is there."

I stared at the sheet a second before taking it. "You knew it would be me. Why else would you bring this with you?"

"Let's just say that after seeing your psi tests, I suspected you might be the one. I also watched several of your classes.

You did amazingly well for someone of your—shall we say—background?"

Before I could decide whether or not I was insulted, Smith picked up the conversational ball.

"How old are you?"

"Thirty cycles. Why?"

"Because I'm thirty-four. That means Gertz created you after me, and I don't believe for a second that he wouldn't have used what he'd learned from my process and even made improvements on it. Do you heal fast?"

"I don't know. I've never been hurt."

She arched a brow. "Never? Not even cuts, bruises?"

"No." I was frowning now. "It's not like I indulge in bar fights, you know. Where would I have gotten cut? Until recently the most strenuous thing I ever did was dance."

"How about during your combat training? Those instructors can be pretty heavy-handed, and they aren't prone to cutting the students any slack."

I stuck my nose in the air. "They're also so slow I could have run rings around them. It looks to me like the government would hire a better quality of instructors for this place."

Smith's lips turned up in a smile as she glanced at Dr. Daniels. "She's like me, all right. No doubt about it. At the very least, a normal GEP would take a healthy share of bruises during training. I suspect if one of the instructors did manage to get a hit in, she healed so fast no one noticed she'd been injured."

He put his cup down on the small table between our chairs and stood. "I'd better go order a ship prepared for her."

Was it my imagination, or did Smith's smile turn a bit nasty? "Give her to Lillith. I have a feeling they were made for each other. Plus, it will get the ship out of Max's hair. She has a horrible case of hero worship and is driving him to distraction."

"Excellent idea," Dr. Daniels said. "Agent Adams, you might want to return to your quarters now and pack. You'll be leaving first thing tomorrow morning."

I finished off my wine and set the glass aside. "Who, exactly, is Lillith?"

"She's an artificial intelligence Surge Zephyr, just like my ship," Smith said. "Oh, and when you're packing? You might want to lose the designer clothes and pack a good supply of jumpsuits. They'll last longer."

Right, I was going to take fashion advice from someone who stuck a strip of material between her legs and called it good.

Without further adieu, I took my leave. I was all the way back in my quarters before I realized the dratted dragon bird had followed me.

Ignoring the creature, I sank down on the end of the bed, my entire body shaking. Yeah, I put on a good show, but the truth was, I'd never been so scared in my whole life. I wasn't created to be an agent. I was created to excel at management and organization. Even with all my retraining I was doomed to fail, because I didn't have a clue how to go about this agent business. I was only biding my time, pretending to go along with the status quo. GEPs are long-lived, especially with rejuv treatments, and I figured sooner or later the furor over Gertz's creations would die down and I could go back to doing what I'd been designed to do.

I could go back to doing what I'd been designed to do as long as I didn't have any psi abilities. One whiff of talent and my old bosses wouldn't let me come back under any circumstances. Which gave me a huge problem if Dr. Daniels was right about those psi tests, a problem I was going to do my best to deny existed.

Faking my way through life wasn't helping my state of mind, though. For the first time ever, there was nothing for me to organize, nothing to manage. And I'd never felt so lost, so inadequate, so alone. Let's face it. I'm no Kiera Smith and never will be.

I desperately wanted my old life back. Instead, I was setting out for who knew where, to do who knows what, with an unknown psi ability waiting to ambush me and ruin all my chances at normalcy. The uncertainty was making me crazy.

Yes, Kiera Smith should eat worms and die. And take her damn dragon bird with her.

CHAPTER 2

It was amazing how many colors jumpsuits came in, I decided, admiring my reflection in the plate-glass window at the front of Alien Affairs docking station. Not only did the bright pink make me look good, it was a nice contrast to Peri's iridescent purple feathers. I'd even found boots and a holster for my blaster in the same shade of amethyst.

Yeah, yeah, I know. I don't like animals. But the silly thing made such a racket when I tried to leave without her that everyone was staring. I had to let her sit on my shoulder just to shut her up.

And at least we were color coordinated.

Now, to find my ship. Checking the orders in my hand, I compared the docking slip location to the numbers lit up along the back wall of the station. Looked like my ride was at the far end.

Good thing I didn't have a lot of luggage to tow along with me. I'd sent most of my clothes to storage and had all the jumpsuits I'd ordered delivered straight to the ship, except for the one I was wearing. My carry-on held a few fancy dresses and accessories I couldn't bring myself to part with.

After all, a girl never knows when she'll have to dress for a party at a moment's notice, and it's best to be prepared.

I strutted down the aisle, aware of all the admiring glances I was getting from the males working around the docking station. But there was no time for fun and games right now. I was scheduled to undock in fifteen minutes and I'd never been late in my entire life.

When I reached the ship, I let my carry-on slide to the floor and stared at the closed hatch. What now? I had no idea what the rules were for boarding one's ship, and there didn't appear to be a latch.

Taking a deep breath, I knocked on the smooth surface of the entry. "Lillith?"

"Who goes there?" The strident voice was that of a middle-aged female. It issued from a speaker I hadn't noticed, and immediately set my nerves jangling.

"I'm Agent Echo Adams. I have orders to report to this berth."

"Identification."

Okay, enough. The ship damn well knew who I was. Everyone who passed through the doors of this place was identified to a fare-thee-well. Even without my biochip I had been scanned and my DNA and brainwaves compared to what Alien Affairs had in their databases. That information was checked against the orders on file and instantly transmitted to an agent's assigned ship. Plus, the hard copy of my orders had been instantly verified by a hidden code embedded in the electronic laminate page.

"How's this?" I drew my blaster and pointed it at the speaker. "If you don't open that hatch in two seconds, I'm going to start firing."

"There's no need to get ugly about it," the voice said with a sniff. The door slid open silently. "You can't be too careful these days, what with all the riffraff hanging around stations."

My teeth ground together as I put my blaster away, picked up my carry-on and stepped through the opening into the air lock. "Are you implying I look like riffraff?"

There was a brief and deliberate hesitation as the outer panel closed behind me. "Of course not. It's just that I've never seen an agent dressed so . . . colorfully before."

"Get used to it. Just because I'm alone on a ship doesn't mean I'm going to start wearing those drab, cheap uniforms. I have standards."

"You mean all your uniforms are that bright?"

"Of course not." The ship gave a sigh of relief before I continued. "I got one in black just in case I have to sneak around at night."

Ahead of me, the inner door slid open and I stepped through onto the ship's bridge. It was bigger than I'd expected, and roomy in spite of the equipment consoles lining the space. At the very front, two stationary chairs faced a command center over which a broad, tempered plexisteel window let in light from two of Alpha Centauri's suns.

"Your quarters are down the hall, first door on the left," Ms. Snide-and-Superior informed me. "Sick bay is on the right, and there's a gym in the rear. The deck below this one has three guest quarters and a mess hall. . . . Oh! You have a dragon bird!"

That last came out in a syrupy sweet tone and I figured I'd just gone up a couple of notches in the ship's estimation. "What did you think this lump on my shoulder was, a growth?"

"Well, now that you mention it—"

"Her name is Peri," I said curtly.

Now that we were on board and the creature in question had decided I was stuck with her, she was sitting up and peering around the command center inquisitively.

"If you know Kiera well enough to have your own dragon

bird, you must know Max, too," Lillith gushed. "Isn't he wonderful? So smart and strong. And wow, what a hull."

"Sorry to burst your bubble," I said, moving down the hall. "But we've never met." I rolled my eyes. Only I could wind up with a ship deep in lust. "Peri attached herself to me yesterday during a meeting with Kiera Smith."

"But Max and Kiera—"

I held up one hand to cut her off as I stepped into the room she'd designated as my quarters. "I don't want to hear it. Isn't there something you should be doing? Like taking off, heading out, getting the show on the road?"

My new quarters weren't bad, considering they were on a flying love machine. They had plenty of space—even a full-sized bed against one wall, and lots of storage. There was even a big mirror over a built-in dresser. Peri hopped off my shoulder and strutted in front of her reflection, extending her wings as she admired her image.

Vain creature.

I deposited my carry-on on the bed, moved over behind her and checked my own appearance as the ship continued. "It would help if I knew where we were going, *Agent* Adams."

"You mean you don't know?" Instantly, my palms started sweating. "Didn't Dr. Daniels give you the locations of the six most plausible quartz-bearing planets?"

"Yes, he did." Her voice was caustic. "Would you like me to go 'eenie meenie'?"

Taking a deep breath, I stiffened my spine and lifted my chin. If I was going to fake being an agent, it was time to start pretending I knew what I was doing. "No, I'll be right there."

Leaving Peri examining the lav, I went back to the bridge and took one of the seats. "Show me a map with the systems marked."

A holovid of the Milky Way sprang to life in front of me, its spiral arms extending outward from a flat central disc comprising billions of stars. The six systems, all marked with red arrows, were spread out across the Orion arm.

I stared at them intently, waiting for inspiration to hit, but my attention kept drifting to a spot in the Sagittarius arm, close to where it intercepted the main disc.

And every time I looked at it, the Imadei would pulse against my skin. Faintly, but enough that I could perceive the change.

"What's right here?" I asked, pointing.

"Where?"

"Here." I jabbed my finger through the holo.

Lillith ruminated for a second. "That's the Trinal system. It has three lone planets, and Madrea, the last in line, is the only one with sentient life."

Giving a satisfied nod, I leaned back. "Madrea. That's where we're going."

"Oh, no we're not. It's not even one of the choices."

My lips turned down in a scowl at her impertinence. "Yes, we are," I ground out through clenched teeth. "Who's the agent here, me or you?"

Her response was sulky. "You, I suppose. But I really think you should get Dr. Daniels's permission first."

"Did Kiera Smith get his permission before she acted?"

"Well, no . . ."

"And did Max argue with every decision Smith made?" I asked triumphantly.

"No, of course not. But then, she never told him to go to the Trinal system, either."

"What's so bad about the Trinal system?"

"It's banned, off-limits to all Federation traffic. That's all I know, because the information is classified."

Well, schite. Didn't it just figure? "Patch me through to Dr. Daniels."

"Excellent idea," the ship said, back to being her smug, know-it-all self.

There was a flicker from my right and I swiveled my chair around in time to see Dr. Daniels's image materialize on the deck. "Agent Adams. Having problems already?"

"Nope." I shook my head. "No problem. I just need all the information you can get me on the planet Madrea in the Trinal system."

His eyebrow arched and a worried expression filled his eyes. "Why Madrea?"

"Because that's where the Sumantti is."

"You're sure?"

"As sure as I can be without knowing more about this thing." I touched the stone concealed under the front of my jumpsuit.

Wearily, he lifted a hand and rubbed his forehead. "Then we have a big problem." He lowered his hand and sighed. "The Madrean king shuns the Federation because he thinks our advanced technology threatens his rule. The planet was colonized by a group of technophobes, and he has the charter to prove it. As a result, the planet was banned to all Federation traffic. Unfortunately, the situation is a lot more complicated than merely honoring the king's wishes, or we might have won him over with diplomacy. A wrong step on Madrea could plunge the Federation into a civil war."

He hesitated, reluctance to divulge potentially dangerous information lining his face. I decided to help him out of his dilemma. "I still have a top secret clearance from my previous job, so there shouldn't be a conflict in giving me what I need."

"Yes, I know." With a sigh, he leaned to the right and did something out of the holo's view. "I'm sending the information to Lillith's data banks. Don't share it with anyone. And make sure no one finds out you're an agent for Alien Affairs. Not only could it spark a battle we don't want, you could end up very dead."

Curiosity filled me as he straightened and drummed his fingers on his desk thoughtfully, but I reined it in as he continued. "Once you're there, contact a man named Marcus Kent. He runs a bar, called the Terpsichore, that's near the main castle in the capital city of Bastion. I'll arrange to let him know you're coming."

"Who is he?"

"A former agent of ours who passes on interesting tidbits of information from time to time."

"A spy?"

"Of course not." His lips tilted the tiniest bit on one side. "We would never stoop to spying."

"Of course we wouldn't. Sir," I gave him a smart-ass salute and his smile became full-blown. "Requesting permission to continue, sir."

"Permission granted. Be careful Agent Adams. We don't want to lose you." His image vanished and I suddenly felt very much alone again.

I swiveled my chair back around to face forward. "Have you got the info yet, Lillith?"

"It's still loading. There seems to be quite a bit of it. This may take a few minutes."

"How long will the jump to Madrea take?"

"Approximately four and a half days."

"Okay." I stood. "Let me know when the info is finished loading. I'll look at it later."

"Where are you going?"

I smiled in anticipation. "To organize and color code my clothes."

"You mean you have more colors?" The ship sounded appalled.

"Yes, I do. Wait until you see the lemon-yellow jump-suit." I sighed in pleasure. "It's made of a synsilk and linen blend, and I have gorgeous lime-green boots and a matching holster to go with it."

"Sit!" the ship bellowed.

Automatically, my butt hit the chair. "What?"

"You can start reviewing the first of the material now, while I download the rest."

"What's the fritching hurry? I mean, we have almost five days."

"The hurry is because you're going to need new clothes. I can transmit the order and your measurements ahead to space station ZT Twelve and they'll be waiting when we arrive. But you have to pick them out first, and they have to be typical wear for the Madrean culture. You certainly can't go dirt side looking like you do now. They'd spot you two seconds after you landed." The ship mumbled something I missed.

"What was that?"

"I said, a person on Old Earth with a pair of binoculars wouldn't be able to miss you in those jumpsuits."

"Hmph. There hasn't been anyone on Old Earth since the last big plague. You're just jealous because you can't wear nice clothes. And it's a good thing. You obviously have no taste. But don't worry, I have enough for both of us. When this job is finished, I think we should have your hull done over in a nice shade of turquoise with deep violet trim."

"No," the ship sputtered. "You aren't touching my—turquoise? Really?" She sounded thoughtful.

"Really," I assured her. *Round Two to my side*, I thought a bit smugly. Leaning back in my chair, I crossed my arms.

"So, how am I supposed to know what typical Madrean clothing looks like?"

"There are vids included in the information. From what I can tell so far, it seems we had agents on the planet until five cycles ago."

"Okay, let's see what you've got."

A vid sprang to life in front of me. It was an open-air market, located on a well-trod, grassy field. Overhead, the sky was a deep blue with fluffy white clouds drifting by, and in the background loomed a massive mountain range. Some of the peaks were so high they were draped in a blanket of snow.

Masses of people swirled through and around booths that held merchandise of every sort imaginable. Voices rang from every direction as the recorder moved through the crowd, some murmuring, others calling attention to their wares. There was a feeling of merriment that dominated the whole affair.

Most of the shoppers were men, but here and there small groups of women eyed trinkets or bolts of material, and a few haggled over live fowl or produce.

And every single one of them was covered from their neck to their toes.

I started to frown as I looked them over. It was obviously a warm day, since most of the men were dressed in sleeveless jerkins. But the women wore long skirts in drab colors, long-sleeved tops, and their hair was tortured into stark knots at their napes.

It was the most horrid clothing I'd ever seen.

Just as I opened my mouth to protest, a flash of color captured my attention. "Stop! Go back."

Lillith paused the vid and then slowly reversed it until the woman I'd seen filled the image. She was beautiful. Her straight blonde hair fell almost to the small of her back, and she was dressed in a gauzy skirt belted low enough to show her belly button. Her top was some kind of halter that snuggled around her breasts and tied behind her neck. Each ear was adorned with dangling gold that matched the bangles on her wrists.

A woman after my own heart, I thought with a sigh. Then I hesitated. "Why is she dressed so differently from the other women?"

"I don't know," Lillith said. "I'm still downloading the information. Hang on a second and let me see if I can find anything in what I've got so far."

The second stretched into a full minute before she answered. "It's possible she's one of the Bashalde, the nomadic tribes that inhabit the deserts of the planet. They appear to be less stringent in their moral code."

Yeah, that made sense. Every nomad tribe I'd heard of or read about usually dressed their women more flamboyantly than other cultures. Look at the Old Earth gypsies. There was also the bonus that it would give me an excellent cover story. City people wouldn't expect to know every nomad that wandered through the streets. And if I met another nomad, I could always tell them I was from a different clan than theirs.

I'll admit, it also beat the schite out of wearing those miserable-looking sacks the other women had on.

"Okay, order me one of those outfits she's wearing, but in a better color. Something bright and eye-catching, like red. No one would expect me to be under cover if I'm dressed to attract attention."

"Just one?" Lillith asked, starting the vid again.

I shrugged. "That's probably all I'll need. How long could it take to get a lock on the stone, grab it, and leave?"

"I'll order two just in case it takes a few days to find the crystal."

I glanced back at the vid as Peri zipped in and landed on the back of my chair. Her feathers were a bit damp and she smelled like amberberry shampoo. Since I'd experienced one of her baths earlier that morning, I suspected the lav floor was now covered in three inches of water.

With an inquisitive *cheep*, she sat back on her haunches and hooked her left front talons in a lock of my hair for balance. Her head tilted to one side as she looked at the vid. I checked to see what had captured her attention and blinked in surprise.

Whoever was recording the vid had left the market and stopped on the edge of a cobblestone square. In the foreground, groups of men were engaged in battle. In the background rose the stone wall of a huge building.

"Shall I stop it now?" Lillith asked.

"No, wait." I studied the men. They weren't wearing uniforms of any kind, but I got the impression they were soldiers engaged in a training exercise. There was no blood, no screams of pain. Most of them were bare from the waist up, and sweating profusely. Squared off in pairs, they moved in a graceful ballet of barbarity that seemed almost choreographed.

While a few were practicing hand-to-hand combat, most of them were armed, and the weapons ran the gamut from wooden staves to broadswords to bows. There was very little talking, but the clack of wood on wood and the ringing of metal against metal mixed with grunts of exertion or shouts of triumph when one of the men bested another. I could almost smell the dust and sweat rising from the vid.

Abruptly, a male voice lifted over the noise and all the action came to a staggering halt. From the direction of the stone wall two men strode into view, the others parting like water to give them room.

The one in the front was middle aged but in good shape.

His hair was a light brown threaded through with silver. He was about average height and his shoulders were wide, his stomach flat. The only thing that set him apart from the other men was his manner of dress. His tunic was a golden-colored silk that complemented his hair, and the belt around his waist was studded with topaz and diamonds.

But it was the man behind him who made my breath hitch.

He towered above the tallest of the others by a good four inches, and even though his clothing was plain, all eyes were drawn to him.

His face was a dichotomy of extremes. A wide forehead and dark brows shadowed deep-set eyes of a piercing crystalline blue. Sharp, high cheekbones highlighted the inward curve of cheek that led to a square, hard chin. His mouth was the definition of sensual, with a slash of upper lip playing against a full lower. It was a mouth that looked like it didn't know how to smile, but might stop feminine hearts if it ever did.

Mine was sure giving it hell. Especially when my gaze wandered over those long, muscled legs encased in tight russet-colored material, and snug boots that went almost to his knees. Or roamed over his broad shoulders, where a coarse off-white shirt stretched its seams. Even the muscles in his forearms, exposed by partially rolled up sleeves, were hard and taut.

All in all, he was a walking, hunk-o-luscious advertisement for testosterone overload. Even through the vid I felt an odd magnetic pull toward him. It was an unsettling feeling, and I forced myself to shake it off.

Peri must have picked on my interest, because she leaned so far forward that she did a somersault and landed in my lap. With a gurgle of embarrassment, she righted herself and hopped to the console for a better look.

I didn't blame her. I seriously wanted to crawl into the vid and swarm all over him.

While I was in the process of trying to get my eyeballs back in my head, he moved to face the decked-out dandy, a beam of sunshine picking out copper highlights in the dark chocolate hair that waved gently in a slight breeze. To my horror, the dandy drew a jewel-encrusted sword from the scabbard attached to his belt and took aim at the unarmed object of my lust.

I completely forgot that this had happened at least five cycles ago. My hands tightened into a death grip on the chair arms as the sword whistled through the air toward the man's neck. Only by the time it reached him, he wasn't there anymore. In a blindingly fast move for such a large man, he whirled and stooped as the sharp metal edge passed over his head. And when he straightened, there was a sixteen-inch knife in his hand pointed directly at the dandy's gut.

Breath I hadn't realized I was holding whooshed out of me as the surrounding group of trainees whistled and cheered. The dandy laughed and clapped the man on the shoulder before returning his sword to its sheath.

As I leaned back in my chair, the vid shut off and my entire body went into mourning. I wasn't done looking at him yet, damn it all. "Who is he?" I asked Lillith.

"I believe that was Reynard du'Marr, commander of the king's army. The man with the jewels was King Politaus. According to my information they often put on exhibits for the common soldiers. It keeps up morale to know their ruler is just a man like them." She gave a delicate snort. "As if."

"Du'Marr," I mused, ignoring everything else she'd told me.

"It means 'to move like lightning,' in their language."

Immediately I perked up. "You have a language program?"

"Yes, it was included in the download. It seems to be based on Galactic Standard, so by tomorrow you'll speak Madrean like a native."

"Excellent. I'll be able to communicate with him."

She let out the equivalent of an AI gasp. "What do you mean, communicate with him? Are you out of your mind? On the list of Madrean men you must avoid at all costs, he's Number One."

Instantly, my heart sank. "Why isn't the king Number One?"

"Because, while the king might grab your ass, he wouldn't really *look* at you. Reynard du'Marr would. The man didn't get to be commander of the imperial army by being a slacker. He's sure to notice every little detail, and according to my files he's totally loyal to the king."

My lips formed a pout. "I bet I could pull it off and he'd never realize I was an off-worlder. Just for an hour." I thought that over. "Okay, maybe three hours. With not much talking involved."

Her voice took on the stern tones of a judge handing down a sentence. "You have been a full-fledged, certified agent for all of eight hours. You have no practical experience. This man is a warrior, trained to be observant, and he's dealt with members of the Federation before. Promise right now that you won't seek him out, or arrange to meet him 'accidentally.' If you can't give me your word, I'm turning around right now and heading back."

Surprised, I turned to look out the side window. Sure enough, I'd been so absorbed in the vid that I hadn't noticed her taking off. Already, Centaurius was a silvery dot, and the suns were dwindling rapidly. Even Primus, the small red sun usually rendered invisible by the brighter rays of the two yellow stars, was discernible.

A hard, hollow knot formed in my chest as I watched the

planetary system fade away into the distance. It was temporary, I assured myself. I *would* get my old life back.

"Well? I'm waiting."

I swiveled back to face forward and sighed. "Fine. I promise not to go looking for him, or try to meet him accidentally. As much as it pains me, I will do everything in my power to avoid the man."

"And if you do happen to run into him, you will not speak or even bat your lashes at him."

"Oh, come on! What if he asks me a question?"

"Pretend your throat has been cut."

"Yeah, that'll really fool him."

"I can always arrange to make it real," she said, her voice taking on a silky tone, as if the idea pleased her.

"No, you can't." I grinned. "You're programmed to protect your partner. And you can't change who you were created to be, any more than I can. So why don't we call a truce and try to get along?"

She grumbled for a bit, and then gave in. "Truce."

Satisfied, I leaned back in the chair. "Do you have any more vids with Reynard in them?"

"Agent Adams!"

"Well, I have to start somewhere," I told her. "Maybe if I watch him enough it'll get him out of my system." But even as another vid sprang up in front of me, I knew I was lying. I'd never been so instantly attracted to a male before. No way was watching a few vids going to get him out of my system.

CHAPTER 3

Time really flies when you're immersed in learning about the culture and politics of a planet full of people, even when the facts are limited. After all, the Federation only had a half cycle to gather info before they were kicked off Madrea, and that was five cycles ago. But what they did get, along with what they pieced together from old records and added to the modern political brouhaha surrounding the new planet, was fascinating.

Madrea's original settlers had boarded the *Zodiac*, one of the first privately owned colony ships to leave Centaurius.

According to Bureau records the human cargo had consisted of two groups that had stayed segregated after migrating to Centaurius from Old Earth. The first was a branch of the Romany people called the Bashalde, and the second comprised descendants of people from Spain, Italy, and France. The groups had only two things in common: a shared language and a hatred of modern technology. Each group longed for the days when life was simpler and work was done by hand. In other words, Dr. Daniels had been right. They were technophobes.

The Bashalde were nomads, their society pastoral. They

claimed the southern deserts on the largest land mass of Madrea, traveling from city to city, selling or trading the animals they bred, offering up their crafts and performing.

Although they roamed separately in family groups, the Bashalde were one people, ruled by one man, Chief Lowden. In the Bashalde culture, he was the spirit and heart and law of the clan. Anyone not belonging to a Bashalde tribe was considered a *Gadjee*, or outsider.

The second group was basically a bunch of farmers, using their agrarian roots to turn the alien landscape into arable soil suitable for their Earth-normal crops. They claimed the northern part of the largest continent, and, as most social humans are prone to do, built cities.

The majority of these municipalities were small communities, with the only really big city being Bastion, where the king's castle was located. After so many generations, they'd forgotten the city was named after Francois Bastion, the captain of the *Zodiac*, had even forgotten their ancestors originated on Old Earth. They barely remembered Centaurius. And the rest of the universe had forgotten them, until an exploration team stumbled across Madrea six cycles ago.

In itself, finding a lost human colony wasn't that unusual. It happened every decade or so. What was unusual about Madrea was how closely they'd stuck to their original charter, barring anything that remotely smacked of high technology. Which was why, after the shock of first contact wore off, the king had arbitrarily banned the Federation from the planet.

That was his excuse, anyway. The Federation had a different take on the matter. As they saw it, King Politaus thought rule by democracy endangered his job security, and he wasn't going to let his people get any bright ideas on the subject.

Whether or not to force the issue had been a hotly debated topic in the hallowed halls of the Galactic Federation, because it turned out that Madrea was rich in sunstones, which the Federation desperately wanted to get its hands on.

Since I'd been gone from the Department of Protocol for some time now, I'd only heard vague rumors of sunstones. I searched the files until I found an explanation. It seemed sunstones were an opalescent rock that produced energy in massive quantities all out of proportion for their size. The Federation scientists theorized that a two-pound rock could provide power for an area the size of eight city blocks on Centaurius for several cycles. Team one up with a surge crystal that amplified power and the possibilities were endless. Unfortunately, until Madrea was discovered, they were rarer than surge crystals and worth more, ounce per ounce, than Orpheus crystals.

And the native Madrean population had no idea what they were sitting on. They used the sunstones, which gave off a soft glow, as a light source. All over the inhabited continent of Madrea, billions of credits' worth of sunstones, controlled primarily by the Bashalde, sat idle in glass lamps.

It was enough to drive the greedier element in the Federation Council to the brink of war. This faction was led by Helios One, a resource-poor system in the Perseus arm of the Milky Way Galaxy.

Although if you asked me, Losif Strand, the hereditary ruler of Helios One, was more interested in lining his own pockets than in helping his people. At one point, he'd been under charges for war crimes against the Federation, but his slimy, high-priced lawyer had slid him through a legal loophole and Strand had gone free.

I'd never met him, but I'd heard his speeches to the Federation Council and I'd seen him from a distance, across the grand ballroom at the social gatherings held after each council session.

He was a tall, hawkish man with dark hair and odd amber

eyes. Not bad-looking, per se, just too austere and self-absorbed for my tastes.

But the law is the law, and Strand had to leave Madrea alone. And in case any of the worlds in his coalition got too bold, the more conservative worlds were standing by to enforce any breaches of the Federated Constitution. All in all it was a very touchy situation, and I could see why the Federation enforced the king's ban on the planet. Just by being there I could tip the uneasy peace that was currently holding by a thread.

Not to mention what would happen if it were discovered that Madrea's abundance of quartz had suddenly turned the world into a potential secondary source of Orpheus crystals, thanks to the Sumantti's presence on the planet. And one not controlled by the Buri at that.

Immersed in the data as I was, five days zipped by almost without my noticing. My only breaks were for meals, sleep, and the brief time I was on ZT Twelve, picking up my Bashalde clothes.

A word to the wise: never take a dragon bird on a space station filled with boutiques and jewelry stores. They have an affinity for anything that glitters, and no concept of payment for goods received. It took some fast talking on my part to keep from being arrested for shoplifting fifteen minutes after we stepped out on Level Six.

And to add insult to injury, I ended up paying for the gaudiest necklace ever created just to keep the creature happy and occupied while I finished my business. It had flowers the size of Peri's head in garish colors, and the center of each flower was a fake gemstone. It was also long enough to wrap around her five times, so I had no idea what she planned to do with it, except gloat like a miser over his gold.

"Are you ready?" Lillith's question interrupted my attempts to forget we'd reached Madrea and I was about to be dumped in the mountains, in the dark, surrounded on all sides by raw, uninhibited nature. Let's face it. Being created for the Department of Protocol and raised in a crèche with other GEPs of the same bent just doesn't prepare a gal for this kind of thing.

"No. Not that it makes any difference." I gave my image one last glance in the mirror. Not bad, if I did say so. The pale beige skirt was just thin enough to give a hint of legs and just thick enough to conceal all the pertinent parts, including a close-fitting weapon sheath attached to my calf. The material swirled around my ankles every time I moved, soft and sexy.

A wide, lemon-yellow belt of soft leather nestled low on my hips, showing off my belly button and stomach. The silky halter top matched my belt, and also served to hide the Imadei, which I'd tucked beneath the silk. It nestled between my breasts, a warm, living stone. The gold bangles on my arms and ears jingled when I walked.

"Are you absolutely certain they don't have the technology to spot your landing?" I asked Lillith.

"I'm sure. Remember, the original colonists signed a charter shunning any form of technology they couldn't make with their own hands. They wanted a strictly agricultural world. Now the king keeps all the Federation's toys away from Madrea, so there's no detection equipment capable of spotting me. The only ships that land here belong to the black-market scum whose main business involves selling information. And even the black marketeers are few, since they have to get by the Federation outposts without being stopped and searched. The only way to get close is to jump right into the system the way I did, which is very dangerous for ships that don't have an artificial intelligence in control. Most black marketeers can't afford AI ships. But to be safe,

I just did a scan and there are no ships currently in the area, so no detectors."

Suppressing a shudder of anxiety, I picked up the artificially aged leather pouch from my bed and tossed a cloak over my arm. "If there are no detection devices, why can't you drop me closer to the city?"

"Because, even with my lights off, there's too much risk of someone seeing me closer to the city. I've scanned the area where I'll drop you and there's no one around. It's not that far a walk, so stop griping."

"What if I get lost?" I made my way to the command deck with Peri following. "Seriously, one tree looks pretty much like another to me."

"I'll be right above you in a geosynchronous orbit, tracking you through your transmitter chip. If you start going the wrong way, I'll tell you."

Nervously I lifted a hand to touch the tiny scar behind my right ear. This particular type of chip was nothing like the biochip used as ID on Centaurius. This one had been implanted shortly after Alien Affairs bought my indenture, and it served as a voice transmitter, receiver, and tracking device for my ship. I'd been heavily trained in its use. Learning to communicate through subvocalization had been one of the hardest things I'd ever done, but now I was thrilled I'd mastered the ability. Being able to talk to Lillith without anyone knowing gave me a sense of security. Sort of.

At least it would allow her to locate my cold, lifeless body when some huge beast had me for breakfast. Or a small beast. Or a bug.

"What if my chip breaks?" I fretted.

"Echo, it's not going to break. It's too small to break. And if it were going to fail, it would have done so long before now."

"If I die, it's your fault," I muttered.

"I've handled first-time agents in conditions a lot worse than this and they survived to tell about the experience. Besides, you're a Gertz GEP. The only way someone can kill you is a direct shot to the head or heart. Anyplace else and you'd heal right up in seconds. All you have to do is pay attention to what I tell you and stay out of trouble."

"Fine, Oh Great One. Speak."

She let my sarcasm slide and concentrated on the details. "As you know, Madrea was one of the earliest planets colonized by Earthlings, but their ship's tracking devices went awry and no one knew where they went until six cycles ago. So any animals you encounter will be of Earth origin. Do you have your knife?"

I lifted my skirt enough so she could see the sheath clinging just below my knee. It held a knife with a wickedly sharp twelve-inch blade. Then I gasped as what she'd said sank in. "You don't expect me to actually fight an animal with nothing but a knife, do you?"

"You probably won't have to. I'll let you know if there's anything dangerous in the area. However, even with infrared scanners I can't see inside caves, holes in the ground, etc. If the unexpected occurs, wouldn't you rather have a weapon?"

Indignantly, I let my skirt fall. "I'd rather have a cannon. Or at the least, my blaster."

"It's too dangerous. One glimpse of a blaster and everyone would know you're Federation. Now, I'm going to drop you in a valley about forty-five minutes before sunrise. Wait there until it's light enough to see where you're going, and then walk toward the rising sun. When you reach the top of the hill, you'll be able to see the spires of the castle. Head straight for them and you'll avoid the outlying farms. You should reach the city late in the evening."

"What? I thought you said it wasn't that far a walk!"

"It's not. Remember, even though their weeks are eight days long, the Madrean days are two hours shorter than Centaurius's. And if you jog part of the time, you'll get there faster."

I glanced down at the sandals strapped to my lower appendages. "I'm pretty sure jogging is not an option in these things. They wouldn't last a kilometer, and there's no way I'm getting nature on my bare feet."

A clanking noise caught my attention and I looked around in time to see Peri stagger out of my quarters dragging that stupid necklace with her. She must have realized we were getting off the ship and gone back for it, and it was too heavy for her to carry when she was flying.

"Oh, no you don't," I told her. "You're going to be hard enough to explain even without you hauling that thing along behind you. You'll have to leave it here."

For the last two days I'd picked up her emotions, faintly at first, then stronger. Now she glared at me and rebellion rolled off her in waves.

"Okay, look, will you leave it here if I promise to let you play with my bracelets when I'm not wearing them? Lillith will take good care of the necklace for you, and it'll be here when you get back."

She studied my bracelets for a second, then gave a happy *cheep* and took the necklace back to my quarters.

"If anyone asks about her, tell them she came from the Dark Continent. None of the Madreans have ever been there and lived to tell about it, and occasionally, odd creatures from there wash up onshore. No one will know the difference."

"Why haven't they been there?" I moved to one of the windows and looked down at the planet as the ship began a rapid descent. Peri came back, flying this time, and landed on my shoulder.

"Superstition, probably. There's a mean current off the continent, and lots of submerged rocks. The Madrean ships aren't sturdy enough to handle being repeatedly bashed into stone. The ones that tried were likely wrecked and never heard from again."

Before we reached the atmosphere, all the ship's lights went off and our speed picked up. "Hang on," Lillith told me. "This landing area is going to be a tight fit."

I gripped the console in front of me as darkened treetops rushed toward us, my breath catching at the sudden conviction that we were crashing. Before I could comment—or scream—there was a gentle bump and I heard the air lock doors open. I tried to move, but it felt like my feet were glued to the deck.

"Go!" Lillith's urgent whisper got through to me and I darted through the tube and down the stairs she'd extended.

The stairs withdrew, the doors closed, and the ship silently lifted from the ground. Before I could blink twice she was gone, leaving me all alone in the dark with no company except a tiny dragon bird.

"You aren't alone." The ship's voice came from the chip behind my ear.

"What? You're a mind reader now?" I subvocalized. My eyes were straining to pierce the darkness around me and my skin was clammy in spite of the chill night air.

"I don't have to be. I know you. There's nothing to worry about. The only life forms nearby are so small they'll be more afraid of you than you are of them."

Life forms? Eeek! I whipped around wildly, trying to see anything that might be creeping up on me. From off to my left came the sound of a splash and I jumped high enough to nearly make it back on board the ship.

"What was that?"

"A fish. There's a pond in that direction."

I tried desperately to slow my heartbeat. "Ew. You mean a real, live slimy fish? Not the kind that comes on a plate?"

A sigh sounded in my ear. "None of them start out on a plate. Now take a deep breath and try to relax."

Following her advice, I inhaled deeply and then coughed. "Good grief. What's that smell?"

"It's called fresh air," the ship told me caustically.

"Yeah? I've heard of that." I took another sniff and wrinkled my nose. All kinds of unknown odors assailed me, and I didn't know what to make of them. Some of them were kind of tangy and intriguing. Others were damp and nasty. I tried hard not to breathe those last in, and concentrated on my surroundings.

"Why is it so cold? I thought you said it was late spring."

"It is, but you're at a higher elevation, where the nights are still cool."

Right. I knew that.

I reached for my cloak, but before I could get it unfurled Peri took off, the dark closing around her immediately. Hastily, I whipped the cloak open and swung it around my shoulders. "Peri? Peri, you come back here right this minute!"

She popped out of the night right in front of my nose, and I recoiled in surprise before she cooed at me in reassurance. "Don't do that again," I scolded her. "You scared me. Until I can see where we are, you stay on my shoulder."

"It shouldn't be long now," Lillith said as the dragon bird returned obediently to her perch. "The sun is coming up."

My eyes were finally getting used to the dark, and I realized she was right. The tree trunks were now visible as ghostly black hulks against a deep gray background. I huddled inside my cloak, taking comfort from Peri's presence, and waited quietly.

Overhead, the sky went from black and star filled to a midnight blue, then gradually lightened until the stars faded away. Fog swirled around my feet, adding an eerie quality to the setting I could have lived without.

Abruptly, the top edge of the sun appeared over the hill in front of me and fired golden beams of light into the valley. I blinked in surprise at how close the trees were and how small the clearing was. It was a miracle Lillith had managed to squeeze into the space.

Squaring my shoulders, I set off gingerly through the dew-drenched grass. Peri launched herself from my shoulder and hovered above a patch of flowers, humming in pleasure before she dived in and delicately sipped nectar from a blossom.

Walking carefully to spare my sandals, it took the better part of an hour to reach the top of the hill, and by then the hem of my skirt was damp and sagging. I held the material away from me so the morning breeze could dry it a bit as I paused on the summit to look out over the land below.

The downward side of the hill was rockier than the climb up had been, and the trees were smaller and fewer in number. At the base, the land sloped into green pastures interspersed with cultivated fields and areas of forest. Here and there I saw large animals grazing, and way off to my right, there was a small cottage with a wisp of smoke coming from its chimney.

The air was pristine, with no smog or dirt to hinder the view. Far to the north, sunlight sparked off the tops of battlements and towers that glittered as if they were jewel encrusted.

"Lillith? Why does the castle sparkle like that?" I asked.

"Quartz," she replied in an ominous tone. "The stone for the castle was cut from it."

Great, just great. That meant the Sumantti would try to colonize the building. "Can you tell if any of it is infested with the life form that inhabits the Orpheus crystals?"

"Not without examining a sample under a molecular microscope. Besides, I doubt the Sumantti has been here long enough to send her colonies out very far. Are you picking up anything from the Imadei?"

I pulled the stone from under my top and curled my fingers around it, eyes shut to enhance concentration. Nothing happened.

I opened my eyes and tucked it away. "No, not a thing. I haven't felt anything from it since it indicated the Sumantti was on this world. The crystal could be anywhere."

"Well, the castle is the most logical place, and you have to start somewhere. Now get a move on. Time is wasting."

Peri whizzed by me, her iridescent feathers flashing shades of blue and green amidst the purple as she flew. She was radiating happiness at finding so many flowers. Even though Lillith had stocked a good supply of nectar in hope that Kiera's dragon birds would visit so she'd have an excuse to contact Max, Peri apparently preferred finding her own food.

I went down the slope after her, giving a couple of small, nasty looking lizard-like creatures a wide berth. It wasn't easy navigating the loose gravel while keeping a wary eye on them in case they attacked. Sliding as much as walking, I was soon out of their reach. It didn't take long after that to reach the bottom, and when I was on solid, relatively flat ground, I reached into my pouch and took out a high energy Zip Bar, eating it as I walked, my nose wrinkling with every bite. If it hadn't been covered in chocolate, I couldn't have swallowed the nutritious gunk.

By noon, I'd shed the cloak. I folded it into my pouch when I stopped to pull out the water skin and take a drink. So far, I hadn't met any people, but signs of civilization were becoming more frequent. I'd crossed several dirt lanes, and stumbled across a rock building that must have served as a barn, from the smells it emitted, hidden among a grove of trees. Animal shelters became more frequent, too, and unlike the first barn, the stables were occupied. I could hear snorts and the shifting of large bodies inside.

From the data Lillith had, the Madreans relied on horses for transportation and heavy work. I suppose it made sense to keep them close to the city.

I'd often escorted dignitaries and their families to the Earth Zoo on Centaurius, so I knew what horses looked and smelled like. And I knew that where there were stables full of horses there had to be handlers, but so far, I'd seen no humans.

The sun was going down when I finally entered the outskirts of Bastion City, and I was getting hungry again. I'd only brought one Zip Bar because it wouldn't do to let a local get their hands on the Federation rations, and the scent of cooking food drifting on the air made my mouth water.

Setting my hunger aside, I looked at the buildings with interest, surprised at how neat they all looked. They were small but well built, with stone walls rising to thatched roofs. Flowers of all colors and shapes lined the fronts on each side of the doors, making Peri hum with excitement.

Oddly, the houses weren't lined up with any symmetry. It looked like some giant had gathered them in his fist, given them a few shakes, and then tossed them to the ground, letting them fall where they may. And that was where they still sat. Narrow cobblestone streets wound around and through the city like pebbled snakes. The effect was strangely agreeable to the eye and made me feel like I'd been dropped into a fairy-tale kingdom.

It took a few seconds for me to realize there was an eerily still quality about the city. I could hear low voices inside the homes, but no children were outside playing, no men coming and going, no women visiting with neighbors.

A sudden rash of goose bumps crawled down my arms, and I rubbed them to soothe the sensation. "Lillith, what's going on? Why aren't there any people out?"

"I don't know. Something isn't right." She paused for a second. "Maybe there's a danger I don't perceive. There are too many soldiers on patrol in the streets. It might be a good idea to avoid them until we find out what's going on."

"Any suggestions on how I'm supposed to do that?" I called Peri back to my shoulder, afraid she'd attract unwanted attention.

"There's a building with no heat signature and a recessed door not far from your location. Turn left at the next inter-section, then right. The building is three down. Wait there until it's full dark."

I followed her directions and found the building with no problems. It was a huge edifice, made of square-cut stone, and it dwarfed the houses around it. Even in the twilight it had a dark and eerie feeling. The front of the building faced away from the setting sun, so the entry was full of shadows. Moving all the way to the back of the entryway, I took my cloak from the pouch. It was a dark blue and would help conceal me.

Pausing in the act of putting it on, I stared at the face etched on the door. It was a woman—a beautiful, devastat-ingly sad woman. A cowl covered her hair, leaving only that perfect face to draw the eye.

"What is this place?" I asked Lillith, unsettled because it felt like the woman was watching me in sorrow.

"I believe it's a church," she answered. "There are dozens of similar buildings scattered throughout the city."

"I don't remember seeing anything about religion in the files."

"That's because you skipped that part. The original colo-nists practiced Catholicism, but over the centuries, the father and son got left behind. Now they only worship the mother.

The sociologists believe it evolved in that direction because men outnumbered the women settlers by five to one. The balance between the sexes is still skewed on Madrea, so motherhood is revered as the highest calling a woman can have, with girl children being highly prized. The Bashalde practice a totally different type of religion. They have so many gods it's hard to keep track of them."

Maybe I should have studied the files a little more, I thought, trying to get comfortable in spite of the woman looking down on me. I'd barely settled when Lillith's voice whispered in my ear. "There are two soldiers coming your way. Don't move."

My breath froze in my lungs and I did my best to shrink into the wall. Time seemed to stand still as I waited for them to discover my hiding place.

They sauntered into view and I lowered my gaze, unwilling to take a chance they might feel my stare. But I'd seen enough to know they weren't acting like men expecting trouble. Both were dressed in tight black pants, knee-high boots, and ocher tunics topped by brown leather vests. The only weapons they carried were swords attached to belts around their waists.

One made a low-voiced comment and the other laughed. Neither slowed nor so much as glanced at my refuge as they went by, and my puzzlement deepened.

The sound of their footsteps faded into the distance, and as soon as I was sure it was safe, my breath whooshed out in relief and muscles I'd tensed went limp.

"None of this makes sense," I told Lillith. "It's like they're out for an evening stroll."

There was no answer.

"Lillith?" Incipient panic tinged my voice.

"Wait." She was silent for another second as the twilight deepened. "I think I know what's happening."

"You want to clue me in?"

"A ship just came out of hyper-drive and is approaching the planet. No Federation markings, and the outer lights are off. It's armed to the teeth."

Alarmed, I straightened. "Can they see you?"

"No. I'm parked beside a large asteroid. If they used detectors, they'd think I was part of the rock. But so far, they haven't scanned the area. I'm betting King Politaus ordered everyone to stay inside tonight so they wouldn't see the ship land."

"The soldiers will see it."

"Yes, but he can control them better than he can the entire population. He probably wants to keep rumors to a minimum. Unless he's stupid, which I doubt, he must know the Federation has spies in the city. The good news is, the soldiers don't expect anyone to be out, so their guard is down. If you stay in the shadows, they'll never see you. Now, go right."

I slipped away from the door, clinging to walls and darting across the open spaces in the descending darkness. Twice more I had to dodge soldiers, one pair coming so close my cloak fluttered in the wake of their passage.

Long before I reached the castle, full night arrived, and the huge building was more something I felt than saw. It loomed over me, deeper patches of darkness indicating the many angles and ells that made up its exterior.

Instead of approaching the front, with its wide stone steps, colonnades, and well-lit massive doors, Lillith directed me to the western side. At this point, my only plan was to get inside and hope the Imadei would let me know where the Sumantti was hidden. With that in mind, I tiptoed along the wall, searching for an unlocked door.

"The ship landed," Lillith told me.

I paused in a pool of shadow, a locked door behind me.

"Did they unload any cargo?" For a fleeting moment, I wondered if they might be bringing the Sumantti, but they couldn't be. The Imadei wouldn't have indicated this star system if the stone hadn't been here yet.

"No cargo. Three men and two female children got off. They entered the castle through a door in the back. Without a full medical scan I can't be one hundred percent positive, but it appears that the larger girl was drugged. She wasn't unconscious, but acted dazed and sluggish, as if she'd just awakened and was still disoriented."

I pondered the information, not sure what to do with it, if anything. Before I could reach a conclusion, the door behind me swung wide and a man stepped out, flooding my hiding place with light. Blind panic swept over me as he halted, his gaze locked on mine. His mouth opened to yell, but he didn't get the chance.

Abruptly, my reflexes took over and time slowed to a crawl. My cloak and pouch went flying as I spun, lashed out, felt my foot connect with flesh and bone.

He crumpled at a snail's pace, the words still trapped in his throat, his body giving the appearance of a rag doll with part of the stuffing removed.

Frantically I looked around for other attackers, only to realize something odd was going on. Off to my right, the cloak and pouch were inching their way through midair, and Peri's wings moved in slow motion on the beginning of the down stroke she'd started when she first launched herself from my shoulder.

Damn.

I inhaled a shuddering breath and shut my eyes, convinced I was imagining what my sight insisted was true.

Damn.

Slowly, I got my heart rate under control and relaxed muscles primed for action.

Damn.

Immediately, everything around me resumed its normal pace. Peri gave a squawk of surprise just as I heard the pouch hit the cobblestone.

"You went into overdrive!" Lillith's voice was tinged with awe. "It was like you vanished."

"Don't be ridiculous," I snapped, turning my attention to the soldier. Zin, was he dead? Had I really gone into overdrive? My heart started pounding again, and my head joined the party.

I'd never exhibited any abilities beyond what was normal for GEPs before. But then, moving at super speeds wouldn't have done much for me on a dance floor, and nothing had ever frightened me enough to trigger an automatic reaction, either.

What else was I capable of that I'd never had occasion to discover?

Pushing the confusion away, I leaned down to check the man for a pulse. To my relief I found one. I certainly hadn't meant to kill him. I hadn't even meant to hurt him. It was like my body had reacted with no conscious direction from my mind.

"You! Halt!"

The voice came from the hall on the other side of the still open door, accompanied by the sound of pounding feet. Three men were charging toward me, swords drawn and murder in their eyes.

"Run!" Lillith yelled in my ear. "But don't go into overdrive. It's dangerous!"

I didn't hang around to argue. Besides, I'd read Kiera Smith's journal, too. I knew what the physical results of going into overdrive would be if I kept it up. Without stopping for my cloak or pouch, I took off along the side of the wall, only to be brought up short by an angry screech from Peri.

Whirling around, I was just in time to see her eyes go bloodred with rage as she dove at the front-runner, beating him with her wings, her small talons scratching his face.

Oh, Zin. She was trying to protect me.

"Peri," I yelled. "Follow me!"

She shot into the air, barely avoiding a wildly swung sword, and came after me.

Once I was sure she wouldn't attack again, I turned and kept running.

"They're gaining," Lillith informed me grimly. "You need to find a place to hide."

I rounded a corner, too busy to reply, and saw a door ahead with a lamp shimmering over it. That door was my only chance. If it was locked, I was screwed.

Still on high, I grabbed the handle and wrenched. To my stunned amazement, there was a splintering reverberation and the wood tore loose from the hinges.

Holy scritch, had I done that? Maybe the wood was rotten.

"Stop gaping and *go*!" Lillith yelled at me.

The sound of feet hitting the cobblestones, mixed with loud yells, had me squeezing through the gap between the door and the frame. Once inside, I paused long enough to see that the hallways made a *T* with its stem stretching out directly in front of me. Since that was the obvious choice, I turned right, for all intents doubling back in the direction I'd come from.

Peri zipped by over my head and darted into a smaller side passage just as the yells of my pursuers were answered by others already inside. They seemed to come from all directions at once, and I slowed as I followed the dragon bird into the dimly lit corridor, trying to determine where the soldiers were located so I wouldn't run straight into them.

"Lillith, which way?"

"I can't see you anymore," she wailed. "Try to find an empty room you can lock from the inside. Maybe you can hide and wait them out."

Wonderful, just wonderful.

There were three doors along the hall and I tried each in turn. All were locked, and for a second I was tempted to try tearing one of them from its frame. Unfortunately, that would be a clear indication of where I was hiding.

The castle was like a maze, halls extending in every direction with no rhyme or reason. I chased Peri through three more turns, by now so disoriented I didn't have a clue where I was. But I had to go to ground, and soon. The noise of the soldiers was getting closer, and it came from both behind and in front of me. Somehow, they had neatly boxed me in.

Only one more door lay between me and the next hallway, and I could hear the sound of many feet coming from just out of sight in the passage. Peri was hovering anxiously in front of the last door as though urging me through.

Taking a deep breath, I silently lunged the remaining few feet and tried the handle. Hallelujah! It opened.

Keeping one eye on the end of the hall, I slid through and held the door just wide enough for Peri to follow me inside. Gently, I eased it closed, ignoring Peri's satisfied squeak while I looked for a lock.

There! A metal latch was positioned on a pivot in the center of the door. When swung down, it would fit perfectly into a corresponding notch on the frame.

I lowered it softly and then turned to face the room. And came to a shocked halt, my gaze locked on the naked man who was frozen in the act of stepping from a tub of bathwater.

Standing before me in all his unabridged glory, mouthwatering rivulets streaming down his bare, lusciously bronzed skin, was the one man I was supposed to avoid at all costs.

Reynard du'Marr, commander of the king's guard.

CHAPTER 4

I pressed my back against the door, thinking faster than I'd ever thought before, while he reached for a drying cloth and wrapped it low around his hips. His piercing eyes never left me.

Peri, damn her feathered hide, had somehow led me right to him, and it was now up to me to salvage the situation.

"Please, sir," I whispered, making sure my voice was low and quivering with terror. Which wasn't much of a stretch in my current condition. "Can you help me? I'm new to your city and men are chasing me."

A heavy fist hit the outside of the door, making me jump for real. Without a word, Reynard stepped forward, moved me aside, and lifted the latch to pull the door open. Its heavy panels shielded me from the man who waited on the other side and gave me a great view of Reynard's heavily muscled bicep. I was so impressed I almost forgot to be scared.

"Commander, I'm sorry to disturb you. A Bashalde girl came this way and we're searching the rooms for her. Have you seen her?"

"Commander?" Lillith's voice screeched in my ear. "You promised!"

"Blame Peri," I subvocalized. "She led me here. Now shut up so I can listen."

"What has this girl done?" Reynard's voice was rich and deep, with a tone that implied he was used to being obeyed without question.

"She downed Furgan, and when we discovered her leaning over his body, she fled through a damaged door into the castle."

"Furgan is dead?"

A subtle menace filled the question, and I held my breath, fear working hot sticky fingers up my spine. The man had been alive when I'd checked. If he'd since died, I didn't know what they'd do to me. Only one thing was clear. My mission would be over before it even started. I would have failed. That prospect sent such stark terror through me that I had to fight to keep from wilting into a puddle of quivering GEP at the commander's feet.

"No, sir. He was regaining his wits by the time the healer arrived."

A wave of relief washed over me. Not only wouldn't I be executed for murder, I still had a chance to complete my job.

"I see." There was a brief hesitation. "The girl is with me. Call off the search and remain outside my door while I question her. And send someone to convey my apologies to the king. Tell him I've been delayed."

"Yes, sir."

Reynard closed the door and turned to face me, his gaze running over my body before coming to rest on my face. "Your name, girl."

I didn't even think about lying. Besides, I had no clue what a typical name for a Bashalde girl would be. "Echo."

He moved to the bed where clothing was laid out and dropped the drying cloth after making sure he was facing away from me. "Did you attack Furgan?"

It took an effort to think with my attention locked on his fine backside and my stomach doing gyrations worthy of a contortionist, but I managed. Briefly, I considered telling him the man was already unconscious when I'd come across him. But if Furgan were waking up, he'd contradict that story.

I forced my gaze to a spot over his shoulder so I could concentrate. "Yes, but not deliberately. I thought I was alone and he startled me. When I turned, I accidentally hit him. I'm not sure how I managed to knock him out."

There was a splash from the direction of his bathing tub and I glanced over just in time to see Peri pop her head out and flip to float on her back, spread wings moving her in a lazy circle. A happy gurgle issued from her chest. Apparently her protective instincts went south when the choice was me or water.

Reynard was watching her, too, one dark brow arched as he did something to fasten the tight black pants he'd pulled on. "What manner of beast is this?"

Lillith whispered frantically in my ear, and I repeated what she was telling me. "Her name is Peri. I found her washed up, nearly dead, on a beach of the eastern sea when I was last in the area. I nursed her back to health and she's been with me ever since."

He reached for a silky white shirt and then held it while he studied me minutely, his face without expression. Nervous under those pale blue eyes, I shifted from foot to foot and brushed my damp palms against my skirt.

"What were you doing outside the castle?"

Again Lillith prompted me. "I was looking for an establishment called the Terpsichore. I'm to work for the owner, Marcus Kent. I was told it was near the castle, but not the exact location, and I saw no one about to ask directions of."

Suddenly I was thankful everyone had been ordered

to stay inside tonight. Otherwise, my story wouldn't have worked.

Slowly he pulled the shirt over his head and it slithered down his body, the hem hugging his slim hips. Abruptly, I forgot I was afraid. There should be a law against men like him wearing a shirt that clings to every ridge and muscle. Didn't he know what it did to those of the female persuasion?

"You traveled without escort?" He put a black belt studded with blue stones the color of his eyes around his waist and buckled it.

"No!" Lillith yelled in my ear. "Remember, women on this planet don't travel alone. He must be suspicious. Think fast and try to look sincere!"

I stopped blinking so my eyes would tear up, stepped forward, hands held out beseechingly, and improvised like crazy. "My father hired two men he mistakenly trusted to bring me here, but they left me near the mountains this morning with only the clothes on my back, and a skin of water to sustain me. Claiming to have business in another city, they pointed me in the right direction and then departed. I believe they were crooks, sir, only after my father's coin. I could have been in danger from wild beasts, alone as I was."

"You're overacting," Lillith told me. "Turn it down a couple of notches."

Deliberately, I ignored her and let my bottom lip tremble.

To my surprise, one side of his mouth kicked up in a tiny smile, exposing one very dangerous dimple. Dangerous to my peace of mind, anyway. It was all I could do to keep from jumping him on the spot.

Especially when he crossed to me, stopping close enough that my skirt tangled against his legs. Putting a broad callused hand under my chin, he lifted my face to his gaze.

"You are a pretty one," he murmured. Then his voice hardened. "Too pretty to be such a good liar."

I let out a gasp of outrage and jerked away from him. "I'm not lying!" Okay, I was, but there was no way he could know it, not for sure.

Before I could blink twice, he had my skirt up and my knife in his hand, the tip pressed against my throat. "Helpless females such as you're pretending to be do not carry such weapons," he said. "Now, I'll have the truth."

Here's the thing. I'd only completed intensive combat training a few days ago, and Alien Affairs instructors are very thorough. Because an agent's life depends on it, they teach us to react to a threat first and think about it later. We're drilled repeatedly, until our responses to danger are automatic. Plus, I had no practical experience to temper my reactions.

With no conscious decision on my part, my training took over and I was moving before he finished speaking. My left hand went over his arm and slammed it downward. The move shifted the knife from my throat and numbed his muscles so he loosened his grip. I caught the knife with my right hand and swung it up in an underhand arc.

The only thing that kept me from gutting him navel to breastbone was Lillith screeching in my ear and Peri slinging water everywhere as she dived at us.

Both Reynard and I stood frozen in place, staring down at the knife pressed to his stomach, him in surprise, me in horror. It's one thing to theoretically practice killing a human during training. It's another thing entirely to realize you'd almost done it for real, and involuntarily at that. Especially when the human in question was one I'd been lusting after not a second before.

A small sound escaped my throat and I dropped the knife like it had turned into a poisonous insect.

Reynard stooped, scooped it up, and offered it to me hilt first. "Nicely done, girl. Who taught you to fight?"

Hesitantly, I took the weapon, lifted my skirt and returned the knife to its sheath. Peri settled watchfully on my shoulder, her eyes tinged with red. The action gave me time to get my tongue working again. It also helped that Lillith was providing me with all the answers.

"My father. He was a weapons master. As his only child and a female, he made sure I could defend myself when he was no longer able to protect me."

Moving to the one chair in the room, he sat and pulled on a pair of black knee-high boots. "He's dead?"

"Yes. When he sickened, he made arrangements for me to come here after he was gone, to Marcus Kent. They were friends once. I left the day after my father's burial."

"What of your tribe? Was there no uncle or promised husband to take you in?"

"No." I was afraid to move, to express any emotion at all, lest I give myself away again. "The Bashalde called my father *Gadjee*, so we lived alone for the most part. After my mother died, her people stopped coming, except for the two men my father occasionally hired to bring supplies. I have no other close relatives."

He stood and went to the door, opening it to speak with the soldier waiting in the hall. "Send someone to find Marcus Kent. Tell him I need to see him immediately, and don't mention the girl. Oh, and have someone bring food."

Scritch. I should have realized he'd send for Kent. The man would literally be walking into a trap of my making. It was just one more thing that proved I didn't belong in this job.

Before I could slump in defeat, Lillith whispered, "Don't worry. I've been repeating everything you've said to Marcus and he's been feeding me your cover story. He's waiting on the soldier sent to fetch him and knows exactly what to say."

"You've talked to him? How?"

"He has an implant. The frequency was in the data Dr. Daniels gave me. And by the way, your father was named August. Marcus says the name will hold up if the commander decides to check it out."

I barely caught a sigh of relief before it escaped, and then checked to make sure Reynard hadn't noticed. He had picked up a comb and moved to stand in front of a mirror, but he was watching me in the reflection while he ran it through his hair.

Automatically, I reached for his drying cloth, folded it, and hung it on the rail at the foot of his bed, and then straightened the personal items lying on a table nearby for maximum efficiency. When that was done, I gathered the soiled clothing he'd discarded before his bath and folded them.

He was obviously dressing up for his meeting with the king. Would the people from the ship be there, too? I wanted to ask but didn't dare. Instead I decided to take a roundabout approach and see if I could learn anything of interest.

I glanced at him over my shoulder. "I'm sorry I made you late for your meeting with the king. Will it cause you problems?"

He had given up all pretense of grooming and was still watching me in the mirror, a slight frown on his rugged face. It was only then I realized old habits had taken over and I'd been organizing his room. I forced my hands behind my back, locking my fingers together to keep them still, and faced him as he answered.

"No. The king expects his unmarried officers to join him for the evening meal once in an eightday, but my duty comes

before socializing. It won't be the first time I've been delayed, and undoubtedly won't be the last."

"Oh. You're dressed so finely I thought maybe tonight
was a special occasion."

He arched a dark brow and shifted to lean one shoulder
against the wall, arms crossed over his chest. "We are always
required to dress for the king's meal."

Before I could answer, there was a knock at the door
and two women entered pushing wheeled carts. They were
dressed in the drab, modest clothing the majority of Madrean
women wore, and stared at me with open curiosity.

Silently they uncovered steaming dishes that filled the
room with scents appetizing enough to make my mouth
water. When they were done, the elder of the two turned to
Reynard. "Will there be anything else, Commander?"

"Nothing. You may go."

They dipped their heads and left, the soldier closing the
door behind them. Once we were alone again, Reynard
moved to the carts and filled a plate until it was heaping, then
brought it to me, motioning me to sit on the sole chair.

He saw my surprise at such consideration and his mouth
kicked up again. "You said you'd walked all day with only
water to sustain you. I'd rather you didn't pass out from
hunger before Marcus arrives."

"Thank you." I took the food and dug in like I hadn't
eaten in a week, while Peri examined the carts and then
lost interest in favor of drying her feathers on the arm of
the chair. Even taking into consideration how long it had
been since I'd filled my stomach, I was extraordinarily
starved. If my brief foray into overdrive had caused this,
I'd be wise to only use it in the direst of emergencies. After
all, it wouldn't do to drop dead from starvation in the midst
of a crisis.

Suddenly I was feeling a lot more sympathetic toward

Kiera Smith. Maybe she'd had a reason to angst after all. Being a Gertz GEP was turning out to be a bit more complicated than I'd expected.

I was swallowing the last bite of roasted fowl when there was another knock on the door. This time the soldier ushered in a slim man of average height, a bit beyond middle age. His pale blond hair, pulled back into a neat queue, was liberally streaked with white, and his deeply tanned face was creased from spending time outdoors. Dark brown eyes that mirrored fatherly concern swung from the commander to me. Then he opened his arms.

"Echo, sweetheart."

"It's Marcus," Lillith told me.

Promptly, I leaped to my feet and launched myself at him, the now empty plate clattering to the floor. His arms closed around me, and he rocked us gently from side to side. And I felt strangely comforted, as though I'd finally found safe shelter when the rest of my world had turned into a swirling mass of confusion.

"I was so sorry to hear about August," he said, just loud enough for his voice to carry to Reynard. "He was a good man. I'll miss him."

"Thank you," I murmured. "He considered you his most trusted friend." I didn't dare look at Reynard, but I could feel him watching us with interest.

Marcus took me by the shoulders and shifted me back so he could look down at me. "Now, what's going on here? I expected you to arrive this morning and come straight to me. Is something amiss?"

I gave him a briefer version of the tale I'd told Reynard about being dumped by two men, only without the theatrics, as well as how I'd come to be in the castle. When I was done, Marcus sighed.

"The men weren't evil, just idiots," he said. "Next time I

see them you can be sure they'll hear about this from me."
He turned to Reynard, keeping one arm around my shoulders. "My apologies for the disruption, Commander. August was something of a recluse and kept Echo away from people for the most part. Because of her isolation she's a bit naive. She meant no harm. May I take her home now? I'm sure she's exhausted from her adventure."

While I did my best to look all tuckered out, Reynard straightened and clasped his hands behind his back. "Of course. She'll be living with you?"

"Yes, and working at the Terpsichore to earn her keep."

I was? News to me. But I didn't think it was the time to argue. And at the moment, I was busy worrying about Peri. She was watching Marcus's arm where it rested on my shoulders and emoting a great deal of resentment.

Friend, I sent her. *But you're my favorite.*

She gurgled happily and her feathers settled. Silly creature. And now that I thought about it, why hadn't she resented it when Reynard touched me?

"Just one more question, if you will, and then you may go." Reynard's voice yanked my attention away from Peri and focused it on him. Marcus nodded his consent and Reynard continued.

"She said her father was a weapons master. Whom did he work for?"

Marcus smiled. "He was teacher to Lowden, chief of the Bashalde."

"He was *that* August?" Reynard's gaze swung to me, a speculative look on his face. "I hadn't realized he had a child."

"Very few know. Echo was born shortly after August and his wife vanished into the desert."

"I see. Then you'll be pleased to know that Lowden and the Bashalde will arrive here tomorrow for the yearly gathering to renew their treaty with the king. I'm sure he'll want to honor the daughter of his old teacher."

Me, Miss Happy-To-Be-a-GEP, suddenly had a past so convoluted it would confuse a Natural. I decided that silence was the better part of valor and looked to Marcus for a response.

"I'll see to it that she's introduced," he told Reynard.

"They'll camp outside the city as usual, and the gathering will begin on the day after tomorrow. It would be my pleasure to escort both of you."

"And it will be our honor to accept." Marcus gave a slight bow. "Now, we really should be going."

Reynard went to the door and opened it, then spoke to the soldier waiting in the hall. "Escort them out of the castle, please, and then return here."

"Yes, Commander." He held out my cloak and pouch. "These were found outside near where Furgan was felled."

Reynard took them and turned to me. "Yours?"

I nodded. "I dropped them while fleeing your men." And there was no doubt in my mind they'd been thoroughly searched. Good thing I'd finished off that Zip Bar.

Moving away from Marcus, I draped the cloak over my arm and settled the pouch strap on my shoulder before calling Peri to roost. "Thank you for your hospitality, Commander. The meal was much appreciated."

"You're welcome. I look forward to seeing you dance."

What? Hold the phone, here. Who said anything about dancing? "Lillith, what in Zin's name is he talking about?"

"Marcus's tavern. It's named after Terpsichore, the goddess of dance."

Now wasn't this just dandy? I go from being a respected employee of the Department of Protocol, to a job I'm horrible at with the Bureau of Alien Affairs, and abruptly I'm demoted yet again. Only this time I get to be a glorified stripper. Whoopee. What was next? Cleaning outdoor toilets? By hand? Without a shovel?

Sure I'd danced in my previous job, but that was different. Mostly because I'd always had a partner and hadn't been dancing alone to entertain large groups of men. *That* dancing had been personal recreation, even if it was part of the job.

In lieu of addressing Reynard's comment, I moved into the hall, Marcus beside me. Reynard followed us as far as the doorway and then paused, his gaze on Marcus.

"I'll be watching, Kent."

Again Marcus gave him a short bow. "I would expect nothing less, Commander." He took my arm and steered me down the hall behind our escort. When we were almost to the end of the passage, I looked over my shoulder.

Reynard was still watching, his manly form limned in the light spilling from his room. Was he really staring at the sway of my hips? A thrill tingled through my stomach and shot straight to my chest. Before I thought about the consequences, I lifted my hand and sent him a small good-bye wave.

He returned it right before we went to the left and I lost sight of him. I faced forward again just as Lillith spoke to me.

"Marcus said to tell you that if you have questions, ask them through me. He says it's not safe to speak aloud until you're in his home."

"Great. Ask him what Reynard meant by that last statement."

There was a pause before she responded. "The commander is either attracted to you, or suspicious. Marcus thinks it's a bit of both. There's also a third reason. As I mentioned before, men here outnumber the women by a good margin, so in their culture women are protected at all costs. Rape and abuse are almost unheard of, and the penalty for either is a very painful death. It's a matter not only of honor, but of preserving a rare and precious commodity necessary for the continuation of their race. By confirming your story and taking you in, Marcus has declared himself your guardian, and it's an unusual arrangement considering you aren't related to him. The commander was serving notice that he wouldn't tolerate any licentious behavior toward you on Marcus's part. In other words, he's decided its part of his duty to make sure you're protected, even from your guardian."

Well, that certainly gave me the warm snuggies. All except the suspicious part. I'd have to be real careful around Reynard. And I had no doubt I'd see him again soon.

Another thought occurred to me as the soldier led us to an outside door. "What if this August person shows up alive and well, and denies I'm his daughter?"

"He won't. Marcus was on the original exploration team that discovered Madrea, and has been here ever since. He came to know August well. The man died nearly a cycle ago. After he left Lowden's service, he wed a Bashalde woman and had a daughter. Enough people knew about her, including Lowden, that the commander can verify the information. What no one but Marcus knows is that the child died of a fever when she was five cycles old, along with her mother. After that, August became even more reclusive. Marcus was his only contact with people, and only because Marcus insisted on taking him supplies, so the story will stand up."

"He came up with all this on the spur of the moment?" By now, we were outside and Marcus was heading down a dark street leading toward the front of the castle, our escort left behind at the castle. Peri abandoned my shoulder and flitted busily from flower to flower.

There was another pause before Lillith answered. "No, he

says Dr. Daniels contacted him about you several days ago. He had time to consider all aspects of your cover, and this was the one he settled on as most believable, especially since he knows you only recently finished your combat training."

I arched a brow as we turned down another street. "What does that have to do with my cover story?"

"He knows how agents are trained. It was only a matter of time before you reacted violently to something or someone the way you did the commander. Women on this world aren't trained to fight. August's daughter would probably be the one exception. Apparently, he wasn't too fond of rules."

"Okay, Marcus is obviously a genius." From the corners of my eyes, I saw him smile.

"He thanks you, and says you've reached his home."

Taking my arm again, he steered me up a rock walkway to a door bordered on both sides with flowers, opened it, and ushered me inside. Peri zipped in right before he closed the door, and then she began to explore the dark house. When I opened my mouth to speak, he put a finger to his lips and moved to a small chest resting on a shelf. Its wooden sides were adorned with stones, and he pushed one of them in like it was an on/off button.

"There, we can talk now."

Outside the window the moon was full, and in its bluish light I eyed the chest with interest. Other than its ornate style there was nothing unusual about it. "What did you do?"

"Activated the motion detectors I've placed strategically around the yard. If anyone gets close enough to overhear our conversation, a light on the box will blink."

He moved around the room, lifting opaque covers from transparent containers. Immediately, a soft white-gold glow filled the interior of the house.

Curious about the sunstones, I moved closer to a lamp and studied it while we continued our conversation. "Aren't

you afraid someone will discover the motion detectors?"
The glow made it difficult to be certain, but it looked like the
container was full of shinning pebbles. Gingerly, I touched it
with one finger, surprised to find it cool even though I'd read
about the phenomenon in the data files.

"Since the bases look like ordinary rocks and most people
on this world haven't a clue what technology can do, no."

He took two glasses from beside the chest and poured
wine while I abandoned the sunstones and looked around
the room. It was good sized and contained both a sitting area
and kitchen. There was a large fireplace in one wall and several wooden chairs with padded seats facing it, a low table
between them.

On the other side of the room there was a table with four
chairs and lots of shelving for food and dishes. In the back,
two doors led to other rooms and a third outside. All in all it
looked snug and cozy.

"Sit." Marcus gestured toward a chair as he handed me
one of the glasses. "I'll show you your room after we chat.
It's small, I'm afraid, but should do for now. The privy is
out back."

I stared at him suspiciously as I deposited my bag and
cloak near the door and took a seat. "I don't have to clean it
out, do I?"

"The privy?" He chuckled as he took the other seat. "No.
It's not up to Alpha Centauri standards, I'm sure, but the
Madreans do have rudimentary plumbing. Basic hygiene is
all that's called for since I hire a housekeeper for the rest
of the cleaning. The Terpsichore has its own kitchens and a
wonderful cook, so I rarely eat at home."

"That's good. The housekeeper, I mean." I took a sip of
wine. Not bad for a domestic. "Where is your tavern?"

Peri landed on the mantel and began examining the items
displayed there.

"It's the big building on the other side of this house. Normally, it would be lit up and busy, but since the king ordered everyone to stay inside we closed for the night."

I leaned back in the chair, relaxing completely for the first time since Lillith had dumped me on this planet. "Do you know why he issued the order?"

He rolled his glass between his hands. "I imagine it had something to do with the ship that landed behind the castle."

"Lillith said three men and two young girls debarked, and that one of the girls appeared to be drugged."

A frown marred his previously friendly face and I suddenly realized he could be a very dangerous man if crossed.

"Braxus." He nearly spit the word.

"I beg your pardon? Who or what is Braxus? There was no mention of anyone by that name in the files."

"He's the king's brother. I'm not surprised the Federation doesn't know about him. I suspect most Madreans have forgotten he exists. He was born with a skeletal deformity and prefers to stay out of sight and work behind the scenes. For the last month, though, ships have been landing on a regular basis. Since the king eschews all things Federation as well as any technology that requires an energy source other than human or animal power, I knew it had to be Braxus's doing. In spite of his appearance, the man is extremely intelligent and spends most of his time reading. So usually the king allows black marketeers to bring in books for his brother. Normally that only happens once every few months, and yet lately, the rate of landings has increased drastically. I know something is going on, but haven't been able to find out what."

He lifted a hand to rub his forehead. "Now that I know about the Sumantti, there's only one conclusion I can reach.

Braxus has the crystal and he's bringing in female children with psi ability to try and use it."

When my heart started pounding in reaction, I knew he'd hit the nail on the head. I didn't even need to ask why the man was using children. The answer was obvious. Children would be easier to control than an adult female with psi abilities.

"They'll die," I blurted out. "Anyone who tries to use the stone without first being prepared by the crystals will die. Oh, Zin. There's no telling how many he's already killed if numerous ships have been arriving. Why is the king allowing him to do this?"

"That's something we'll have to find out." Marcus's face was downright grim. "I think it's time we discussed your mission. Dr. Daniels gave me the pertinent parts, but I'd like to hear what you know about the Sumantti."

I snorted. "That should take all of two seconds." After I repeated everything Kiera Smith had told me, and explained about the Imadei, he nodded.

"You have no idea how to use the Imadei?"

"No, not even a tiny clue. I've tried holding it and concentrating, but so far that hasn't worked."

"May I see it?"

Oddly enough, I was reluctant to take it out. Since that seemed rather silly, I shrugged. "Sure." I tugged the stone from under my top, slid the chain over my head, and held it in my palm where he could see it.

I expected him to reach for the stone, but he didn't. He leaned over the chair arm and gazed into the inky depths for what seemed liked ten minutes. And the longer he stared, the more my head ached.

Abruptly, I couldn't take any more. I curled my fingers around the Imadei, hiding it from his view, and with the other hand massaged my temple.

Marcus blinked like a man coming out of a trance, and then frowned. "Put it back on and never let anyone see it again. And if you value your life, don't allow it to be touched unless you trust the person implicitly. For better or worse, the stone is linked to you now, and until you learn to control it, rough handling of the Imadei could either kill you or destroy your mind."

I stared at him as my headache eased. "How do you know that?"

"When you've lived as long as I have, you pick things up here and there."

Abruptly, my internal radar went on high alert. "Exactly how old are you?"

"Six hundred and twenty-eight cycles."

My mouth gaped and I had trouble forming a sentence for a second. "You're a super GEP."

He smiled and shook his head. "Not on the same level as Kiera Smith, or you, apparently. But Gertz wasn't the first to experiment with GEP DNA. He just took it further than most."

If he was that old, how long could *I* expect to live? My brain spun even though I was still in shock. "What are your abilities?"

"Extremely good health and a long life."

"No psi abilities?"

"None whatsoever." He hesitated and then shrugged. "What I have is an innate skill at deductive reasoning and all those years of experience to draw from. Sometimes that's enough for intuitive leaps in logic that others might miss. But there's one thing I know that doesn't have to be guessed at. Braxus has to be stopped, and you're the only one who can do it."

So much for not cleaning out the privy. Because if solving this problem depended on me alone, we were up to our eyeballs in shit with no shovel in sight.

CHAPTER 5

The first rays of sunlight stabbed my tightly closed eyelids with knife-like precision, and with a groan I pulled my pillow over my head. Just ten more minutes would do me, or even five. But there was no getting around the fact that I was awake and suddenly conscious of a feeling of dread that blanketed me for no apparent reason.

Until I remembered where I was and the conversation I'd had with Marcus the night before.

With a sigh, I tossed the pillow aside and sat up, blinking at my surroundings. The room was smaller than my quarters on board Lillith, with just enough space for a single bed and a chest. The one window was wide open, panes of wood-framed glass pulled back against the plaster of aged yellow walls to allow perfume-laden air to circulate.

It kind of freaked me out, knowing there was no barrier between me and the wild bugs sneaking around outside. I'd lain awake for hours staring at the window, trying to make sure they weren't about to jump me. And yes, I knew they were there during the day, too, but I was awake and ready for them then, not asleep and vulnerable.

Peri was nowhere in sight, but without even concentrating I could feel her satisfaction as she gathered nectar. For such a small creature she sure spent a lot of time eating. But then, I guess it took a lot of flowers to supply enough food to sustain her. On Madrea she'd hit the jackpot. There were flowers everywhere.

Rubbing my eyes, I swung my legs off the bed and then reached for my cloak. I needed a shower and I didn't want to put on my last outfit until I'd had one. The cloak would keep me from shocking the neighbors witless when I traipsed across the yard to the privy. Clutching my bag in one hand and holding the cloak tightly closed with the other, I left my room.

There were snores coming from the other side of the house as I tiptoed through to the back door, and I envied Marcus the ability to sleep late. Of course, his room didn't have the sun shining through a window at this Zin-awful hour, either.

I wasn't the first person up, though. Already the scent of cooking wafted from the large stone building next door, and I could hear the chatter of voices mixed with the clatter of pots and pans.

Although I'd made a trip to the privy the night before, it had been dark and the small sunstone lamp I'd carried hadn't illuminated much more than the crushed stone path. This morning I took a better look around.

Marcus's home and business were separated by a white wooden fence lined with flowers. Both yards were neat and clean, but where his home yard contained only the privy, there was a building with three doors at the back of the business, and another, even longer, two-story building with numerous doors situated at the back of the lot.

The front one had to be privies for the customers' use, but the back one looked like apartments of some kind. Even as

I watched, a roughly dressed man carrying a hoe emerged from the end door, ran his gaze over me curiously, and then went to work in one of the dozen flower beds.

Okay, guess the building was living quarters for Marcus's employees.

With that burning question answered, I continued to the privy, joined by an enthusiastic Peri, who'd figured out I was going to bathe. I made sure the door was latched and then shed my cloak. The building was divided into two parts. One side contained an old-fashioned gravity-flow toilet and a sink; the other was a walk-in shower with a drain in the floor. A large tank on the roof, heated only during the winter months, I'd been informed, supplied the water.

"Lillith, did you contact Dr. Daniels and tell him what was going on?" I stepped into the shower, pulled on the rope hanging down, and moved under the tepid sprinkle of water that resulted, scrubbing vigorously with the cake of soap I'd found on a shelf. It smelled like flowers.

Peri landed at my feet, flapping energetically in the water and suds that pooled around the drain, slinging droplets to all corners of the stall.

What was it with this place and flowers? I made a mental note to ask Marcus about it later.

"Yes," Lillith responded to my question. "Plus, it's all going into my archives. Dr. Daniels is going to check into any reports on missing girls, but he said the chances of finding out anything about the ones brought to Madrea are extremely slim. It's a big universe and children go missing from all over, every day. However, he does find it interesting that King Politaus is allowing ships to land, given his attitude toward anything that smacks of the Federation."

"Yeah, that occurred to me, too. Marcus thinks Braxus is behind the Sumantti being stolen and the girls being brought here, but at the least the king has to know about and condone the ships. He's the one who gave the order to keep people inside so they wouldn't see them land."

"At least we can be relatively sure the Sumantti is somewhere nearby. Otherwise, there'd be no need to bring the girls to Bastion City."

I rinsed quickly and shut the water off, grabbing a drying cloth from a shelf. "Is the ship still here?"

Peri tiptoed out of the stall, jumped to the sink edge, and began drying her feathers.

"No. The three men got back on board and it lifted off an hour before sunrise. As soon as it was away from Madrea's gravitational field it went into hyper-drive. The girls weren't with them."

With a sigh, I toweled the excess moisture from my hair. "So, what now? If I get caught sneaking around the castle again, they'll know something is up. I don't think they'll believe I could get lost there twice."

"Now we bide our time and lie low until you learn to use the Imadei. Once you do, you should be able to pinpoint the exact location of the Daughter Stone. You'll still have to go get it, but knowing where it is will minimize the risk. And, it would help if we knew what your psi ability is."

"Regardless of what the tests say, I've never shown any indication of an ability. And what's more, I don't want one."

"Sooner or later you must face the fact that you have psi talent and learn to use it. You won't have a choice in the matter."

"Yeah? Well, you just watch me. We always have a choice."

Staring at my reflection it dawned on me that I had no way to fix my hair. No dryer, no styler, nothing. I was lucky I had the comb Marcus was loaning me. Maybe there was a reason Kiera Smith constantly wore her hair in a braid.

Well, if she could do a braid, I could at least do a ponytail. Using my knife, I stripped a piece of leather from the flap on

my pouch and then pulled the comb through the heavy mass
to smooth out the snags. It took me three tries to get the hair
pulled back and the tie around it, and when I was done, what
I had was an off-center, tangled mop of hair with drying ten-
drils escaping in every direction.

Okay, maybe I couldn't do it.

I shook my head and watched my hair go crazy, one fat
lock falling to hide my left eye while the rest fluffed up like
each individual strand had its own force field that repelled all
the other strands. Wonder what Reynard would think of my
new wild-woman do?

Instantly, a mental image of the commander formed in
my mind. He was sitting at a long table with other men, all in
the uniforms of the king. The table groaned with the weight
of food, and there was much laughter and talking.

My eyes drifted closed as I inspected him minutely. Damn,
he was one fine-looking man. In spite of being hungry again,
it sure wasn't the food that had my mouth watering.

Suddenly Reynard went tense, his head lifting alertly as
he scanned the room.

My eyes popped open. Wow, talk about an imagination.
I shook my head again and the image vanished. I really
needed to stop daydreaming. There simply wasn't enough
time. I had lots to do, like getting dressed, finding something
to eat, and then lying low.

Yeah, I could do that. At least I was pretty sure I wouldn't
screw up the getting-dressed-and-eating part. How hard
could it be, after all? I'd been doing it my whole life.

Lying low, however, might be a problem.

I pulled my last skirt and top from the pouch and put them
on. The belt and halter were a silvery sage that made my
eyes stand out. Not my first choice in color, because I preferred bright vivid shades, but I had to admit, the hue looked
good on me.

After tidying the privy, I made my way back to the house, Peri abandoning me for the flowers again. Once inside, I returned my pouch to my room and straightened the bed. By the time I finished, Marcus was up and waiting for me. He blinked at my hair, but was too polite to comment.

"Ready for breakfast?" he inquired mildly.

"I passed ready an hour ago," I replied, following him out the back door. "So, what exactly are my duties going to be while I'm working for you?"

He clasped his hands behind his back as we strolled across the yard, aiming at a gate set in the white fence. "You'll take orders from customers and deliver those orders back to them. At least twice a night you'll dance. And most important of all, you'll keep your ears open. The soldiers let their guard down when they're relaxed and drinking, and we need all the information we can get."

"No problem."

Peri fluttered by with a chirp of greeting for Marcus as we went through the gate, and then hovered over another batch of flowers before making her selection.

"You do know how to dance, don't you?"

I gave him a satisfied smile. When you're created for the Department of Protocol, knowing how to dance is incorporated in your DNA. "Yes."

Truth was, one of the first things I'd been taught in the crèche was all the traditional dances of the Federation member planets, and I was a quick study. According to my instructors at Alien Affairs, my ability to dance was part of what made me so good at hand-to-hand combat.

My dance repertoire was vast and spanned several centuries of culture. Give me a beat and I could move to it. If pressed, I could even carry a passable tune, although I didn't think it would be smart to try that here. At least, not until I learned some of their songs.

"Excellent," Marcus said. "We'll need to get you a costume before tonight, but you and Treya are about the same size, so that shouldn't be a problem. You can borrow one of hers until we get something made."

"How many people work for you?"

He tilted his head a moment to think. "I believe there are twelve now, but the numbers vary with the seasons, and most of my regulars do several different jobs."

We reached the back of the Terpsichore just as the blonde woman from the vid I'd watched my first day on board Lillith stepped outside. Even taking into consideration the five cycles that had passed since the vid was shot, she was beautiful.

She stopped the second she saw us and her gaze swept over me, a frown marring the smooth skin between her emerald eyes. "What have you brought me now, Marcus?"

"Treya, this is my ward, Echo. She's going to be working at the Terpsichore with us."

"I see." She circled me slowly, assessing my worth. "A bit on the slim side, but well toned." When she stopped in front of me, we were eye to eye. "Smile, girl."

I bared my teeth at her.

"Good, although when you're working, try to put more feeling into it." She glanced at Marcus. "Her hair is extraordinary. The men will all want to get their hands in it."

Huh? My hair was a mess! Maybe the men on Madrea were all frustrated beauticians.

To my surprise Marcus was nodding agreement. "I'll make sure Bim keeps an eye on her when she's working the tables."

I opened my mouth to tell him I could take care of myself, and then closed it again. On this world, I wasn't *supposed* to take care of myself and I needed to remember that.

But Treya wasn't finished yet. She motioned with one

hand. "Walk to the door and back so I can see how you move."

I did as she asked, putting an extra swing into my hips just because she got on my nerves.

"Excellent!" She clasped her hands together and smiled at me. "Fluid and natural, with just enough curves to be delicately feminine. I know just the costume for her."

Maybe she wasn't so bad after all. She was obviously a connoisseur when it came to the female form. If her taste in clothes was on a par with mine, we were all set to be best buds.

"Now go, eat." She made a shooing motion. "When you are done, we will work on your dancing."

"Treya is in charge of all the dancers," Marcus said, ushering me into a huge bustling kitchen.

Heat rose from three large cast-iron stoves tended by a short, slim woman wielding a spatula. She glanced around long enough to beam at us, her brown eyes sparkling, red hair standing on end from the steam rising out of bubbling pots.

A long table capable of seating dozens was positioned to one side, away from the work area. It was currently populated by three women dressed like me, a giant of a man shoveling in food with a single-mindedness that was awe inspiring, and four normal-sized men ranging in age from early twenties to late fifties.

All of them but the giant stopped eating to stare at me while Marcus made the introductions. The women were my counterparts, both servers and dancers. The four men were musicians. The giant was the aforementioned Bim, Treya's brother and chief head banger when the customers got a little too merry. The cook was named Leddy and she obviously had a letch on for Marcus, fussing over him until even I got embarrassed. But when I tasted the food she slid in front of me, I forgave her.

There were perfectly cooked eggs, thick slices of ham, gravy, and fluffy biscuits the size of my fist. I'd be willing to bet there wasn't a synthesized protein on the plate. And best of all, there was real coffee—hot, black, and strong. I wondered if they realized how rare coffee was in the rest of the universe. Probably. No doubt they'd made a fortune on it before the king closed the planet.

Silence descended while everyone chowed down, and once again my thoughts strayed to Reynard. Only this time I pictured him outside the castle, frowning at the door I'd torn from its frame.

"We may have a problem," Lillith told me.

I banished Reynard's image and swallowed hurriedly. "What?"

"The commander is examining the door you tore out last night."

If I'd still had food in my mouth, I would have choked on it. As it was, I must have made a sound, because several of my dining companions glanced in my direction. Marcus arched a questioning brow at me, and I gave my head a slight shake.

"What was that noise?" Lillith asked.

"Nothing. It was me." I took a deep breath, more than a little freaked. As coincidences went, this one was way out there. And I refused to think about the ramifications right now. Do you think he suspects I did it?"

"Let me see." Her voice was laced with sarcasm. "It was a perfectly solid door. The wood is now splintered around the lock and the hinges. The soldiers saw you go that way. So do I think he suspects you? No, of course not. He probably thinks it was a muscular termite." She snorted, an artificial intelligence's equivalent of scornful hilarity.

"Remind me to laugh at your brilliant wit next week," I told her. "In the meantime, what am I supposed to do?"

"Deny everything. He might suspect you're not what you seem, but he can't prove it."

"Right. Lie through my teeth. I've been around politicians all my life. Should be easy. I'll tell him the door must have been like that when I happened across it and that's why I was able to open it. After all, lying went so well for me the first time I tried it with him." I was babbling. To stop myself, I gripped my cup and took another sip of coffee.

Before I could break down into total hysteria, the back door opened and I looked up as Treya came in. She surveyed my empty plate and then motioned with her head. "This way. We'll see what you can do."

Unwilling to waste a precious drop of coffee, I slugged back what was left and then followed her to a room off the kitchen. The four musicians trailed us and picked up instruments that were resting on a small table against the wall. They included a guitar anyone on Old Earth would have recognized, an oddly shaped percussion apparatus, and two strange-looking pipes. They moved to chairs positioned in a corner, and for a few minutes a horrible cacophony of sounds rose as they made sure their instruments were in tune.

When silence fell, Treya sent me to the middle of the floor and nodded at the men. Immediately, exotic music filled the air, lent a sensual quality by the pipes. Mentally I ran through my repertoire and settled on a mating dance from the bird people of Denbigh. Their ambassador had taught it to me right after I'd left the crèche.

I'd barely started when Treya grimaced and waved a hand. The music stopped and she marched over to me, hands on her hips.

"What is this? You look like a flea on hot sand! This is not dancing. If hopping around is the best you can do it will be cycles before you're ready to dance in public."

I mimicked her stance and matched her glare for glare. "Why don't you show me what you want instead of criticizing? I promise, any dance you can do, I can do better."

A slight smile lifted the corners of her lips. "Impertinence. I like that. Shows you have spirit. Now I will teach you how to dance."

I moved back as the music began anew, and watched carefully as she undulated. It looked like a muted, stately version of a belly dance to me.

Before she'd danced through two bars of music, I joined her, only there was nothing muted or stately about my movements. I let the haunting melody take me, dancing for the sheer joy of putting my body through its paces. It had been so long since I'd had a chance to dance.

It wasn't until the music faded away that I realized Treya had stopped and was watching me intently. And it wasn't just her. The men were watching me too, a look of awe on their faces.

"Who taught you to dance this way?" Treya asked me, her voice carrying an odd note.

Oops.

Frantically, I scrambled to come up with a good lie, but my mind remained blank. "Um, no one, really. I just like dancing, and can usually pick new ones up quickly."

"Who was your mother?"

"Lillith, do I have a mother?" I subvocalized.

"Rilyana," she replied.

I repeated the name to Treya, but she only looked more suspicious.

"What tribe was she from?"

"I don't know. My father kept us apart from others, and

my mother died when I was very young. My father never spoke of her afterward."

"Only an Apsaras, or the child of one, could dance this way."

"What the frag is an Apsaras?" I asked Lillith.

"In their culture, it's a supernatural being who takes the form of a beautiful young woman. They excel at dance and singing, but perform only for the Bashalde god Invet, and for fallen heroes."

"No," I shook my head vigorously at Treya, a knot in my stomach. Since a Natural who knew nothing of GEPs might consider one of us supernatural, that was getting a tiny bit too close for comfort. "There's nothing supernatural about me. I just have a talent for dance."

She went back to glaring. "If word spreads that Marcus has an Apsaras performing here, his business will increase tenfold. The more coin he makes, the more we are paid."

Ah, the light dawned. She wanted to use the Apsaras as a marketing ploy. Smart woman.

"Fine. You can tell the customers whatever you want, as long as you understand I'm not really an Apsaras."

This time her grin was full of smug satisfaction. "We will open soon for the midday meal. By this evening all will know, and will come to see the Apsaras dance. You are excused from serving for now. It will increase the mystery and curiosity if no one sees you except when you perform."

"And what am I supposed to do until then?"

"Help Leddy in the kitchen."

Right, I was going to help in the kitchen when my idea of cooking was pushing a button on the food prep unit and watching a tray slide out. On the other hand, that's where the coffee was.

Preparations for the midday meal were in full swing by

now, so I grabbed a cup, poured myself some coffee, and then found a spot out of the way to watch and sip. It didn't take me long to realize that the kitchen was an organizational disaster. I was surprised poor Leddy had feet left. She had to run from one side of the room to the other to get seasoning, make another trip for a particular pan, and yet another for a spoon or platter to dish the food up.

Immediately, a blueprint of the kitchen formed in my mind, only in this one, everything was right where it needed to be for maximum efficiency. Quietly I set to work, making the reality match the picture I'd conjured. And since the musicians weren't doing anything constructive, I put them to work, too.

By the time we were done, it was late afternoon, and only a few diehard customers remained from the lunch crowd. All the utensils Leddy used most were right next to her on a table I'd had the men carry in from the common room. Half the shelves over the stoves now contained the pots and pans I'd noticed were her favorites, and the other half contained spices and seasonings. A few steps behind her I'd positioned the food prep table that had been all the way on the other side of the room. One end of the table now held a neat stack of bowls and platters.

Peri had spent the time alternating between visits to the flowers and zooming into the kitchen to "help." Her idea of assistance was to toss dishes and utensils from the table onto the floor while chuckling gleefully as she watched them hit. Luckily, they were stout and only one plate actually broke.

"It's wonderful," Leddy told me, eyes shinning with pleasure. "I barely have to move two steps in any direction to reach what I need. Don't know why we didn't think of this cycles ago. Marcus should let you work something out for the taproom. The girls have to come right through the kitchen to reach it."

Yeah, I'd noticed that. I was on the verge of telling her I'd see what I could do when Lillith intruded.

"Don't you dare volunteer. You're not here to organize the planet. You're here to retrieve the Sumantti and the first step to accomplishing that goal is to learn how to use the Imadei. Stop avoiding your mission."

"I'm not avoiding," I told her, turning to adjust some extra dishes. "I'm merely blending in, following orders, trying not to look like I'm working for the Federation."

"Uh-huh."

"Okay, so maybe there's a tiny bit of avoidance there. Truth is, I don't have any idea where to start with the Imadei. Suggestions, please?"

"Find a quiet spot and try. If you don't try, how can you ever succeed?"

Great. Now she was a philosopher. Wasn't that just wonderful? Not to mention really helpful. Before I could tell her just how I felt about her little pep talk, Marcus appeared in the doorway, glanced around, and then came straight for me.

"You've got about an hour before you have to dress for the act. Go rest. I'll handle Treya." He arched a brow and tipped his head toward the house next door.

With a sigh, I headed out the back door. "You tattled, didn't you?" I asked Lillith as Peri joined me with a chirped greeting.

"Of course I did. A big part of my job is making sure you do yours. Marcus understands and says not to forget the motion detectors."

"Sure. People might start thinking I'm Federation if they see me staring at a black rock." I rolled my eyes as I went through the gate and crossed the backyard of Marcus's house.

"No, but give even an idiot enough pieces, and eventually they'll put them all together and solve the puzzle. Why help them out any more than we have to?"

Okay, maybe she had a point. I wasn't going to admit it, though. No sense inflating her ego even more.

I entered the house through the back door with Peri following, and moved through the living room to the box on the mantel. As soon as the motion detector was set, I went to a chair, sat down, and pulled out the Imadei. "I'm ready," I told the ship. "What now?"

"First, relax. Empty your mind of everything except the Sumantti. Then try looking 'into' the crystal as opposed to looking 'at' the stone."

Relax. Easy for her to say. I took a deep breath, closed my eyes, and willed tense muscles to loosen. Letting an image of the Sumantti form in my mind, I raised the crystal and gazed into its depths.

It really was a pretty stone, I realized. The separate crystals were hexagonal in shape, giving the facets an odd glimmer instead of a sharp refraction of light. The effect was rather hypnotic, and the longer I stared into its depths, the more my eyelids began to droop.

A wave of vertigo swept over me, and I was only minimally aware of Peri perching on the chair arm, crooning so hard her body vibrated.

"Echo?" Lillith's voice seemed to come from a long way off. I tried to answer her, but the words stayed stuck in my head. Wasn't I supposed to be concentrating on something?

Wait. It had to do with children and the castle, didn't it?

"Echo, what's wrong? Answer me!" The ship sounded frantic now, but I couldn't respond no matter how hard I tried. The dizziness was getting worse and darkness was edging in at the corners of my vision.

Abruptly, I wasn't in Marcus's house anymore. I was standing in a plain dark room that looked vaguely like a bedroom. There was something familiar about what was happening, something that set my heart hammering in fear. I turned already knowing what I'd see. A small bed with a fragile little blonde girl strapped down, her body riddled with tubes attached to beeping machines.

Except that wasn't what I saw. There was a bed, yes, but no tiny blonde girl, no bright lights or tubes or beeping machines.

A feeling of disorientation swept over me, and I put out a hand to brace myself on a post at the foot of the bed. And then stared stupidly when my hand went right through it.

What in the name of Zin was going on?

"Please," a small voice whispered. "We're frightened. Are you here to help us?"

My head shot up, heart in my throat as I located the source of the question. There was a girl after all, although not the one I had expected. She uncurled from the blankets and stared at me beseechingly, tears glimmering in emerald-green eyes before streaking down one dirty cheek. Her dress was thin, ragged, and looked as if it had been designed for a warmer place than this room. Her long hair was a golden red and in dire need of a good washing, as were the thin legs protruding from beneath the tattered hem of her skirt.

Beside her, the blanket stirred and I saw another face emerge, this one a bit smaller and so white I wondered if there was actually blood flowing through her veins. Her hair was coal black and dull with mats. The palest blue eyes I'd ever seen stared at me blankly from purplish circles that lined their lower lids.

In spite of the difference in size, I got the feeling they were about the same age.

"I'm Gaia and this is my sister, Banca. She doesn't feel good. If you can only help one of us, please help her."

It was the red-haired girl who had spoken. Even though I tried to answer, my brain still couldn't get around what was happening and no speech escaped my suddenly useless mouth.

I took a deep breath, prepared to try again, but abruptly, pain like I'd never known sliced through my head and the world went black.

CHAPTER 6

I came around with Marcus gently tapping my cheeks and calling my name. Awareness roared back and I lurched to my feet, scanning the room anxiously. "Where is she, where's Pelga?"

Marcus's eyes were dark with worry. "Who? Echo, are you all right? Lillith called me when she couldn't get a response from you, and I found you unconscious. What happened?"

"Pelga," I said, frantically moving toward the door. "I have to help her."

"Stop right there." He stepped between me and the exit, blocking my path. "Who is Pelga?"

I froze as the name finally registered in my pain befuddled mind. "No one. A little girl I knew in the crèche. Except she said her name was Gaia. I must have been dreaming." I pushed the name away and pressed on my temples with both hands. "Zin, my head hurts. Do you have any analgesic?"

"Of course." He moved to the kitchen side of the house, poured a glass full of water from a pitcher, and added some kind of powder. Giving the contents a swirl or two, he crossed the room and handed it to me. "It's fast acting, so the pain should be gone soon."

I took a sip, grimaced at the bitter taste, and then held my breath long enough to down the rest of it. Almost immediately my headache began to ease and I sighed with relief as I handed the glass back. "Thanks. That's much better."

"Echo, exactly what happened here? Start at the beginning." He put the glass on a counter and motioned me to sit.

With a frown, I reclaimed my previous seat as Marcus took the one beside me and Peri fluttered to perch on the mantel. "I don't really know. Lillith suggested I look 'into' the crystal instead of closing my eyes and trying to feel something. That's what I did. I remember getting dizzy. Next thing I knew, you were waking me up."

He arched a brow. "And nothing happened in between?"

"No." I hesitated. "Well, except the nightmare."

"And the nightmare was about this Pelga?"

"Yes. No." I shook my head in confusion. "I thought it was, at first. But the girl I dreamed about wasn't Pelga. She had red hair instead of blonde, and she was older, maybe seven or eight cycles. Pelga and I were only five cycles the last time I saw her."

"Tell me, where did this dream take place?"

I didn't much care for the way he'd gone all squinty-eyed as he watched me, but I answered, anyway. "I'm not sure. It was a small, dimly lit room and I didn't see any windows. The only things there were the bed and the girls."

"There were two of them?"

"Yes. Gaia and Banca."

He gave a brief nod of acknowledgment. "What were the girls doing?"

"Nothing, until I showed up. Then Gaia sat up and begged me to help them."

Marcus straightened abruptly. "They saw you?"

"Of course they saw me. It was *my* dream, for Zin's sake. Why wouldn't they see me?"

"Clairvoyance?" he murmured.

"No," Lillith responded, somehow managing to communicate with both Marcus and I at the same time. "The psi test would have recognized clairvoyance. There has to be more to it than that. Especially if the child could see her, which also rules out astral projection."

"Teleportation?" he asked.

"That's fairly common, also," the ship told us. "Besides, I'm tracking her constantly and she never left this room."

Realization swept over me in a wave of panic and I leaped to my feet, hands fisted at my sides. "Oh, no you don't. It was a dream, nothing more, and I can prove it. When I first got there, I reached for the bedpost. My hand went right through it, like I was a ghost. Now, if you'll excuse me, I'm going back to the Terpsichore. Treya must be waiting for me to change into my costume."

Peri, picking up on my emotional turmoil, fluttered after me, shrilling in dismay as I marched from the room. I slowed enough to allow her to settle on my shoulder just to quiet her down. Frag it, I did not have any psi ability, and no was going to force me to admit I did.

So what if odd things were happening, like seeing Reynard examining the door I'd destroyed right before Lillith told me he was doing exactly that? It was this Zin blasted crystal doing all the woo-woo stuff, not me personally.

I refused to let it be me.

Inhaling a deep gulp of the pristine air, I focused on my surroundings enough to realize that the sun was sinking from view in a blaze of red-and-gold glory, leaving fingers of deep blue twilight to creep over the land. As I went through the gate that gave entry from Marcus's yard to his business premises, two things happened simultaneously.

The hair on my nape stood erect, and Peri stiffened, her eyes tinged with faint shades of red as she stared intently at the Terpsichore. I came to an abrupt stop, scanning the deeper shadows around the base of the building, muscles tensed for action.

"Lillith, can you check the area? I think someone is watching me," I subvocalized.

"There are countless heat signatures around the inn," she said. "They all blur together. And I can't use my night vision because there's still too much sunlight in the upper atmosphere. I have to use my infrared scanners and it's hard to pick out a single person when the inn is full. Wait—" There was a slight pause. "It looks like someone is pressed against the outside northern wall, moving toward the front of the building."

I turned rapidly in the direction she'd indicated. "Try to keep a fix on them." Peri launched from my shoulder and zoomed ahead, silent for once.

"Stop! What are you doing? It could just be a customer returning from the privy," the ship told me.

"Sneaking along the wall? I don't think so. Whoever it is, they were watching me. If someone suspects I'm not what I seem to be, I'd at least like to be able to identify them."

When I reached the stone wall, I slowed and edged along its length. I wanted to see the person who'd watched me, not trip over them and cause a confrontation.

Just as I reached the front corner I felt a sense of frustrated puzzlement coming from Peri. Carefully, I poked my head far enough around the building to see the entrance. And discovered why Peri was so frustrated. A steady stream of people, exclusively male, paraded through the door, with smaller groups stopping to chat here and there before going inside. None of them was paying undue attention to my location, or to Peri, who hovered several meters above their heads.

"Lillith, was there anything distinguishing about him?" I asked.

"Not really, since details don't show up infrared scans. All I can tell you is he was average height and average weight."

Which could describe more than half the men I saw. With a sigh I withdrew, calling Peri off the search as I walked slowly around the building to the back door of the Terpsichore. She was emoting her reluctance to give up, and I could certainly share the sentiment. It was creepy knowing someone was spying on you, with no idea who it was or what their intentions might be.

But it was either give up for now, or tackle each male and hold him captive while I interrogated him. That could take a lot of time, considering how many men were in attendance tonight. Not to mention the undue notice it would bring me. The king probably wouldn't approve of my taking out a hundred or so of his citizens. I would, however, keep a close eye on those in attendance tonight.

Leddy looked up from a pot she was stirring and smiled when I entered the kitchen. "Treya is ready for you," she said. "Through there." Her head tilted toward the room where I'd danced earlier that morning. "She found the most amazing costume for you to wear tonight."

"Yeah?" I immediately perked up at the thought of new clothes. "What color?"

She waved a hand and grinned. "See for yourself."

The room was now devoid of musicians, but I could hear a melody drifting in from the common room of the inn mixed with the continuous murmur of masculine voices. I'd barely cleared the threshold before Treya grabbed me and hauled me across the room to where a folding screen partitioned off one corner.

"Hurry, change into your costume. I've never seen the inn so full. Even Reynard du'Marr is out there."

I came to a quick stop, my heart suddenly giving it hell. "Here? He's here?"

"Yes, and his visits are rare. He must have heard the rumors about an Apsaras dancing tonight."

"Uh, yeah. He probably heard the rumors." I nodded vigorously, reluctant to tell her I suspected he'd shown up just because he knew I was working here. I'd managed to fully arouse his suspicions. If Lillith hadn't said my watcher was average height, I might have suspected the commander. As it was, he could have set one of his troops on the job. It was imperative that I stayed on my toes from here on out, both figuratively and literally.

With that in mind I continued behind the screen and then blinked in wonder at the costume hanging from a hook on the wall. The silky halter and waist band were red. Blindingly, brilliantly red, and I fell instantly in love with the costume.

Reverently, I took the bottom half down and examined the skirt. It was fuller than the normal Bashalde apparel, transparent to the point of being see-through, and it was shot with golden thread. Every rustle of the material set gold spangles glimmering in the gossamer stuff.

And that wasn't all. A fine gold chain girded the low-cut leather waist and from it dangled shorter chains adorned with tiny gold bells that would sway and chime seductively when the wearer moved.

I stripped out of my own clothes in record time and carefully donned the costume, tucking the Imadei out of sight under the halter top. Now I needed a mirror, and luckily, there was one attached to the wall in the practice room.

Still barefoot, I stepped from behind the screen just in time to see Peri dive headfirst into a pile of gold jewelry Treya had put on a table. A spate of cursing erupted as the blonde made a grab for her, followed by a hiss of warning from the center of the heap.

"Peri, no!" I jumped across the space separating us and fished her out of the shiny mound. "Sorry." I gave Treya a weak smile. "She has a thing for jewelry. Here." I pulled off the lightest of my bracelets and gave it to the sullen dragon bird. "You can play with this for now."

Still pouting, she eyed the bracelet for a second, weighing it against the larger treasure trove, then grasped it in her front talons and carried it to a corner, mumbling with ill-concealed indignation.

Treya shook her head. "Useless creature."

Okay, that got my hackles up. Maybe I hadn't asked for a dragon bird, and maybe I didn't care much for animals in general, but Peri was different. Peri was *my* animal, and no one was allowed to malign her but me. "You like jewelry, too. Does that make you useless?"

She turned from Peri to glare at me. "Loyalty and spirit are well and good, but remember who you work for, girl. Now sit down."

I had to bite my tongue to keep from telling her who I really worked for, and that I could break her in half with one finger. Clenching my teeth on a response that could only get me in deep schite, I took the chair she'd pulled out and sat down.

Ignoring my anger, she grasped my chin in one hand, tilted my face up, and proceeded to apply makeup to my eyes. When that was done to her satisfaction, she took a short veil that matched my skirt and fastened it so it covered the lower half of my face. Next came the jewelry. While Peri watched jealously, Treya loaded down my arms and even my ankles with slender gold bangles.

"There." She stood back and motioned toward the mirror. "You're ready. See what you think."

I stood, musical tinkling accompanying every move, and walked to the mirror. Then gaped in shock at the mysterious, sexy stranger staring back at me. Her lids were lined with kohl, making her eyes look big and luminous. The costume concealed barely enough to be decent, and yet still conveyed a sense of maidenly modesty.

Even my wild-woman do added to the exotic appearance Treya had achieved. How in Zin's name had she pulled this off? I was still goggling and wondering if Alien Affairs would let me keep her when the stage door opened a crack and Marcus stuck his head into the room.

"Is she ready? The band is waiting. . . ." His voice trailed off as he saw me, then he stepped all the way inside and closed the door. "Oh, my. It might not be a good idea to have her serve after her acts. We could have a riot on our hands."

Treya shrugged. "It will prolong the mystery if she stays away from the men, and that means larger crowds and more money."

Okay, she really, really liked money. Maybe if I offered her half my salary, she'd come with me when this job was over. It would take me longer to pay off my indenture, but hey, if she could make me look like this it was worth the sacrifice.

Unaware of the direction my thoughts were traveling in, Marcus nodded. "I'll introduce her as soon as you get the lamps covered." He went back through the door as Treya slid a cover over the nearest glass cylinder and headed for another.

"Why do the lamps need to be out?" I asked, positioning myself beside the door Marcus had just used.

The room got darker as Treya moved around it extinguishing the light. "The back of the stage is dark. With the lamps out, no one will see you enter. It will be as if you simply appeared. Stay in the dark area until the music starts, then just move forward."

As she reached the last lamp she hesitated and shot me a

questioning glance. "Are you nervous? This will be your first time performing in public."

"A little," I lied. After all, I was supposed to be a girl who'd been raised by a reclusive father, not the organized employee of the Department of Protocol who dealt with hundreds of Naturals every day.

She seemed satisfied with my response and even gave me an encouraging pat on the arm. "That's perfectly understandable. Just dance as you did this morning, for the joy of it, and you'll be fine."

Cupping her hand around the last cover, she lowered it over the sunstone container and plunged the room into total darkness. "Go."

Just as I opened the door and slipped through onto the stage, there was a rush of air and Peri landed on my shoulder, waves of excitement rolling off her. Great, this was just what I needed. How could I dance with a hyper dragon bird clinging to me?

Doing my best to ignore her, I scanned the common room and suddenly faltered. The place was wall-to-wall men. I'm talking packed in like sardines, with not so much as a single inch of space unoccupied. And every one of them was staring intently at the stage as Marcus finished his introduction and left to join a table near the front. A table where Reynard du'Marr was seated with two other men.

Okay, maybe I hadn't lied about being nervous, because my tummy suddenly erupted with butterflies in full riot, all trying to make their escape to freedom. Quickly I shut my eyes to block out the men and forced myself to take deep calming breaths. This was no big deal, I assured my suddenly alert nerves. It was all part of the job.

As the band played the first chords, calm washed over me and I realized with surprise that most of it was coming from Peri. Slowly I opened my eyes, raised my arms over my head and began a gentle hip-swaying rhythm as I moved forward, one small step at a time.

Right before I was fully revealed, Peri launched from my shoulder and swooped over the audience. Her action drew the men's attention away from the stage long enough for me to step into the light as murmurs of wonder followed her flight. By the time they looked back, there I was. It must have looked like I'd just suddenly materialized from thin air.

Useless, my rear end. That was one smart dragon bird.

The song was the same one the band had played for me this morning. It started off measured and stately, then gathered speed and exuberance. I kept my movements in line with the tempo, my gaze locked on the commander to block out the other men.

Peri rejoined me onstage, dipping and rising, circling me in time with my movements. Warbling an intricate thread that wove its way through the melody, she bobbed and weaved, wings fluttering madly as she mimicked the steps in midair.

The audience was enthralled. Not so much as a whisper rose from the watching men as I gyrated, undulated and spun. And for a while, I forgot they were there. Once again I danced from the sheer love of moving, from the joy of doing something I was created, at least in part, to do.

Until I remembered that one of the men in the audience had been spying on me earlier.

My steps faltered a beat before I found my pace again, but now I scanned the faces turned toward me, the hair on my arms prickling erect. You don't pull surveillance on someone if your intentions are good.

Somehow, someway, I had aroused suspicions. Now I needed to know who thought I wasn't what I seemed. My gaze went to the commander. If it was him, I had to find out, and there was only one way to accomplish that goal.

"Lillith," I subvocalized, "tell Marcus to bring the commander back after I'm done. I need to talk with him."

"You agreed to stay away from him," she reminded me in her best general-to-the-troops voice.

"I know. But this has nothing to do with lust. It's business. Please, just do as I ask."

"Fine. I hope you know what you're doing."

So did I. The music began to slow toward its final notes, and with each step I moved nearer the darkened part of the stage. By the time the last echo from the pipe died away, I was in total darkness again. Peri did one more flyby over the audience and then joined me, radiating smug satisfaction as we slipped through the door together.

"Did you tell Marcus?" I asked the ship. Off to the side I heard a sliding noise and one of the lamps flared to life under Treya's hands. She moved around the room, uncovering the others.

"Yes," Lillith answered. "He's not sure it's a good idea, either, but said he'd bring the commander right back."

"Good."

When the last lamp was glowing, Treya turned, hands on her hips, and surveyed the dragon bird on my shoulder. "So, she's not useless after all. Did you train her to do that?"

"No." Peri was preening so vigorously I couldn't shake my head. "She did it all on her own."

"Will she do it again for your next act?"

"Probably. She likes to participate in whatever I'm doing."

Before she could continue, the door to the kitchen opened and Marcus ushered the commander into the room. Right before my eyes Treya transformed from a money-grubbing taskmaster into a quivering pile of cooing mush.

"Commander!" She went forward with her hands reaching for his, full lips in a playful pout. "It's been months since you've stopped in for a visit. I thought you'd forgotten me."

"Of course not." He gave her a vague smile, but he was looking at me over her shoulder. "My duties are many. I'm afraid I have little time for anything else."

My eyes narrowed as I took in Treya's body language and a nasty suspicion made the rounds of my gray matter. "Lilith," I subvocalized. "If women are treated like a precious commodity here, what do the unmarried men do for sexual release?"

Marcus glanced at me and I saw his eyebrow arch right before the ship responded. "There are Bashalde women who have no fathers or husbands that are willing to accommodate them for a price."

Yeah, that's what I thought. And I'd bet half my next pay voucher that Treya was one of them. It was time to break up her little party, I decided.

Practically muscling my way between them, I took Reynard by the arm. "Commander, thank you for coming." I glanced at Treya. "Would you mind getting the commander some wine?"

Her expression made her look like something nasty had crawled into her mouth and died. "You know each other?"

"We've met. And we have some private business to discuss. So, if you don't mind . . ."

She turned to Marcus as though hoping he'd override my requests, but before she could speak he nodded. "I believe your act is up next?"

Shooting me an angry glare, she turned in a swirl of skirts and marched through the door, slamming it behind her so hard the walls rattled.

I gave the commander my best innocent look. "She seemed upset. Maybe she thought you came back to see her?"

Marcus muffled a cough behind his hand as the commander looked down at me, his mouth lifting on one side. "No woman directs my actions. By my sworn oath, my first and only loyalty is to the king. Now, what did you wish to see me about?"

The opening door interrupted us as Leddy bustled in, a tray balanced on her hip. With a smile for Marcus, she went to the table where jewelry had been spread earlier and set out a bottle of wine and three glasses. As she went by me on her way out, she reached over and patted my arm. "Good for you," she whispered. "Treya's had that coming for a long time." The door closed gently behind her.

Ignoring her comment, I gestured to the table. "Why don't we sit?"

Marcus poured the wine as the commander held a chair for me and then pulled one out for himself.

Once both men were comfortable, I cleared my throat. "Commander, did you order me watched?"

His eyes narrowed as he studied me. "Why would you think I might?"

"Because someone is watching me, and you're the only one I can think of who might have a reason. After all, I did accidentally hurt one of your men and stumble into the castle. Plus, my father was an experienced arms master who taught me well. Combined, I can see why you might feel a need to keep an eye on me."

His piercing gaze swung to Marcus. "You knew about this?"

"No, this is the first I've heard." At my original question to the commander, Marcus had stiffened, his hand tightening on the glass of wine he held. He knew, even better than I, what was at stake here if someone discovered my true identity.

"I haven't had a chance to tell him," I told Reynard. "The event occurred only a short time before my act."

"Tell us exactly what happened," the commander ordered.

"I was leaving Marcus's house just as the sun was setting, and the base of the Terpsichore was in darkness. There was a man in hiding in the shadows, watching me."

"Maybe it was someone who'd heard the tales Treya was spreading about an Apsaras dancing here and wanted to get a look at you," Marcus said.

"Peri didn't think so," I told him. "And she's very good at picking up human emotions. She thought he was up to no good and gave chase. If he were only curious, why did he move away from us and mingle with the crowds so we couldn't locate his position?" The dragon bird bobbed her head as though agreeing with what I'd said.

"You saw this man?" the commander asked.

This was where it got tricky, because I'd felt more than seen him. Lillith was the one who'd "seen" him. "Not clearly enough to identify him," I answered. "I can only tell you he was average height and weight."

"You were not harmed?"

"No. He ran as soon as I started toward him."

"I gave no order to have you observed," the commander said. His fingertips drummed the table for a second. "But I will assign a man for your protection."

Uh-oh. That was a reaction I hadn't anticipated. No way could I allow one of his soldiers to watch my every move. I was doing mental gymnastics trying to find a solution to the problem when Marcus saved me the trouble.

"Thank you for the offer, Commander, but Echo is my ward and my responsibility. I'll see to her protection. He may not be the brightest stone in the lamp, but Bim would die before allowing any harm to come to her. And, as you've seen for yourself, Echo is not without her own resources. Together I'm sure we can handle any situation that might arise."

Reynard stared at Marcus for a long, tense moment, as if

trying to make up his mind whether or not he could trust the barkeep with my health and well-being. Finally, he nodded. "In that case, I will have my men try to discover who would wish her ill. And if any further problems occur, you will notify me at once."

"As you wish," Marcus responded.

Reynard pushed his chair back then paused to smile at me. "I regret that I cannot stay for your second dance, but I will arrive after the breaking of the fast tomorrow to escort you and your guardian to the Bashalde gathering."

"I'll look forward to it," I told him, returning the smile.

With a final nod, he left through the kitchen door. As soon as it closed behind him, Marcus arched a brow at me.

"Why didn't you tell me someone was watching you?"

"Truthfully?" I shrugged. "It didn't even occur to me. I was too busy getting ready for my act and wondering if the commander was that suspicious of me."

"I'm going to assign Bim to escort you, and stay with you when I can't. We won't have to worry about him repeating anything he sees because he can barely speak. And the next time you think someone is stalking you, alert me through Lillith. Maybe we can trap them between us."

"Did you believe the commander?" I sipped the wine that had gone ignored until now.

"Yes and no." He sighed. "He's suspicious, no doubt about that. But I don't think he'd set his men to watching you. He's the type who would do it himself. The question is, who else would want to keep an eye on you, and why? We need those questions answered soon. It also worries me that the commander didn't ask the same things." Brow furrowed, he stood and pushed his chair up to the table. "I'm going to send some food for you and have a talk with Bim. Rest here until your second act, and then go straight home."

He left by the same door the commander had used and I

didn't see him again before my second dance. I ate and then waited until Treya, tight lipped with anger, returned after her act. She marched right up to me and poked me in the chest with one finger.

"You overstepped your bounds, girl. I am in charge of the dancers. When you want something, you go through me. And you do not invite men to visit without my permission."

I grabbed her hand and bent her wrist back until she winced with pain. "Now, you listen to me. The only bounds overstepped here are yours. I'm not just another dancer, I'm Marcus's ward. When it comes to dancing, I'll *allow* you to direct me, but anything else is my business and you will stay out of it.

"Furthermore, if this little show of power is because of the commander, you should understand that by his words, you don't own him. So if you've been deluding yourself that sex with him implies some kind of commitment, get over it. From this point on, the commander is off-limits to you. Am I making myself clear?"

She nodded and I released her wrist. "Good. Now, I believe it's time for my last act."

Casually, I strolled to the table where I'd left my jewelry for Peri to play with and began putting it on, but I kept one eye on Treya in case she decided to try something.

Rubbing her wrist, she glared at me for a moment longer, then turned and flounced from the room. Peri watched her go, a satisfied guess-you-showed-her air coming from the dragon bird. But even though Treya had pushed me into acting, I regretted having to let her know who was boss, and I knew another talk with her was in order. If there was one thing I didn't need on Madrea it was another enemy. Especially not one who was in charge of my costumes and makeup.

CHAPTER 7

"Treya told me what happened," Marcus said, sliding a plate of food in front of me. We were in the small kitchen of his house, awaiting the commander's arrival before heading off to the Bashalde gathering.

"Did she?" I toyed with the food, too tired to eat. It had been a strange night, full of odd dreams I couldn't quite remember. But it felt as if I'd gone on a four-day trek with no sleep and had just returned. "I'm sorry if I caused a problem."

"No problem at all." He dug into his own food with gusto. "You were absolutely right, even by Madrean standards. As far as anyone knows, you're my ward, and as much as I care about her, Treya is an employee. I can make her behave, but unfortunately, I can't stop her jealousy. You'll have to deal with that on your own."

"Uh-huh."

At my lackluster response he set his fork aside and arched a brow at me. "What's wrong?"

"Nothing, I'm just tired." I forced myself to take a bite of the food.

"Is something wrong with your bed?"

"No, no, the bed is fine. My dreams made me restless, that's all."

"I see." He pushed back from the table and went to the counter, where he poured water into a glass, then added some powdery concoction from a jar that sat on a shelf near the stove. After a quick stir, he handed it to me. "Drink this."

I took the glass and sniffed its contents. It didn't smell horrible, but it did make my senses whirl. "What is it?"

"A potion I keep handy. Make it myself from local herbs. It should make you feel better."

"Well, I'm all for feeling better." First, I sipped gingerly, then drank heavily when I caught the pleasant, smoky taste. Immediately I felt warm, soothing energy flow through me. "That's amazing," I told him. "You should bottle this stuff."

"Wouldn't sell, I'm afraid." He resumed his seat and nonchalantly picked up his fork. "It only works on people in the first stages of verge sickness, and has no effect on anyone else."

I'd been reaching for my own fork when he dropped that verbal bomb. Now I sat frozen, my hand suspended over the utensil as I stared at him. "What? What are you talking about? I'm not sick, I never get sick. I was just tired from a restless night, that's all."

"You're in the first stages of verge sickness, Echo. I've seen it before. And as long as you keep denying your psi ability, the sickness will continue to get worse. Soon, very soon, my potion won't help you anymore."

"He's right," Lillith interjected. "It's a well-documented reaction among those with psi ability."

"I don't believe you, either of you." The heat from my coffee mug drew me and I wrapped suddenly icy hands around it. "I'm thirty cycles. If I have psi ability, why would it wait until now to manifest?"

"Normally, it wouldn't." Marcus finished eating and

pushed his plate aside. "And we don't think it did this time. Lillith and I believe you've always had it, but something happened that made you suppress not only the ability, but even the memory of having it. Close and constant contact with the Imadei has made it surface again."

"In that case, I'll just stop wearing the Imadei." He watched with interest as I fumbled for the chain, pulled the stone from under my silk top. And then winced in agony as I tried to place it on the table.

I couldn't stand it. Without any conscious decision on my part, I put the necklace back on and tucked the stone out of sight before breathing a sigh of relief.

And then blinked at Marcus in surprise. "I'm doomed," I told him.

His mouth kicked up on one side. "I wouldn't go that far. All you have to do is start using your ability and the verge sickness will go away."

"How am I supposed to do that? Assuming I really do have psi ability, how do I use it when I don't know what it is?"

Before he could answer me, Peri zoomed into the room, landed on the table and stared at the front door, her entire body vibrating with anticipation. A second later, someone knocked.

"We'll continue this conversation tonight," Marcus said as he moved to open the door. "Commander, you're right on time. Please come in."

Hastily I ran my fingers through my wild hair and plastered a smile on my face.

"Your heartbeat just accelerated to an alarming degree," Lillith told me.

"Go away and leave me alone," I subvocalized, stepping forward to meet Reynard. He reached for my hand, and when his larger, calloused palm closed around my fingers, I not only forgot my aversion to having my hands held, I almost forgot what I was going to say. "Commander, thank you for taking the time out of your schedule to escort us. Would you like a cup of coffee before we leave?"

"Thank you for the offer, but we should be off." He smiled down at me. "I spoke with Chief Lowden about you before our meeting yesterday. He's anxious to meet the daughter of his old teacher. So is King Politaus, who also knew your father. Unfortunately, he won't be at the gathering today. Instead he requests that you and Kent join him for the evening meal at week's end."

"We'd be delighted." I saw Marcus arch a brow at my rapid response. "Tell Marcus this could be my chance to meet Braxus," I told Lillith.

"Not to mention spend more time with the commander," she shot back.

There was that, I thought with a smile as I took the commander's outstretched arm and let him escort me through the door. It took a great deal of effort not to run my hand over the hard muscles in his forearm.

"How far is it to the gathering?" I asked him as Peri did loops around us and Marcus brought up the rear.

"Within walking distance," he said. "The Bashalde always set their tents in the field behind the castle."

Made sense, I decided. And now that I looked around, people were converging on the castle from all directions: men, women, and children alike. Most were walking, but a few rode horses, with other equines following them on leading ropes. Occasionally, a wagon holding an entire family or produce creaked by, the horses' harness jingling as they easily pulled the load. There was a festive air about the population that even the women's drab clothing couldn't dampen.

Two giggling young boys darted by, clutching coins tightly in their fists. They paused to ogle Peri in awe before dashing ahead.

I watched them vanish into the crowd in front of us, then reached down and checked the small coin pouch attached to my belt. Marcus had given it to me first thing this morning. I'd been loath to take it, but he assured me I'd earned it the night before. Plus, anything extra I spent would be reimbursed by Alien Affairs, and I really did need more clothes.

Marcus moved up to walk beside us. "I know it's been less than a day, Commander, but have your men found anything yet?"

"I'm afraid not," Reynard answered. "There are so many people in the city for the gathering that finding one particular stranger will be almost impossible. Especially without a good description. But I've ordered them to keep their ears open for any rumors concerning your ward."

"Please, call me Echo," I told him, my stomach doing a quick flip when he smiled at me.

"In that case, you must call me Reynard."

"Reynard." I gave him a quick grin. "It's such a strong name. Your mother must have been very pleased at your birth, to give you such a name."

"Stop flirting," Lillith ordered.

"Shut up, you old cow," I told her and received an indignant gasp in response.

"I don't know," the commander was saying. "I never knew my parents. The king's mother found me wandering alone when her company passed through a village near Bastion City, and she had me brought to the castle to serve as a companion to her son."

"You have no relatives?"

"None that came forward to claim me."

I tried to picture him as a lost little boy no one wanted and my stomach clenched for a different reason this time. "You must have been very lonely."

One broad shoulder lifted in a shrug. "There were compensations. I benefited from the same education given the king, and we became fast friends. His family saved me."

No wonder he was so loyal to the king.

By now we'd reached the castle and started around it. Marcus had joined a group of men in front of us, close enough to preserve his position as chaperone, but far enough away to give us some room to chat. Peri was off hovering over a batch of flowers.

"What of you?" Reynard asked. "You must have been lonely growing up without friends."

Immediately, an image of small, delicate Pelga flashed through my mind. What the hell was going on with my memory? I hadn't thought about Pelga since I'd left the crèche, and now she seemed to be constantly in my thoughts.

I shoved her visage away and concentrated on weaving my lies together. "Not really. You don't miss what you've never known, and I had my father. He was parent, teacher, and playmate, all rolled into one."

"You must miss him terribly."

"Yes, but his illness was progressive, so I had time to prepare for his loss."

The words were barely out of my mouth when we rounded the end of the castle. My reaction to the sight spread out in front of us almost gave me away.

"Oh!" I gasped in wonder. "It's beautiful."

Realizing too late what I'd said, I shot Reynard a glance from under my lashes. "This is the first time I've seen a full gathering," I explained. "My father refused to go. He hated crowds."

The castle sat on a slight rise that sloped gently down to an eight-hectare field, giving us a view of the entire gathering all at once. Silk tents in every color known to man undulated softly in the gentle spring breeze. They took up the entire open area, stretching from tree line to tree line.

A small stream wound its way across the field and around tents, sunlight glinting off its rushing water. It was spanned in several locations by rustic wooden foot bridges that gave access to both sides of the meadow, while trees growing here and there on its banks offered cooling shade.

From all directions rose the faint sound of voices hawking wares, overlaid by the tinkle of distant music. The air was redolent with the spicy scent of cooking food that made my mouth water even though I'd only finished eating a short while before.

It was a sensory overload for a GEP used to mile-high plexisteel buildings, plascrete walkways and canned air. The only grass on Centaurius was in state-supervised parks, and the rules governing their use were strict to the point of being prohibitive. You could look but not touch, and until now that had been fine with me. Nowhere on Centaurius did anything remotely like this mad chaos of color and humanity exist. Even our parties were stately and formal and I was filled with an inexplicable sense of loss.

Maybe I had a tiny bit of nature girl in me after all, although I wasn't going to get carried away and actually touch dirt.

The commander was watching me closely, his crystal eyes entirely too knowledgeable, so I cleared my throat and gestured at the mayhem below us. "Which tent belongs to Chief Lowden?"

"His is the large green and gold one in the center of the field. The slightly smaller tents scattered around it belong to the heads of families."

From the data I'd studied on board Lillith, there were fourteen Bashalde "families" on Madrea, and their heads made up the Bashalde council. They were the ones who upheld tribal laws, settled disputes among their families, and advised the chief, although Lowden had the last word on any larger issues that might arise. The Bashalde also controlled the majority of the sunstone deposits.

A million questions crowded my mind as I studied the tents, like what the treaty with the king involved and were there any current disputes between the two groups, not counting the wars they'd waged against each other in the past. But asking Reynard would expose how very little I knew of what was supposed to be my own people, so I tucked them away for later discussion with Marcus.

As we crossed the first bridge to merge with the crowd, Peri returned to perch on my shoulder. The silly creature trilled a musical greeting to everyone we passed, drawing even more attention than she normally would. So many people stopped to gawk that we caused a jam in the flow of foot traffic.

Hush, I told her. *We're supposed to be inconspicuous, not putting on a show.*

With a rebellious ruffling of her feathers, she settled down to watch a colorfully dressed man juggling balls, her head tilting from one side to the other as she studied him, her curiosity flowing over me in waves. For that matter, I was curious, too. He was the first male Bashalde I'd seen and I couldn't help noticing how strikingly attractive he was with his dark looks and slim build.

He caught me staring and winked, his ebony eyes flashing with merriment. Beside me, Reynard stiffened just enough for me to notice. When I glanced up to see what the problem was, I discovered him glaring a warning at the juggler.

Chuckling, the man turned back to entertain the group that gathered around him, seemingly paying no attention to the coins being dropped into a cup near his feet.

Could it be that the commander was jealous? A warm rush

of happiness set my blood singing, but it faded quickly when I realized his protective stance might have more to with my unknown stalker than lust for my person.

As if to verify my suspicion, Marcus waited for us to catch up with him and then fell into place on my left. Since the commander was with us, he'd given Bim the day off from his guard duty.

"There's an excellent garment maker just ahead," he told me. "If you'd like, we can get that out of the way so you can enjoy the rest of the gathering."

When I replied in the affirmative they steered me to an open booth with a small red-and-white tent behind it. A middle-aged woman, slim and pretty, glanced in our direction and then put down her sewing and came to greet us with a smile. "Marcus, I hoped you'd come to the gathering today. I have a package for Treya. You can pick it up when you're ready to leave."

"I'll be happy to."

The smile he gave her was that of a man very familiar with the woman he was aiming it at, and I took a closer look. Did I say she was pretty? Striking would be more apt, with a single lock of stark white forming a widow's peak in an otherwise inky sea of thick, shiny hair.

"In the meantime," he continued, "I'd like you to meet my ward, Echo. She's in need of new clothing, so of course I brought her to you. Echo, this is Cammi, the best garment maker around."

Her gaze shifted to me and I nearly squirmed under the close scrutiny of her clear hazel eyes. "So, this is the one that's set tongues wagging throughout the gathering."

"And what are they saying?" the commander asked, retaining possession of my hand by the simple expedient of placing his free one over mine.

I saw Cammi take in the gesture before she looked up

to meet Reynard's steady gaze. "Many things, Commander. Some say no Bashalde girl should be the ward of a Gadjee when her own kind would happily find a place for her. Others speak of August, her father, and his skill with arms, wondering if he broke tradition and taught his daughter to fight. Some, like me, remember Rilyana, her mother. I imagine everyone at the gathering knows she's here by now and will be trying to get a look at her."

She glanced back at me. "I knew your mother when we were children, before she met and married August." Once again her gaze skimmed my face. "You don't look much like her, or your father either."

"Think fast!" Lillith hissed in my ear.

But I'd already prepared for this eventuality and didn't even hesitate. "I'm afraid I don't remember my mother. She died while I was very young. But my father always said I looked like his mother."

"August had a mother?" She snorted delicately. "I always thought the man was spawned by Invet's demon horde. No offense intended, of course." This time she smiled. "It's just that he was so silent, and so deadly, it was hard to think of him as human. But enough chatter from me." With a graceful wave she indicated the piles of material and leather scattered around the booth. "Let's find something you like and then I'll get your measurements."

With a mixture of reluctance and relief, I eased my hand from under the commander's and joined her. We wandered the aisles, stopping now and then to discuss colors and fabrics. Before we were done, I chose red silk for a top with matching red leather for the skirt's waistband. And then to be on the safe side, I picked another set in emerald green.

We were on our way to the tent so she could measure me when I spotted a glimmer of rich purple sitting alone on a table and paused. Noting my sudden interest, she picked the material up, shifting it slightly so I wouldn't miss the silver threads sparkling in its depths.

"Can you make it into a costume for my dancing?" I asked, breathless with longing as I stared at the shimming translucent material.

"Of course." She smiled. "And the color is perfect for you. It makes your eyes turn violet."

Not to mention it matched Peri's feathers. But I hesitated. "How much?" I had to force the words from my reluctant throat.

"For you, nothing. Since it's to be a costume, I'll charge the price to Marcus." She patted my arm. "Don't worry, he can afford it."

I glanced back to where Marcus and the commander were waiting, Marcus watching me closely, the commander constantly scanning the area around the booth. Marcus gave a slight nod when I held up the material and arched a brow in question.

"Fine, I'll take it," I told her with a sigh of happiness.

She ushered me into a small tent with two openings, one in front and one in back. The back flap was closed and she lowered the front one as we entered. With a smile, she pulled a tape measure from a niche in the stand sitting to one side as Peri left my shoulder to investigate all the nooks and crannies in the stand. No doubt Cammi was mentally counting the coins she'd just made on the sale.

"I know just the design for the costume. It will put Treya's to shame."

Okay, she wasn't thinking about money. "You know Treya?"

"Yes, I know her. Too well." She measured my bust and then moved on to my waist, using what looked like a slim stick of charcoal to jot the numbers on a thick sheet of vellum. "All that one thinks of is money and snagging a rich, important husband. Lately her eye has been on the commander, but it seems he favors you. I'm sure she's not happy about that, but she'll move on to the next man on her list soon."

Just as she finished measuring my hips and straightened to note down the figure, I caught a glimpse of movement from the back of the tent and sunlight flashed off the metal of a blade.

I reacted instinctively, going into overdrive as the knife flew toward us. With one quick scoop, I moved Cammi out of the line of fire, turned, and caught the knife in my right hand. Without slowing, I spun in a half circle and aimed the knife at the wooden pole holding up the front of the tent. The blade went three inches deep and stuck, the shaft quivering from the blow.

Only then did I realize the commander was standing in the front opening, his eyes wide with disbelief as I came out of overdrive. Shocked silence descended as our gazes locked, and then Cammi started babbling, her voice drowning out Peri's indignant squawk as she launched toward me.

"Sweet gods above, what happened? Did someone throw a knife at us? Did they miss? Are you hurt?" She rushed to my side, hands running over me frantically as she searched for wounds.

I tore my gaze from the commander to reassure her as Peri settled back on my shoulder. "I'm fine, really. They missed completely. See?" I pointed to the knife still buried in the pole. Another two inches to the right and I'd have hit Reynard in the chest.

That thought scared me more than the look on his face.

Without a word, the commander went to the back of the tent, pushed the flap aside, and stepped out. He was back by the time Marcus rushed in from the front.

"What happened?"

Reynard glanced at me before answering. "Someone tried to kill Echo. There are hundreds of people out there. It could have been any one of them."

Cammi was looking at the knife, a surprised expression on her face. "It's Bashalde. Why would one of her own people want to hurt her?"

"Good question," the commander said.

Both of them were staring at me again, and I shrugged. "I don't know. Maybe someone had a grudge against my father that I'm unaware of. Marcus, do you know of anything?"

"No, nothing specific. But August was a powerful man. I'm sure he made enemies in his lifetime." He reached over and pulled the knife loose. "Besides, just because it's a Bashalde knife doesn't mean the person throwing it was Bashalde. I have a similar knife that I bought at the last gathering."

Through this whole episode, Lillith had been suspiciously quiet. While Marcus was speaking, I decided to find out why.

"Lillith?"

"Hush, I'm busy," she replied.

"Well, thank you *so* much for your concern." It's not easy to be sarcastic when you're subvocalizing, but I managed.

"I knew you were safe, and right now it's more important to track the man who threw the knife."

I stiffened. "You saw him?"

"Yes, although I didn't know he tried to kill you until you reacted. But he was the only one near enough to the tent opening to have done it."

Marcus continued to speak, but I tuned him out to concentrate on what Lillith was saying. "What does he look like, where is he going?"

"Average height and weight, brown hair, white shirt, dark pants. And he seems to be heading toward Chief Lowden's tent in a roundabout manner." There was a pause. "Yes, he definitely went into the chief's tent."

This made no sense at all and my mind whirled with questions, one in particular rising to the top. Why would Chief Lowden want me dead? The only feasible reason was that he suspected my real identity. And that would imply he was connected to the Daughter Stone in some way.

Something else suddenly hit me. The knife thrower hadn't wanted me dead. If I hadn't moved, the trajectory of the knife would have impaled it in my upper arm.

A chill ran over me. They either wanted to see how fast I healed or see if I could stop the attack, and there was only one explanation for that. Not only did they suspect I was a Federation agent, they wanted to see if I was a Gertz GEP.

And I'd made the stupid mistake of showing them. I might as well have hung a sign around my neck. Even the commander now knew I wasn't what I'd claimed to be, and I had no idea why he was remaining silent.

"Echo, are you sure you're okay?" Marcus had stopped talking and was looking at me with concern. "I think we should take you home. You've had quite a shock."

"No. No, I'm fine." Quickly I pulled myself together. "I believe the commander said Chief Lowden is expecting me. We certainly can't disappoint him."

Not to mention, I desperately wanted to get a look at the chief myself, and test his reaction to my presence.

"Are you sure?"

"Yes, absolutely. I'm not going to let this spoil the day." I turned to Cammi, pulled the coin purse from my belt and gave her half the contents for the everyday clothes, leaving Marcus to worry about paying for the fancy costume. "I'm sorry you were involved in this. Please have the clothing delivered to the Terpsichore when it's done."

"Of course." She patted my arm again. "I'll make sure you have it by week's end. And don't worry about Treya's order," she told Marcus. "I'll have it delivered at the same time."

Marcus leaned over and whispered something to her that caused her to smile, and then the three of us left the tent and made our way out of the booth in silence. I figured it wouldn't be long before the commander voiced his suspicions, and I was right. We hadn't gone ten steps before he took my arm and pulled me to a stop.

"I'd like to speak with your ward, Kent. Alone."

"Do you think that's wise, under the circumstances? Someone did try to kill her."

Before he finished the sentence, Lillith whispered in my ear. "Marcus wants to know if he should insist on staying with you. He says maybe he can keep the commander from asking questions you don't want to answer."

Mentally, I sighed. "No, we might as well get this over with. The commander saw me go into overdrive. He's not going to ignore that even if Marcus is chemically bonded to my side."

"I think she'll be safe with me." The commander's tone would brook no argument, and finally, Marcus nodded.

"As you wish. I'll wait for you outside the baker's tent." He pointed to a blue-and-yellow pavilion not far away.

Without waiting for Marcus to leave, the commander steered me toward the stream and down the gently sloping bank until we stood in a relatively flat space at the edge of the water. There were a few small trees between us and the crowd and they provided a bit of privacy.

The scent of damp earth rose around us as he stopped and turned to face me. "Who are you? And if I don't get the truth this time, I'll lock you in a cell until I do."

Now wasn't that a choice? Naturally, there wasn't a

wooden or barred cell on the planet that could hold me. I'd proven that when I tore the door off the castle. But the very act of breaking out would expose me. And I couldn't sit in a cell and do nothing, knowing those children would be destroyed when they were forced to use the Sumantti.

A feeling of resignation swept over me. I'd known this would never work. I simply wasn't cut out to be an agent. Straightening slowly I forced myself to meet the commander's gaze, my decision made.

"My name is Echo Adams. I'm an agent for the Bureau of Alien Affairs." I held my hand up, palm out in the universal symbol for peace. "Greetings from the Galactic Federation, Commander Reynard du'Marr."

CHAPTER 8

"Are you out of your mind?" Lillith screeched. "You're supposed to be undercover! You'll have to kill him now. I'd do it, but someone might notice the beam. And I'll have to report this to Dr. Daniels immediately."

Eek!

"Just wait," I told her hastily. "We need to see what his reaction is before I do anything rash like murder him." My entire body went into mourning at just the thought of wasting such a glorious male specimen. Plus, I wasn't at all sure I could actually kill someone deliberately and in cold blood.

From my shoulder, Peri leaned forward and cooed softly. Reynard's gaze swung to her and he studied her intently before looking back at me.

"You're like that Smith woman, aren't you? And your creature is a dragon bird. I've suspected as much since you downed Furgan and ripped the castle door off. Now your speed proves it."

My mouth dropped open, and then closed with an audible snap as irritation washed over me. Frag Kiera Smith! Even here, on a banned world, she was ruining my life.

"How do you know about Kiera Smith?"

He hesitated and then sighed. "Black marketeers are allowed to bring books to the king's brother. I also read them. One was this Smith woman's journal."

"Yes," I reluctantly admitted. "I'm like Kiera Smith, only I'm not an empath." Now that I thought about it, maybe the fact that he'd read her journal would make my life easier. He already knew about the Limantti, or Mother Stone, so he wouldn't think I was making the story up out of space dust.

"Why are you here? The king has forbidden this world to the Federation."

I glanced around at the people passing on the other side of the trees as they enjoyed the gathering. We were out of earshot, but the longer we stood here, the more attention we'd draw, and I couldn't take a chance on someone strolling over to see why an unescorted Bashalde woman was alone with a Gadjee. As it was, they probably thought we were negotiating for sexual favors.

One man in particular seemed to be watching us closely as he strolled on the other side of the trees, and I blinked. There was something familiar about him. I narrowed my eyes to see him better, and then shook my head. What would Losif Strand, leader of Helios One, be doing at a Bashalde gathering? And how would he have got here without Lillith spotting his ship? Must be my imagination. I forced my attention back to Reynard.

"Look, I'll be more than happy to tell you everything, but not here. There's too much chance that someone might overhear. For now, you'll just have to take my word that the situation is desperate or I wouldn't be on Madrea."

"Then we will return to Kent's home."

"No. I have to see Chief Lowden, remember?"

"Why?" His eyes narrowed in suspicion.

I held up my fingers and ticked my points off. "One, because you told him about me and got me invited to this party.

And two, the man who just threw a knife at me went into the chief's tent."

He reached for my arm again, his grip tight. "You saw him? Why didn't you tell me?"

"Because I *didn't* see him. My ship did. She tracked his movements to Chief Lowden. She said he's average height and weight, has dark hair, and is wearing a light shirt and dark pants."

"Right," Lillith snorted. "Spill your guts. And be sure to tell him all about your closet full of gaudy jumpsuits while you're at it. I'm sure he'll be fascinated."

"Oh, shut up," I mumbled under my breath. Reynard, who had automatically looked up when I mentioned my ship, refocused his attention on me.

"I beg your pardon?"

"Nothing. I was talking to Lillith, my ship. She's not real happy with me at the moment."

"Where is this ship?"

"Right above us, acting like space trash." I smiled sweetly when Lillith let out an indignant sputter. Two could play the sarcasm game, and I wasn't about to let her win. "We really need to find Marcus now," I added. "We've been here too long."

I started to turn, but he stopped me.

"Wait. One more question. Does Kent know who you are?"

It was my turn to hesitate. Marcus's secrets were his own, and I had no right to cause him problems. On the other hand, the commander seemed unusually talented when it came to picking out my lies. I decided part of the truth would be my best bet.

"He knows who I am and why I'm here, but he isn't on the Federation's payroll." Being recompensed for expenses didn't count in my book, so it was mostly the truth.

Reynard studied me for a moment, then nodded and took my arm to assist me up the slope and back into the gathering. "A word of advice," he murmured just before we merged with the crowd. "Tell no one else who you are, and if Chief Lowden challenges you, don't accept; find a way to avoid showing off your skills. From what I've seen, you're an even better fighter than August was reputed to be, and much stronger than a normal female. There's no need to verify what they must suspect."

I couldn't stop the smile playing around my lips. The commander was on my side, whether he realized it or not. He could have immediately called for my arrest, but he hadn't. Instead he was giving me tips on how to keep my secret from Lowden.

"Don't look so smug," he told me, his thumb gently rubbing my skin, raising goose bumps in its wake. "I may still arrest you. I'm reserving judgment until I hear the whole story."

My smile promptly vanished as I glared at him. "Don't tell me you're a damn mind reader, too?"

"No." He smiled. "You just have a very expressive face."

Oh, wonderful. Didn't every agent want to hear that anything she thought showed up on her face? More proof that Alien Affairs had put me in the wrong job.

While I was scowling over that remark, we reached the baker's tent, where Marcus was waiting for us, chatting with an elderly Bashalde man outside the entrance. He didn't so much as arch a brow in my direction, so I knew Lillith had kept him updated on what I'd told the commander.

Both men stopped talking as we joined them and the elderly gentleman smiled at me. "Marcus, will you introduce me to my young cousin?"

Cousin? Schite! Since August was a Gadjee, the man must be related on my "mother's" side, and I had no idea Rilyana had living relatives.

Marcus lifted a hand to my arm. "Echo, allow me to introduce Jancen, the head of the Lovara family. He's a distant relative of your mother's. Jancen, my ward, Echo."

Jancen gripped my shoulders and planted a peck on each of my cheeks. "Welcome, child, welcome." He beamed with pleasure as he released me. "I could only be happier if you had come to us instead of this reprobate when your father died."

I liked him, I decided. Even though he was slightly stooped and the skin on his hands was wrinkled and thin enough to show the blue veins, he exuded kindness and the spirit of someone much younger. If it were possible for me, a GEP, to claim relatives, I could do worse than this nice old man.

"Now, Jancen," Marcus interrupted my thoughts. "I told you that it was August's last wish that she come to me. Echo is merely honoring her father."

"That doesn't mean she can't visit whenever she likes." His watery blue eyes twinkled with merriment. "Just send me a message, child, and I'll arrange an escort to our camp. You can stay as long as you wish."

"Thank you." I returned his smile. "I'll take it into consideration."

Satisfied with my answer, he turned his attention to Reynard. "Well, Commander, have you managed to sway the king from his stance yet?"

"Unfortunately, he remains steadfast in his refusal to open the planet to the Federation, Jancen. I'm afraid nothing will change his mind."

I was so surprised I could barely grasp what I'd just heard. The commander wanted Madrea opened? Why? I couldn't ask him now, so I settled for asking Jancen.

"Why do you want the planet opened?"

"For trade, of course." He twinkled at me. "It's our life, our very blood. You've lived too long with a Gadjee, or you would know this. Every cycle at gathering, Chief Lowden and the heads of the families petition the king to reopen Madrea. We consider the commander our best ally in this goal, since he advises Politaus. To our regret, the king has so far refused to heed our pleas, but we continue to try." He shrugged. "Maybe next cycle we will succeed."

Now that was interesting. I'd been under the impression that everyone in power on Madrea was in agreement about the ban. And I was pretty sure the Federation had no clue, either, or it would have been mentioned in the data Dr. Daniels had given me.

I was so busy thinking about the ramifications of this revelation that it took a moment before I realized something was wrong with my surroundings. They were taking a slow, stately spin to the right. Tents, people, grass, everything was moving. And no one else seemed to notice.

Brow furrowed in puzzlement, I stared at the phenomenon, ignoring Peri's sudden squawk as she fluttered frantically on my shoulder. What the fritch was going on?

"Echo?" The commander's grip on my arm tightened, and his voice seemed to come from a long tunnel. I could hear the alarm in it, but I couldn't respond.

Black seeped into the edges of my vision, blocking out the sunlight, and at the same time, the Imadei, safely tucked under my top, gave a violent pulse. Instinctively, I lifted a hand to grasp the stone. With no time to brace, I was suddenly somewhere else, somewhere dark and full of pain. Somewhere so alien I couldn't get my balance. A weak cry that was a combination of my fear and confusion, mixed with the frantic emotions that bombarded me from every direction, escaped from deep inside me.

At the same time, I could feel the commander supporting my body, hear the distant babble of voices as I collapsed. I pushed those impressions away, needing all my strength to cope with what was happening in the dark.

Where, I thought frantically. *Where am I?*

Dark. The response was so loud I winced, even though it wasn't aimed at me. *Hurt!*

The tone was impossibly young, that of a mere child, and yet there was nothing human about it. Every emotion it emitted vibrated with enough power to reduce Madrea to a dust cloud with one thought.

Holy Zin, it was the Sumantti! At the same instant I realized who it was, it became aware of me.

WHO ARE YOU?

I cringed in agony at the force of the question. *Please! Stop. I'm here to help you. The Limantti sent me.*

The Mother? This time the tone was slightly calmer, questioning, and I felt the desparate longing flowing from the crystal. *The Mother sent you?* There was a brief hesitation, then a sense of surety. *You are not a Shushanna.*

No, but the Limantti gave me something to help. It's called the Imadei*, and it lets me act as your Shushanna even though I haven't been prepared.*

GET ME OUT!

A scream welled in my throat as the strength of the command speared through my mind, and I had to fight to retain consciousness. *I'm trying,* I told her. *But you're hurting me. You have to stay calm.*

I'm sorry. The tone was contrite now, like a child who'd been chastised.

That's better, I assured her. *Just don't yell. Do you know where you are?*

Dark. A weird sound came from around me, one I interpreted as pain. *They won't let me out.*

Can't you get yourself out? This was important, because from what Dr. Daniels had said, they hadn't known if the Sumantti was stolen or if it had fled on its own. That meant it should be capable of escape.

Tried. Tried many times. Can't get out, can't move.

Mentally, I took a deep breath. *Okay, anything you can tell me may help me find you. Have you been able to send out colonies?*

No, they can't go out, either. Only humans can move. They bring unprepared Shushannas. Hurts. Another whimper of pain echoed in the darkness as my blood chilled.

How many Shushannas have they brought?

Four, four have tried. I reach out for them, but then they go away. Now there is another, stronger than the others, but still unprepared. I can feel her nearby.

Listen to me, I told her urgently. *Since this girl has not been prepared by the crystals to become a Shushanna, she will die if you try to bond with her. That's why it hurts. When they bring her to you, do not reach out. You have to trust me. I will find you, and I will get you away from the people who have you now.*

When?

I don't know. I don't know where you are, but I'm going to keep looking. Just be patient. The Mother wishes it, I added on a stroke of genius. It was the only thing I could think of that might keep this powerful, unruly child in check.

There was a hesitation, then a tired sigh. *I will try.*

I needed to get my mind and body back together, fast. The thought was barely formed when there was a twisting motion in the darkness, and suddenly I was alone.

My return to consciousness wasn't a slow spiral upward, but an abrupt, fully alert awakening. It was a good thing, too, because my room in Marcus's house was full of concerned people. What if I'd blurted out something I shouldn't have?

When my eyes did pop open, I almost screamed. Peri was gripping a section of the headboard with her hind feet, dangling upside down so she could stare at my face. From two inches away. Assured that I was awake, she gave a merry gurgle, flipped over, and flew to perch on the windowsill, where she could keep an eye on the proceedings.

The commander was sitting beside me, holding my hand tightly while Leddy waved something that smelled Zin-awful under my nose. Near the end of the bed, Marcus and Jancen stared at me, worry clear in their expressions.

Even Treya was there, glaring at the way Reynard hovered over me.

The room was small to start with. Now it was so tightly packed I barely had space to breathe.

Pushing Leddy's nasty concoction away, I sat up and swung my legs off the bed. "I'm fine. Really, I'm good. Did I faint? How did I get back here?"

Maybe if I babbled out enough questions it would distract them from the ones I didn't want asked. Questions I wasn't at all sure I could answer, even if I wanted to. Surreptitiously, I touched the Imadei with my free hand and barely stopped myself from biting my lip. I'd expected the stone to do something, just not this, and I wasn't sure how to react.

Reynard arched a brow at me, then let go of my hand and stood. "Apparently the knife attack affected you more than we believed. When you fainted, I carried you back here. Jancen sent a messenger to Chief Lowden, explaining why you couldn't keep your appointment to meet with him."

He was covering for me. Probably wanted to grill me all by himself and then toss me in the dungeon, I thought sourly.

"Did someone really throw a knife at you?" Treya asked, her eyes wide.

"It missed me by this much," I told her, holding my fingers a centimeter apart.

"I don't understand. Why would anyone want to kill you?"

Marcus patted her shoulder. "We think it might be someone who had a grudge against Echo's father. Since August is dead, he's taking his anger out on Echo."

"If it's one of our people, I *will* find the culprit," Jancen said. "It's a disgrace to attack a woman, and they'll be punished accordingly." The twinkle in his eyes had turned to a steely glint and his voice held a menacing note. Suddenly I could see why he was head of the Lovara family and on the chief's council.

There was a clatter from the front room, and Leddy looked toward the door. "There's Bim. I sent him for soup." She waved her hands in a shooing motion. "Now, everyone out. Echo may think she's fine, but she needs to rest and eat."

Everyone filed out except the commander. He gave Leddy a dark stare, daring her to object. "I'm staying. I'll see to it she eats."

We both waited silently until the door in the front room banged closed, then I stood and checked to make sure everyone was really gone. The commander followed me into the main room, watching as I peeked out the front window. Peri was close behind us. She landed on the table, strutting its length while she cooed at the commander.

Marcus, Leddy, and Treya were heading next door to the Terpsichore, and Jancen toward the gathering. Bim stood solidly at the end of the crushed stone walk with his back to the house, thick arms crossed over his chest as he suspiciously watched every male who went by. As if one look at the axe strapped across his back wouldn't scare away any sane person, innocent or guilty.

Forcing a smile, I turned. "Alone at last." And then sputtered in shock as Reynard crossed to me in two strides, lifted me in his arms, and let his lips crash down on mine.

For a surprised minute, I just hung on and tried to keep breathing. Then, as he gentled the assault, his mouth moving against mine, I decided breathing was overrated anyway.

The room blurred around us and time seemed to stop. Without knowing how it happened, my arms were around his neck, and I was returning the kiss with all the passion I'd felt since I first laid eyes on him.

The heat he roused had me tingling from my toes to the top of my head. I was dizzy with need, and more than ready to head back to the bedroom.

A groan sounded from deep in his throat, and he drew back, lightly nipping my lower lip as he went. It was hard to tell which of us was more shaken, him or me.

I'd been kissed before, naturally. Lots of times. Kissing was pretty much de rigueur in the Department of Protocol. I'd had friendly kisses, serious kisses, nice-to-see-you kisses, even let's-find-a-dark-spot-fast kisses. But none of them caused the turmoil inside me that Reynard's kiss had, and it was a little scary.

Trying for nonchalant and failing miserably, I gazed up at him. "Does this mean you aren't going to arrest me after all?"

His mouth turned up on one side in a half smile. "I'm reserving judgment. But I've wanted to get my hands on you from the minute I first saw you, sneaking into my room. Today, when you suddenly went limp, I thought I'd permanently been denied the opportunity. I wasn't going to waste this second chance."

His arms were still around me and I was leaning into his hard, muscled body, in no hurry to move. "Scared you, huh? Well, apparently, I'm pretty hard to kill, so you don't need to worry."

"Apparently? You aren't sure?" Reluctantly, he released me and stepped back to put some distance between us.

I clasped my hands behind my back to keep from reaching for him again. "Oh, I'm sure now. But I didn't realize I was like Kiera Smith until very recently."

That eyebrow arched again. "How could you not know?"

With a shrug I walked over to examine the soup Bim had brought. It smelled wonderful and I suddenly realized I was hungry. "Because no one told me, and my job with the Department of Protocol didn't require me to perform feats of superhuman strength, move at super speeds, or get into life-threatening situations that would require me to heal near-fatal wounds to my person. And if anything out of the ordinary *had* happened, I probably would have just chalked it up to being a normal GEP."

I ladled up two bowls of thick chunky soup and gestured to the chair across from me. When we were seated, I continued. "Then, when I was transferred to the Bureau of Alien Affairs and went into training, I thought the instructors they assigned to me were simply inferior." Taking my first taste of the spicy stew, I chewed thoughtfully for a second. "Maybe I really didn't want to know, because the signs were there during training. I just ignored them. It wasn't until I'd completed training that Kiera Smith suggested I was probably like her, and to tell the truth, I wasn't prepared to believe anything she told me."

"You know her?" Reynard had paused with his spoon halfway to his mouth when I mentioned her name.

"We've met." I scowled at him. "And if you start telling me how wonderful she is, this soup is going to end up on your head."

He merely smiled and continued eating for two beats. "You said you were not an empath like her."

"That's right." I was still scowling, and I'd lost my appetite.

"Then what is your mental ability?"

The spoon I was holding hit the bowl with a clatter. "I don't have one. No one can make me have one, I don't care how much Marcus goes on about verge sickness or how Lillith keeps insisting the tests say I do. If I had a psi ability I'd know it."

"The same way you knew you had these other abilities?"

I leaned back and crossed my arms in irritation. Why did everyone want me to have psi ability? "It's not the same at all."

He took in my closed-off posture and slowly nodded. "Tell me why you're here."

With a sigh of relief at the subject change, I told him about the Sumantti, how we were sure now it had been stolen, about the Imadei choosing me, and how it had indicated the Daughter Stone was on Madrea. He listened patiently, never interrupting, and it was with some surprise that I realized I'd finished my soup while I talked.

For a moment after I completed the story, his fingertips drummed the table and he stared fixedly off into some distant place I couldn't see. Finally, his gaze returned to me.

"King Politaus is an honest man. He would have nothing to do with stealing the Sumantti. Is there a reason you believe it's in the castle?"

"Logic, for the most part," I told him. "The ordinary people on Madrea wouldn't even know the crystal existed, much less have a way to steal it. It has to be someone with power, enough power and opportunity to put men aboard a Federation vessel and then arrange their escape from that vessel with the Sumantti. Believe me, it wouldn't be an easy feat. Any other ship approaching a Federation vessel would be treated as an adversary until they could prove differently, and then they'd still be closely watched. The most sensible option would be to have a man planted on the ship as a crewmember. If he found some way to contain the Sumantti, he could pass it off at one of the ports when the ship docked. I think that's what happened, and it would take someone with power and influence to pull it off."

That reminded me of something. "Lillith," I subvocalized. "Can you find out where Kiera Smith is? I need to talk to her."

"Of course. One second, please." I'd barely drawn a breath when she replied, "Max is currently jumping from ZT Twelve to Orpheus Two. Their estimated time of arrival is late tonight, our time. We should be able to contact them first thing tomorrow."

While talking to a ship during jump wasn't impossible, the lag made it damn annoying. I resigned myself to waiting.

Unaware of my side conversation, Reynard continued. "That still doesn't mean it was the king. There are others on Medrea who have the power to do something like this."

"Like who?" I asked.

"Chief Lowden, for one, or the heads of the Bashalde families. There are even those among the king's court who might manage the theft."

I reached across the table and covered his hand with mine. "Reynard, I know you owe the king a lot and that you're loyal to him. But even if he didn't actively participate in the theft, he has to know about it. Not only does he order people to stay inside on the nights they arrive, the ships bringing the girls are landing behind the castle, and the children are taken inside."

He stiffened, his gaze sharpening as he pulled his hand from mine. "What children?"

"The Sumantti is useless to whoever has her without a Shushanna to wield the crystal's power," I reminded him. "Whoever has the stone knows that. They've been bringing in young girls with psi ability and forcing them to make the attempt. But without being prepared by the Orpheus crystals, anyone trying to use it will die. So far, they've killed four girls. Two more were brought the same night I arrived."

"How do you know?"

"I know because Lillith tracked the last ship from the instant it came out of hyper-drive. She recorded its landing, and the party who debarked, and she scanned the children, one of whom appeared to be drugged. The information is now permanently stored in her archives."

"And the other four? She saw them also?"

"No, I got that data from another source."

"You will tell me who this source is."

His tone indicated he would brook no argument, but I hesitated. So far I hadn't told anyone about my conversation with the Sumantti. Oh, what the hell. I'd already told him enough to ensure I was fragged if he didn't believe me. Might as well trust him with the rest, especially since I needed all the help I could get.

I inhaled slowly and then let it out. "You know when I fainted today? Well, I didn't really faint. The Imadei made contact with the Daughter Stone. I was talking to her, and she told me four girls had attempted to become her Shushanna, but that they all went away. The Ṣumantti is very young and I don't think she realized the girls were dying. She promised me she'd try not to reach out for this next one, but I'm not sure she can help herself. She said one of the girls feels stronger than the others."

Lillith let out a screech that had me wincing. "Why didn't you tell me this?"

"Because I haven't had time," I told her, watching Reynard.

He stood so abruptly the chair almost turned over, and began to pace around the room. "This is an abomination," he ground out through clenched teeth. "It must be stopped immediately." His hands fisted as he turned to face me again. "Did the Sumantti tell you where the girls were being held?"

"No, she doesn't know. It's dark and for some reason she can't send out colonies."

"And what of the children?"

Again I hesitated, and then sighed. "I think they're in the castle somewhere. A few days ago I tried to use the Imadei to locate the Daughter Stone and instead, I saw the girls. They were in a small room with only a bed. There were no windows, so I couldn't tell where it was located."

"It must be an inside room, then, or below ground in a cell."

He spun and marched toward the door. I caught him just as he reached for the handle. "Wait! Where are you going?"

He looked at me as though the answer should be obvious. "To organize a search for the girls, of course."

CHAPTER 9

"You can't." I pushed my way between Reynard and the door and put a hand on his chest to restrain him.

A growl rumbled deep in his chest as he stared down at me and I could feel the tension in his muscular body. If I didn't convince him fast, he was going to walk right through me. Or at least he'd try, and I really didn't want to hurt him.

"Please, just listen to me for a second. If you organize a group of men to search the castle, whoever's holding them will figure out what you're doing. They could move the girls, or even kill them and dispose of the bodies. After all, they've already brought in six girls, so it wouldn't be much of a problem if they have to kidnap a few more."

His head tilted slightly and some of the tension left his body as he listened. I took heart and kept going.

"They already suspect who and what I am. That's why someone has been watching me, why they attacked this morning. But they *don't* know I've confided in you, and that you believe me. That gives us a real advantage. You have access to the castle that I don't, and you can question your men, subtly, so they won't wonder what's going on."

From her position on the table, Peri sent me waves of encouragement. I took it as an affirmation that I was getting through to the commander, since she was apparently picking up his emotions, too.

"Reynard, I promise you, I'm going to do everything in my power to make sure they don't hurt these children the way they have the others. And while I don't like it, I need the girls to stay where they are for now. If I can continue to contact them, it may help us locate the stone. Because the most important thing we can do is find the Sumantti and return it to the Federation. Without the crystal, they have no need for the girls. We also don't need them to move the crystal to an even more remote location."

His hand fell away from the door's handle and he nodded. "You're right. When we find whoever is doing this you may retrieve the Daughter Stone. *But* justice for the children is mine."

From the look on his face, I wouldn't want to be in the culprit's shoes when he found them. But there was one more thing that had to be settled before I agreed.

"And what if your king is in on the whole thing? Will you be able to dispense justice for him?"

His jaw clenched, but he spoke clearly. "He's not. He would never participate in such an atrocity. But if he is, I will deal with him accordingly."

"Madrea is your world, the laws they're breaking are yours. Therefore, you may deal with them however you deem fit, with two exceptions." When he started to protest, I held my hand up and he stopped.

"One," I ticked the points off on my fingers. "If any of them are citizens of the Federation, the Federation will deal with them. And two, if I'm attacked, I reserve the right to defend myself regardless of who might have jurisdiction. Agreed?"

Reluctantly, he nodded. "Agreed."

"Good. Then why don't we sit down and have something to drink? I know Marcus has a bottle of wine here somewhere."

Apparently recognizing that the crisis had been averted, Peri warbled and then shot into my room, heading for the open window so she could visit the flowers. Which reminded me of something I'd wondered about.

"Tell me, why are there so many flowers on Madrea?" I asked while rummaging in the cabinets. "Your people grow them like they're a work of art."

"They are." He moved to one of the chairs in front of the fireplace and sat just as I located the wine. "According to the old records I've found, the flowers the colonists brought to Madrea had a difficult time with the alien soil, and there was no indigenous insect to provide pollination. They brought bees with them, but something about this world disagreed with the insects and they died out quickly. Most of the flowers also had medicinal qualities, so they couldn't afford to lose them."

I poured the wine into glasses and joined him. "It looks like they succeeded in saving them."

He took the glass I held out and sipped. "Yes, people learned how to do the pollination themselves and made the soil more acceptable, but not before numerous species were lost. At first it was merely a race to save as many as possible, and each success was met with much fanfare. But as generations passed, the reasons for saving the flowers became buried in the past while the prestige of growing them remained. Now they have become not only a status symbol, but also a form of art. No self-respecting Madrean would have barren gardens and walkways."

"Well, Peri certainly appreciates it, and she's probably saving some people the trouble of hand pollinating." Drawing one knee up onto the chair, I shifted enough that I could see him without straining my neck. "How did you know to look for the old records? I thought the Madreans didn't remember their origin until the Federation showed up."

"We didn't. But when we found out, I searched the oldest sections of the castle and found a very old diary, along with some reports made by those in charge."

He'd made several comments about reading, now. I tilted my head and studied him. "You're something of a scholar, aren't you? Is that why you want Madrea opened again?"

He lifted a hand to rub his forehead, and then sighed. "I believe the Federation has much to offer Madrea. My people should have the right to choose which path they want to take instead of blindly following a charter that was written centuries ago by people who have little to do with the present. Unfortunately, the king thinks of himself as a father, protecting his children from a harm they can't see, and none of my arguments has swayed him from that belief."

Mouth tilting in a wry grin, he glanced over at me. "Of course I'm thinking of myself, too. There's nothing I want more than to travel to Alpha Centauri, see all the modern wonders, visit the libraries. A member of the Federation who was here before the king placed the ban told me they're vast beyond description."

I returned his smile, amazed at the sharp mind enclosed in such a wonderfully masculine body. "They are. And the best part of all: the information is available by simply touching a screen and asking for what you want. You don't even have to leave home if you don't want to."

"Did you go to the university there?" There was a touch of envy mixed with a good dose of longing in the question.

"No, but I had the same education. GEPs mature faster than Naturals. We're adults by the age of thirteen cycles, so all of our learning is very intense and very accelerated. It's done in the crèche with the best instructors on the planet."

He reached over and took my hand, the one not holding my wineglass, and toyed with my fingers. "Tell me about your life there, what living on Centaurius is like."

"Before or after Kiera Smith's journal was released?" I asked sourly.

"Didn't you work for the Federation in both jobs?" His tone was curious.

"You could say that. But there's a huge difference between the Department of Protocol and the Bureau of Alien Affairs. In Protocol, they kind of frowned on the employees killing other life forms. With Alien Affairs it's almost a requirement. Did you know they taught me fifty-six ways to kill with one finger?" I snorted. "Talk about bloodthirsty. I mean, what if I forget and accidentally poke someone the wrong way? After all, I was created to make nice, to solve problems through diplomacy. I wasn't created to be a killing machine."

"I don't understand." His brow furrowed in perplexity. "If this Dr. Gertz made you like Kiera Smith, shouldn't you be able to do the same job?"

My glare pinned him to his seat, and I yanked my hand back. "Look, Commander. Logic won't win you any favors from me. I'm in deep denial and I fully intend to stay there. I want my old job back. I don't *want* to be an agent like Kiera Smith. What Gertz did to me is irrelevant."

Calmly, he took my hand again, and this time kept a firm grip on it. "We all fight change in our own way. Especially those changes we didn't ask for and don't understand. Politaus didn't ask the Federation to discover Madrea. So now he fights to keep our world locked in a timeless prison of sameness without considering the benefits that the Federation's technology could bring. He sees only danger instead of possibilities."

"And you're saying that I don't see the possibilities?"

"Do you?" His smile was so slow and sexy it set my stomach twisting like a ribbon around a pole in a high wind.

Taking a deep breath, I forced my gaze from his mouth and concentrated on the conversation. "I see there's a good possibility that sooner or later I'm going to wind up wading through a swamp teaming with nasty bugs and slimy, crawly things."

"What of the people you can help by using the talents you were gifted with?"

"I can help them just as well from behind a desk on Centaurius."

He did that brow-arch thing again. "If you were on Centaurius, who would be here trying to help those young girls?"

Abruptly, I became aware of the Imadei, warm against my skin. If Dr. Daniels was to be believed, I'd been the only person responsive to it. And without it no one would be able to communicate with or control the Sumantti.

Maybe Reynard was right. Maybe the children's lives did depend on me, personally, being the agent sent to Madrea.

I'd never thought of it quite like that before.

"Okay, you win." I sighed. "There's no one else who could help them the way I can. I'm obviously meant to be here. But that still doesn't mean I'm cut out to be an agent for the rest of my life."

We sat in silence for a moment, contemplating the conversation we'd had. At least, I was contemplating. I noticed Reynard's mind had strayed in other directions when I saw him squirm uncomfortably in his chair, a tinge of red inching up his cheeks.

"May I ask you something personal?" He was staring intently down at my hand, and I glanced over to make sure my fingers weren't dirty.

Nope, clean as a whistle. "Sure. Fire away."

"Do all GEPs receive sexual training the way Kiera Smith did?"

Aw, wasn't that cute? He was embarrassed! Before I answered, I lifted my glass and drank to hide my grin. "Yes, it's mandatory."

Still addressing my hand, he forged ahead with grim determination. "Then you aren't a virgin?"

Deliberately, I pursed my lips. "No, no, I'm not. GEP females have their hymens surgically removed before they begin sexual training. It eliminates the fear of the sex act and reduces the risk of any potential trauma."

He gaped at me, shock written all over his face. "You mean they—you . . ." Carefully, he put the glass down on the small table between us and ran a hand over his face. "I don't understand."

I put my glass beside his and patted his hand in sympathy. Even Naturals who are used to GEPs sometimes have a hard time understanding us. That Reynard had done so well up until now said a lot for him.

"Let me see if I can explain," I told him. "In archaic societies where it's important to the males to ensure their genes are the ones being passed on, a virgin bride is important. It proves she's not carrying the get of another male. So, the only real function of the hymen is to prove that the female hasn't had sex before. In our society, where birth control is easy and abundant, the need for a hymen is eliminated. On the other hand, the first penetration for the female is usually painful, especially if the male isn't careful. And not many are," I added.

"For GEPs the situation is much the same, but for different reasons. Normally, we can't reproduce, so there's no worry about whose genes are being passed on. Plus, we have no societal taboos where sex is concerned. There's nothing shameful or wrong about the act. It's just another bodily function, some-thing natural that's meant to be enjoyed."

"But the GEPs created by this Dr. Gertz *can* reproduce."

I could almost see his brain working. "Yes. Apparently he wanted to make sure the bloodlines he created aren't lost. But luckily, the crèche doctors realized early on that I was fertile. They thought it was an anomaly in my creation. To rectify the problem I was given an oral dose of a contracep-tive that will prevent conception until the antidote is taken." I thought for a second. "Kiera must have taken the antidote, because she has a daughter now."

He squirmed again, and then cleared his throat. "Ah, do you take money for your favors?"

I blinked. Now what the scritch was this all about? "No, of course not. I was created for the Department of Protocol, not to be a pleasure GEP. When I have sex with someone it's because I want to."

Red was tinting his cheeks again. "Have there been many times you wanted to?"

"Not as many as you're probably thinking. I'm very se-lective." An evil grin crossed my face. "What about you? Have there been many women in your life?"

Mumbling something indistinguishable, he dropped my hand and jumped to his feet like the chair had bitten him. "I've been here too long. It's unseemly. And I need to begin questioning my men."

Before I could respond, he was out the door.

How curious. "Lillith, do you have any idea what just happened?"

"Naturally," the ship responded, her tone smug. "There's a very high probability that he was trying to determine what kind of woman you are. Remember, in his society, there are only two types, and while all women are respected, he would only have premarital sex with a prostitute. All other females are off-limits. And you just informed him that you don't take payment for sex."

"But he kissed me!" It's hard to wail subvocally, but I pulled it off.

"I imagine that even in this society, kisses are stolen on a regular basis by courting couples. In the commander's defense, he's male, he wants you, and you'd just scared him out of his wits by passing out in his arms. It was more an instinctual reaction rather than a thought-out act of deliberation."

"She's right." I spun as Marcus strolled through the door. Lillith must have been repeating the conversation to him verbatim. "The commander would never have touched you without declaring a formal courtship if he hadn't been so relieved you were recovered. That he slipped even that much is a measure of the way he feels about you. And he was right to leave. Being alone with you for as long as he was could very well hurt your reputation as a respectable young woman, and truthfully, I shouldn't have allowed him to stay."

I gaped at him. "For Zin's sake, Marcus, I'm a GEP. We don't *have* reputations to protect where sex is concerned!"

He helped himself to the wine I'd opened and carried it to the chair Reynard had vacated so abruptly. "To all of Madrea you're a Bashalde girl and my ward. Unless you intend to declare your real identity, it's imperative you follow the customs here. Especially since Jancen has taken the view that you're a member of his family regardless of who your guardian might be. I wouldn't enjoy being called out on the field of honor by a man of his age for neglecting my duty to protect your virtue."

"You're right." I rubbed my temples, trying to ease the faint pounding I'd ignored when the commander was here. "I apologize. I forgot who I'm supposed to be."

"It's understandable, given the circumstances." He sipped the wine thoughtfully. "And for what it's worth, I think you were right to tell the commander the truth. He's a fair man and very honorable. He'll make a powerful ally. And I'm sure once he gets over the shock of hearing about a GEP's sex life, he'll start to see the advantages. The commander is very logical and straightforward, and he has a mind like a steel blade."

Finishing off his wine, he put the glass aside, stretched out his legs, and folded his hands across his stomach. "Now, tell me about your conversation with the Sumantti."

Involuntarily, my brow arched, mimicking Reynard's favorite expression. "Didn't Lillith tell you?"

"She gave me the facts. I'd like to hear your impressions of the exchange."

My head tilted slightly as I considered the conversation I'd had with the stone. "She was angry. So angry in fact, that I'm worried about what she'll do if she gets free." I hesitated. "It was like talking to a child, Marcus. An extremely powerful, very scared child." I shook my head. "I tried to convince her not to reach out for the girls they've stolen and she agreed to try, but I'm worried she won't be able to help herself. Not if she sees it as a chance to get away from her captors."

The fingers of his right hand drummed on his left for a moment. "How are they holding her? If she's that powerful, how do they keep her contained?"

"I have an idea, but I'm not even sure it's possible."

"From your description, it sounds like they have her in a stasis box."

"Exactly." The pressure on my temples wasn't helping much, so I closed my eyes to block out the fading sunlight. "But what's confusing is that if it works on the Sumantti at all, would I even be able to communicate with her? I need to talk to Kiera. She knows more about the crystals than anyone else. Lillith contacted Max, and they're in the middle of a jump back to Orpheus Two. As soon as Kiera is dirt side, I'll have Lillith get in touch with her."

Marcus's chair squeaked and I knew he'd shifted to study me. "Your headache is getting worse, isn't it?"

Narrowly opening my eyes, I looked at him through my lashes. "Yes. I don't suppose you have any more of that stuff you gave me this morning?"

"I do, but it would be dangerous to give you more now. And if it's worn off this fast, it wouldn't help, anyway." His tone was deadly serious. "Echo, you *must* find out what your psi ability is and start using it. Until you do, the headaches will only continue to get worse. Do you understand that this could kill you?"

Forcing a smile took all my strength. "You're being melo-dramatic, Marcus. My headache is a result of the Sumantti yelling in my brain. You have no idea how loud and forceful she can be. I'll be fine after I get some rest."

His sigh echoed around the room as he straightened and leaned forward. "No, Echo, you won't be fine. Think of it like this: your psi energy is water spilling into an enclosed reservoir. If none of the water is used, the reservoir will fill to capacity. But the water is still being pumped in. The reservoir can't hold it all and pressure builds. At some point, one of two things will happen. Either someone begins to remove the water at a faster rate than the reservoir can fill, or the force of the water will cause the reservoir to rupture."

This time the grin came easier. "Are you saying I'm going to explode?"

His expression was grim enough to make the first flutter of fear start in my chest. "That's exactly what I'm saying. Until you acquired the Imadei, you had your reservoir blocked so no water could enter it. Even the simplest Orpheus crystals amplify psi ability. But the Imadei is a powerful crystal and your ability isn't meager. It's extraordinarily high. Since the moment you put it on, that crystal has been pouring metaphoric water into your reservoir at an enormous rate. And it's starting to ooze through the cracks in your defenses. The verge sickness and the headaches are symptoms of the leakage.

"If you don't start using it voluntarily, the ability will blast out on its own and you'll have no control over it. Depending on what your talent is, it could destroy you and everyone around you."

I made a heroic and futile effort to tamp down the fear that was suddenly choking me. "What if my so-called talent is growing plants? How would that threaten anyone?"

"Imagine this planet suddenly overgrown with a jungle so thick no one could cut through it."

"Lillith, is he exaggerating?"

"No," the ship responded. "If anything, he's downplaying the danger. You need to listen to him, Echo. It's not only your ability we have to worry about, but the Imadei. Remember, for all intents it's a small Mother Stone, and we know how powerful they can be. It is imperative that you be in control of the stone, and that won't happen until you can acknowledge and control your psi ability."

By now my head was throbbing in time with my heartbeat, but that didn't stop me from jumping to my feet and pacing frantically around the room. "Okay, I've got psi ability! Now tell me how in Zin's name I'm supposed to use it when I don't have any idea what it is."

From somewhere in the distance I felt Peri's startled query at my vehemence, and knew she was already winging her way back to the house.

"Admitting you have psi ability is a good first step," Lillith said. "And we do have some clues as to what it might be."

"You've been discussing me?" I paused to look suspiciously at Marcus.

"Of course we have," he answered. "At least, we've talked about your probable talent."

"Fine." I threw my hands up and then winced as pain shot through my temples at the movement. "What are these clues you've come up with?"

"You contacted the girls, the ones they brought in on the black marketeers' ship," Lillith said. "It wasn't a dream, Echo, and we don't believe it was the Imadei. The stone's primary goal would be to connect with the Sumantti. Has that type of 'seeing' happened at any other time?"

Saying I had psi ability and admitting it to myself were two different things, and for a moment I wrestled with what I wanted the truth to be versus what it really was. If I did this, I'd be giving up any chance I had of returning to my former employer. I'd be an agent for the rest of my life.

It was a horrifying and scary thought.

On the other hand, it seemed I was to have no choice in the matter. Unless I was ready to die. Even *I* wasn't that stubborn.

With an odd sense of relief I stopped fighting fate and answered the ship's question. "Yes. Twice now I've seen Reynard when he was somewhere else."

Marcus was fully alert now, his gaze pinned on me. "Was he aware of you?"

I hesitated. "Maybe. The first time, he was eating breakfast with a large group of men. After I observed him for a second, he suddenly looked up and scanned the room, like he felt someone watching him."

"And the second time?" Lillith asked.

"It was later the same day. I saw him examine the castle door right before you told me he was doing exactly that."

Marcus got up and uncovered the sunstone lamps to alleviate the falling darkness, and brought me a cup of herbal tea.

Peri zoomed into the room and hovered in front of me, cooing encouragement as I drank the liquid. When I returned the glass to Marcus, she landed on my shoulder, sending waves of love and support. My headache didn't go away, but it eased a little, as much because of Peri as anything else.

"Sit," Marcus put the cup away and gestured to the chair. "We need to figure out exactly what's going on with your ability."

I perched on the edge of the seat, too tense to relax, as he continued.

"Lillith, I know you've been running probability programs and feeding what information we have to the psi examiner on Centaurius. Have you come up with anything?"

"A few theories. For lack of anything better, we're calling Echo's ability *ghosting*, since she can appear to other people but can't manipulate her environment. It seems to be a combination of clairvoyance and astral projection with elements common to neither."

"What elements?" I asked. My headache was slowly changing, the pain turning into something I'd never felt before. It was as if my head was stuffed with thick cloth, making it difficult to think, to hear, and I had to concentrate to hear Lillith's response.

"With clairvoyance you could see events occurring in other places, which you seem to be able to do. With astral projection, your essence, or spirit, travels to another place. You did that, too. However, in neither case should anyone be able to see you or communicate with you, and the girl did. That's the element we're trying to understand."

Marcus tapped his steepled fingers against his chin. "We

don't know for sure if the commander actually saw her. A lot of people are able to sense if they're being watched. I'd think a man with his training would be one of them. And maybe there's something about Gaia that allowed her to see Echo."

"Pelga," I mumbled. "She's Pelga." All that cloth in my head was suddenly doing a slow shuffle, making it feel like something was crawling around inside my skull. I could barely think now.

"Interesting," Lillith commented. "I did some checking after you mentioned this Pelga. She was your crèche mate, but she died at the age of five cycles from Chekhov disease and her DNA was retrieved for reprocessing."

Chekhov disease was a childhood illness, usually mild, that produced flu-like symptoms in its victims that lasted about a week. Only in rare cases was it fatal, and no one knew why.

But that was wrong. My forehead wrinkled as my brain tried to function. "Pelga was recycled." I forced the words out through suddenly clumsy lips. "She got her lesson wrong, and they took her away. They took her away and strapped her down to a bed under bright lights, and then they stuck needles in her. I saw her."

"You couldn't have seen her," the ship said. "The hospital they had her in was on the other side of Centaurius and— Echo? Echo!"

Well, Marcus had said I was going to explode. From my shoulder Peri let out a scream that echoed around the room, but I could only think one thing as my surroundings faded.

Boom.

CHAPTER 10

I opened my eyes to the sound of hundreds of dragon birds screeching in alarm. They darted into the air, swooped in synchronous patterns, and then finally settled on convenient perches, peering at me in puzzlement while they chattered frantically at one another. For as far as I could see, a tropical jungle stretched the landscape, with adobe buildings snuggled between towering trees.

Panic closed my throat as several extremely large, stunningly beautiful men paused in what they were doing and headed in my direction. Holy Zin, were those spears they were carrying?

"Echo?"

The voice came from behind me, and I spun. "Kiera?"

I went weak-kneed with relief when I recognized the other woman. She was standing beside an older female who held Teeah, bouncing the child on her hip.

A perplexed expression flitted across Kiera's face as she stared at me. "Yes, we just got back. Max didn't tell me Lillith was here. That's not like him."

"She's not here," I whispered.

Her mouth turned down in a frown. "I don't understand.

If she's not here, how did you get . . ." She trailed off, her eyes going wide as she stared at me. "Great Goddess, with the sun behind you like that, I can almost see right through you. What's going on here?"

The men had reached our location, but she waved them back as I tried to answer her.

"My psi ability."

Her gaze sharpened. "You've figured out what it is? Does Dr. Daniels know?"

Dr. Daniels's name was still on her lips when his image flashed through my mind. A rush of vertigo swamped my senses and abruptly I was standing on a white crushed-shell garden path beside a pink bench. Flowers native to Centaurius bloomed in controlled abandon from bushes that drank the strong early-morning light.

An involuntary whimper escaped, alerting the man a few meters away of my presence. He whirled abruptly, his eyes widening when he saw me.

"Agent Adams?" Dr. Daniels looked around wildly. "How did you get by my home security? Why aren't you on Madrea, doing your job?"

As soon as he mentioned Madrea, I thought of Marcus. Before I could blink, the vertigo hit me again. Peri's hysterical screaming turned to angry scolding as she hovered in front of me, and I could hear Marcus's voice as he bent over my body.

"Ignore the damn demands! Agent Smith and Dr. Daniels will just have to get in line. We've got an emergency here."

There was a slight pause during which, I assumed, Lillith was answering him. "Of course I'm trying to wake her up! She's not responding. How are her vital signs?"

Another pause. "Well, that's good, at least. Peri, will you please shut up?"

The dragon bird cut off in mid-scold and cooed at me.

The change in tone caught Marcus's attention and he turned his head to see what was going on. With a shocked gasp, he stumbled back two steps and tripped over the small table, landing on his rear end with a thud.

"Echo?" His gaze whipped from me to my body and then back again as he scrambled to his feet. "I must say, even though we had an idea of what was happening, it's a bit unsettling to see you twice in the same room. Can you get back in your body now?"

"I don't know how! Every time I think of someone, I'm there with them. How do I stop?" The fear built until I didn't know how I could contain it.

Marcus's head tilted before he answered. "Lillith says you need to calm down. Your heart rate is increasing dramatically."

Calm down? Calm down? How in Zin was I supposed to calm down when my spirit was all the way across the room and I didn't have any idea how to merge it with my corporeal body? I needed help. I needed—Reynard!

The unreasonable certainty that he was the only one who could save me washed through my mind as the vertigo spun me again. I expected to appear in his room at the castle, but to my surprise, I landed in a room four times the size of Marcus's house. The only usual furniture was a table with two chairs set near the front of the room. Every square inch of the wall space was taken up by row after row of actual paper books, and more shelves spanned the room with narrow aisles between them. There had to be thousands of books here.

For a split second, I simply gaped at the display, temporarily shocked out of my panic. When Reynard had talked about the king's brother getting black-market copies, I'd been picturing electronic books. Paper versions hadn't been made in centuries, except for rare special orders that cost enough to pay off my indenture. Even the sheets for scribbling notes were made of reusable electronic paper that could be cleared with one swipe of a hand. How was the king reimbursing the black marketeers for all these?

My mind was still whirling when I ripped my gaze from the obscene wealth of paper and looked toward Reynard. He was at the table, bent over a book, head cradled in his hands. A sunstone lamp burned in front of him, casting its light over his face as well as the pages he perused so intently. It was a thick tome, and I leaned closer to see the title at the top. *Genetically Engineered Persons: From Creation to Adulthood.*

Well, his foray into all things GEP would just have to wait. I was in trouble here. The fear returned with a vengeance and my voice quivered.

"Reynard?"

He jumped and lurched to his feet, one hand automatically going to his knife before he saw me and halted the action. "Echo? How did you get in here?" His gaze sharpened as he stared at me. "What's wrong?"

I raised a hand in supplication. "Help me. Please. I can't stop. I don't know how to get back in my body."

With no hesitation, he stepped toward me. "Where are you?"

"Marcus's house."

And by simply speaking the words, that's where I was again. Both Marcus and Peri were expectantly watching the spot where I'd been last time, but now I was behind them.

"Back here." I waved to get their attention. They both turned to see me better. "Please don't mention any names."

Marcus was frowning intently. "Lillith wants to know if you see any white filmy cords attaching you to your body."

"No, there's nothing connecting me."

"So, it's not any form of astral projection," he mused. "But there has to be a way for you to get—"

The pounding hooves of a horse going full speed sounded outside, punctuated by the noise of a sliding stop. Marcus's words were cut off by the sound of raised voices that drifted in through the windows. Abruptly, the door flew open and Reynard charged into the house, shaking Bim off before slamming it shut again. He must have had the horse waiting right outside the library to get here so fast.

Without pausing he went straight to my body, knelt and tugged the chain around my neck to bring the Imadei into view.

Marcus yelled as the commander reached for the stone, and I braced myself for the pain of his touch.

It never happened.

As Reynard's hand gently enfolded the stone, a feeling of warmth and bliss washed over me, and my eyes drifted closed. I could literally feel the power of his will as he pulled my spirit back into my body. In spite of my relief, the analytical, obsessive part of me watched how he did it with a sense of awe. And by now I was so connected to the stone that I knew I could duplicate his actions all on my own, mentally, without the physical contact.

When I opened my eyes again it was to see the commander leaning over me, still cradling the Imadei in his palm, a light sheen of sweat coating his forehead. With one hand I reached out and cradled his cheek for a moment.

"Thank you," I whispered as Peri cooed from the back of my chair. "You may have saved my life."

Our gazes met and held until Marcus cleared his throat. "I'd better go calm Bim down. I'll be right back."

We both ignored him, concentrating too deeply on each other as the door closed to hear anything else. "How did you know what to do?" I asked.

He shrugged. "I can't explain what happened. It just seemed like the right thing. How do you feel?"

I did a mental rundown. My heart was still pounding from the aftereffects of terror, but the headache was gone as if it had never existed. All in all, I felt better than I had in days.

"Amazingly good," I told him. "I'm not even tired."

"You said you weren't like the Smith woman that way." There was a question in his eyes now, and I sighed.

"I'm not an empath, Reynard. No one seems to know exactly *what* I am. And I didn't want to admit I had any psi ability at all, because that would mean there was no chance of getting my old job back. But it doesn't look like I have a choice in the matter now." I rubbed my forehead, despair and confusion roiling inside me, and then pushed it all away. My old life was over. I had to accept that once and for all.

"Either I learn how to use this talent or it will kill me," I continued. "Fortunately, after watching how you did it, I think I can get back to my body next time."

"Excellent," Lillith commented in my ear. "We need to do some experiments."

Damn, I'd forgotten about her. "Can't it wait until tomorrow? It's been a long day." And I really needed time to sort out everything that had happened.

"You just said you weren't tired and Dr. Daniels has gone back to Alien Affairs headquarters to confer with the psi testers and run probabilities. He's very excited that you've narrowed in on your ability and wants to know its exact limits."

So much for some personal alone time. I grimaced and sat up straighter as Marcus came back in. Reynard immediately stood and moved two paces away. At my side, Peri ruffled her feathers and then settled watchfully. "What does Dr. Daniels want me to do now?"

"He wants you to try and visit someone you've never met before. Maybe someone you've only seen an image of."

"Is he thinking this is some form of distance viewing?" Marcus asked.

"No, they have some theories, but at this point they need more information to either prove or disprove them."

After thinking for a second, I nodded. "Okay, I'll try to 'visit' the king."

Reynard arched a brow. "You've seen him?"

"Yes, in a vid." I didn't tell him that I'd barely noticed the man because I was too busy drooling over him.

I took a minute to think about what, exactly, had happened the first time. It wasn't easy to analyze because I'd been dizzy and confused. We had been talking about Pelga, but my mind had been thinking about Kiera, how I wouldn't be in this fix if not for her. And suddenly her image had formed very strongly in my head, followed by a pushing feeling. I took a deep breath. "Okay, here goes."

Eyes closed, I took a deep breath and brought the king's image into my mind. Once it was firm, I put myself into the picture, saw myself standing next to him, and then pushed.

Nothing happened.

Closing my hand around the Imadei, I tried again, this time straining with all the strength I had in me and drawing on the crystal for more.

Still nothing. Finally, I opened my eyes and shook my head. "It's not working. I can *feel* it not working. It's like there's some vital piece missing with the king that I had with Dr. Daniels and Kiera and Marcus."

"Dr. Daniels says that's excellent. Now try Jancen."

Because I was paying more attention this time, I felt something that I can only compare to rapidly flipping pages, followed by an infinitesimal click as though something had locked into place.

Abruptly, I was standing in a darkened space. Jancen was in front of me, stretched out on a narrow cot, snoring gently.

Scattered rustlings from here and there told me we weren't alone in the tent. Others were sleeping nearby. Smiling at the old man, I pictured myself sliding back into my body the way I'd don a comfortable robe. With no notable transition, I was back.

Marcus was looking at me, waiting patiently, and Reynard had moved back to my side, ready to intervene if necessary. Peri didn't seem the least bit concerned. "It worked."

Quickly, I told them what had happened, and knew Lillith was relaying my words to Dr. Daniels. There was a moment of silence before she responded.

"Dr. Daniels says he thinks they have enough information now to come up with a reasonable explanation for what you do and how you do it. He says to get some rest while they run it through the computer and he'll talk to you in the morning."

"Well," Marcus stretched and glanced meaningfully at the commander, "guess I'll head off to bed."

"Just a second." I stood and waved a hand at the table where there were enough chairs for the three of us. "Let's all sit down. There's something else I want to know."

In my ear, Lillith sighed, and I figured she knew what was coming and hadn't wanted to talk about it. When we were seated, with Peri perched on the back of the empty chair, I cleared my throat.

"Here's the thing. When Reynard touched the Imadei, it should have hurt, badly from the information we have. But it didn't. Not only was he able to touch it, he used it to help get me back in my body. Since the Imadei is attuned to my brain and no one else's, how did he do it?"

The commander looked vaguely surprised as he turned to Marcus for an answer. When Lillith spoke, Marcus repeated her answer aloud so I was hearing it in stereo.

"Because his brain is operating on the exact same electrical wave pattern as yours, Echo. It shouldn't be possible. Even identical twins have different electrical brain-wave patterns."

"Then how . . . ?"

"It's an anomaly I can't explain. But it did make me curious about the rest of the Madreans. After I scanned the commander the first time and realized he was different from other Naturals, I checked a large sampling of the other people on this planet. And I found something very amazing. The Madreans have evolved into the equivalent of normal GEPs, and from their brains' electrical impulses, some exhibit the beginnings of rudimentary psi ability."

I'd be hard put to say who was more surprised, me or Marcus. We both sat there with our mouths open, while the commander looked more puzzled than ever, and Peri chuckled deep in her throat as though laughing at a private joke only she had heard. I finally got my mouth closed enough to ask one of the zillion questions darting through my mind.

"Why wasn't this information included in the data Dr. Daniels gave me?"

"Because the Federation didn't know until I told them. Remember, they were only here for half a cycle and the Madreans are very wary of scientific equipment. I'm sure the Federation would have realized it sooner or later, but for the short time they were on Madrea, the scientists simply chalked the Madreans' good health and lack of disease up to their natural style of living. It was only because of the commander that I did a more in-depth study of their physiology and discovered the direction their evolution has taken. Of course, I'd really love to do a DNA study now, but that will have to wait."

Reynard was frowning now. "Is this ship saying I'm like you and the Smith woman?"

"Not exactly." I touched his hand. "She's saying something in your environment has caused you Madreans to evolve faster than the average humans. You're stronger, smarter, and healthier than Naturals."

I paused to gather my thoughts. "Lillith, does the commander have a psi ability?"

"Yes, I believe he does. I've analyzed every interaction you've had with him, and one hundred percent of the time he knows when you're lying. That's statistically impossible without the aide of an ability. The only times he's missed are when you add truth to the mix, or lie by omission. And even then I can tell from his heart rate and blood pressure that he's suspicious, as if he senses he's not getting the entire story."

Marcus studied the commander. "Have you always been able to tell when someone is lying?"

Reynard's frown had eased. Now he just looked thoughtful. "It's more that I know what's right from what's wrong. Like in combat, I know what the right action will be to counter any attack as soon as my foe begins to move. The same way I knew what was needed to bring Echo back to her body. When someone lies, the words feel wrong. I've always just accepted the results without thinking too much about the why, the same way I accept breathing or eating. It's part of who I am."

I couldn't restrain a snort. "No wonder you didn't believe a word I said that first night in the castle."

He grinned at me, that single dimple flashing. "No, but I did find the telling very amusing. It was like watching a play."

"Oh, thanks a bunch. So happy I could entertain you. Why didn't you call me on it right then and there?"

"Because you made me curious. I'd never met anyone like you before, a beautiful woman who fought the way you obviously could. You moved so fast I had no time to come up with the correct countermove. That had never happened to me before. I wanted to know more, so I waited and watched."

"And I obliged you by going into overdrive."

"Yes, you did. It was amazing to behold, as if you simply vanished for a fraction of a second. At that point, I'd already decided you were from the Federation. Seeing how you reacted to the thrown knife made me realize you were like the Smith woman, and the situation must be dire indeed for Alien Affairs to not only violate the ban, but send someone of your caliber to Madrea."

"Which brings us back to the Daughter Stone," Marcus said. "And who has it. Any ideas?"

"It's not the king." His eyes turned chill and his chin formed a tight, stubborn line with the answer. "As you said, I would know if it were."

"How?" I asked him. "Have you mentioned a stolen Orpheus crystal to him and gauged his reaction? Have you told him six girls have been kidnapped and brought here, and that four of them have died so far?"

"No, but I have no need to ask him these things. I grew up with him, spend part of every day in his company, hear his judgments and see his dealings with our people. I know him better than anyone else alive, as if we were brothers. He's an honorable man down to his soul, one who would have no part in the killing of children."

"Even good men can be tricked, Reynard. Honorable men can do the wrong thing for all the right reasons, but they'll still be wrong. The king knows the ships bringing the girls are landing. He even orders people to stay inside on the nights they arrive."

His fists clenched on the table and he looked down. "Politaus breaks his own rules and allows the ships out of a sense of guilt. As the firstborn son, his older brother, Braxus, should be king. Only his twisted body and constant pain prevent him from taking the throne. And the king never forgets that he rules at his brother's expense. He'd do almost anything to bring some bit of peace to Braxus, even allow the delivery of contraband books. Braxus has so little to live for, this seems like a small thing in comparison."

His hand rose, then banged down on the table, causing me to jump with surprise. "But not even for Braxus would Politaus allow the deaths of innocent children."

I nodded. "Okay, for now we'll take your word that the king's not involved. But someone in the castle knows what's going on and is actively participating. If it's not Politaus, the next likely candidate is Braxus. How do you feel about him?"

His face became expressionless as he answered. "He is the king's brother."

"And you're loyal to the king, so you won't say anything bad about his family."

"He doesn't need to," Marcus said. "I can tell you. Braxus is a bitter, hateful man. He never misses an opportunity to remind Politaus that he rules only because of Braxus's infirmity and pain. I believe his mind is as misshapen as his body—maybe more so."

I drummed my fingers on the table while I thought. "I'm inclined to believe he's in this up to his twisted little ears, but what reason would he have to steal the Daughter Stone?"

As soon as the words were out of my mouth, it hit me. "Oh, Zin. He's read Kiera Smith's journal, how she fixed the Buri females so they could have children and how she healed Thor's blaster wound. Now he thinks the Sumantti can make him whole again, and he doesn't care how many children he kills to do it."

"Could it make him whole?" Reynard asked.

In my agitation, I leaped to my feet and paced the length

of the room. On the table, Peri marched from one end to the other, mimicking my actions. "I don't know. In both cases where Kiera used it to heal, it was one specific thing that needed fixing. From everything I've heard, Braxus's condition is congenital. If it were fixable, the Federation scientists who were here five cycles ago would have offered to cure him, but they couldn't fix the Buri, either. It took Kiera with the Limantti, or Mother Stone, to accomplish that feat, so maybe if she tried, it would work."

I raised my hands in a helpless gesture. "But there's another aspect of this that Braxus couldn't know. The Daughter Stone is too immature to be as rational as the Limantti. And right now, she's very, very angry. If she gets the chance, she's more likely to kill him than cure him, even *with* a Shushanna in control. No matter how powerful those girls' psi abilities might be, they aren't Shushannas. And the Sumantti may not stop with her immediate surroundings. So, even though she's not as powerful as the Mother Stone, she's plenty strong enough to wipe out this solar system and maybe a few more for good measure."

"Will you be able to stop her, with the Imadei's aide?" Reynard asked.

I touched the crystal, a grim knot forming in my chest. "That's the theory. Or at least, that I'll be able to act as her Shushanna without going through the preparation ceremony."

"You will succeed," Reynard told me. "I don't doubt it for a second."

His gaze was so warm that heat suffused my body in response. This time it was Marcus who cleared his throat.

"Well, if there's nothing else, I'll be off to bed." He stood and waited for Reynard to do the same. "Commander."

"I'll walk him out the back way," I told Marcus. "We don't want to upset Bim again."

"Don't be long." He gave me a meaningful look.

I nodded, and then waited until he was closed inside his room. "This way, Commander," I gestured toward the back door, calculating just how much time I had. Not as much as I'd like, but enough to make some progress on the personal front, maybe.

Peri watched with a great deal of interest, but stayed where she was on the table as the night closed around me and the commander.

It was clear out, stars visible in the black sky, although they seemed to be in the wrong place to someone used to seeing them from Alpha Centauri. The air was warm enough to stave off chill, but not hot enough to make you sweat, and heavy with the scent of flowers.

After a slight pause to insure no one was around, I turned to face the commander. He was staring down at me, that intense look still in his eyes.

"Will I see you tomorrow—"

I cut his words off by the simple expedient of going up on my tiptoes, wrapping my arms around him and sealing his lips with mine. For a split second his body went taut with shock, but then he scooped me off my feet and dived right in.

The desire that had simmered since I'd first seen him burst into full heat and shot through my body with a force that left me shaken as he deepened the kiss. No one had ever affected me this way before and I had a horrible feeling no one ever would again. If there really was such a thing as a soul mate, I'd met mine in Reynard du'Marr.

And if the way he shook was any indication, he felt the same about me.

When we finally drew apart it took me three tries before I could speak. "There's something we need to get straight, Commander."

He let me slide down the length of his body until my feet touched the ground, but kept his arms around me. "What would that be?"

"Books are fine if you want to learn about GEPs in general, but if you want to know about me in particular, then I'm the one you should ask. And I'm going to save you the trouble. I'm not a Madrean woman. The fact that I don't charge for sex has no bearing on who or what I am. If I needed to charge for sex to earn credits for my own support, I'd do it without a qualm and it wouldn't make me less a person than what I am now."

My hand curled into a fist and I thumped him gently on the chest. "As I told you earlier, when I have sex with someone it's because I want to. That means I take responsibility for my own actions and I'm not expecting a marriage proposal to make me an honest woman afterwards. I *am* an honest woman, and the only one who can change that is me. Sharing myself with someone I care about doesn't have a thing to do with my honesty."

I wrinkled my nose at him. "Are you afraid yet?"

His lips twitched. "Terrified."

"Good. You should be. Because there's something else I have to tell you. When I want something badly, I go after it and I don't stop until it's mine. And I want you."

Before he could answer, a loud thud sounded from Marcus's room. I couldn't decide whether to sigh or roll my eyes at his none-too-subtle reminder.

"However," I continued with a grimace, "it seems now isn't the time or place. Marcus has to live and work here on Madrea and I don't want to jeopardize his reputation as my guardian."

Reluctantly, I freed myself from Reynard's embrace and stepped back. "But be warned, Commander. I plan on having my way with you first chance we get."

Slowly, he lifted his hand to run a finger gently down my cheek. "I'll be looking forward to it." With the same deliberation, he kissed me again and then leaned down, his lips brushing my ear. "You won't have to fight for me, Echo. I surrender."

And then he was gone, swallowed by the darkness, leaving me with a confusing mix of longing and elation. I almost danced my way into the house, deliberately making enough noise to let Marcus know I was back. When I was sure he'd gotten the message, I followed Peri to my room. The dragon bird was positively oozing smug satisfaction as she settled on the bed's headboard. She'd had the same reaction when Reynard had used the Imadei to pull me back into my body, as though she'd known exactly what he was going to do, and why he was doing it.

It made me wonder. If she picked up my emotions, and Reynard's brain operated on the same frequency as mine, she might be picking up on his feelings, too. At this point, nothing would surprise me. She'd been enthusiastic about him from the beginning. Lucky for me, I was fine with that, but it would be nice to know for sure.

I stripped, folded my clothes and climbed into bed, but sleep was the furthest thing from my mind. It had been a hell of a day, and I needed a few minutes to go over it, let the events soak in. Especially the part where I had to admit I was endowed with psi ability, thereby ending any hope, however futile, of getting my old job back.

And of course, it *had* been futile. Part of me had known it from the beginning.

That didn't change the fact that I wasn't created to be an agent or that I had no desire to be one, so the question now became, What could I do about it?

Easy, I decided after a few moments of ruminating. If I

couldn't have my old office job back, then I'd find a niche for myself in the upper echelon of Alien Affairs. And if I were going to aim for an office job, might as well go for broke. A smile crossed my lips. Dr. Daniels's job would do very nicely. Very nicely, indeed.

CHAPTER 11

The sun had barely cleared the edge of the planet the next morning before I was up, energized by the decision I'd reached the night before. I had a goal now, one that felt absolutely right this time, as if the Director of Alien Affairs job had been made specifically with me in mind. Don't know why I hadn't seen it before. Too busy being upset with the unasked-for changes in my life, maybe.

Oh, I knew it wouldn't be easy. I'd have to work my way into the job. But Dr. Daniels was getting on up there in age, and sooner or later he'd want to retire. With my background in political relations and organizational skills, I'd be uniquely qualified to step into his very large shoes.

There were only two stumbling blocks to this plan that I could foresee.

First and foremost, I'd have to complete this mission. Successfully.

My chin went all stubborn as I thought about it. I could do it. I was created to be a problem solver. Now that I was invested in getting this done, the bad guys didn't stand a chance.

Imbued with new energy for my task, I jumped out of bed, wrapped my cloak around me, and headed for the shower. My cheery call of "Good morning!" to Bim, who had just returned from his breakfast break, startled the stoic man, and I could feel him watching me in surprise as I tripped down the path to the privy.

Peri zipped inside with me, and I was under the shower, scrubbing away and trying not to step on her as she flapped vigorously near the drain, before I let myself think about the second problem.

Reynard.

Every time I pictured myself in Dr. Daniels's office, doing his job, Reynard was by my side.

He would love Centaurius. Love the universities and museums. Love all the modern gadgets, and technology, and information available. I could even see him working for Alien Affairs. His ability to distinguish truth from lie would make him an invaluable asset, and he had so much more than that to offer.

But I also knew, right down to my toes, that he would never abandon his duty to King Politaus. His loyalty to the man was unwavering, preceding Reynard's own wants or needs.

I couldn't—wouldn't—ask him to change. His honor and loyalty were as much a part of him as his eye color or height. And it was part of why I was rapidly falling in love with him.

My problem, I thought, as I stepped from under the water and toweled off. One I wouldn't inflict on Reynard. I'd simply have to live with the knowledge that he could only be mine for as long as I was on Madrea, and enjoy him while I had the chance.

As much as I wanted to rush through everything I had to do, I forced myself to slow down enough to insure I got my clothes on properly, and then combed out my wild mass of hair while Peri preened and fluffed her damp feathers. When we were both presentable, I headed for the Terpsichore with Bim close on my heels.

The kitchen was bustling with early-morning activity, and all the usual people were either eating or working. Leddy smiled as I came in and gestured at the eggs currently simmering in a large skillet.

"Hungry?"

"Starved." I returned her smile. "But can I get a tray for me and Marcus, along with a pot of coffee, to take back to his house? We have some business to take care of today."

"Of course. I'll fix it for you." Efficiently, she began heaping food on plates, positioning them on a large tray.

Treya came in from the front of the inn just as the cook finished adding a basket of homemade biscuits to the other bounty. "Will you be dancing tonight?" The blonde asked.

"No, not tonight. Marcus and I are to have dinner with the king. Apparently he knew my father. But I promise, I'll be here tomorrow tonight."

"Hmph. See that you are," she commented before sweeping back out.

I sighed, and Leddy took a second to pat my arm. "Ignore her. She's just jealous. Until you came, she was the top draw around here. Taking second place is good for her character."

She picked the tray up and handed it to Bim. "Carry this for Echo, then come back for another cup of coffee. You don't have to stand guard when Marcus is with her."

His brows lowered and I got the impression he wanted to argue with her, but he didn't. Holding the heavy tray like it weighed no more than a single flower petal, he opened the door for me, then kept his pace even with mine as we returned to the house. Quiet though he was, his eyes were sharp, constantly checking our surroundings for danger, and that massive axe was always within easy reach on his back.

If *I* were up to no good, I sure wouldn't want to take Bim on. The man was solid as a rock and built like a mountain. And he was, apparently, devoted to Marcus from tip to toe.

He escorted me into the house and deposited the tray on the table, then stood shifting in indecision. I could hear Marcus stirring in the bedroom, so I touched Bim's arm.

"Go get your coffee. Marcus is awake, and we aren't going anywhere. We'll still be here when you get back."

He shot a look at Marcus's door, hesitated briefly, and then nodded. Silently, he made his way out the back door and was gone.

By the time I got the tray unloaded and our places set, Marcus put in an appearance, sniffing as he took his seat. "Coffee," he croaked, cradling the hot cup I poured for him.

After the first long sip, he sighed with pleasure. "I don't know how I managed to survive in the Federation for so long with only cafftea to wake me up."

"I know. I'll miss it when I have to go back."

Putting down the cup, he picked up a fork and dug in. "I think there's something you'll miss more than coffee. Or should I say, someone."

I smiled as I raised my own cup. "Yes, but I'll live. Now, eat. We've got things to do today."

He nodded around a bite of eggs. "Which first, Dr. Daniels or Kiera Smith?"

"Lillith, is Dr. Daniels ready for me yet?"

"He will be by the time you finish eating," the ship responded. "He wants you to come to him, if you don't mind."

"Of course. So, I guess it's Dr. Daniels first."

"I really don't think there's much danger now that you've

figured out how to get back in your body, but I'd like to stay just to be on the safe side. I'd hate for whoever threw that knife yesterday to come across you when you weren't able to protect yourself," Marcus said.

"Thank you. The same thing occurred to me, so I hoped you'd stay. I'm still not comfortable with this leaving-my-body-defenseless thing."

We finished the rest of the meal in silence and then stacked the dishes back on the tray.

"Where do you want to do this?" Marcus asked.

I thought for a second. "Since I don't know how long it will take, maybe I should stretch out on my bed?"

"Good idea." Bringing a chair with him, he waited while I went to my room and got on the bed, and then he blocked the doorway as he sat down. Even as Peri darted into the room, humming with curiosity, I noted that Marcus could cover the window, too, from his position. He wasn't taking any chances, and that made me more comfortable with what I had to do.

Eyes closed, I took a deep breath and let it out slowly. Then I began to construct a mental image of Dr. Daniels. When it was complete, I gave a slight push and literally felt the sensation of rapidly flipping pages followed by a click, and abruptly I was in his office.

Two men lurched to their feet when I appeared, and I recognized the second one as Dr. Shilly, head of the Alien Affairs psi department. He was holding a metal rod in his hand, aimed right at me.

"What's that?" I asked, suspicious in spite of myself.

"Now, now," Dr. Daniels patted the air to calm me. "It's nothing to get upset about. Dr. Shilly merely wanted to find out if you leave any kind of signature in this state."

"Oh." I looked at the elderly man in his rumpled suit. His

thin hair was standing on end as if he'd been running his hands through it all night. Of course, he always looked like that. "Do I?"

He fiddled with a control on the rod, and then smiled. "No, you don't. Not even an electrical pulse. As far as the machine is concerned, you aren't here at all. This is absolutely amazing."

"I'm thrilled you like it," I told him sourly. "But the question remains, what *exactly* am I?"

Dr. Shilly put the rod away while Dr. Daniels moved to sit behind his desk. "There's no name for what you do, Echo, so for now we'll just stick with *ghosting*. It works as well as anything."

"According to all the data we've gathered, and the probability programs we've run, I think we know how it is you're doing this." Dr. Shilly sat down on the sofa. "It seems you're somehow able to lock onto an individual's DNA and then travel to them instantaneously. It's like you're tracking them. And what's more, you seem to be able to do this without expending excess energy."

"Or, more likely," Dr. Daniels interjected, "the Imadei is replacing the energy you use."

"Yes. But to continue," Dr. Shilly said. "Once you've met someone in person, you somehow store their DNA code and are able to access it at will."

My thoughts spun. "You mean, I gather DNA just walking down the street? Good grief. I've lived on Centaurius for thirty cycles. Is it even possible that I've stored the code for everyone I've passed?"

"No, not at all," Dr. Shilly said. "That would be counterproductive to the ability's efficiency. According to all our probability programs, an individual would have to be fairly close to you before you picked up and stored their DNA code. And there's no way to be sure how long you store the code without more testing. I imagine those you spend the most time with are the ones whose codes will last longest."

I wanted to fidget, but I was afraid I'd accidentally walk through a chair, and that thought tended to freak the schite out of me. Instead I forced myself to stand still and merely flexed my fingers.

"So how did I 'track' Gaia? I'd never met her before."

"In a sense, we think you have," Dr. Daniels told me. "When your crèche mate, Pelga, died from Chekhov disease, her DNA remained in the storage bank, since there was nothing fundamentally wrong with her. Simon Gertz had access to the bank. When he left, we believe he took DNA samples with him, including Pelga's. We checked last night and the sample used to create her is gone."

I started to rub my forehead and then stopped. If walking through a chair was freaky, what would it be like to stick my hand through my head? An involuntary shudder ran over me. Was I ever going to get used to this? It took an effort but I refocused on what they were telling me.

"You mean Gaia is actually Pelga? But they don't look alike. Well, not much. Gaia has red hair. Pelga's hair was an almost-white blonde and I haven't seen her since I was five cycles."

"No, she's not Pelga," Dr. Daniels assured me. "But she was created from Pelga's DNA. And even though Gertz made changes to that DNA, enough of the original remains to allow you to track her. The fact that you have such a traumatic history with Pelga makes your attachment to her deeper than to most other people, especially since you spent your first five cycles with her. It actually makes sense that she would be the first one you involuntarily tracked when your psi ability began to manifest after you bonded with the Imadei."

My brow furrowed in puzzlement. "I don't understand. *What* traumatic history?"

Dr. Shilly glanced at Dr. Daniels, got a nod, and picked up the story. "When Pelga became ill, she was hospitalized on the far side of Centaurius in an institution that specializes in Chekhov disease. There's absolutely no way you could have visited her that night unless you used your psi ability. You were so young, it was probably the first time you'd managed it."

He sighed heavily. "It must have been a terrifying sight to see your friend in that condition. If we'd known about it we could have given you appropriate therapy, but we had no idea in those days what Gertz had done to the GEPs he created. So, with no other rational explanation for what you'd seen, your young mind attributed Pelga's removal to her inability to correctly do her lessons, when in fact, her failure was due to her illness. And the first use of your ability provided you with an experience that must have looked like torture. The two events got all mixed up in your mind. That's part of why you've always been obsessed with being perfect, and it's also why you subconsciously blocked your ability for so long."

I stared at him, shock mixed with an eerie kind of recognition. He was right. Deep down inside I knew it.

While the child that I had been still insisted my friend had been tortured, as an adult I now recognized that what I'd seen was medical equipment. Pelga hadn't been punished for failing.

An enormous sense of relief swept over me, a weight lifted from my shoulders that I hadn't known was there. *I* didn't have to be perfect.

Oh, I knew it wouldn't be that easy to get over a lifelong fixation, but I suddenly realized I didn't have to be another Kiera Smith to be a good agent. I could be a good agent my own way, and the Federation wouldn't come to an end if I made one wrong step.

Except, in this case, Madrea and the surrounding space might cease to exist if I failed to control the Daughter Stone. So, even if I made mistakes along the way, I'd simply have to insure I succeeded in getting the fragging stone to trust me. Somehow.

Dr. Daniels was nodding his agreement with Dr. Shilly. "Now that her ability is back to normal, it will be interesting to discover its parameters."

I perked up. "Parameters?"

"Yes. It does have limits, obviously, since you can't track someone through images. Also, your hand goes through anything solid, but you have no trouble standing here even though we're twenty-five stories up. Why don't you sink through the floor?"

As soon as he mentioned it, I began to slowly slip downward. Eeek! Hastily, I stepped forward and up, giving a huge sigh of relief when I stayed put.

Both men had stopped talking and were watching me with a great deal of curiosity.

"Interesting," Dr. Shilly commented. "Apparently if she needs something to be solid, her ability treats it as such. That would imply that she *can* manipulate her surroundings if she thinks she can, at least to an extent."

Dr. Daniels nodded. "I imagine it will take some practice, though. And I have a feeling we're only seeing the tip of the sword where Echo's ability is concerned. She tested much too strong for this to be all there is of her ability."

"There's more?" I swallowed hard. "I just accepted I had an ability yesterday. I'm not sure I can handle any more surprises."

"In my experience," Dr. Shilly told me, "it's a very instinctual process. Rather like yanking your hand back from a flame once you feel the heat. The full range of your ability will be there when it's needed, and you won't even realize you've used it until afterward."

"Great. That makes me feel so much better. Kind of like a blaster with the trigger half depressed. Now, unless you gentlemen have more good news for me, I need to be on my way." I glanced at Dr. Daniels. "Can you make sure Lillith gets a copy of everything you've found out? It will save a lot of time if I don't have to explain it all to her myself."

"Of course." He stood and pushed a few buttons on his desk console. "All taken care of. I understand you've asked to meet with Kiera. Excellent idea. She's probably the only person in the Federation who has any chance of understanding what you're going through." An expression more serious than any I'd seen before crossed his face. "Be careful, Agent Adams. Remember, while Gaia may seem like a helpless child, Gertz created her. We have no idea what she's capable of doing, and as Dr. Shilly mentioned, use of psi ability can be a reflex action. If she's scared, she could lash out, even against those trying to help her. And we have no information at all on Banca, except she's obviously not Gaia's biological sister, no matter what the girls believe. She's a total mystery."

Wonderful. Something else I hadn't thought about. I'd sure be thinking about it now, though. Me, Miss I-don't-like-kids suddenly had not one but three to deal with. One was a superhuman with unknown capabilities, another was a little girl with spooky eyes, and the last was an alien with the potential to destroy universes. And at least two of them were scared and dangerous. If that didn't make your knees shake, nothing would.

Trying to maintain my confidence, I gave him a curt nod and then closed my eyes, pictured Kiera, and pushed.

When I opened my eyes again, it was to the sound of

squabbling dragon birds and the rush of a waterfall somewhere nearby. I was standing in what appeared to be a giant
birdcage attached to the back of a stone building. On the
floor, two kittens the size of medium canines snarled and
tumbled and mock-stalked each other, barely sparing me a
glance when I appeared.

Before I could stop myself, I inhaled deeply and caught
the scent of growing things mixed with traces of a recent
rain. Maybe there was something to this "wishing it to be so"
thing, because I wouldn't have thought I'd be able to smell
anything in this form.

There was so much to look at that it took me a second to
focus on Kiera and the man beside her.

Holy Zin. While I might prefer Reynard's rugged visage
and piercing blue eyes, there was no denying that Smith's
mate was the most gorgeous male I'd ever seen. And there
was no doubt whatsoever that this was Thor. He was huge,
with inky black hair and ebony eyes that reflected a deep-
seated wisdom and kindness.

I tried not to ogle all those rippling muscles under warm
bronze skin, instead forcing my gaze on Kiera. She was
standing in front of a waist-high pedestal that held the biggest black crystal I'd ever seen. Even in my current bodiless
condition I could sense the power flowing off that stone. To
say it scared me silly would be an understatement of epic
proportions. All I could do was gape at it.

"Echo, I don't believe you've met Thor, my mate," Smith
lifted a hand to the man beside her. "Thor, this is Echo
Adams. I thought maybe Thor could help, since his people
have lived with the crystals for thousands of cycles."

I tore my gaze away from the Limantti long enough to
acknowledge Thor with a nod, then nervously looked back
at the giant crystal.

"You get used to it, eventually," Kiera said, reminding me

yet again that she was an empath. "And luckily, she wants only the best for all life forms."

"Unlike her daughter?"

Smith frowned. "What do you mean?"

I told her about my experience with the Sumantti the day before. "That's why I wanted to speak with you. I need to know everything you can tell me about the Daughter Stone, about the alien life form that inhabits the crystal. The Sumantti may want the best for everyone in theory, but she's so young I don't think she's developed any self-control yet. And she's trapped, unable to get away from her captors. I'm afraid that in her panic, she could very well take out the people who are trying to help her. Namely, me."

"I see what you mean." She glanced at Thor, and I got the impression a conversation was going on just below the level of my hearing. Finally, Thor spoke in careful Galactic Standard, his voice deep and rumbling.

"We do not understand how these captors are holding her, or why the Limantti can find no trace of her daughter."

"I can't be positive, but it felt to me as if she were in a stasis box. Is that even possible? If she's powerful enough to destroy a star system, I don't know why she couldn't escape from a stasis field."

Smith put her hands on the Limantti, her eyes unfocused. She stayed that way for a second or two, and then nodded. "The Mother Stone says it would explain why she can't locate the Sumantti. Her daughter has no experience with stasis fields. While no one could hold *her* this way, the Sumantti is still very immature. But the Daughter Stone will, eventually, determine how the field works, and then her captors won't be able to contain her." She lowered her hands.

"Zin help us if that happens before I can calm her down."

I sighed. "And I can't even start trying until I understand exactly how this life form operates. For instance," I gestured at the crystal. "Why did the brains of the bunch end up in black quartz, as opposed to another color?"

Smith glanced down at the huge stone. "The easiest way to put it is that black tastes better than other colors to the psynaviats that make up the hive mind. The color each colony prefers depends on the workers' psi function, but all are tied to and created by the brains of the life form." She tilted her head toward the Mother Stone. "Think of her as the queen bee. It makes things simpler."

"Psynaviats?"

"Yes, it's what we've named them, for lack of a better term. It means psychic energy."

"Okay. Psynaviats it is. But is the Limantti really female?"

She hesitated. "Only in the sense that it replicates, or gives birth. *Female* is our word, not hers. You have to remember, this isn't a single entity we're dealing with. Both the Sumantti, or Daughter Stone, and the Limantti contain millions of living beings, all too small to see, even with a molecular microscope. You have to go to the subatomic level to get a glimpse of them. They make viruses look gigantic. Just as an example, they move *between* the molecules of the quartz, not through them."

Midway through her explanation, Thor touched her arm lightly, and then vanished through a curtained door into the building, the kittens scrambling at his heels. A scarlet-feathered dragon bird darted after them, pausing long enough to loudly scold a blue-green dragon bird and swat him with one wing before ducking under the curtain.

Smith chuckled at their antics. "Sorry about that. It's almost time for Rayda to mate again, and she's giving Gem a hard time. Now, where were we?"

"The organism that lives in the quartz," I reminded her.

"If there are that many of them, won't they eventually consume the crystal?"

"That's what we thought at first. Turns out, they don't consume the quartz at all. Quartz is a conduit for electricity, even minor quantities like what it absorbs from sunlight. The entities feed on that energy. And while we aren't sure how they manage it, they can even produce more quartz. That's how the quartz for the Daughter Stone was created."

"I thought it was mitosis."

Smith nodded. "For the psynaviats, it was, but they had to make the quartz for their new halves to inhabit first."

My mind spun with questions. "So the form that operates as the brain can't survive outside the crystal?"

"Oh, it can, and has in the past. It just prefers staying in its quartz." She frowned again. "At least, I think it does. The truth is, we wouldn't know if came out and went for daily walks, since we can't see it. And it does send colonies out every time it lands on a quartz-rich world."

"Okay, I think I'm getting the basic idea of how this works. Maybe that will help if the Daughter Stone gets loose and throws a fit, although I'm not sure how."

"Don't forget the Imadei," Smith told me. "It should help you control her. And now that we know which planet the Sumantti is on, the Mother Stone will be watching, too. If there's anything we can do, I promise, we'll do it. You aren't alone in this, Echo, even if it feels that way sometimes."

"Thanks, I'll take all the help I can get. I just have one more question. Are there any more of them floating around in space, waiting to fall into the wrong hands?"

Smith looked shocked and I figured she'd never thought of that possibility before. Her eyes went unfocused again as she consulted the Limantti. Whatever the conversation, it seemed to take longer this time, and she appeared troubled when she finally answered me.

"The Mother Stone says she encountered three others in her travels through space. Two continued on and she lost track of them when they left this galaxy. She believes the third crashed on a deserted planet, because it vanished from her sight and she hasn't seen it since then."

Not a comforting thought, but I could only deal with one catastrophe at a time. Casting a last look at the massive crystal, I said good-bye and then pictured slipping into my body.

When I opened my eyes, both Marcus and Peri were leaning close, looking at me, Peri from the headboard, Marcus from beside the bed.

"We were beginning to worry," Marcus said, straightening while Peri cooed at me. "You've been gone for over two hours."

"Zin, three planets, scattered all over the galaxy, in two hours." I grinned at him. "I'm starting to see the advantages of this ability. But there's one more thing I need to try."

It had occurred to me that maybe I could get a lock on someone's DNA when I was in ghost form. And I had a perfect subject to practice on now.

Closing my eyes, I let Thor's image form in my mind, and then pushed. Abruptly, I was back on Orpheus Two, standing outside a large adobe building. Thor was in front of me, along with three other male Buri, and all of them were staring at me in surprise.

A whoop of glee escaped before I could stop it, causing all the Buri except Thor to jump. He merely smiled at me, his thick black hair lifting in a gentle breeze.

"My mate wishes to know if you forgot something."

"Yes." I grinned at him. "I forgot to tell you good-bye."

His head dipped in a regal nod, as if ghost women popped up in front of him every day. "Good-bye, Echo Adams. Fare thee well."

Aw, now wasn't that just the sweetest thing ever? I could see why Kiera Smith liked him so much. Before I could respond, Kiera spoke from behind me.

"He's taken, Adams. Go get your own man."

A laugh burst out of me. "I already did. See you later."

This time when I returned to Madrea, Marcus had his arms crossed over his chest, glaring at me. "What just happened?"

I sat up and swung my feet to the floor. "Did Lillith tell you what Dr. Daniels and Dr. Shilly discovered about my ability?"

"Yes."

"Well, I just found out I don't have to meet people in my normal form to get a lock on their DNA. I can do the same thing in my ghost form. That should help."

"How are you feeling? You must have expended quite a bit of energy."

I did a quick inventory. "Maybe, but I feel fine. Probably a little hungrier than I normally would be a few hours after eating breakfast, but that's it."

"In that case, we might as well go to the Terpsichore and grab a snack. We still have a while before we'll need to get ready for tonight, and I'm expecting a wagonload of wine from up north today at the warehouse."

"Sure. Leddy wanted me to organize things so the women wouldn't have to go all the way through the kitchen to get drinks for the customers. I can keep busy with that."

Peri gave an inquisitive *cheep*, and I waved her toward the window. "Go ahead and visit the flowers. You must be starved by now."

She trilled happily and fluttered out of sight, but I could still feel her nearby. It made me think of Rayda, and the fact that she'd mate soon.

Which presented a problem I hadn't thought about before

now. Sooner or later, Peri would be mature enough to mate. What we were going to do then? As far as I knew, other dragon birds were nonexistent on Centaurius.

Well, schite. It looked like I was going to end up owning yet another dragon bird in the future. Didn't that just figure?

With a sigh, I followed Marcus from the house.

CHAPTER 12

"Y ou cut a hole in the wall of my storage room!" Marcus roared.

I winced, and then continued calmly putting on my bracelets, watching him from the corner of my eye as I stood in the main room of the house. "You don't have to yell. Bim will think we're being attacked."

"You cut a hole in the wall of my storage room," he said through clenched teeth.

At least he didn't rattle the windows this time.

Carefully, I reached over and patted his arm. "It's for the best. When you see how much time it will save, you'll thank me."

"I had kegs of ale stored against that wall. Now you've cut my storage space down by a fourth of what it was."

Pausing, I tilted my head to study him. "You didn't go into the storage room, did you? You just saw the opening from the common room." With a put-upon huff, I propped my hands on my hips. "If you'd bothered to look, you'd have noticed I rearranged your stock so that it's not only more efficient, you have twice the storage space you had before. Furthermore, if you put a man inside to fill the mugs, which,

I might add, are now within reach of anyone standing behind the counter in the opening, it will speed up the flow of the servers. Everyone else loves it, including Treya." I glared at him.

"Fine!" He threw his hands up. "I'll go look at the storage room." Stomping every step, he went through the back door, letting it slam behind him.

By the time he came back, much subdued, I'd finished getting ready for our meeting with the king. "Well?"

"You were right. It's much better." He looked at me curiously. "How do you do it? How do you know exactly where to put everything to make the most use of a space?"

"It's no big mystery." I shrugged. "The image of how it should look just pops into my head, like a diagram, all nice and neat."

An inscrutable look crossed his face. "So you always know just what's right for a space."

"I guess you could put it that way."

"Rather like the commander knows what's right or wrong when someone speaks to him."

Surprised, I nodded slowly. I'd never made the connection before. "Lillith did say our brains operated on the same electrical frequency. I guess this proves it. The only difference is he focuses on people, I focus on spaces."

"Did you think I was lying?" the ship asked.

"No, I'd simply never considered how it might affect us."

"Given your upbringings, I suppose it's natural that you use this talent differently," Marcus mused.

"What do you mean?" I asked him, watching Peri attempt to get a spare bangle bracelet over her head.

"Well, you were created for the Department of Protocol, so you were taught to organize events. And that included the spaces they were held in. In the commander's case, he was alone at an extremely young age. His very survival depended on his ability to judge the people he encountered, figure out whom he could trust and whom he couldn't."

"That makes sense." I took the bangle bracelet away from Peri and picked up one made from a slender chain. Looping it around her neck twice, I fastened it and stood back to survey the effect while she happily preened. It was still loose, but at least it wouldn't impede her wings. "There, you look gorgeous. Definitely fit to visit the king."

"And if I don't get changed, you two will be the only ones allowed into the royal dining room," Marcus said, vanishing into his room.

When he was gone, Peri waddled across the table, looked me in the eye, and sent me an image of herself holding a stick of makeup.

"No," I hastily told her. "Not a fragging chance. Dragon birds do not wear makeup. You don't need it," I added, hoping to head off a trend. "You're beautiful just like you are. I should be so lucky."

Impatiently, I blew at the lock of hair that insisted on hanging over my left eye. It seemed like the harder I tried to do something with the mop, the worse it got. I'd finally given up entirely and just let it do what it wanted.

At least Treya had loaned me a dressier outfit for the night. It wasn't as elaborate as the costumes used for performing, but it was a beautiful shade of sapphire blue, adorned with golden chains at the waistband. There were even matching sandals and a velvety cloak to go with it.

"How do I look?" I asked the dragon bird, and then blinked in surprise when she sent me an image of myself glowing like I'd swallowed a sun. "That good, huh?" I chuckled.

Kiera had told me that Peri would pick up my emotions and broadcast hers, but lately it seemed the exchange had gone way beyond emotions. The fact that Peri answered a question with an appropriate image boded well for future communications on a higher level.

"Are you two finished admiring yourselves?" Lillith asked. "The commander just left the castle and is headed your way."

"Right on time, as usual," Marcus said, carrying his boots as he came back into the main room.

I couldn't help staring at my "guardian." "Zin, Marcus. No wonder so many women are in lust with you. If you dressed like that more often they'd be falling at your feet."

His tight pants were made from a fine, chocolate-brown material that delineated the long muscles of his legs. The boots he pulled on were a darker, shinier brown and came to his knees. His shirt was a light, silky tan, set off by a jeweled belt holding an ornamental short sword. The colors set off the silver-threaded blond hair that had been pulled into a queue and tied with a matching ribbon.

An attractive flush tinted his cheeks at my words. "It's hard to dress like this when I do manual labor most of the day. Besides, there aren't that many women in 'lust' with me."

I shot him a wicked grin. "I've been here a week and I can already name two. Maybe I should be *your* guardian." I took a simple offensive stance, arms raised to strike. "I'm pretty sure I could take Leddy. Cammi seemed a little more determined, though."

"I can defend my own honor, thank you." Marcus chuckled as I straightened. "You're certainly in a good mood tonight."

"Of course I am. I get to have dinner in a castle with a king, escorted by the two most handsome men on the planet."

"And maybe get closer to the Sumantti?" he asked shrewdly.

"That, too," I told him. "I really need to get a better idea of the way the castle is laid out, plus, get a lock on as many people's DNA as possible. If I can't search the place in my corporeal body, maybe I can do it in ghost form."

"You know, you can always ask the commander to help you with the layout."

"I could." Sobered, I shook my head. "But it would put him in an untenable position, Marcus. He's already compromised his loyalty to the king by not telling him the truth about me. I don't want to push him any more than necessary. It may come down to that to save the girls, and if it does, I'll use him. But until we reach that point, I won't force him to choose between me and the king more than he already has."

Before he could respond, there was a brief tap on the front door, and Bim opened it to allow Reynard entry. One glimpse of him and my knees went weak; my heart gave one hard knock and then started hammering at a rate it had never achieved before. I forgot all about how good Marcus looked or that he was even in the room.

Reynard was dressed in black from top to bottom, the silk shirt clinging to a well-defined chest and snuggled lovingly against his flat stomach. The sleeves were long and full, cinched tightly at his wrists.

His slim waist was encircled by a wide silver belt studded with blue stones the same shade as his eyes. Attached to the belt hung a silver scabbard containing a sword that wasn't the least bit ornamental.

An ornate medallion holding the same kind of blue stone hung from a silver chain around his neck. It looked official, and I suspected it was the formal badge of his office.

Peri saved me from making a complete idiot of myself by strutting across the table, chortling proudly as she fluffed her feathers, tilting her head from side to side, all to better display her necklace.

With a grin that highlighted his dimple, Reynard bowed to her. "How magnificent you look tonight, my lady. The king will be most impressed. As he will be when he sees your beautiful mistress."

The look he sent me simmered with heat as he extended an arm. "May I have the privilege of escorting you?"

"Of course." After donning my cloak, I wrapped my hand around his muscled arm as Peri settled on my shoulder. The commander and Marcus greeted each other and then we exited through the front door.

And I came to a screeching stop, causing Peri to scramble for purchase.

Bim was holding the reins of three gigantic animals. At least, they looked gigantic to me. They shifted, snorted, and tossed their heads until their gear jingled.

Immediately, I released Reynard's arm and took two quick steps in reverse until my back was pressed to the door. Unaware of my sudden terror, Marcus continued on, stopping to talk with Bim.

"What's wrong?" Lillith asked. "They're just horses."

"I know what they are," I told her, my voice shaking while Reynard turned toward me, concern on his expressive face. "And I'm not getting on one of those evil beasts."

"They aren't evil, Echo," Reynard told me, and I realized I'd been speaking aloud. "They're animals, with no concept of right or wrong."

"Then why are they looking at me as though they want to see how I taste?" I asked him.

Lillith's snort mimicked those of the horses. "Even if they bit you, you'd heal instantly."

"Yeah, well, knowing that in theory and experiencing it in actuality are two different things. Besides, it would still hurt even if it didn't kill me, and my instincts are telling me that if I get on that creature's back, I'll die. Not to mention,

I have no idea how to steer the things, or where the brakes are. I don't even own a fragging PTV. The tubes or the public beltways have always served just fine to get me where I'm going."

"A PTV?" Reynard asked.

"Personal transportation vehicle," I explained.

"You'll ride with me," Reynard decided abruptly. He held out a hand. "I swear, I'll let no harm come to you."

Well, schite. Now I had no choice in the matter unless I wanted to insult him.

Reluctantly, I put my hand in his and let him lead me closer to the monstrous beasts. Lillith must have repeated the conversation to Marcus, because he calmly mounted the reddish-brown animal, and took the reins of the gray. "I'll lead this one."

"Thank you." Reynard nodded to him and then patted the huge black horse we'd stopped next to on the neck. "This is Arrow. I raised him from a foal and saw to his training myself."

The inky-black animal turned his head and stared at me, his mouth making chewing motions on the metal bar between his teeth.

"Bite me, and so help me Zin, I'll break your nose," I muttered at him. "Believe me, I'm a lot stronger than I look."

The threat seemed to leave him supremely unconcerned.

"He's merely curious," Reynard told me. "Your scent is unfamiliar to him."

Without another word, he scooped me up, put his foot in the stirrup, and suddenly we were on top of Arrow's broad back, me in front of Reynard. Frantically I clutched him, burying my face against his neck as the animal began to move.

With an indignant squawk, Peri squirmed out from between us, deciding it was better to fly than get squashed.

Reynard's right arm came around me, holding me securely against his body. Beneath me, I could feel the shift of muscles as he used his legs to control the horse.

"Are we there yet?" I mumbled against his warm, clean skin.

"No." His head lowered until his lips brushed my ear. "And I'm thinking of taking the longer way, if it will keep you in my arms like this."

I was still melting when, from our right, Marcus cleared his throat. "Nice evening, isn't it? Lots of people out enjoying the weather."

"Marcus says if you don't stop, you're going to be engaged to the commander before you reach the castle," Lillith told me. "As your guardian he will personally see to it."

This guardian thing was turning out to be a real pain in the butt. With a sigh, I gathered my courage and forced myself to sit up straighter, barely suppressing a gasp when I saw how far away the ground looked.

Gripping the commander's arms, I glanced around and realized why Marcus was so concerned. The sun was barely down, but enough light remained to show me the people who had stopped along the road to gape at us.

Lifting my chin, I schooled my features into a serene expression and gazed straight between the horse's ears. If I could fake being an agent, I could fake being calm, even though my heart was still pounding.

Faster than I would have thought possible, we reached the front of the castle. A man ran forward and took the reins Reynard handed him, then held the horse while we alit. I was tempted to fall down and kiss the ground, but managed to restrain the urge. Instead, I took a closer look at my surroundings.

Since I'd avoided the front of the castle on my first attempt to get inside, I'd only seen it from a distance. The porch made a half circle abutting the stone building, and it was so big that twenty men lying stretched out wouldn't reach from one end to the other.

Ten wide marble steps followed the entire length of the arc, and ten marble columns supported the roof.

Thanks to large sunstone lamps attached to each side of every column and adorning the walls on both sides of the huge double doors, the area was lit up like the Federation Council during a five-day filibuster.

Every inch of marble was stark white shot through with veins of clear quartz crystals. The only spots of color came from the many-hued flowers filling round marble planters that flanked each pillar and weighted the air with scent.

Reynard took my hand and led me up the stairs to the doors, Marcus and Peri following. The doors were made of solid wood, and so big I had no idea how the liveried men next to them would get them open.

Easily, as it turned out. One of the men gave the commander a brisk three-fingered salute and then gripped a handle. Without a sound, one of the massive doors swung outward. Not until then did I notice the slight indentation of a tack in the marble floor where weight-bearing rollers could glide, making moving the door effortless. Apparently Politaus feared no enemy attack.

But then why should he? The only other people on Madrea were the Bashalde and they seemed content with their nomadic existence. And as I'd learned early on, his soldiers were more than capable of stopping the random intruder.

Tucking the information away, I followed Reynard inside. The hall was as wide as both doors, and the sound of music and voices drifted from just ahead. Peri bounced with excitement as she landed on my shoulder and then bobbed her head in time to the melody.

Reynard smiled down at me as we walked, Marcus close beside us. "Nervous?"

"Not in the least, now that I'm off that animal. I'm used to events like this. But I have to tell you, I'd prefer to walk home afterwards."

"Arrow will be devastated." His smile remained in place as he ushered me forward, so I knew he was teasing. "He doesn't often get the chance to carry such a beautiful lady."

"I'm sure he'll get over it," I told him wryly. We'd stopped in the entryway of a great hall filled with people, and the murmur of conversation died as they saw us. A quick scan told me I was the only female present dressed in the Bashalde manner, so I wasn't sure if they were staring at me or Peri, or simply because I was with the commander. Maybe it was all of the above.

Ignoring them, I took a longer look, checking for anyone who might be Braxus. If he was there, I couldn't pick him out. All I saw was a sea of faces turned in our direction, sparkling lights, and walls adorned with colorful tapestries.

At one end of the hall, men and women wearing the drab, modest clothing that was normal in Bastion City mingled with men who were obviously Bashalde. To my surprise, there were equal numbers of commoners and merchants mixed in with what seemed to be the gentry.

The other half of the room was set with long tables punctuated with floral arrangements between white dishes edged in gold. From numerous doors behind them wafted the delicious scent of roasting meat and spices.

Directly across from where we stood, the hall was divided by a dais holding a large, hand-carved wooden chair. The man occupying the seat was probably the only one in the room who hadn't immediately stopped what he was doing to stare at us. Instead, he leaned over the arm, talking earnestly to Jancen, who stood beside him, head tilted as he listened intently to whatever the man was saying.

King Politaus. I recognized him immediately from the first vid I'd watched of Madrea. Tonight he was dressed in a flattering green-gold combination that went well with his coloring, his belt set with emeralds and topaz. A slim gold band that sat low on his head was the only sign of his station.

I noted all this in only a second or two while Peri launched into the air, circling us as Reynard's hands went to my shoulders to remove my cloak and give it to the waiting doorman. Her antics drew the attention of those on the dais, and Jancen smiled as he looked over and motioned for us to join him.

When we started forward, the voices resumed, louder now, but I ignored them, my focus on the dais as Peri resumed her favorite seat. Another few steps and surely I'd be close enough to lock on to the king's DNA. And because I was paying more attention this time, I felt it when it happened.

It was a bit like catching a pleasant scent and then having it settle in your memory, forever linked with the first time you encountered it. From now on, I'd be able to lock on and visit the king no matter where he might be. Unfortunately, I was close enough to touch him before it happened.

There was one step ascending to the dais, and the king stood as we reached it. Keeping his hand on the small of my back, Reynard gave a short bow. "Your Highness, may I present Echo, daughter of arms master August and cousin to Jancen?"

"Your Royal Highness." I executed a deep curtsey, holding it until I felt a strange hand on my arm, lifting me erect.

"Please, there's no need to be so formal." His voice was rich and kind, and filled with humor, surprising me yet again. "Especially since I feel as if I know you already. Not only have you turned my usually stoic commander's head, Jancen can't stop singing your praises."

"Thank you, sire." I graced him with my most brilliant smile. "I've heard much about you also."

"Oh?" His brows arched in an invitation to continue. "You've aroused my curiosity."

"Well." I paused for effect. "The commander considers you his friend as well as his monarch. His faith in you is unshakable. He says you're kind, wise, and fair."

Politaus nodded. "Reynard is like a brother to me. I would expect nothing less." Briefly, his eyes clouded and I wondered if he was thinking of Braxus. But the expression was fleeting before he wiped it away. "And who else has spoken of me?"

"Jancen," I promptly replied. "He says you're a pig-headed, stubborn old woman for not allowing the Federation access to Madrea."

Jancen winked at me as the king threw his head back and roared with laughter, drawing stares from all over the hall. "Oh, my. I can certainly see why the commander is enamored of you, my dear. He always has valued direct speech. As do I. You remind me of your father in that respect. August was never one to withhold his opinion, whether solicited or not. Will you and your party sit with me at supper and tell me your views on the topic of the Federation?"

Talk about irony. "We'd be happy to, sire. Have you met my guardian, Marcus Kent?"

"I have." He turned to Marcus with a friendly slap on his shoulder. "Kent. Why has it been so long since you've accepted an invitation to join me for supper?"

Marcus gave him a short bow. "My apologies, sire. I've only recently returned from an extended trip to restock my wine."

Interest sparked in the king's eyes. "Did you visit that small winery in the hill country this time?"

"I did." Marcus smiled. "And as you requested, two barrels of their red now reside in your cellar."

"Excellent, excellent!" He rubbed his hands together in anticipation, and then glanced at Jancen. "You'll want to try this wine, old friend. It's extraordinary. I'll have some brought up to go with our meal."

"I'll look forward to it," Jancen told him. As the king's attention went back to Marcus, the older man moved closer to me.

"How are you today? The last time I saw you, you were unconscious."

"I'm perfectly fine, I promise." I patted him on the arm. "It was just a reaction to the events of the day."

His gaze turned shrewd as he leaned down next to my ear. "I would have thought August's daughter would be made of sterner stuff than to faint over a failed attempt on her person."

Uh-oh. I swallowed hard. This old man saw way too much.

"Caught me," I whispered to him, noting that Reynard came to attention at Jancen's words and stepped nearer, one hand resting casually on the hilt of his sword. Even Peri went still. I didn't dare tell him about the Daughter Stone, so once again I was being forced to tell half-truths.

"Honestly? I faked it because I didn't want to meet Chief Lowden right then."

"Why not?"

I checked to make sure the king was still involved with Marcus and no one else was close enough to overhear, then lowered my voice even more. "Because the man who threw the knife at me went into Chief Lowden's tent."

He reeled back a step, and I steadied him with a hand on his arm before he could draw unwanted attention. "But why would one of Lowden's men want to hurt you?"

"I don't know. And without more information it wasn't prudent to throw myself into a situation I was uncertain about."

"Well, I certainly can." He almost vibrated with indignation. "You can be sure I'll get to the bottom of this as soon as I return to camp."

Alarm streaked through me. I *liked* Jancen. No way did I want him in the middle of whatever was going on with Lowden.

"No, please, for my sake, stay out of it. Let me handle this my own way."

He stared at me intently for a moment. "There's more to this than you want me to know, isn't there?"

I let my head dip in a slight nod. "Yes."

A sigh lifted his chest. "When it's over, will you tell me everything?"

Again, I nodded. "Yes."

"Then I'll have your promise that if you get in trouble you'll come to me."

"I promise."

He hesitated. "There's one more thing. Zeller, Lowden's cousin and ambassador to the court is here tonight. He's been watching you closely since you arrived. I thought his interest was because he found you attractive, but now I have to wonder. I've never trusted him," he added.

My first instinct was to turn and look for the man, but I restrained myself. There was a slim possibility his faction thought I was the type that swooned at the first sign of danger. If that was the case, I wanted them to stay deluded. At the least, I didn't want him to know I was suspicious of Lowden.

"Thank you for the warning," I told Jancen just as the king's attention focused back on us.

He smiled expansively as he waved us away. "Reynard, why don't you introduce Echo around? I'm sure there are many here who would love to meet her. Kent can stay here and keep me company until supper."

Peri had stayed quiet throughout the entire meeting with the king, but she perked up as Reynard led me from the dais, ruffling her feathers as she peered around to see if anyone was admiring her.

"That was interesting," I told Reynard. "The king was nothing like I expected him to be."

Keeping a hand on my arm, he smiled as we paused a few feet from the crowd. "What did you expect?"

"A lecher. Lillith said he'd probably grab my—rear."

The ship snorted in my ear. "He knows the commander has already staked a claim on you. *That's* why he didn't grab your ass. And you need to be more careful. Another few minutes and you'd have spilled your life story to Jancen."

"Since you'd be so much better at this than I am, would you like to trade places?" I subvocalized. "Oh, wait. You might have problems getting into the outfit." I let out a dramatic sigh. "Guess you'll just have to *let me do this my way.*"

"There's no need to get huffy about it," she replied.

Reynard arched a brow at me. "What is she saying?"

"How did you know I was talking to my ship?" I asked.

"Because you always get this look in your eyes, like you're doing battle, when she talks to you."

"Oh." I thought about that, then decided he was probably right. "She didn't say anything important. But I do have a question. Why isn't Politaus married? I'd think it would be important for him to produce an heir."

He nodded, a lock of dark chocolate hair falling over his

forehead. "It is important. But men outnumber our women three to one. Finding a suitable female to marry isn't easy, even for a king." He glanced back toward the dais. "Fortunately, arrangements have been made with one of the northern families who have a daughter of marriageable age, and the wedding will take place in eight months. She's a handsome girl with a good heart. She'll be the perfect wife for Politaus and provide him with many children."

Another thought occurred to me. "What would happen if Politaus were to die before he had an heir? Who would take the throne then?"

The commander's face was without expression when he answered. "Braxus would be our only alternative. At least until we could choose someone more fit to rule."

I glanced back at the dais, suddenly very, very worried. "Reynard, I'm not trying to tell you how to do your job, but you might want to seriously consider assigning more guards to the king. I've got a really bad feeling about Braxus."

"Duly noted," he said, his eyes going grim. "Especially if he has the Daughter Stone."

CHAPTER 13

"Does Politaus know every single person on Madrea?"
I asked Reynard, trying not to scowl as I locked onto
the DNA of yet another shopkeeper I'd brushed
against in the crowd. Was there a limit to this psi ability of
mine? What if I reached my saturation point before I locked
onto Lowden's ambassador?

When I had the time, I really needed to experiment, see
if there was a way I could pick and choose whose DNA to
store in my head.

"For the most part. It's what makes him a good ruler. Not
only does he go out in public and patronize the shops and
businesses, he also sits in judgment on disputes once every
four eightdays and he holds these suppers twice a month. The
guests vary each time, so everyone is eventually invited."

"No wonder Treya and Leddy didn't act surprised when I
told them I was having supper with the king."

Reynard had casually pointed out Lowden's ambassador
earlier and I scanned the crowd, looking for the bright blue
of Zeller's tunic. It was starting to feel like the man was
deliberately avoiding me. Every time we wended our way in
his direction, he'd head for the other side of the hall.

When I finally spotted him, he was in conversation with another man, his back to us, and closer than he'd been all evening long.

With barely a touch on the commander's arm to get his attention, we strolled toward the ambassador. "Who's he talking to?" I murmured.

The man was about as plain as they come. Average height, average weight, simple clothes, brown hair and eyes. He was the kind of man who could fade into the background and no one would ever remember he'd been there.

"That's Chine, Braxus's man," Reynard said, his voice as low as mine.

"Good. I really need to get a lock on him. Maybe I can catch him near Braxus later tonight."

He looked at me curiously. "Can you travel in your other form?"

Good question. I'd never tried it, but I'd taken a step forward in Dr. Daniels's office, so I had to assume it was possible. "I think so."

"Then it doesn't matter if you collect Chine's DNA. I can wait outside Braxus's living quarters and you can simply come to me."

I shook my head. "Reynard, I don't want to get you any more involved in this than absolutely necessary. Besides, there may come a time when I need to find Chine and you won't be able to help." A woman to our right was leaning in our direction, trying to overhear our conversation. I sent her my best political smile as we moved closer to Zeller and Chine.

"You have a point about Chine, but I am involved," he responded calmly. "How could I not be, when those two children are in danger? Besides, my loyalty is to Politaus, not Braxus, and the king would agree that by helping you I'm doing what's best for Madrea."

"If you're sure." When he nodded, I continued. "I don't have to talk to them. We can just walk by. A few steps seems close enough for my ability to register their DNA codes."

We both remained silent as we moved nearer the two men, and I held my breath, waiting for them to notice us. They were so intent on their conversation that we were almost within range, when the king's voice rang out from the other end of the hall.

"My friends, supper is served. Please join me at the tables."

Instantly, both men stopped talking and looked up, straight at me and the commander. Zeller's eyes went wide, and Chine paled as they began to back up. It didn't take a genius to figure out they knew I wasn't who I claimed to be, that I was, in fact, an agent of the Federation.

Well, schite. I couldn't let this opportunity pass when I was so close. From their reactions, I wouldn't get a second chance.

Go to Reynard, I ordered Peri. *Now*.

The instant her feet left my shoulder, I went into over-drive. Without wasting time thinking about it, I charged the men, getting near enough to touch them. And felt two mental clicks so close together it was hard to distinguish one from the other as I stored their DNA codes.

I continued in a circle that brought me back to my original starting position at Reynard's side just in time to see Peri fly to his shoulder. A little smugly, I watched Zeller and Chine's pants legs flutter in the breeze of my passage. Both of them looked around as though wondering where the sudden draft had come from before continuing their retreat.

"Got it," I told Reynard with a grin. "Let's go eat. I'm starved."

The food was every bit as delicious as it smelled, and the dishes were varied and frequent. No one noticed I was eating a bit more than usual because they were doing the same, everyone taking advantage of the king's largess.

The king sat to my right, Reynard to my left, and Peri kept everyone at our table entertained by inspecting each type of food that made the rounds, cooing at the floral centerpieces, and strutting between the place settings to show off her chain necklace. Politaus was so amused by her antics that he pulled an intricately woven, golden pinkie ring from his hand and gave it to her.

From Peri's reaction, you'd think he'd given her keys to the crown jewels. It took her a few tries, but she finally managed to get it on her right foreleg, and then sat back on her haunches the better to admire it. I had a feeling the king was her new best friend.

The meal was finally winding down, and I was wiggling in my chair with the desire to get back to Marcus's house. I had things to do, places to go, people to spy on. Plus, I needed to check on the girls again, make sure they were okay and try to determine where they were being held.

Unfortunately, I was well versed in protocol and knew it was impossible to leave until the king departed. Instead, I eyed Zeller, who was seated at the far end of our table near Jancen. He still appeared to be avoiding me, so it was something of a shock when he looked straight at me and raised his voice.

"I understand August taught you to fight."

Well, schite. He was definitely up to something. "That's correct. Since we had no close relatives, he tried to insure I was able to protect myself if he was no longer able."

"You know I've often said there's no reason to coddle our women. They should all be taught self-defense. But there are those among our people who believe women are incapable of learning the skills needed for fighting. Would you be willing to give us a demonstration?"

Eeek! "What do I do?" I asked Lillith, praying my panic didn't show.

"Say yes. You really have no choice."

"But what if I accidentally kill someone?"

"Just remember your life isn't in danger, no matter what happens. Try to think of it as a practice match with one of your instructors. Maybe your instincts won't take over."

Oh, sure. Nothing like showing a little encouragement to help build my confidence.

Keeping a stiff smile in place, I dipped my head in a nod. "If it's the king's wish. Sire?" I turned to Politaus, hoping he'd put a stop to the suggestion.

"What an excellent idea!" He scrubbed his hands together in anticipation. "I'll have a wide selection of weapons brought in, and you can choose whichever you prefer."

"Thank you, but I have my own knife. And I'd really rather we do this hand to hand, so no one accidentally gets hurt."

His eyes lit with anticipation, and he ignored everything I'd said except the part about the knife. "You have a knife with you? Did August make it? May I see it? His weapons are much prized."

Double schite! I'd chosen the plainest knife in the Alien Affairs armory, but it was still a technical marvel compared to the handcrafted weapons used on Madrea. I could only hope that August was ahead of his time when it came to weapons, and no one noticed the blade that never dulled, or the non-skid grip that was all one piece with the blade and not attached separately. Or the fact that it was made from a metal alloy that didn't exist on Madrea.

Reluctantly, I reached under my skirt, pulled the knife from its sheath, and handed it carefully to Politaus.

He examined it reverently, almost holding his breath as

he turned the blade in his hands. "Amazing. Such balance. This has to be August's finest work. When did he make it?"

I watched anxiously as he passed it down the table for others to admire, including Zeller. The loss of its weight against my leg left me feeling strangely unsettled, naked almost. "It was the last he forged, sire, and therefore very dear to me."

And why was Jancen checking my weapon so closely? My nerves were screaming by the time he passed it back in my direction, the look in his eyes speculative.

"Ah, I was hoping you might consider selling it, but I can see now that's impossible." The king retrieved the knife and gave it back to me. "Hand to hand will be sufficient," he continued, as though I'd only just made the request.

Reynard leaned forward. "It would be my pleasure to engage Echo, sire."

"I would also volunteer," Zeller chimed in.

Choices, choices. I was pretty sure Zeller had offered because he wanted to do me in. Accidentally, of course, which I wasn't about to allow. And stopping him would expose me.

Since Reynard knew all about me, that would solve all my problems. I wanted to kiss him for suggesting it.

"Nonsense." The king smiled at him as I sighed in resignation. "You're the best fighter on Madrea, possibly even better than August. I want the girl to have a fair chance. And Zeller, both you and Echo are Bashalde. I don't want anyone to accuse you of favoritism. This should be a fair endeavor." He lifted an arm and motioned to a guard standing near the doors.

Damn. Talk about up-and-down emotions.

As the man started forward, I leaned into Reynard, noting his resigned expression. "Who is he?"

"His name is Durtran. Other than myself and the king, he's the best fighter we have."

"Any weaknesses?"

"Only one." He looked down at me. "He's never sparred with a woman before. Use it if necessary. And try not to kill him."

Sheesh. Why was everyone so convinced I couldn't control myself? Even Marcus looked worried. Okay, so I almost gutted Reynard the first time I met him, and maybe my own knee-jerk reaction was fear for the man I'd be pitted against. Now that I remembered my defensive reactions were programmed to be instinctive, I was better prepared to contain them.

As I saw it, my biggest problem would be remembering that I was only supposed to be as strong as a normal female. That would limit what I could do to him, since he was almost as big as Reynard.

I watched him approach the king, frowning and glancing in my direction as he received his instructions in a lowered tone. He argued for a moment, and then stiffly nodded. It was obvious he didn't like the king's orders a bit, and I felt a little sorry for him. After all, men on Madrea were taught from birth that women should be respected at all costs. Now he was being told he had to fight one. It was a no-win situation for the man.

Unless I did something that went completely against the grain and let him beat me.

I pondered all angles of the solution as he turned to me and bowed. If I could do just enough to make him think he'd worked for his win, it might cause Zeller and company to underestimate my strength and ability. As far as I was concerned, that was a good thing, and my ego wasn't so big that I had to win just for the sake of winning.

Standing, I pushed my chair back and followed Durtran to the other end of the hall, where we'd have space to move. "Stay with Reynard," I told Peri. She made an annoyed sound, but obeyed, settling on his shoulder.

The tables emptied quickly as Durtran and I divested ourselves of weapons and put them on the floor out of reach. By the time we were done, everyone in the room had formed a wide, loose circle around us.

We took our place in the center and again, Durtran bowed to me. "My lady. Please know I do this reluctantly, even though it's at my king's order. There is no honor in fighting a woman."

"Just try to think of me as a shorter, lighter man in a dress," I told him.

Balancing on the balls of my feet so I'd be ready to move in any direction, I waited for him to attack. And waited. Then waited some more.

Okay, this was getting ridiculous. We couldn't stand here staring at each other all night. I had to do something to motivate the man.

"Did you know August?" I asked him.

"Yes, I did. Your father was a great fighter, my lady."

I sent him a cocky grin. "I'm better."

His eyes went wide a split second before I dropped to one hand and used my legs to sweep his feet out from under him.

He'd barely started to fall before I was upright again. But instead of crashing to the floor, he used the momentum to roll back to a standing position. Without giving him time to recover, I aimed the edge of my hand at his neck.

As I'd hoped, I wasn't the only one with automatic responses built in. He blocked me, grabbed my wrist, and used the motion to spin and toss me over his shoulder.

If one of my instructors had executed the throw, I'd have landed on my feet with no problem. But since I was supposed to be a normal female, I let myself hit the polished marble floor.

Yeowch! Zin, that hurt! For a split second, pain lanced

through my hip, and then was replaced by warm, sweet relief. This super-fast healing thing was worth its weight in sunstones.

I got to my feet just in time. Durtran looked like he was in more pain than I'd been, and was on the verge of helping me up.

This couldn't be allowed to happen. I had to make the man fight so hard he'd forget I was a woman.

With no more hesitation, I attacked, raining blows to his body and limbs, forcing him to retreat with each contact in an effort to defend himself.

Fortunately, it finally dawned on him that he needed to take the offensive if he was going to get out of this with his manhood intact, and he launched his own attacks.

Okay, now we were getting somewhere, even if it did feel more like dancing in slow motion to me than fighting. Up until now all my sparring had been down with GEP instructors, and the action with them was so fast it would look like a continuous blur to a Natural. Now, because it *was* so slow for me, I had time to choreograph every move, gauging Durtran's response before he made it, and making sure he held his own.

I even had time to make sure the outfit Treya had loaned me didn't get damaged in the fray. The thought of having to tell her I'd ruined it was *almost* scarier than an angry Sumantti.

After twenty minutes of constant sparring, it occurred to me I had a problem. While the activity might seem slow and easy for me, my opponent was getting a real workout. Sweat rolled down Durtran's face, and his hands were slick with it. I, on the other hand, was cool and dry, not even breathing hard. And while I could pretend to pant, there was no way to fake sweat.

So how could I let him win when he was obviously in more distress than I?

"Tell Marcus to do something to stop this!" I told Lillith. "I don't dare let Durtran win, and I won't beat him. He'd be humiliated for life. Not to mention confirming Zeller's suspicions about me."

As Durtran drew in an exhausted breath and came at me again, I saw Marcus straighten, hesitate for moment, and then lean toward the king.

Blocking the guard's move, I danced out of reach, trying to give Marcus more time with my evasion tactics.

To my relief, the king nodded, and then stepped forward, hands raised. "Enough! I hereby declare the match a draw. You've both represented yourselves very well indeed. Durtran has upheld the standards of my guards, and Echo has proven without a doubt that women can be excellent fighters."

There was a smattering of polite applause as Durtran swiped his sleeve across his damp brow. "You've taught me a valuable lesson today, my lady," he said before the others reached us. "Never again will I underestimate the skill of an opponent based on sex alone."

"Well, I'm not exactly your average female," I told him modestly.

"No, you're not. Your father exceeded himself with your training. Don't think I'm not well aware you could have bested me from the beginning. I owe you for allowing me my pride. If I had lost, it would have meant resigning my commission. If ever you need my assistance, please ask."

I was trying not to gape at him when Reynard, the king, and Marcus reached us. Everyone else drifted away, and I saw Zeller duck out the door. My attention was still focused on his retreating back when the king grabbed my hand and raised it to his lips.

"You were wonderful, my dear. If I'd seen you first, Reynard wouldn't have a chance of winning you from me."

Gently, I extracted my hand from his grip. Because I'd been created for the Department of Protocol, my repugnance at having my hands touched wasn't as great as it was for other GEPs, but it had taken intensive aversion therapy for me to reach this level of tolerance. And nothing was ever going to make me like it.

"Thank you, sire. If I might be excused, I'd love to find a place to freshen up a bit." And even more, I'd love to see what had Zeller rushing from the room.

"Of course." He beamed at me like a proud father. "Reynard can show you to a room."

Marcus opened his mouth to protest, and I hastily contacted Lillith. "Tell Marcus to shut up. His reputation as my guardian will simply have to suffer this time. I need to catch up with Zeller."

His mouth closed and he gave a grim nod.

Taking the commander's arm, I urged him to quicken his steps as Peri took to the air and darted ahead of us. Although it seemed like hours since Zeller left, it had only been a few minutes, and the second we were through the doors, I looked in the direction he'd gone.

The hall was well lit and I had no trouble seeing the three men huddled together, halfway down, talking in furious murmurs.

Unfortunately, they didn't have any trouble seeing us, either. Both Zeller and Chine glared at me, but the third man turned away quickly and faded into the room behind him.

He was too late, though, because I'd recognized him instantly. Losif Strand, leader of Helios One. It really *had* been him I'd seen at the gathering.

With one final optical death ray aimed in my direction, Zeller and Chine hurried into the room behind Strand.

"Lillith, send a red alert to Dr. Daniels," I told the ship, actually speaking aloud so Reynard would know, too, as we went down the hall. "Losif Strand is on Madrea."

"Sending. Did he recognize you?"

"Oh, without a doubt. We've never formally met, but we've been in the same room often enough that he'd know who I was. How did he get on Madrea without you seeing his ship?"

"They probably approached from the other side of the planet, and then landed just out of my sensors' range."

"That would imply they know you're up there."

"Yes, it would." She sounded downright grim. "I wish I could deploy my satellites."

"Ask Dr. Daniels to send a Federation ship to monitor the space from a distance."

"I will, but it could take a few days. A large percentage of the unattached fleet is conducting maneuvers near Andromeda, and the ones that are patrolling outside Madrea's planetary system are too large to jump in closer. They'll have to use conventional engines to get here."

"Fine, but tell them to come as fast as they can."

I hadn't paid attention to where we were going, concentrating on my conversation with Lillith instead. We stopped outside a door that looked vaguely familiar, and the commander opened it and ushered me inside.

No wonder it looked familiar. He'd brought me to his quarters. There wasn't time to think about those ramifications, however. As Peri settled onto a table, gave a prodigious yawn and curled into a tired ball, I moved to the bed, sat down and looked at Reynard.

"That room the men went into, does it have another exit?"

"Yes. It's one of the king's small central meeting rooms, and can be entered at either end. It's often used as a shortcut so people can get from one side of the castle to the other without going around the long way."

"Okay." I took a breath and braced my body. "When my psi ability first began to manifest, I 'saw' you having breakfast without actually showing up in front of you. I'm going to try it again with Zeller."

He frowned. "What if it doesn't work and they see you?"

I shrugged. "They can't hurt me in my ghost form. At worst, it will simply expose my ability to them. And while I'd rather that not happen, knowing what they're doing is more important right now."

Eyes closed, I concentrated on building an image of Zeller in my mind. Medium height, stocky build, greenish squinty eyes. Instead of letting it reach the page-ruffling stage, though, I tried to mimic what I'd done with Reynard and treat this as I would a daydream.

He would be with Chine and Losif Strand, so I sketchily added the other two men to my mental picture, and made the room around them deliberately hazy. When I had it fixed to my satisfaction, I gave a gentle push.

Abruptly, my image of the room solidified to include a glossy table surrounded by four chairs, and a desk full of scrolls. Both Zeller and Chine were staring at Losif like he'd grown a second head.

"You're sure?" Zeller asked.

"Positive," Losif's smile was feral. "Not only is she a Federation agent named Echo Adams, two cycles ago her indenture was purchased by the Department of Alien Affairs because it was discovered that Simon Gertz was her creator."

At Gertz's name, Chine went pale, but Zeller only looked puzzled. "Who is Simon Gertz?"

Losif glanced at Chine. "Why don't you explain?" He went to a sideboard and poured a glass of wine.

"Simon Gertz is a rogue geneticist who tampers with the DNA of those he creates, giving them unknown psychic abilities. According to the book Braxus has about the Smith woman, the Gertz GEPs are also stronger, faster, smarter and nearly impossible to kill, since their wounds heal instantly."

"And it's all true," Losif added, swirling his glass. "The only thing we don't know is what her psychic ability is. But be assured she has one. Gertz is well known for his ingenuity."

"What are we going to do?" Zeller blurted. "This changes everything. We thought there would be more time before the Federation discovered where the crystal was located. Now they not only know we have it, they've sent a woman we can't hurt to stop us and retrieve the crystal."

Losif drained his wine and then sat the glass aside. "The only thing this changes is our timeline. We'll have to speed things along, put our plans into action now. Once we have control of the Sumantti, not even Echo Adams will be able to stop us."

He crossed to the other two men and slapped Zeller on the shoulder. "Come, I want to see if the men have started loading my ship yet. And you can reassure your chieftain that the woman won't be an obstacle much longer."

As soon as they left, I banished the image and opened my eyes. Reynard was crouched in front of me, a worried look on his rugged face, and Peri was snoring away from her position on the small table.

"Well, schite. Not only do they know who I am, they know *what* I am. The only thing they *don't* know is what kind of psi ability I have."

"Did they see you?" he asked anxiously.

"No, they didn't. This ability does have its good points, and unlike you, they weren't even aware that someone was watching. What bothers me is that Losif Strand didn't seem too worried about me. From what he said, he has plans to stop me from completing my mission."

The commander surged to his feet and reached for the hilt of his sword. "He plans to hurt you?"

Now wasn't that the sweetest thing ever? He wanted to defend me. It was enough to make my heart leap with joy, and it was an effort not to smile from sheer happiness. But since I didn't want to hurt his feelings, I kept my expression serious when I answered.

"He didn't say for sure, but he knows enough about Gertz GEPs to understand that hurting me won't work. I'll heal too fast. He also knows I'm not easy to kill. From what Kiera said, it would take a direct blaster shot to the head or heart, and if I know it's coming, I'm fast enough to dodge. I suspect he has something much more diabolical in mind. I just wish I knew what it was."

"Whatever he plans, he'll have to go through me first. I've never cared for the man."

I arched a brow at him. "You know him?"

"Yes, but not as this 'Losif Strand.' He's the black marketeer who takes our sunstones in exchange for the books Braxus wants."

"Well, that explains how he can move around the castle so freely. But he's no trader, legal or otherwise. He's the leader of Helios One, and he wants control of Madrea's sunstone trade." A troubling thought occurred to me. "How many sunstones has the king given him?"

"Several chests full. Why?"

I chewed on my lip for a second while I thought it through. "Because each sunstone is worth a sizable fortune in the Federation. And I have a feeling he's taking a ship full of them every time he comes to Madrea. I heard him tell Zeller and Chine he wanted to go see if his men had started loading the ship yet. So what is he doing with them?"

We were silent for a minute, mulling over the possibilities. "Lillith, see if there's been a sudden influx of sunstones on the market."

There was a pause as she checked. "There's been a few turn up, but not what I'd call an influx, and the Federation *does* have a small supply they use for research."

"Trace them down. If there's even a hint of a sunstone for sale in the Federation, I want to know who's selling it and where they got it."

"This could take a while," the ship told me.

"That's fine." I smiled at Reynard. "There's something I've been wanting to do, anyway. Now seems to be the perfect time." I stood and moved in on him.

CHAPTER 14

"Lillith, tell Marcus not to wait up for me." I flattened my hands on Reynard's tight abdomen and slid them up to his well-muscled chest, relishing the feel of hot skin under the warm silk of his shirt.

"I've finally got you to myself." My smile was sultry as I looked up at him. "No guardian to protect you from my mercenary clutches."

My heart rate went up a notch when he slid his hand down my arm, and I leaned closer to inhale his scent. He smelled so damn good. Like soap and shampoo, but with an underlying scent that was uniquely his. It was, I decided, sexier than any exotic male cologne I'd ever smelled before in the hallowed halls of the Federation Council.

"Reynard." I kept my tone soft and low. Keeping a tight rein on my emotions, I went up on my toes and teasingly brushed his lips with mine. Then I pulled away enough to see his face. "Are you still worried about propriety?"

Scarlet flooded his cheeks, but his eyes heated with desire. "To hell with propriety."

He curved his hand around the back of my neck under my hair, his thumb caressing the skin just below my ear as he pulled me against his body. The motion sent chills of anticipation all over my body.

The mixture of elation and desire that slammed into me left me weak and shaking. Holding me tightly against his hard length with one arm, he tilted my chin up with his free hand. As soon as our lips met, mine parted. He let his tongue skim the opening, teasing me as I had him, tasting, tempting until I was dizzy with the sweetness of his actions.

When he finally let his tongue slip farther inside, I made the same sound he had made, the one that had been driving me crazy since I'd first heard it, and I couldn't stand it another minute. My mouth took possession of his and I plunged all the way in. He met my parry thrust for thrust, fighting for control of the kiss, and I almost came unglued.

A groan of loss tore its way from deep inside me when he eased back.

Gently, he took my hand and raised it to his lips. "Echo, I want you so badly it's killing me, but before we do this you must understand that as long as my vow to the king stands, I'm not a free man."

"Neither am I, if you want to get technical about it. Alien Affairs owns my indenture and I have to work for them until it's paid off." I slid my hands down his chest and unbuckled his belt, tossing it and the sword onto the chair. "Reynard, I'm not asking you to marry me. I'm only asking for this."

I brushed my hand over the front of his trousers and encountered exactly what I'd expected to find.

"Echo." His voice was strangled, and I knew any thought of denying this pleasure had fled right out of his head.

There was a look on his face I'd never seen before, a sudden gleam of determination. And more, so much more. When his mouth claimed mine this time, I knew there would be no stopping for either of us.

Again, his arms slid around me, and he realized I was

standing on tiptoe, straining to reach him. He straightened, bringing my feet completely off the floor while he supported me. "Put your legs around me," he murmured against my lips.

Worked for me. As I complied with no hesitation at all, he slid his hands under my bottom, pulling me tightly into him. We held that position for a while, kissing deeply. Then he turned toward the bed and lowered me to the blanket spread over the plush mattress that smelled fresh and clean.

Sitting back on his heels, he gazed down at me before his hand skimmed over my halter top, grazing a breast that instantly hardened. The action caused my eyes to glaze and I inhaled sharply. As he let his fingers trace the mound, outlining its erect shape, my head went back and I arched against his hand.

Suddenly touching wasn't enough. I wanted to feast my eyes on his naked body, explore until he was moaning with pleasure. I wanted to torment him with pleasure until he was writhing in the same agony of desire that tormented me.

Moving carefully, I sat up, tugged his shirt loose, and pulled it over his head. Next, I slid off the bed and removed his boots. With that out of the way, I undid his trousers and maneuvered them off his legs. And while I was stripping him, he was busy returning the favor, dodging my hands to unfasten my halter top and loosen my skirt until it pooled at my feet.

For a long time, we simply filled our senses with each other, and his gaze was so filled with desire and yearning that a lump formed in my throat. No one had ever looked at me that way before, like I was special, like I really meant something to them.

It made me realize how much I'd missed out on, how very badly I'd miss it again when it was time to leave him behind.

"Echo," he whispered, refocusing my attention. He pulled me back onto the bed, and while his hands found my breasts, his mouth covered mine again just in time to catch my whimper.

He moved to my neck and traveled downward as he slid his hand over the warm skin of my abdomen, and for a moment he let it rest there, driving me insane with anticipation before he moved on.

I'd been right. He was even more glorious now than the first time I'd seen him, stepping out of the tub. My oft-repeated memory of the event hadn't done him justice. Had there ever been another man like this one?

Not that I could remember, and I was pretty sure I *would* remember if I'd felt this way before. Right now it was enough to know that he really cared for me, but I had a horrible feeling I was going to pay dearly for this night. Because with every sigh, every touch, I was falling a little deeper in love with Reynard du'Marr. The one man I couldn't have.

When he leaned over to kiss me again, this time deeply, slowly, thoroughly, I turned to meet him. I wanted to feel his body pressed tightly to mine, all the way down.

It seemed like an eternity before his mouth trailed down to my breasts, but when he took a tender nipple between his teeth and flicked it with his tongue it took all my willpower to keep from screaming with pleasure. It took forever for his hand to find its way back to the throbbing ache between my legs, but when it did, when he caressed me with light circular motions, I knew ecstasy was moments away.

His murmured reassurance was lost in the pounding rush of my own heartbeat. Then he was kneeling between my thighs, his hands on my hips pulling me into him. I could tell he wanted to plunge, bury himself as deeply as possible, but he didn't.

With his teeth clamped together in effort, he entered

slowly, just a little at a time, pausing with each movement to give me time to adjust. What seemed like hours later, he was finally fully encased, and I was afraid to move, afraid to even breathe. The sensation was so exquisite that even the smallest twitch could send me hurtling into space.

Reynard lost control. Holding my hips in place with his hands, he drove into me, withdrew, and then drove again, my name a groan on his lips. My scream of joyous release yanked his gaze to my face, and what he saw there destroyed what little restraint he had left. "Oh, sweet mother," he gasped. "Echo!"

I was in the throws of yet another wave of spasms when he exploded, endlessly, intensely, his moan of release bouncing off the walls, seeming to shatter into a million pieces. With no choice, he followed me into oblivion.

I had no idea how much time had passed when I finally began to surface back to the here and now, Reynard's weight adding to the lethargy that pervaded my body.

Unwilling and unable to withdraw, he rolled onto his back, taking me with him. After a moment he brushed away the wild mop of hair that hid my face. "Echo?"

"I was wrong," I whispered.

He wrapped his arms around me, his hands sliding possessively over my back as he began to move gently again. "Wrong about what?" He could barely get the question out.

A moan escaped from deep in my throat as my body matched his rhythm. "I thought I could stop myself from falling in love with you. But I was wrong. *I love you*, Reynard."

Lifting a hand, I covered his lips. "You don't have to say anything. It's my problem, not yours."

His body went still as I spoke, and then he sighed. "From the moment you walked through my door the first time, I knew you were the one, the same way I know what is right and what is wrong. No other woman has existed for me since that day, and never will again. *I love you*, Echo."

Tears filled my eyes as we made love again. He couldn't leave and I couldn't stay. All we had was now, and it would have to last us a lifetime.

"Echo. Echo!"

"What?!" I opened my eyes and glanced around, taking in Reynard's room.

"If you want to make it back to Marcus's house before you mortally embarrass him and cause Jancen to issue a challenge, you need to go now," Lillith told me.

"What time is it?" I asked, sitting up reluctantly and pushing the mop of hair out of my eyes.

"About ninety minutes until sunrise. Some of the shopkeepers are already out and about."

I glanced down at Reynard. He was sprawled facedown on the bed, the blanket barely covering him enough to be modest. We'd made love several times during the night, napping or talking in between, and I hated to wake him. On the other hand, if I didn't, he'd be upset with me. Just because we'd made love didn't change the fact that he was a Madrean male through and through.

As though to prove it, he turned his head on the pillow and gazed up at me. "Don't even think about sneaking off without me."

He was so sexy with his eyes all sleepy, his hair mussed and spilling onto his forehead, and heavy stubble on his jaw. So much that I couldn't stop my grin. "Wouldn't dream of it." Reaching over, I patted his butt. "But as cute as that part of your anatomy is, you need to get it out of bed before Marcus has to fight a duel on my behalf."

I jumped out of bed and began gathering clothes, sorting mine from Reynard's as I went, and tossing his on the bed. When there was no noise from that direction, I glanced over my shoulder and frowned. He'd rolled onto his back and stacked his hands behind his head.

"Why aren't you getting up?"

He grinned. "Because I'd rather enjoy the view."

"Ha ha." I threw his shirt at his head, forcing him to catch it or get slapped in the face. "Enjoy later, dress now."

"Will there be a later?"

"Count on it, even if I have to smuggle you through the window. After all, Bim can't stand guard forever. The man has to sleep sometime."

Taking my word for it, he finally got up and began dressing while I finished. When I had my knife back in place, I looked around the room and cursed.

"What?" Reynard pulled his shirt over his head, momentarily muffling the question.

"I left my cloak in the great hall."

"I'll find it and return it to you later. We'd be noticed if we looked for it now."

"Thanks."

Peri still hadn't stirred, so I poked her. "Come on, lazy bones. We have to go."

She opened one eye, grumbled at me, and went back to sleep.

With a sigh, I picked her up and cradled her warm body in the crook of my left arm, being careful of her wings. She didn't even twitch.

"Ready?" I asked Reynard.

"Yes." He went by me and opened the door. "We'll go out the same way you did the first day you were here. There are fewer sleeping quarters in that direction, but we'll still need to be quiet."

Together, we moved silently down one hall after another, until we reached the small door leading outside. Reynard stepped through it and looked in both directions before motioning me forward.

After that it was a short trip to Marcus's house. With a final lingering kiss, Reynard left me at the back door just as the first pale rays of light broke over the horizon.

Carefully, I eased the door open, praying it didn't squeak, and then jumped in surprise when it was pulled out of my hand from the inside. Instinctively, I reached for my knife before I recognized the person staring back at me.

Guiltily, she held a finger to her lips and leaned closer to me. "I'll keep your secret if you keep mine," she whispered.

"Of course," I answered. "Why are we whispering?"

A satisfied smile lit her striking face. "Marcus is still asleep, and it's better he doesn't know we ran into each other. Men can be so silly about things like this."

I thought about Reynard sneaking me through the halls of the castle, and nodded. "You're absolutely right."

She touched my arm and then slid by me. "I'd better go. I've already stayed later than I should have. I left a package in your room. It's on the bed."

"Thanks." I watched as Cammi hurried around the side of the house, heading for the main road that would take her back to the field where the gathering was being held.

Huh. No wonder Marcus hadn't insisted on leaving the supper with me and Reynard. I let out a soft snort. The old letch. I just hoped Leddy hadn't seen him bringing Cammi home for the night. She might stop cooking such wonderful food for the Terpsichore if she got upset.

Making sure the back door was firmly shut, I tiptoed to my room and deposited Peri on the pillow before picking up the large cloth-wrapped bundle Cammi had left.

Gingerly, I unwrapped it and then stared in wonder at the costume on top. It was the purple one, the one that was the same color as Peri's feathers, and shot through with silver thread.

Cammi was undoubtedly a genius with needle and thread, because it put the red outfit Treya had loaned me for my first dance to shame. The top was halter style, as were all the Bashalde women's, and there was a short veil to go with it. But the skirt was completely different. Instead of flaring from the belt as usual, the material was crossed in the front and pulled tight so it would cup my bottom snugly. From there, it swirled to full, beginning at the top of my thighs and continuing to ankle length.

Cammi had even included a packet of silver jewelry to go with it. I glanced quickly at Peri to make sure she was still asleep and then hid the pouch in a drawer before turning back to the costume.

It was the most gorgeous outfit I'd ever owned, and I decided that when I left Madrea, it was going with me even if Lillith had to land in the middle of Bastion City so I could retrieve it.

Spreading it across the chest so it wouldn't get mussed, I took out the other two everyday outfits and inspected them. Again, the workmanship was wonderful, and I picked the emerald green one for today. The red one I'd save for tomorrow. To think, when I'd first started this mission I thought two outfits would be more than enough. Now I'd been here an eightday with no end in sight. It just showed how naive I had been a mere week ago.

But I'd changed, I realized. I wasn't even as worried about wild bugs as I'd been before.

Well, not much, anyway.

Gathering up my clothes and a towel, I headed for the shower. It came as no surprise to discover Peri had exited my room via the window and beat me to the privy. She fluttered eagerly outside the door, sending me images of cascading water with suds flying in all directions.

"Yeah, yeah. You couldn't wake up enough to fly home, but you're bright-eyed and enthusiastic the second I think about taking a shower."

She agreed with a happy chirp.

By the time I stripped and stepped into the shower stall, she was dangling from the pull rope, doing her best to get the water going. Since she weighed maybe one and a half kilograms, or three pounds, on her fat days, it wasn't working.

Reaching over her, I gave it a tug, fastened it to the hook on the wall, and then stood under the tepid trickle, letting it soak me while Peri splashed vigorously at my feet. I took my time so she could get her fill, but she still sulked when I finally released the rope to turn the water off.

"Even you can't stay in the shower all day," I told her. "You'd look like a big purple prune with feathers."

Ignoring me, she found a perch on the sink and began the task of fluffing and drying her plumage. I returned the favor by taking care of my own morning rituals, and we finished at about the same time.

The day was bright and warm by the time I headed back to the house so I could leave my soiled clothes, although there were clouds gathering in the west. Looked like we might get some rain by nightfall.

"Don't go too far away," I told Peri as she headed off in the direction of the nearest flowers. An uneasy feeling was creeping over me. I glanced around casually, but no one was in sight.

Maybe I was getting paranoid. Of course, knowing Losif Strand was out to get me was a fragging good reason to start looking over my shoulder every few seconds. While we'd never been introduced, gossip had it that everyone in the

Federation Council mistrusted the man. He was diabolical, evil, and brilliant.

Shaking off the chill bumps that crawled over my skin, I entered the house and went to my room. Cammi must have worn Marcus out, because there was still no sound coming from his room. I contemplated waiting for him, then my stomach and the scents wafting from next door made me decide against it.

Bim had just arrived to take up his post when I headed for the Terpsichore, and he fell into step beside me with a nod of greeting. His solid presence was welcome today since I was still jumpy.

The kitchen was bustling with activity as usual, and I sniffed appreciatively as Leddy handed me a cup of hot coffee.

"Sit down, I'll bring your plate to the table."

"Thanks, Leddy."

Treya and the other women were already eating when I pulled out a chair, careful not to spill a drop of the coffee. "Good morning," I told them.

All of them replied in kind except Treya. She stopped eating to look over at me. "How was your supper with the king last night?"

"It was fine, very interesting."

"We heard you held your own sparring with Durtran. You didn't hurt my clothes, did you?"

"No, I didn't hurt your clothes. I'll have them cleaned and returned to you."

She nodded. "See that you do. And don't forget you're dancing tonight. I've already spread the word, so we'll have a good crowd."

Leddy slid a plate full of food in front of me before I could answer, and I dug in. "Don't worry about finding a costume for me. I had one made. I'll wear it tonight."

"I hope it goes with your coloring. Pale colors would wash you out."

"It does."

Leddy hovered near me, clutching the coffeepot. When I glanced at her, she nervously refilled my cup. "I haven't seen Marcus yet this morning. He hasn't left on another trip, has he?"

"No, he's just sleeping in today. I think the king kept him late last night."

"Oh, in that case, I'll keep his breakfast warm."

Treya gave me a knowing smirk as the older woman hurried away, but she kept her mouth shut.

I was just finishing up my food when the musicians came in, so while the other women served the customers in the common room, I waited on the guys and helped Leddy dish up eggs, ham, biscuits, and coffee.

Things were starting to slow down when Marcus finally showed up, a sheepish expression on his face. I merely arched a brow at him and pointed. "Leddy saved you some breakfast. Since the crowd is thinning out, there are some things I need to take care of at the house."

"Of course." He took the plate full of food and sat down. "Just be sure Bim goes with you."

The sun was approaching midday as I crossed the yard with Bim, and the clouds were closer, piling up like white fluffy mountains in the sky. Peri zipped by me with a chirped greeting before angling toward another bed of flowers.

When we reached the house I paused with my hand on the backdoor. "I'm going to take a nap," I told Bim, just in case he grew some curiosity and peeked in the bedroom window.

Moving quickly, I snuck into Marcus's room and rummaged until I found what I wanted, then went to my own room, hid the bundle, and stretched out on the bed. When I was comfortable, I pulled the image of Gaia from my memory. The pages ruffled, there was a mental click, and suddenly I was in the same small room where I'd seen the girls before. There was a table this time, holding two plates, one of them untouched, the other empty.

Both girls sat on the bed, staring at me. The smaller of the two, Banca, looked much better this time. There was color in her cheeks and the black circles were gone from under her eyes.

"Are you going to help us this time?" Gaia asked hopefully.

"I wish I could," I told her. "But I still don't know where you are."

"Then how did you get here?"

Good question. So how did I answer it in a way that would make sense to a child?

"That's a little hard to explain. You see, I have this special talent that lets my spirit go places my body can't go. So even though you can see me and we can talk, I'm not really physically here."

She nodded sagely and then looked worried. "You aren't a Gloom, are you?"

I frowned. What the scritch was a Gloom? It didn't sound pleasant, so I made a judgment call. "No, I'm not a Gloom."

"That's good. We don't like Glooms."

I glanced at the other girl, only to be met with that vacant stare. "Banca looks better. Is she still sick?"

"No." Gaia shot an uncomfortable look at the girl she called sister. "She ate."

"You should eat, too," I told her, remembering only one of the plates had been empty.

"Oh, I did."

Okay, this was getting weird, but at least the girls weren't being starved into submission. Strand probably wanted to make sure they were healthy enough to wield the Sumantti's power when the time came. Which brought to me one of the reasons I'd come.

"Gaia, do you know why those men brought you here?"

"No. They just keep telling me to shut up when I ask questions."

"Well, I won't tell you to shut up. They want you to do something bad. You see, they stole this big black crystal, and because only special girls can use it, they're going to try and make you or Banca use it for them."

"Why?"

I wasn't sure if she were asking why it had been stolen, or why only special girls could use it. Both at once, I decided.

"Because the crystal is very powerful. It's inhabited by an alien life form with great psychic ability. This stone is so strong it can destroy worlds." I took a tentative step forward, relieved when I found I could actually move.

"But there's something they won't tell you, Gaia. The girls who use the crystal have to be prepared in a very unique way or they'll die."

She went a shade paler. "Can't you fix it so we can do what they want?"

"No, I'm afraid not. The only way to prepare someone is to take them to a planet very far away from here. Those men aren't going to let that happen. What you *can* do is stay as far from the crystal as you can get, and whatever happens, don't touch it. Do you understand?"

"Yes."

I glanced at the smaller girl. "Banca, do you understand?"

"She does," Gaia answered hastily.

Again, I frowned. There was definitely something odd

about the other child. Even the way she looked at me, with no expression whatsoever, made me uncomfortable. Enough so that I turned away from her gaze.

I wasn't a coward, I assured myself. There was just one more thing I wanted to try before I popped back into my body.

"What are you doing?" Gaia asked as I moved across the room.

"I'm going to try and walk through the door. If I can, maybe it will give me an idea of where you are."

She watched with interest as I took a deep breath and stepped forward. And slammed into the door like I was in my physical body.

Backing off, I stared at the wood in perplexity. This should have worked. While I expected some limitations on my ability, I *had* put my hand through a solid wooden bedpost the first time, and later started to sink through Dr. Daniels's floor. So why couldn't I walk through the door?

There had to be something else going on here. I thought hard for a few minutes, sorting it all out in my head, and then motioned for Gaia. "I need you to come stand by the door."

Obligingly, she slid off the bed and walked to my side.

"Okay, stand right there and don't move. If this works, I'll be right back."

This time, I went through the door like it wasn't there and knew I'd found one limitation. I could only get a few meters away from whomever I'd locked on to, which meant exploring the castle in my "spiritual" ghost form was out of the question.

But at least I could check out the immediate surroundings.

It was dark in the hall I'd entered, with just enough ambient light to let me see stone walls, damp in large patches from trickles of water that oozed between the cracks. As far as I could tell, the passageway extended equally in both directions, with blacker squares that indicated more doors along its length.

I was contemplating checking another of the rooms when a scraping sound came from my left, followed by the murmur of low voices. Panic shot through me. Someone was coming, and I didn't dare get caught here. Quickly, I went back to the girls' room.

"I have to go," I told Gaia. "Someone is coming."

"Wait!" She tried to clutch me, but her hand went right through my skirt. "When will you come back?"

"As soon as I can. Gaia, I promise I'll get you out of here somehow. Just be patient and give me time."

She nodded slowly. "I don't even know your name."

From outside the room came the sound of voices. I could see a glimmer of light through the cracks in the door, and hear the jangle of keys. My time was up.

"It's Echo," I told her, right before I jumped back into my body. "Echo Adams."

CHAPTER 15

I opened my eyes and then lay very still, listening hard to insure I was still alone. The only thing I heard was Bim shifting restlessly from foot to foot as he stood watch.

The sun was high enough in the sky that it made a mere puddle of light on the floor beneath the window of my room, so it was a bit after midday. That meant I hadn't been gone long.

Good, there were a few more people I needed to visit.

First, Losif Strand. I wanted to know if he was still on Madrea and what he was up to.

I closed my eyes and tried to bring his image into focus. I didn't want to appear in front of him, but I did want to "see" him. Nothing happened. No page ruffling, no click, no daydream, nothing.

Hmm, interesting. I'd locked onto Thor's DNA while I was in spirit form, but not Strand's. Eavesdropping must not count, I realized. I had to "be" in the room and close to the person to get a lock, not just listening. And while I'd been in the "room" with Strand back on Centaurius, apparently I'd never been close enough to get a lock on his DNA.

Next on my list was Chine. Since I figured he would

notice if I started following him around all day in my ghost form, this was going to make it difficult to get close enough to Braxus to gather his DNA.

However, I *could* take a peek and see what Chine was up to.

I let his image float into my mind, hazy and insubstantial, leaving his surroundings vague. He was holding a tray, I thought. A tray with dishes on it.

The daydream snapped into clarity as he addressed a man with his back to the room. "I've brought your lunch, Your Highness."

I recognized the space immediately. It was the library filled with real paper books, where I'd found Reynard poring over the text on GEPs.

"Put it there." An obscenely deformed hand emerged from the sleeve of a hooded robe and gestured, giving me a glimpse of an open book in front of him. The thick brown robe prevented me from really seeing him, but unlike his bent form and misshapen hands, his voice was smooth and cultured.

Chine deposited the tray and then stepped back. "The new crate of books arrived from Strand a few moments ago. I told some of the men to bring it up after lunch."

"Good, good. Has Strand finished loading his ship yet?"

"No, sire. It will take several days. He also wants to be here to see your plans set in motion."

"As he should, since he was instrumental in bringing them to fruition." Ignoring the tray of food, he turned a page. "Is everything in place?"

"Word has spread that she'll dance tonight. The man has been instructed and is prepared."

"Excellent. It won't be long now, Chine. Soon I'll be whole, able to rule Madrea in my brother's stead."

"A happy day that will be, sire."

"Yes. Before you go, hand me that book on increasing crop yields. I believe it's on the back of the left center shelf."

"Yes, sire." Chine turned and moved to the shelf, vanishing behind the stack of books.

This could be my chance, I realized. Maybe the only one I'd get. I just hoped Chine wasn't so far away that my psychic tether wouldn't reach to Braxus.

Quickly, I pushed the daydream farther, felt the pages ruffle and then the click. I was standing halfway between Braxus and the shelf that hid Chine, and knew I had to be fast.

Silently, I glided closer to Braxus, careful to stay behind him so he wouldn't see me. Just as I came within range, felt the click that locked his DNA in place, he went still.

"How many times have I told you not to sneak up on me?" His voice was laced with annoyance.

"Sire?" Chine's voice obviously came from behind the shelf, and Braxus stiffened.

Schite! Somehow the man knew I was back there. I had to get out. Now.

He was already turning when I slid back into my body. Had he seen me? I couldn't be sure.

Lifting a shaky hand to my forehead, I wiped away the light sheen of sweat that had formed. It would be a disaster if they discovered I could listen in on them whenever I wanted.

But it was what I'd heard that had really shaken me. They were going to put their plans for me in motion tonight.

I chewed on my lip for a second, thinking about the ramifications. If I told Marcus and Reynard, they'd not only keep me from dancing, they'd probably try to lock me up somewhere. It wouldn't work, of course, but they'd try.

So I wouldn't tell them. I'd just be extra watchful. It was

only one man after all, and truthfully, I was better equipped to handle any attack than they were.

That decision made, I sucked in a deep breath, held it, and then released it slowly to calm myself. There were still some things I needed to do, and panic wouldn't help.

When my heartbeat was back to normal, I concentrated on making a daydream of Zeller. It was easier this time, like practice really did make perfect.

He was in a tent, facing a man I assumed was Lowden, leader of the Bashalde, since he was the right age and so richly dressed. The man was shorter than I'd expected, and very slender, although he had the dark coloring normal for the majority of the Bashalde.

"I don't trust him, Zeller." He paced the length of the tent and back. "Strand has his own agenda, and he's not the kind of man to let anything get in his way, not even his allies."

"Then we'll watch him more closely."

Lowden made a dismissive noise and stopped, hands on his hips as he looked at Zeller. "It doesn't matter how much you watch a snake. They'll always find a hole to crawl through." His brow furrowed in a frown. "Tell me again what he plans for the woman."

"He didn't go into details, just said to assure you that he would take care of her."

"I don't like involving a woman in this. It's wrong, and I don't care who she is or what she can do. I will not tolerate her being hurt." He turned away and scrubbed both hands over his face. "When Strand first came to us, I agreed to help because I wanted to open trade between Madrea and the Federation. What happened, Zeller? When did this idea begin to go so badly wrong?"

"When Braxus became involved. The man's mind is as

twisted as his body. He actually believes Strand has some way to make him whole again so he can depose Politaus and take his rightful place on the throne."

"Invet help us all if that should come to pass." Over his shoulder he shot Zeller a piercing look. "And what of you, my friend? Where do you stand in all this?"

Zeller arched a brow. "My loyalty has always been with you, Lowden. You know that."

"Do I?" He dropped a hand to the hilt of his sword. "Be very careful, Zeller. Betray me and you'll regret it for a very long time before you die."

With those words, Lowden left the tent and Zeller watched him go, a feral smile playing at the corners of his lips.

Opening my eyes, I sat up and swung my feet off the bed. Suddenly my mind was whirling with so much information I could barely process it.

Lowden didn't know about the Sumantti or the girls.

But Zeller did.

I'd really thought Lowden was the instigator here. Now, I was inclined to give him the benefit of the doubt. Oh, he wasn't innocent by a long shot. At the very least he was guilty of conspiring with Strand to have the ban lifted. But that was a Madrean law, not a Federation mandate. And I had to give him big points for not wanting to hurt me.

I needed to talk to Lowden as soon as possible, warn him about Zeller and Strand. Since it was apparent he already knew I was a Federation agent, I wouldn't be giving anything away, and it might just cause Strand and Braxus a few problems.

Unfortunately, I'd have to go through Jancen to get to Lowden, and that would put the older man right in the line of fire.

I sighed and pressed my thumb and index finger against

my eyes. Any action in that direction would have to wait until after tonight so I could deal with the imminent danger to my person.

Abruptly, I frowned. They knew I was a Gertz GEP, knew what I could do. Why were they only sending one man? An ordinary man stood no chance at all against me. I could break the strongest of them in half and not even breathe hard.

Even a normal GEP couldn't hurt me. At least, not enough to put me out of action. Assuming one got in a lucky shot, I'd heal so fast it wouldn't even slow me down.

So what were they planning that one man could accomplish?

I tried to put myself in their shoes, think it through from their perspective. They didn't need to kill me, I realized. They only needed to stop me long enough to allow them free use of the Sumantti.

Because they were afraid I could control it.

After all, I was created by Simon Gertz, just like Kiera Smith, the woman who became Shushanna to the Limantti. If she could control the stone, it made sense that I could, too.

But the only way to keep me from controlling the crystal would be to keep me unconscious. With drugs, maybe? I had no idea how a knockout drug would affect me. Since I wasn't going to oblige them by standing still and letting them give me one, it was a moot point. And just to be on the safe side, I'd take no food or drink tonight.

"What are you doing?" Lillith asked me. "You haven't moved in an hour."

"Thinking," I told her, and then gave her a rundown of everything I'd found out.

"You should tell Marcus," she advised me.

"Why? So both of us can worry about it?"

"No, as a witness when I have to tell Dr. Daniels why I'm returning with your dead body," she snarled.

"Sheesh, Lillith, don't hold back. Tell me how you really feel."

She continued as if I hadn't spoken. "You're not invincible even if you are a Gertz GEP, and you'd better remember it. You've only considered one possibility, when my probability program indicates Strand's choices number in the thousands, many of which could be fatal."

"Like what?" I asked her indignantly.

"Do you honestly think that just because technology is banned on Madrea that Strand doesn't have an arsenal on his ship? How hard would it be to dress one of his men in Madrean clothing and send him to the Terpsichore with a blaster? Can you dodge the beam from one of those?"

"Oh," I murmured, embarrassed I hadn't thought of that.

"Yes, *oh*. Now, don't make me come down there. You *will* tell Marcus."

"Fine!" I threw my hands up. "I'll tell him."

"Tell me what?" Marcus asked from the door. "Lillith said you wanted to talk to me."

"Yes, apparently I do. Tattletale," I added under my breath.

"I heard that," the ship said.

"You were *meant* to," I shot back.

"Are you two going to fight all day, or will someone tell me what's going on?" Marcus asked.

Giving in less than gracefully, I repeated everything I'd found out and added my own thoughts on the matter. Marcus's expression became grimmer and grimmer as I talked. When I was done, he turned on his heel and marched out of the house.

"So much for that," I told Lillith.

I barely got the comment out before he was back. "Bim is sending someone to fetch the commander," he told me. "We're going to need his help."

Well, it wasn't like that came as a surprise. I'd expected it. Didn't men always call for reinforcements when things went bad? It was like they wanted to share the fun so they'd have someone to chat with about their parts in bringing glory to mankind long after the battle had ended.

I bit off a snort of amusement and got back on topic. "While we're waiting, I have to try and contact the Sumantti again, reassure her that we're still here and trying to get her free," I said with a great deal of reluctance. The last time, I'd passed out from the force of her anger. I wasn't anxious to repeat the experience, but I really had no choice. If I didn't reassure her occasionally, she might decide to do something drastic. Like blow up the solar system.

I pulled the Imadei from the neck of my top and cradled it on my palm while I buttressed my defenses, both physical and mental. When I was ready, I dropped my gaze to the stone and reached for the Sumantti.

What met me was a deep, brooding, pulsing anger, and I hesitated, a sense of foreboding washing over me. She'd changed since I'd first contacted her, pulled into herself more. No longer did the crystal seem childlike. It was an extremely powerful alien entity bent on destruction.

I'm here, I sent. *Will you talk to me?*

There was no response, not so much as a hint that she knew I was speaking.

I know you can hear me, I told her. *Please don't give up hope. We're working hard to free you from those men and we won't stop until you're back where you belong.*

A force unlike anything I'd ever felt before slammed into my mind like a battering ram, throwing me back into my own head so hard my teeth rattled. If not for the Imadei's protection I doubt I would have survived.

My entire body trembled with terror when I looked up. "We're in trouble, Marcus. She's become more alien, and far more desperate. I don't think she cares if she kills those children. She doesn't care if she kills us all. As a matter of fact, I think she plans to do just that. She won't talk to me, and she won't listen to anything I tell her."

His face went a shade whiter. "But you have the Imadei; you should be able to control her."

I shook my head. "I'll try. I'll try as long as there's breath in my body. But when the Mother Stone made the Imadei, I don't think she had a clue what her daughter would become. At this point, I'm not sure even the Mother Stone could stop her. Give the Daughter Stone a few more days, and she's going to be powerful enough break loose from the stasis box. We're running out of time."

"Is there anything we can do?"

"Pray for a miracle," I told him. "That may be the only chance we have."

Voices sounded from outside just as Peri zipped in through the open window, dodged Marcus and then hovered in the main room, chittering expectantly at the back door.

"Reynard must have arrived," I said. "Let's go open a bottle of wine before I have to repeat this again. I'm getting dry from all the talking." We both followed the dragon bird just as the commander stepped into sight.

His gaze went straight to me and warmed me to my toes. "I received a message you needed to see me right away?"

I tried to ignore the tingles his look started in my stomach, and waved the bottle of wine I'd picked up in the direction of the table. "Yes. Why don't we sit down?"

Marcus nodded to the commander and then snagged three glasses and took them to the table. After they were filled, I handed them around, taking my own and drinking deeply before I sat down. "Zin, I needed that."

"Shall I start for you?" Marcus asked.

"Please do." I leaned my head against the back of the chair to ease the dull, muzzy feeling left over from the Sumantti's forcible eviction of my consciousness. Concerned, Peri landed on the arm of my chair and cooed at me in sympathy.

Reynard remained quiet except for a few direct questions, focused completely on what Marcus was recounting for him. Finally, the story was told and silence held sway for a few beats.

"Don't even think about it," I told them.

"Think about what?" Marcus asked, all wide-eyed and innocent.

"Trying to stop me from dancing tonight." I shifted my head so I could see him better. "If I don't show up, neither will the man they're sending. We need to catch him, find out what his orders are."

He looked at me with an intensity I hadn't seen from him before. "Only under one condition," Reynard said.

I rolled my head back in his direction. "What condition?"

"The audience will be sprinkled with men I trust, and Marcus and I will be on the stage with you. I believe there are enough shadows that no one will see us there."

"Fine, as long as the men aren't conspicuous. I don't want to scare this guy off."

"That won't be a problem. The Terpsichore is a favorite among my men, so no one will think them out of place. I'll go talk to them now and be back before the sun sets. Until then, do not leave her alone." He aimed that last at Marcus.

"I won't. And Bim will be with her, too."

The commander pushed his chair back, stood, hesitated for a moment, and then leaned down to give me a quick kiss.

I wasn't having that, though. Putting my palms against his cheeks, I held him in place and deepened the kiss.

From across the table, Marcus cleared his throat. "I don't think that is such a good idea—"

I released Reynard long enough to say one word. "Cammi." Marcus's mouth snapped shut and he looked in the other direction, face red.

Assured there would be no more protests from that quarter, I went back to what I was doing, my toes curling with pleasure. Finally, I let him go, satisfied for the moment. "Go, before I change my mind and keep you here," I murmured.

He shot me a grin and left, paying no attention to Marcus's glare.

"Stop that," I told my guardian. "We both know I'm not a Madrean woman and don't need protecting from male attention. As for Jancen, I'm pretty sure he already suspects I'm not August's daughter. And after tomorrow, he'll know the whole truth anyway, so he won't be inclined to challenge you to a duel for violating the rules of guardianship or whatever it is you're operating under."

"What!" Lillith screeched in my ear. "I might as well land at the castle and set off fireworks!"

I considered her suggestion before shaking my head. "While that might give the Madreans pause, it wouldn't stop Strand. We'll save that maneuver for emergencies."

"I wasn't serious," the ship said.

"It might come down to that, though. I'm not ruling anything out."

"Why are you going to tell Jancen the truth?" Marcus asked.

"Because I need him on my side, and he can get me in to see Lowden. Lillith, have you heard from Dr. Daniels yet?"

"Yes, and he's not happy. Strand hasn't broken any Federation laws by being there, but with the political situation being what it is concerning Madrea, this could be just enough to cause an escalation in the hostilities between the two factions in the council. And even more troubling, he's received reports that in the last six months large quantities of munitions have been diverted to all the planets who side with Strand on this issue."

I sat up straight as Marcus went tense. "Holy Zin. The man is planning to start a war with the Federation, and he's paying for it with Madrea's sunstones. What's Dr. Daniels planning to do?"

"He's asked to address an emergency session of the council, but you know how politicians are. It'll probably take several days to get them all to sit down and listen. In the meantime, he's suspended the maneuvers near the Andromeda Galaxy and has sent the fleet to patrol areas near the planets involved. And he said to tell you your mission is even more important now than it was before."

She switched to a recording of Dr. Daniels's voice. "Do not fail, Agent Adams. The entire Federation is at stake."

Oh, sure. Dump the fate of the free universe on the shoulders of one green agent who doesn't know what the scritch she's doing 90 percent of the time. I gave a mental snort of disgust. No pressure there.

Almost as if he knew what was going through my mind, Marcus reached over and patted my hand. "Don't think about it. We have a plan in place. For now, all we can do is stick to it."

He was right. I might be a Gertz GEP, but I was still only human. One step at a time was the only way to handle all the problems.

Suddenly Marcus got an odd look on his face. "What's wrong?" I asked anxiously.

"I just realized something."

"What?"

"I don't think they're going to attack you physically. It doesn't make sense. They have something worse planned, and it starts tonight."

My skin went cold. "What could be worse?"

"Someone important could die, and they'll arrange to have the blame land squarely on you."

"Well, schite." I stood and paced the length of the room. "Any idea who the most likely candidate would be?"

"Unfortunately, no." He rubbed his forehead. "It could be any of the higher-ups, most of whom you met when we dined with the king."

"Well, if they aren't going to attack me, then we don't need Reynard's men."

"Yes, we do. Just because there's no immediate danger to you doesn't mean they won't try something. Maybe we can stop them, or at least find out what it is."

"I'm getting confused." I turned and headed for my room. "I'm going to get my costume and go to the Terpsichore. If the danger isn't to me, I want to eat before I change."

"Bim and I will go with you."

He waited while I carefully gathered the purple outfit and then soothed Peri's ruffled feathers when she discovered I'd hidden the silver jewelry. "Ready," I told him, returning to the main room.

We crossed the yards with Bim sticking even closer than normal, and I figured Reynard had talked to him.

The kitchen was gearing up for the evening, pots bubbling, the staff hurrying back and forth to the common room, and general chaos ruling as food and drinks were dished up and carried out.

Before Marcus would let me put my costume in the room, he checked the place top to bottom. Treya gave me an odd look as he motioned that it was safe to go in, but I ignored her.

When the outfit was safely stowed away, I returned to the kitchen and helped myself to the roast that was perfectly cooked, added some tubers and green vegetables from the communal pot, and took a seat at the table. I was just finishing up the meal when Reynard came in and leaned close to my ear.

"Everyone is in place," he told me.

"Good." I forked up the last bite of meat and stuck it in his mouth. "Did you get a chance to eat?"

He swallowed and shook his head. "Not yet."

"Well, sit down. Leddy can bring you a plate and you can eat while I change."

Treya went by, her chin hard as she gazed from me to Reynard. "Don't be late. We have a full house tonight."

Guess that meant I was on my own with the makeup. Good thing I didn't have to attempt intricate procedures on my hair.

When Leddy slid a plate in front of the commander, I kissed his cheek and stood. "Take your time. Regardless of what Treya said, it will be a while before I'm changed and ready."

While Peri played with the jewelry, I experimented with the cosmetics until I achieved the same mysterious look as last time. Then I stepped behind the screen and stripped down to my skin.

For a moment, I hesitated over my knife, uncomfortable with leaving it behind when someone was out to get me. But it would be clearly visible under the sheer skirt I was putting on, and it wasn't like I was defenseless without it.

I hung it on the hook with my clothes, and then dressed in the new costume. Not only was it gorgeous and shimmering from the silver threads, it fit as if Cammi had sewn it onto my body.

Barefoot, I went to the table and pried the jewelry away from Peri, then fastened on the short half-veil. Just as I finished, Reynard opened the door a crack, saw I was decent, and entered followed by Marcus.

"You are so beautiful," he told me, all serious and sexy.

"Thank you." I smiled at the compliment, but for once in my life, the way I looked wasn't a priority. "Is it time?"

"Yes." Marcus moved around the room, covering the sunstone lamps. "We'll go out first, the commander to your right, me to left. Bim will be floor level, right in front of the stage. Just pretend we aren't there."

He reached the last lamp, the one by the door, and put his hand on the cover as we joined him, Peri radiating excitement as she landed on my shoulder. From the common room the murmur of voices faded as the musicians began to play. "Let's get this over with."

There was a shushing noise as the last cover slid down and plunged the room into darkness, then I felt more than saw Marcus and the commander go through the door. I slipped through behind them, closing it after me, and then paused in the dark to wait for my beat. When it came, I moved forward in time to the music, jewelry jingling in counterpoint.

On cue, Peri launched into the air, her iridescent feathers catching the light from the lamps in the common room as she spiraled and dove around the audience, giving me time to step into view.

Dancing was so ingrained in me that I could do it without thinking. So instead, I spent the time scanning the audience. Reynard's men were easy for me to locate, mainly because they were the only ones not watching the stage.

I was also very much aware of Reynard and Marcus, standing in the dark at the ends of the stage. The tension in the air was so thick it would almost have been a relief if a squadron of armed men had burst through the room and attacked. But it was all a bit anticlimactic.

The dance ended with no untoward movements from anyone, and Peri and I faded back into the dark at the back of the stage to the sound of thunderous applause.

Marcus and Reynard were waiting and we all went silently back into the changing room. Marcus uncovered the first lamp and then moved to the next.

"You might as well change," he said. "I told Treya you were only going to do one dance tonight."

Peri fluttered to the table as I moved behind the screen. Abruptly, I halted, staring at the hook that held my clothes.

"Reynard? Marcus?"

Something in my voice must have given me away because they both rushed across the room, swords out. "What's wrong?"

I pointed at the sheath draped over the hook. "My knife is gone."

CHAPTER 16

"Someone stole my knife." I was more surprised than alarmed as we stepped from behind the screen. Surprised that it hadn't occurred to me someone might take it. "Looks like we know now what they planned to do tonight."

"Are you sure you didn't just misplace it?" Marcus asked.

I simply stared at him.

"Okay, you didn't lose it." He sighed. "You're right. We have to assume this was their plan all along."

"You said you thought they were going to kill someone and blame Echo," Reynard commented. "What better way to frame her for murder than by using her knife to do it?"

"You told him?" I asked Marcus.

"Yes, while you were eating. And he's right. Everyone at the king's supper last night, including the king himself, can identify that knife as yours. Who on Madrea would dispute the word of the king?"

"No one," Reynard said grimly, sliding his sword back into the scabbard. "Politaus is eminently fair. If someone was found murdered by Echo's knife, he'd have no choice but to arrest her."

"Okay, two questions," I said, taking off my jewelry and tossing it on the table, much to Peri's delight. "First, how did they get in here to steal the knife? And second, who would be important enough to get me tossed in the dungeon forever if they were killed?"

"I'll question everyone and see if they noticed a stranger, but it never occurred to us to put a guard at the door of the changing room during your act. The kitchen is always a madhouse in the evenings, and sometimes the customers use it as a shortcut to the privy. Anyone could have slipped in here unnoticed," Marcus said.

He was right, I realized. I'd seen it myself. Finding one particular man was a hopeless cause. We needed to concentrate on the second of my questions, the part about who they were going to kill.

"So who would be the most likely target?" I asked. "It would have to be someone important, someone whose death would further their plans."

"That narrows it down a bit," Reynard said, his face hard. "Putting myself in their place, there are only four men who fill their needs. Chief Lowden, Jancen, Braxus, and the king."

"I think we can cross Braxus off the list," I told him wryly. "But there's one you forgot to mention. You. Everyone knows we're . . . close, and you're totally loyal to the king. There's no doubt you'd do anything within your power to protect him. So, it would be in Strand's best interest to get you out of his way."

"I can take care of myself," Reynard said. "You forget, if someone intended me harm I would know it instantly. They can't take me by surprise, and that would be the only way Strand and his henchmen could hurt me."

"Strand has a reputation as a superior swordsman," I told him.

"I'm better. I'd know every thrust and parry before he

made it," he told me, his arrogant tone bringing a smile to my lips in spite of the circumstances.

"Okay, you'll always be on guard while you're awake, and you'll make damn sure they can't get into your quarters when you're asleep. But we need to talk to the other men. I'd planned to speak with Jancen and Lowden tomorrow. Now I think we should go tonight."

Reynard nodded. "It would be best if you leave the king to me. It wouldn't be wise to let him know you're a Federation agent yet."

"I think you're both forgetting something," Marcus said. "We have no idea when this will happen. For all we know, someone could already be dead."

"Maybe," I said, heading toward the screen so I could change out of my costume. "But I still have to try. It hasn't been that long since they took the knife, so there's still a chance we can stop them. And while it may sound harsh, the more people who know what Strand is up to, the less likely it is he can place the blame on me."

The two men talked quietly while I changed and folded my costume. "Are the Bashalde still camped at the gathering field?" I asked Reynard when I rejoined them.

"Yes. Normally they only stay one eightday, but Lowden has postponed their leaving this time in hopes of making further progress with the king concerning the ban."

"Good. Peri, leave the jewelry and let's go."

She pouted for a second, her gaze going from me to the silver and back, then she came to roost on my shoulder and we all left the Terpsichore together.

A light rain had come and gone, leaving the air clean and full of the scent of damp earth. Most of the bigger clouds had moved on, leaving gauze-like wisps to wrap around the visible stars scattered across the night sky. Luckily, it was warm enough that I didn't need a cloak.

Since it was still early enough for people to be out and about on the main streets of Bastion City, we kept our conversation to mundane matters or remained silent as we walked. By the time we reached the field behind the castle where the Bashalde were camped, the hem of my skirt was wet enough to be irritating, but not soaked enough to drag the material down.

I peered through the darkness at the tents huddled together, some well lit with sunstone lamps, others dark. "Which one is Jancen's?"

"The blue-and-gold-striped tent there, near Chief Lowden's." Reynard gestured. "Its lamps are still on, so Jancen hasn't retired yet."

A young boy darted past us and the commander snagged him by the collar. "Tell Jancen that Reynard du'Marr wishes a meeting."

With a quick grin, the boy pocketed the coin Reynard tossed him, and dashed into the tent. A moment later, Jancen stuck his head out, surveyed our somber party, and then reached back to close the tent flap before he stepped out to meet us.

"What's wrong?"

"We need an audience with you and Chief Lowden, in private. And Zeller can't know we're talking to Lowden. It's an emergency, Jancen," I told him.

He studied me for a moment, as though trying to make up his mind. "Does this have something to do with the Federation?"

I glanced around quickly, but no one was near. "I'll tell you anything you want to know when we can't be overheard."

"Do you know the clearing with the lightning-struck tree near the middle, on the other side of the stream?" he asked Reynard. When the commander nodded, he continued. "Wait for us in the center. It's broad enough that anyone trying to hear our conversation would have to show themselves. I'll bring Lowden there."

He hurried away toward the green-and-gold tent that housed the chief of the Bashalde while Marcus and I followed Reynard to the field in question. I watched a last remnant of cloud play hide and seek with the moon while we waited and noted the fog that crawled knee-high over the ground in this area.

It seemed to take forever and I'd almost decided Jancen hadn't been able to talk Lowden into coming. Suddenly, Peri fluttered her wings and chirruped, her head pointed in the direction we'd come from. A second later, I saw two men step into a shaft of moonlight as they walked from between the trees. One of them carried a sunstone lamp partially shielded and I studied them as they made their way nearer until I was sure it was Jancen and Lowden. As far as I could tell, no one was trailing them, but there were woods all around us except for the path to the clearing.

Marcus and Reynard flanked me as the men stopped in front of us, Lowden staring at me so hard I wouldn't have been surprised if he'd asked to examine my teeth.

"To my knowledge, we all look perfectly normal," I told him. "Well, except for Kiera Smith. There should be a law against making women that beautiful."

Although he didn't move, I saw the shock in his eyes. "Yes, Chief Lowden, I'm aware that you know who and what I am."

"Well, I don't," Jancen snapped. "So why don't you tell me?"

"Of course." I tilted my head in acknowledgment. "My name is Echo Adams. I'm an agent for the Bureau of Alien Affairs. The Federation sent me here to retrieve something that was stolen from one of our ships. I'm sorry I had to deceive you, Jancen. If I *were* Bashalde, I'd certainly want to be part of your family."

He nodded. "I suspected you weren't August's daughter, that you were Federation. But what did you mean, 'what' you are?"

"I'm a GEP. That means I was created in a lab to be faster, stronger, and smarter than Naturals. And because the man who created me thinks he's a god, he altered my genetic makeup so far as to give me psychic abilities."

"Why come to us?" Jancen asked. "We have nothing that belongs to the Federation. We couldn't reach your ships even if the thought occurred to us."

"I'm here tonight because your chief is conspiring with Losif Strand, the man responsible for the stolen item."

Jancen turned to look at Lowden, who hadn't moved a muscle. "Is this true?"

"Yes, to a point." He gazed around our circle. "I don't know anything about a stolen object. Strand came to me and offered a deal. He would get the king to lift the ban on Madrea if I would agree to give him an exclusive contract for the exportation of our sunstones."

"Why?" Reynard asked him.

"Every cycle my people get poorer, Commander. You know this, you've seen it. All we have of value are our animals and the sunstone deposits. Yet the sunstones are no good to us unless we can sell them to the Federation. At least once a cycle we petition the king to lift the ban, a ban we had no part in creating, and each time he refuses. *We're desperate.* I don't like forcing the king's hand, but it seemed the only choice left to us."

"You could have come to us, Lowden," Reynard told him. "Politaus is a compassionate man. If your people need help, all you have to do is ask."

"And give up our tents and wagons, give up our desert

and build stone houses outside your cities so we can wait for handouts? Bah!" He spit to one side. "This world belongs to us as much as it does the Madreans, but does your king give us a say in its laws? No, he doesn't. Why should we be bound by laws that we do not agree with and had no part in creating? The Bashalde are a separate people. We make our own laws. If we want to deal with the Federation, we will and no Madrean ban will stop us."

Jancen had started nodding halfway through Lowden's speech, but I ignored his agreement. "I'm not here to interfere in the internal politics of Madrea," I told him. "That's for you to work out with the king if we survive long enough."

Both men stared at me. "Why wouldn't we survive?" Lowden asked.

"You don't trust Strand, do you?" I asked the chief.

He hesitated. "No, I don't. He's becoming more arrogant and secretive every day. If there were any other way to contact the Federation, I would have nothing to do with him."

"You have good instincts," I told him. "Strand intends to depose Politaus and replace him with Braxus. When he does, they'll wrest control of the sunstones away from the Bashalde."

"But Braxus's infirmity makes it impossible for him to rule," Jancen protested.

"Which brings us to the item they stole from the Federation," I replied. "It's a black quartz crystal infested with a very powerful alien life form, a life form capable of wielding psychic forces the likes of which you've never seen before. And only a specially prepared female can communicate with or use this crystal."

"A female like you?" Lowden asked.

"Yes, like me. But Strand couldn't control an adult female like me. I'd break him into tiny pieces if he tried. So he's been kidnapping and bringing in young girls with psi abilities to try and use the crystal. He's killed four so far, and is holding two more captive. Unless I stop him and retrieve the crystal, they'll die, too."

Both men looked horrified. "Why do you allow his heart to still beat?" Lowden growled, his hand going reflexively to his sword hilt.

"Because we don't know where the girls are, or where he's hidden the crystal. Plus, Strand isn't a lowly black marketeer, as he's presented himself to you. He's the leader of Helios One, and there will be political ramifications if I just kill him without proof of his crimes."

This time, I was the one who hesitated. "You've gone this far, you might as well tell them the rest," Lillith said. "Their lives are at stake, too."

She was right, they really should know. I took a deep breath. "We have a bigger problem than just the girls. You see, Strand has very badly underestimated what being locked up in a stasis box will do to the crystal. She's beyond angry, and she's gathering more power every day. The next chance she has, she's going to strike out and nothing will stop her. Take my word for it, when she strikes, there will be nothing left of this solar system but a dust cloud."

They were silent for a minute, then Jancen spoke. "Is there no way for you to stop this crystal?"

"I'm going to try. And there's another crystal on another planet that has formed a symbiosis with a woman like me. They are watching Madrea, and will do what they can when the time comes. We hope it will be enough."

"So you are our only chance of survival," Lowden said. "If anything happens to you, we're doomed."

I nodded. "Pretty much, unless you have another plan."

"Strand has launched a plot against you." The words rushed out of him. "I don't know what it is, only that he plans to get you out of his way. He assured me you wouldn't

be harmed or I wouldn't have gone along with him. Now
everything has changed."

"Yes, we're aware of his plot, and that's the other reason
we decided to seek you out tonight," I acknowledged.
"Strand had someone steal my knife. We believe he's going
to murder someone important and see to it that I'm blamed
for the death. Both of you are potential targets, as are the
commander and King Politaus. You should be on your guard
at all times. And before I forget, do not trust Zeller. I don't
know what he's been promised, but as you suspected, the
man is betraying you to Strand. He knows about the crystal
and Strand's plan for its use. I suspect he was the one who
threw the knife at me the other day in Cammi's tent."

Jancen went stiff, seeming to grow several inches at the
mention of Zeller's name. "There is only one thing he covets.
Leadership of the Bashalde." He turned to Lowden. "You
must send your son into hiding immediately. Zeller is your
cousin. The only thing that stands between him and his goal
are you and Jolem. We can't risk losing both of you."

"It will be done as soon as we return," Lowden agreed. "I
will personally see to Zeller." When he reached for his knife,
both Reynard and Marcus braced themselves, but the chief
merely offered the blade to me hilt first.

"I regret my part in the troubles that Strand has brought
to Madrea," he said. "If you'll allow it, I'd like to replace
the knife that was stolen from you. If the need arises, Jancen
and I will bear witness to your innocence, and the Bashalde
stand ready to aide you with your mission. Whatever is required of us, we will do without question."

"Thank you." I took the knife and sheathed it. "I accept
both the knife and the offer of assistance. If we make it
through this, I'll personally see to it that the Federation
supplies a trained mediator for talks between you and the
king."

Marcus arched a brow at me, but I didn't have time to react.

"Echo, I'm picking up a heat signature—" The rest of Lillith's words were cut off as Peri hissed, her eyes going blood red as she launched from my shoulder like a rocket and shot toward a section of woods to our left. From her mind I got the image of a man releasing the string of a bow that was aimed directly at Lowden.

The whistle of the arrow was already loud when I went into overdrive. Luckily, Lowden wasn't that far away. In two steps I grabbed him and tossed him out of danger.

Unfortunately, I was busy moving him and didn't have time to stop the arrow. It hit me in the right shoulder, going in my back with the tip protruding in front just below my clavicle.

I staggered and dropped out of overdrive, the pain fierce and hot as it surged through me, taking me to my knees. From the direction of the woods a man screamed and then came the sound of something large crashing through brush.

There was a moment of silence as everyone took in what had happened. Of course, Reynard was the first to react.

"Echo!" Fear laced his voice as he dropped down beside me.

"I'll be fine," I told him through clenched teeth. "Just get it out."

The others gathered round as he examined the arrow. "You saved my life," Lowden said, voice shaking. "How can I ever repay you?"

"Find Zeller," I ground out, "*and kill him.* He's the one who shot the arrow. There's no way he could have heard us, but just the fact that we were meeting must have told him we're joining forces."

"Let me get a healer," Jancen said, his brow furrowed with worry.

"I don't need one," I told him, and then winced as Reynard jostled the shaft.

"I need to break off the fletching," he told me. "It's going to hurt when I push it through."

"It already hurts."

"This will be worse." With no further warning, he snapped the end off the arrow and shoved it through my shoulder with his left hand, the right one pulling from the front.

A shocked gasp escaped my lips, and if I hadn't already been on the ground, I would have fallen. Blood, hot and sticky, coated the front of my top and ran down my back, but slowed quickly as the pain was gradually replaced with soothing warmth.

I breathed a sigh of relief. "Thanks. That's much better."

Lowden and Jancen were staring at the spot where the arrow had entered, awe on their faces. "It's healed," Jancen whispered. "Your skin is just slightly pink where the arrow pierced."

Lowden glanced at my face. "I wasn't sure I believed all they told me about you."

"Believe it," I told him, pushing to my feet while Reynard steadied me with a hand on my arm. "And they don't know the half of it. *I'm* not even sure I know everything I'm capable of yet. My creator didn't let me in on his design plans."

I glanced toward the woods as Peri winged her way back across the clearing, radiating smug satisfaction. "She scratched him up some before he got away," I told them. "Lillith, are you tracking him?"

Jancen and Lowden both looked around. "Who is Lillith?" Jancen asked when they saw no one else.

"My ship. She's a self-aware artificial intelligence." I paused to listen to her response. "She says she tracked him to the river using the heat his body gives off, but when he got wet it cooled him down and she lost him."

"Leave Zeller to me," Lowden said. "I'll send my best men to track him on foot. We'll find him."

"Then we'll leave you to your hunt," I said. "I'm in desperate need of something to eat. That's the only downside of healing so fast."

"Come with us back to the gathering," Jancen said. "It's closer and it would be our honor to see you fed."

"Thank you, but I'll be fine until we get to Marcus's house. I'm sure you both have a lot to do tonight."

With a final bow, they hurried on their way, and I leaned against Reynard until their lamp bobbed out of sight.

"Are you sure you're truly healed?" he asked me as darkness enfolded us again.

"Yes, but I'm a little shaky. Apparently, it takes a lot of energy to heal a wound like that."

He leaned over and scooped me into his arms, holding me snuggly against his chest.

"I can walk," I told him. But I have to admit, my protest was pretty weak. It felt good to be held like that, and his warmth eased a deep chill inside me that I hadn't noticed until now.

"Hush," he said, lips brushing my hair. "It's no hardship to carry you."

"I'll go ahead and make sure there's food waiting," Marcus told us. "Keep a watch out, commander. Zeller may not have gone far, and you don't heal the way Echo does."

"Nor do you."

"Then we'll both be careful," Marcus replied as he hurried away.

"I don't understand why I'm still weak," I murmured as Reynard followed more slowly. "The Imadei provides me with energy. Lillith, do you know?"

"You lost quite a bit of blood, and the wound was severe. It took a lot of energy for your body to repair itself. I've done a scan and you'll be fine after you eat. The Imadei's energy flows at a steady rate, so even if you didn't eat you would be back to normal by morning."

"That's good." I muffled a yawn and let my head rest against Reynard's chest. I must have fallen asleep, because it was the last thing I remembered until we went through the door of Marcus's house.

The scent of food woke me, and I wiggled until Reynard deposited me on my feet, my stomach rumbling in anticipation. You'd think I hadn't eaten in days from the way I felt.

The table was piled with food, so much that Marcus must have emptied the Terpsichore's kitchen. He and Bim were removing the last of it from trays when I rinsed my hands, then sat down and started eating, sending them mental blessings for the hot coffee that accompanied the meal.

"Bim is upset that you were hurt and he wasn't there to stop it," Marcus told me.

Uh-huh. And he knew this how? I stopped chewing to stare at the big man. To my eyes, he wore the same stoic expression as always, and I'd never heard him utter a single word. Maybe Marcus was just so used to him that he could read some body language cue I was missing.

"I'm sorry, Bim. We weren't expecting trouble or we'd have taken you with us," I told him. "And it's really not as bad as it looks."

I probably should have changed out of the blood-soaked top before I ate, but my need for food had been more pressing. I went back to chewing, then noted Bim was still standing there. Apparently, more assurance was needed.

"Next time, we'll make sure you go with us," I told him.

That must have been what he was waiting for, because he gave me a curt nod and backed away to the door, staying on the inside. Guess he wanted to make sure I didn't sneak off without him.

It was a bit of a novelty, having all these different people concerned with my welfare. Reynard was understandable, as was Marcus. But Durtran had made it clear he owed me a debt of gratitude, and now Lowden and Jancen were ready to go to war at one word from me.

I wasn't sure I liked having that much power over the lives of others. Not that I had much choice in the matter.

Unconsciously, I touched the Imadei. My choice had been taken away the second I became aware of the crystal back at headquarters. Everything else I'd gone through, and would go through in the future, stemmed from that one second in time.

Fate was a funny thing. But without it, I'd never have met Reynard, and that made everything else worthwhile.

Now, I'd just have to make sure we all lived to see another cycle. Somehow.

All three men were looking at me with a touch of awe in their gazes by the time I pushed my plate back. "What?" I asked, puzzled.

Marcus grinned. "I don't think any of us have ever seen a woman eat that much in one sitting. Feeling better?"

I did a quick mental rundown of my health. "Much better, actually. Completely back to normal." I pulled on the sticky top. "Well, except I could use a shower. And, scritch it, a different top. This was one of my new ones, and now it's ruined."

"Cammi can make you another," he told me, a slight blush tinting his cheeks. "I'll talk to her tomorrow."

I just bet he would. He'd probably been wracking his brain for an excuse to see her, anyway.

"Are you sure you're recovered?" Reynard asked. "I should go talk to the king, but I don't want to leave you if you're still weak."

"Really, I'm fine. You should go. His life might be in danger." I hesitated. "Are you going to tell him everything?"

"No, just enough to make sure he's alert to the danger."

"I think that's smart," I told him as we stood. "I'd really hate for him to throw me off the planet."

"So would I. I'll see you tomorrow?"

"Of course." I leaned closer and kissed him. "Good night, Commander."

When he was gone I went to my room and gathered up clean clothes. Marcus was stacking dishes on the tray as I returned to the front room.

"I'm going to run these next door. Shouldn't take more than a minute. You can walk out with me."

Bim held the door for us, and then accompanied me down the path to the privy. It wouldn't have surprised me if he'd insisted on coming inside with me, but he merely checked the space thoroughly and then stationed himself outside the door.

Peri was thrilled that we were taking another shower, and splashed for all she was worth, but I rushed through the ablutions in spite of her mutterings at my hurry. There were a few more things I had to do tonight—things I didn't want Reynard or Marcus to know about—and one of them I didn't dare attempt until Marcus was safely asleep.

By the time I dressed and got back to the house, he had returned, and I gave him a small wave as I headed for my room. "I'm going to bed. See you in the morning."

I waited just long enough for Peri to squeeze through, and then closed the door and went to the bed. Without undressing, I stretched out and closed my eyes.

It only took a second for me to lock onto Zeller's DNA, and I didn't bother with the dream state.

He was outside, crouched behind a bush as he watched a

group of Bashalde men search the ground in the light of the lamps they carried. Deep scratches adorned his cheeks and forehead, and I smiled. Good for Peri.

We weren't far from the castle, I realized. Another few minutes and he might have made it safely inside.

My grin was evil as I slid up closer behind him. When I spoke, I deliberately kept my voice to a low, spooky whisper.

"Oh, Zeller."

He glanced over his shoulder just in time to see me step through a tree. "Boo!" I told him.

The man was still screaming when Lowden's troops surrounded him, weapons at the ready.

CHAPTER 17

I was chuckling as I popped back into my body. Who knew being a ghost could be so much fun? Even Peri was quivering with suppressed excitement, although in her case it was more because she'd picked up what was coming next from me. For once, she wasn't asleep two seconds after she hit the bed.

Waiting impatiently, I listened to the sounds of the house settling around me, the creaks and groans, and the rustles as Marcus took to his bed. He shifted a few times, then went still.

It was thirty minutes later when soft snores issued from his room, and I decided it was safe to put my second plan into action.

Slipping out of bed, I retrieved the bundle I'd hidden earlier, and shook out a pair of dark trousers and an equally dark shirt. They were too big for me, but I'd fixed that by swiping a belt, too. Luckily, Marcus had small feet. His boots would be a pretty good fit if I added a couple pair of socks before I put them on.

By the time I stripped and redressed, Peri was on the window ledge, peering into the darkness with anticipation.

She took flight, hovering just outside as I tiptoed to the opening and boosted myself through.

I'd barely hit the ground when a darker, bulky shadow separated from the corner of the house and stepped closer. I was reaching for my knife when I recognized the man's outline.

Well, scritch. I'd expected Bim to retire for the night when Marcus and I were abed. Instead, there he was, staring at me with reproach in his eyes, that massive axe held crosswise over his chest.

My shoulders slumped in resignation, and I let out a deep sigh. I'd have to let him go with me, whether I wanted to or not.

"We have to be quiet," I told him in a whisper. "And I'm going to be moving fast. Can you keep up with me?"

He moved the axe to a sling on his back and gave a curt nod.

If he couldn't, he'd simply have to lag behind, even if it hurt his feelings. I had a lot of ground to cover tonight, and it was important I be back by dawn so no one missed me.

I set off through the backyards of the nearest homes to avoid the main street, keeping to the shadows as we got closer to the castle. Bim moved amazingly well for such a big man, and had no trouble staying with me up to that point.

Things were about to change, though.

The moon was clear, all the clouds gone and the fog had lifted when we stepped out of the woods on the far side of the gathering field. I paused for a moment to get my bearings.

"Which way, Lillith?" I subvocalized as I surveyed the land around me. It appeared to be mostly fields, with the occasional tree here and there showing up as a darker shape in the pale blue-white light of the moon.

"Straight ahead, and a bit to the right," she replied.

I knew that somewhere above me, the ship was sliding away from the cover of her asteroid, making her way in the same direction.

"Here we go," I told Bim, and took off at a very fast ground-eating lope. "Any idea how far, Lillith?"

"I suspect they're about eighty kilometers away, near the base of the eastern mountains," she said. "That's where the largest of the Madrean mines is located."

"Let me know when we're close. I don't want to run right into the middle of a pack of men carrying blasters."

Together, Bim and I ran through the moon-shadowed night, our muffled steps the only sound except for the noise of alien-sounding insects. Peri winged ahead of us, circling occasionally as if to hurry us along.

Again, Bim surprised me. I couldn't go into overdrive for a long period of time because my energy level had taken a beating earlier. But I didn't slow my pace, either, going much faster than the average Natural. Even at a steady lope, I could cover approximately forty kilometers an hour.

And he kept up with me, not even breathing hard as far as I could tell. Obviously, the results of Lillith's scan showing that the Madreans had evolved naturally to a GEP level were right, and I wondered what on the planet had caused the phenomenon. Something in the air? The water? The very ground they walked on? Or maybe a combination of all three.

I just hoped the planet survived long enough for the Federation scientists to figure it out.

We continued on until the ground began an upward slope, Peri alternately flying and riding on my shoulder, and I was wondering if Lillith had miscalculated the location of Strand's ship. The moon had almost reached its zenith before she spoke.

"I have the ship. It's about twenty minutes ahead of you and a bit to your left."

"Is it an artificial intelligence?" I asked anxiously, slowing my pace a bit and noting Bim follow my lead. *Stay*, I sent to Peri when she started to take off.

"Yes, but it's one of the earliest models, very rudimentary. Its higher functions are mostly limited to the mathematical equations needed for navigation."

"And its weapons?" I asked.

"Standard and mostly up to date," she said. "The detection program is turned off, or it would have picked me up and sounded an alarm by now. They must be sure I'll stay over Bastion City."

"Yeah, 'cause they think that's where I am. Almost there," I added aloud for Bim's sake.

Suddenly, something big stomped, and then there was a snort from directly in front of us.

Bim grabbed my arm and towed me to the left while I stared over my shoulder at the hulking shapes of five or six big animals that all seemed to be looking back at me. Horses, I realized. I should have been on the lookout for them. How else would Strand travel here? He certainly couldn't take a PTV when he went to the castle.

After a shudder of disgust, I pulled away from Bim and we continued on side by side until a glow of light appeared ahead of us, and I slowed yet again, barely jogging now. This radiance wasn't the soft mellow shine given off by sunstones. It was the harsh beam of halogen lamps. It became brighter abruptly as we topped a rise, and both Bim and I instantly dropped to the ground. Peri let out an indignant squeak at the action, then hopped to the ground and glared at me.

On our stomachs, we edged forward until we could peer into the small valley below.

A medium-sized ship was nestled at one end near an opening in the side of the hill, from which issued voices and scraping sounds. As we watched, Losif Strand stepped from the ship's hatch and met a man waiting at the bottom of the steps. We were close enough that I had no problem overhearing their conversation, and I ordered Peri to stay silent.

"What was so important that it couldn't wait until morning?" Strand asked the man.

"Zeller has been captured," the man blurted. Even from our perch above them I could see the sweat bead on his brow.

Strand stiffened. "By who?"

"Lowden," the man said. "Chine said he must have discovered our duplicity."

Strand relaxed marginally. "As long as it wasn't the Federation agent, I don't see the problem."

"Braxus is worried. He thinks we should move the plan up in case Lowden talks to the king."

"The plan depends on perfect timing. I'll decide when to put it in action, not Chine. Besides, what can Lowden tell the king?" Strand gave a negligent wave with one hand. "That he's signed an agreement with us to export sunstones? Politaus would toss him in a dungeon for breaking the ban. Even if Zeller spills his guts to Lowden, why would Politaus believe him? To him, I'm just the lowly black marketeer who sells him illegal books, a fact he doesn't want the general population to know about."

"Do not underestimate Lowden, Strand. He's entirely capable of taking matters into his own hands without the king's approval if he thinks you've cheated him, and the man was taught by a master strategist. If it comes to a fight, not even your blasters will stop his people, and they'll follow him unquestioningly."

"Then the sand will run with their blood," Strand said. "The Bashalde can die as easily as any other men."

A low growl came from beside me, and I jumped before realizing it was Bim. I'd forgotten he was Bashalde.

Quickly, I put a steadying hand on his arm and shook my head. Praise Zin, he settled down. I didn't need him charging the ship. That was my job. The entire purpose of this little jaunt was to see if the Sumantti was on board, and if it was, to retrieve it, something I couldn't do in my ghost form. Plus, while I'd been in the same room with Strand on numerous occasions, I'd never actually been close enough to the man to get a lock on his DNA.

That was about to change, of course, since I could go so fast no one would see me. And it needed to be now, while Strand was outside and occupied.

I poked Bim on the shoulder and leaned as close as I could get to him. "I'm going to be gone for a minute," I told him. "Don't move." *Stay with Bim*, I told Peri.

By the time he turned his head to stare at me, I was in overdrive and at the ship. It was as if the whole world came to a standstill while I was the only thing moving through it.

I went by Strand near enough to touch him, and leaped over the steps into the ship, my feet never hitting a single rung. And I didn't slow down, even then. Staying in overdrive, I searched the place top to bottom, nearly tearing the door off a locker because it wasn't meant to be opened and closed that fast.

I looked in every place big enough to hold a stasis box until I could feel my speed begin to outpace my energy input. I'd never stayed in overdrive so long before, and it was time to get out. The box wasn't there. All I found of interest was five chests full of sunstones and a large stash of weapons. I hesitated before deciding against taking a blaster. I couldn't risk getting caught with a Federation weapon, no matter how tempted I was to help myself. I also didn't want Strand to know I'd been inside his ship.

On the bright side, I'd now gotten a lock on Strand's

DNA. I could keep an eye on him and hope he led me to the Sumantti.

Jumping out of the ship, I dashed back up the hill. Strand had only moved a centimeter, and the man with him still had his mouth open on the same word.

I dropped to the ground before coming out of overdrive. Bim was still looking at me, this time in puzzlement. But I didn't have time to worry about him. A wave of dizziness washed over me that had my eyes closing until it passed. When it did, I edged backward, motioning for Bim and Peri to follow.

As soon as we were far enough away, I stood, using Bim's arm to steady myself. Somehow, I had to gather enough energy to run all the way back to Bastion City by morning.

"Is there anything to eat around here?" I asked Bim softly. "Maybe a fruit tree or some edible tubers I could dig up?"

Silently, he reached into a pouch hooked onto his belt and pulled out a wrapped package. When he handed it to me, I caught the familiar scent of spiced meat. Familiar because I'd smelled it cooking before, at the Bashalde gathering.

It was some kind of sausage, I discovered when I unwrapped it and took a bite. And it was apparently fortified with nutrients, since energy flowed through me from the first swallow.

I ate the whole thing and then handed the cloth wrapper back to Bim. "Thank you. It's a good thing you came with me. I might not have made it back otherwise."

He nodded and tucked the cloth back into his pouch as we walked. Soon, we'd have to start running again, but I wanted to be a little farther away from Strand before we did. I also needed to talk to Bim about what he'd heard, even if he didn't talk back.

"I know what you heard back there upset you," I told him. "But I'm going to ask you not to do anything yet."

When he only looked at me, I continued. "Lowden knows about those men and what they're up to. I told him earlier today. That's why he captured Zeller. Well, that and Zeller tried to kill him."

He reached over and touched the spot where the arrow had come out under my clavicle, brow arched in question.

"Yes, I stopped the arrow that was meant for Lowden."

After a moment's thought, he pointed at me, then upward, toward the stars. He was a smart man, even if he didn't speak.

"Yes, I'm the Federation agent Strand mentioned. I'm here because he stole a very dangerous object. All of our lives may depend on my getting it back before he tries to use it. Now, let's move it before everyone on Madrea knows what we've been up to."

We took off at a full run, Peri flying in front of us. "Are you headed back to the asteroid?" I asked Lillith.

"Yes. I only stayed long enough to be sure they were loading sunstones onto Strand's ship, and to get proof if they were."

"And?"

"They are and I did. I just sent the vids to my archives. Nice of them to light the place up so well. Got some good ones of Strand, so he can't say he didn't know about it."

"Good. You might want to alert Dr. Daniels. He can probably use them in the emergency council session he's called."

"Already done."

"You might also want to mention that there were already five chests of sunstones in the ship's hold this trip. With their price on the Federation market, that's enough to fund an entire armada. And there's not much telling how many loads he's taken out before now."

After that, I concentrated on putting one foot in front of the other. Even Gertz GEPs occasionally need rest, and I was dead on my feet. I hadn't slept much the night before, either. Not that I was complaining. Being with Reynard was worth a little sleep deprivation.

We reached Marcus's house just as the last sliver of moon vanished below the horizon, and nothing had ever looked as good to me as that house did.

"Go get some sleep," I told Bim. "That's what I'm going to do."

I'm not sure he believed me, because he waited until I scooted back through the window before he walked away. I didn't check to see if he was truly gone, just stripped and collapsed onto the bed. I barely had the willpower to pull the blanket up.

I fell asleep to the sound of Peri's snores coming from the pillow beside my head.

"Echo." The bed vibrated as it was struck by a booted foot.

I pulled the blanket over my head. "Go away," I mumbled.

The vibration came again. "It's noon. I thought you were simply exhausted from the wound you received yesterday, but I see there was more to it than that."

Lowering the blanket an inch, I opened one eye and peered out at Marcus. He was holding up the black trousers I'd left on the floor.

Well, schite. He'd caught me. "I can explain."

"Uh-huh. While you're at it, you can explain to the commander. He just arrived."

Double schite. I started to sit up and then remembered I wasn't wearing anything. "If you'll give me some privacy, I'll get dressed and be right out."

He eyed me for a second like he was trying to decide whether to trust me or not, then nodded and left, pulling the door closed behind him. The low sound of voices came from the front of the house as I jumped up and dressed hurriedly.

When I was done, I did a mental check on Peri. She was outside, visiting the flowers, and showed no inclination to come protect me. I took that as a good sign. Marcus probably wasn't going to kill me, just yell at me a bit.

Blowing a persistent lock of hair from my eyes, I gathered my courage, pasted a smile on my face, and opened the bedroom door.

Both Marcus and Reynard were holding cups and frowning at me, but I ignored them and strolled to the table as if I hadn't a care in the world. There was a light lunch spread on the table, along with a pot of hot coffee.

"Gentlemen." I nodded a greeting as I sat and poured a cup of coffee, inhaling deeply of the wonderful aroma before taking that first marvelous sip.

"Where did you go last night?" Marcus asked.

Okay, guess the social part of the day was over. "I went to search Strand's ship," I answered.

"Alone?" Marcus roared, almost dropping his cup. Reynard's frown merely deepened.

"No." I snagged some bread and speared a slice of meat to go with it. "Bim went with me."

"Well, at least you're not a complete idiot," Marcus said. He put his cup down and rubbed his eyes. I decided I'd better not mention that Bim only went because he'd caught me sneaking out.

"I was perfectly safe," I told the men. "Strand never knew I was there. And at least we know now that the Sumantti isn't on his ship. Plus, Lillith got some vid of Strand and his men loading sunstones onto the ship."

"Lillith knew about this little trip?"

"Yes, it was her idea, actually. She wanted to find out what kind of ship Strand had so she could be prepared, and I wanted to look for the Sumantti."

"And what kind does he have?" Reynard asked the question this time.

I shrugged. "Not one worth worrying about. Lillith can take it easily if it comes to a fight."

"Echo, I don't think you understand how important you are." Marcus's tone was so serious that I stopped eating to stare at him.

"I'm not important. Getting that crystal back before she can destroy this solar system is what's important."

"And how do you think we're going to do that if anything happens to you?" Reynard asked. "You are our only hope. If you're incapacitated in any way, we're doomed."

"Well, when you put it like that . . ." I trailed off, and then sighed. "Fine. I'm sorry. I wasn't thinking. From now on, I swear I'll tell you both before I do anything drastic. So, did you warn the king?" I asked in an attempt to change the subject.

"Yes, for all the good it did."

"He didn't believe you?"

"He doesn't take the threat seriously, says his guards are loyal and would allow no one, especially not a stranger, close enough to harm him. I've assigned extra men to stay with him, but I'm not sure it will help."

I reached over and covered his hand with mine. "Maybe we should tell him the whole truth, Reynard. I know it's a risk, but it might save his life."

He ran his free hand over his face and shook his head.

"Well, at least think about it," I commented. "By the way, did I mention Zeller has been captured?"

Suddenly both of them were staring at me again and I couldn't stop the smug grin that crossed my face.

"What makes you think Zeller was captured?" Marcus asked ominously.

"Because I saw it. Lowden's men captured him near the castle last night. The crazy man was screaming his head off. Something about spirits trying to kill him," I added innocently.

They were both silent a second before Marcus shook his head. "I'm not going to ask," he muttered.

"This ghosting thing I've got really comes in handy," I told him, reaching for my cup of coffee. It was halfway to my lips when suddenly the Imadei twitched, and then gave off a frantic burst of heat. The cup crashed to the table as I grabbed the stone, wrapped my hand around it over the material of my top. Involuntarily, my eyes closed as I tried to figure out what was happening.

For a moment I was distracted as Peri launched into the room, screaming in fear as she hovered in front of me. Then I knew, and terror nearly stopped my heart.

"What's wrong?!" Marcus and Reynard had both leaped to their feet, and I heard the sound of metal sliding from leather.

"It's the Daughter Stone," I gasped. "She's trying to break free from the stasis box."

"Can you locate the stone?" Marcus asked urgently.

"No." Sweat coated my forehead as I focused all my attention on the Imadei. If the Daughter Stone broke free, I had to be prepared.

"How can I help?" Reynard asked, his voice low and worried.

I shook my head and took a deep breath. Then, as quickly as it had started, the Imadei settled, the heat gradually fading from the small crystal under my hand. Relief flowed through me as I opened my eyes, leaving me weak and shaky.

Peri landed watchfully on the table, still peering at me in concern. "It's over." I let my breath out in a sigh. "She didn't get out this time."

Violently, Marcus grabbed a cloth and swabbed at the coffee I'd spilt. "We have to find that crystal, damn it!"

"I'm open to suggestions," I told him as Reynard sheathed his sword and sat down beside me. "Maybe this is even more reason to come clean with the king. Doesn't he have a right to know what kind of danger his world is in?" I glanced at Reynard. "You said he was a fair man. I'm sure when he knows there's a good reason for me to be here in spite of the ban, he'll understand. After all, it's not like I'm planning to set up a shop to sell advanced technology. As soon as I complete my mission I'll be gone."

Reynard and I looked at each other, and I knew we were thinking the same thing. I didn't want to leave him. The idea of never seeing him again, never touching him or talking to him, was almost more than I could stand.

But we had no choice.

As hard as it would be to resist, I couldn't use my psi ability to pop in for a visit. That would only prolong the agony for both of us when we knew nothing more was possible, that we had no future together.

Reynard dropped his gaze first. "As much as I'd like to tell Politaus the truth, we can't. It's not merely that you've violated the ban, although he wouldn't approve, even under these dire circumstances. But how would I tell him that his brother is involved in this scheme, how would I convince him it's the truth? Even honest men have their blind spots, and he'd rather cut off his own limb than believe Braxus would plot against him. Knowing Politaus the way I do, he'd probably put himself in danger simply to prove his brother's loyalty."

"I'm afraid he's right," Marcus agreed in disgust. "Telling the king would do more damage than good now."

"Then what are we supposed to do?" I asked the two men. "Just sit here and wait for Strand to act or for the Daughter Stone to succeed in getting away from them?"

"Unless you want to break into the castle and start searching room to room." Marcus tossed the cloth onto a counter and hesitated, glancing from me to Reynard. "I'm going to talk to Lowden, see exactly what happened to Zeller and if he got any information out of him. I'll stop at Cammi's on the way and tell her you need another top. It will probably take me a couple of hours, at the least. Don't worry about your act. I've already sent word to Treya that you won't be dancing."

"Where's Bim?" I asked.

"I sent him to get some sleep. Commander, would you mind staying until I return?"

"It will be my pleasure."

Neither of them said anything until Marcus went out and closed the door behind him, then Reynard took my hand and tugged me around the table to sit on his lap.

"He's getting better about this guardian thing, but I'm surprised he left us alone," I said, snuggling into his chest.

"I asked him to give us some time," Reynard said.

"And he agreed? You'll have to tell me what you threatened him with so I can use it."

He rested his chin on top of my head, his arm holding me close, and I felt him smile. "I didn't threaten him, only told him we needed to talk."

"About what?"

"This." He pulled out a small, deep blue velvet pouch and handed it to me.

I held it in my palm for a moment. "What is it?"

"Open it and see."

Gingerly, I opened the pouch and upended it into my hand. And then gaped in shock. It was a gold ring, intricately made from what looked, to all appearances, to be two dragon birds, talons and tails entwined to form the band. In the center of their talons was set a sunstone, the size of the nail on my pinkie finger, which glowed softly in the bright light of day.

"It's beautiful, Reynard," I breathed. "The most beautiful thing I've ever seen."

"The jeweler told me the creatures are mythological beasts called dragons. They're supposed to be good luck. Now I know they are much more."

"Where did you get it?"

"I bought it for you at a Bashalde gathering five cycles ago when I was on my way to meet with Jancen and Lowden. The jeweler's tent was next to theirs. I was almost past it when I stopped and went back. The ring was sitting there as if it were waiting for me, and I knew the instant I saw it that it was yours."

"You didn't know me five cycles ago," I whispered, afraid if I took my gaze off the ring it would vanish.

"I knew you," he murmured, his lips brushing my hair. "I knew someday I'd find you, and you'd be all I had ever dreamed of, and more."

Tears filled my eyes. "Reynard, you bought this for the woman you planned to spend your life with. We both know that's not going to be me." My fist closed around the ring in spite of my good intentions. "You should keep it. Someday you'll wish you had it back."

He pried my hand open, took the ring, and slid it on my left ring finger. "I bought it for the woman who would own my heart, Echo. That's you. It will be you until the day I die no matter how far apart we are. Promise me you'll wear it. It will give me comfort knowing that my gift will always bring light to your life."

The tears spilled over and ran down my cheeks. "I'll wear it, I promise. Forever. And every time I look at it, I'll see you again, and know that my heart, too, is yours alone."

I slid off his lap, scrubbed the tears from my face, and then held out my hand for his. "Come on. We have some time before Marcus gets back. My bed isn't as big as yours, but I plan on showing you exactly what I can accomplish with such a limited amount of space."

He stood, a slight smile on his rugged face. "As I told Marcus, it will be my pleasure." With a quick tug he pulled me into his arms. "And yours as well. I'll see to it."

CHAPTER 18

It was just getting dark when Marcus finally made it back, and we had taken full advantage of every moment, barely getting dressed and back in the front room before he came through the door. And our save was due mostly to Peri. I picked up an image of Marcus from her mind, strolling down the main street of Bastion City, looking very pleased with life in general. It was much the same expression Reynard was wearing as we rapidly dressed.

Bim had returned sometime that afternoon, and I'd just sent him to fetch food for the three of us when Marcus walked through the front door.

"What did you find out?" I asked him, uncovering the lamps to brighten the room.

He moved to the table where Reynard was sitting, trying to look innocent, and pulled out a chair. "Zeller is dead. Apparently it wasn't an easy death, so I won't go into the details. He told Lowden everything he knew before the end, but all that did was verify what we already know. He had no idea where the girls or the crystal are hidden."

"What about Strand's plans for me?"

He shook his head. "Strand didn't trust him enough to go

into details. He only knew it involved stealing your knife. Nice ring," he added, eyeing my hand.

"Thanks." I held it out so he could admire it better. "Reynard gave it to me."

"Good. Since you're promised now, I don't have to worry about my responsibilities as your guardian."

I looked at him blankly. "Promised?" My gaze went to Reynard. He was practically whistling at the ceiling in an effort to appear nonchalant.

"Yes. Didn't the commander explain?"

"No, he certainly did *not*." I scowled at Reynard.

Marcus grinned gleefully at the commander. "Well, on Madrea, there's no such thing as divorce or short-term marriages. When a man gives a woman a promise ring and she accepts it, you're as good as married. The only thing left to do is the formal ceremony, which is mostly a celebration of the union, not a legal joining like it is in the Federation."

"Neglected to mention that little detail to me, didn't you?" I said.

He shrugged, a smile twitching at the corners of his lips. "You aren't Madrean."

"No, but you are," I reminded him.

"Yes, I am." His smile widened. "And you are mine now, no matter where you go."

My fingers drummed the table. "Yeah? You can be sure we *will* talk about this later. People can't just go around claiming other people without telling them about it in advance, pal."

There was a scratching sound outside before the door opened and Bim came in carrying a tray loaded with food. We all unloaded it, and then filled our plates.

"Eat up," I told the commander. "You're going to need your strength tonight."

"Oh?" He wiggled a brow, and I rolled my eyes.

"Not for that. We're going to search under the castle."

Both he and Marcus promptly choked.

"What?"

"Well, it was your idea," I told Marcus. "And I know the girls are there somewhere. I got that much from the hall outside their room. It stands to reason that if they're being kept under the castle, so is the Sumantti, and I have to look for them. If you'd prefer not to get involved," I told the commander, "I can do it alone."

"You aren't going alone," he practically growled. "Do you have any idea how extensive the network of rooms under the castle is? Even I don't know my way around half of it, and I grew up exploring those passages."

"Why are there so many of them?" I asked, puzzled. "I mean, I know you've had wars with the Bashalde in the past, but surely you didn't need that many dungeons. There wouldn't be any Bashalde left."

"They aren't dungeons, for the most part," Marcus told me. "The theory is that the first settlers lived there until they could get crops well established and the planet supporting life on an individual basis. It was a commonsense way to keep supplies and medical care in a central location. The castle was later built on top of the quarters, but they extend outside the castle's foundations."

Suddenly, I sat up straighter, an idea occurring to me. "Are there outside entrances to this place, so a person could get in and out without having to go through the castle?"

"Probably," Reynard said. "It would make sense to have multiple exits, although I've never seen one."

"Lillith, do you have access to scans of the area around the castle from five cycles ago?"

"Yes, of course. The original teams were very thorough."

"Great. I want you to compare them with the most recent scans you've taken of the same area. Look for anomalies like paths that seem to end in the middle of nowhere, and weren't there before. Or maybe a place where the ground has been disturbed recently. Or a big boulder has vanished. Anything that's noticeably different."

"Checking."

We continued eating and were almost finished when she spoke again. "I think I've found what you're looking for. There's a faint path leading from the direction of Strand's ship. It ends in a grassy area to the rear left of the castle several kilometers from the gathering field, and there's a patch of ground that looks yellow and dead."

"She found it." I told Reynard what the ship had discovered. "That's where we'll start. I'm betting the girls won't be far from the entrance, and they'll keep the crystal close to the girls."

"Echo," Lillith spoke again. "I'm not sure this is a good idea. That path is entirely too clear from above when you're looking for it. Why didn't they hide it better?"

"Probably because they didn't think it would occur to me to check. After all, this *is* my first mission. Strand would know that."

"I still don't like it."

"We'll be extra careful," I promised the ship as I scooted my chair back. "Marcus, sorry about your clothes, but I need to borrow them again. I'll be right back."

Peri was on the window ledge grooming her feathers when I went into my room and closed the door. She'd left as soon as Marcus had earlier and stayed out later than usual, but then she'd been tired last night, too, and had slept most of the morning away just as I had.

"Don't go to sleep," I told her as I changed. "We're leaving again."

She gave her feathers one last fluff, and then looked up

with interest, giving an excited chirp as she picked up my thoughts.

I finished changing into the dark shirt and trousers, then attached my sheath to the belt, filling it with the knife I'd gotten from Lowden. It wasn't as well balanced as mine, but it was sharp and well cared for. If I had to use it, it would get the job done, and that was what counted.

"Let's go," I told her, waiting until she was on my shoulder before going back to the front room. At once, both men stood.

"Marcus, I think you should stay here," I told him. "If I'm not mistaken, my chip won't work underground, so I won't be able to communicate with Lillith. And since she doesn't have human DNA, I can't pop in on her. If it is a trap, I may need you on the outside more than I need you with us."

He scowled and then sighed. "Fine, but I don't like it. What am I supposed to do, sit here and twiddle my thumbs?"

"Go to work," I said. "You've got a tavern to run. And it'll make the time go faster. If I need you, it won't matter where you are, anyway. But truthfully, I figure this will take a while. You'll probably be in bed, fast asleep, when we get back."

The look he gave me was wry. "Don't count on it. I won't sleep a wink until I know you're both safe."

Reynard slid the cylindrical covers over two of the lamps and handed one to me. "We'll need these. It's dark in those passages."

I took it, and then gave Marcus a quick kiss on the cheek. "Don't worry. We'll be back before you know it."

He grumbled as we went by him, then stood with his hands on his hips as we went out the door. And ran headlong into Bim.

The big man took one look at the way I was dressed, spread his feet, crossed his arms over his chest, and stared at me. He'd trapped me again, and there was obviously no way out of taking him with us.

Making the best of the situation, I pasted on a smile. "There you are, Bim. We want to know if you'd mind coming with us on a little adventure."

Reynard arched a brow at me, but I concentrated on Bim. He looked downright suspicious, his gaze going from me to Reynard and back again. But really, what could he do? There was no chance he'd let me go off without him. Not when he felt semi-responsible for Zeller's arrow piercing my shoulder, and not when he knew we were trying to help his people.

Finally, he nodded, and we started in the direction Lillith indicated. From the main street came the sounds of shopkeepers closing up and hurrying home for the night, and the laughter of children, stretching their playtime for as long as possible before their mothers called them in to supper.

It should have felt serene, normal, calming. Instead, an uneasy feeling of dread washed over me, causing my skin to pebble.

Was it percipience, a sense that we were walking into something that would change this idyllic world forever? A shiver ran over me and Reynard glanced down.

"Cold?"

"No." I forced a smile. "Just dire thoughts. They're gone now," I lied, forgetting about his ability to detect the truth.

"No, they aren't." He took my free hand. "But we will prevail. You need to believe that. Fear of failure is a self-fulfilling prophecy. If we accept we're going to fail before we start, why try? You might as well sit down and wait to die. This is something all soldiers know deep inside."

"You're right." I squeezed his hand. "Thank you for re-minding me."

We went the rest of the way in relative silence. Since most of Bastion City stretched out in front of the castle, there was little in the way of habitations after we got on the other side. Lillith made minor adjustments in our direction until we stood in the area she'd indicated, up to our knees in green, healthy-looking grass dotted with wildflowers that gave off a slight glow in the darkness.

Once upon a time, this must have been part of the forest. Here and there, large tree stumps poked up from the ground, their bark dark and dry looking.

"Okay, where is the dead spot?" I asked her.

"About twenty paces to your left, closer to the tree line."

"This way," I gestured at Reynard and Bim.

We went slowly, examining the ground until we found the place Lillith indicated. I could see why she thought it suspicious. The grass was much shorter here, stiff and so yellowed that, from her vantage point, it must have looked like a signpost that said, "Enter here." It was also way too symmetrical, measuring three meters by three meters square, with the edges sharply delineated.

The hair stood erect on my nape as I studied it, and I paused to check our surrounds. Had I heard something, or was my imagination running on high? Peri gave no indica-tion that she was aware of a human near our location, but I wasn't convinced. It felt like we were being watched.

"Lillith," I said subvocally. "Are there any heat signatures in the woods large enough to be a person?"

"No. If there were, I would have mentioned it before now. And I still don't like this."

"I'm not thrilled about it, either," I told her, walking slowly around the square of ground. "I'm pretty sure you're right. They know we're coming, watching for us, even."

"How would they be watching? There's no one near."

"A vidport on one of the trees, maybe?" I commented.

She went silent for a second. "I found it." Her tone was grim. "It's operating off a very low voltage battery. That's why I didn't pick up on it before. You should abort this operation now."

"I can't, Lillith." I stooped and ran a finger under the edge of the dead grass. What I found was a two-inch-thick metal hatch, heavy from the weight of soil on top, but light enough that a Natural could lift it if they strained a bit. "They are undoubtedly using those girls and the crystal as bait. But at least we know Strand is expecting us, and if we're careful, this could be our best chance of retrieving them."

Sliding both hands under the trapdoor, I tugged. Reynard and Bim joined me, and together we set the metal plate aside. Below it was a set of narrow stone stairs leading downward into stygian darkness.

"I'll go first." After a brief hesitation, I uncovered the lamp and started down. It wasn't like I was giving away our presence, after all.

Behind me, Reynard followed suit, and then Bim. I could tell from his gait that Bim had removed the axe from his back and now carried it at the ready. Reynard did the same with his sword.

I counted forty steps before we reached the bottom, and realized they had gradually angled back toward the castle. From somewhere ahead water trickled, and the walls I touched were damp and slick with moss.

"Anything look familiar?" I asked Reynard, pausing a few feet beyond the steps.

"No, I've never been here before. I think it's below the level I explored growing up. The main passageways weren't this deep. We didn't even know there was another level."

"Great." I lowered the lamp and studied the floor. "Too damp for dust, so no footprints. Looks like we're on our own." I meant that literally, too. I'd had no communication with Lillith since we were about halfway down the stairs. It was odd, not having the ship to rely on for information, and a little bit lonely.

"On the other hand, the hall outside the girls' room looked like this, too, so it's a good bet they're down here somewhere. Let's keep going."

The hall seemed to stretch forever before we ran into an intersection. Here, we stopped again and with lamps raised, looked in both directions.

"What do you think?" Reynard asked. "Right, left or keep going?"

"All of the above," I told him. "There are doors down each side hall. We need to check them all. It will take longer, but we stay together. Left first, and hope the doors aren't locked."

They weren't. Most of them weren't even completely closed. We checked each one and discovered the dust that was missing from the hall. Dust that hadn't been disturbed in hundreds of years, from the look of things. Otherwise, the rooms were empty.

The other hall yielded the same results, as did the next set of corridors we came to, and the set after that. Several hours passed, and I was beginning to get bored by the time we reached the fourth intersection along the main passage. Immediately, things got more interesting as I peered down the right hall.

"It's not stone," I told Reynard, running my hand down a wall.

He stepped up beside me, gazing over my shoulder. "Neither are the floors. It looks like some kind of metal, but I don't see any seams."

"They must have cast it all at once," I told him. "Either that, or this is part of the original ship that brought the settlers to Madrea. It makes sense that they would scavenge the living quarters and continue to use them, although I'm not sure why the section would have been buried down here."

"Do we need to search this section?" He asked. "You said the hall outside the girls' room was stone."

I thought about it and then nodded. "Yes, because the Sumantti could be anywhere."

This time when I stepped into the hall, my footsteps rang slightly, and instinctively, I slowed down, being careful where I put my feet. There didn't seem to be as many doors here, and they appeared closer together.

On my shoulder, Peri shifted restlessly, and I picked up a feeling of unease from her as I stopped between the first set of doors. The one on the right was almost completely closed. The door on the left was wide open. I raised the lamp and took a closer look inside, then caught my breath.

"Look," I told the men. "There are metal shelves built into the walls." But what really held my attention was the lack of dust, combined with numerous black metal cubes sitting on the shelves. Stasis boxes. I'd recognize them anywhere, had even used them back on Centaurius to keep food fresh for weeks or months on end.

Excitement surged through me as I walked into the room and glanced around. Reynard moved to one of the shelves and reached for a box, but I stopped him. "Don't open them. If the Sumantti is here, we don't want her lashing out in anger. Maybe I can tell if she's here from just touching them. Her container should be the only one that's actually turned on, and the box will be expending a lot of energy to keep her captive."

From my shoulder, Peri muttered darkly, her gaze on the door. I paused, head tilted. "Did either of you hear something?"

They listened for a second and then shook their heads.

"Must have been my imagination." I put my lamp on a shelf, went to the first of the boxes and put my hands on the sides. Nothing.

"How do you tell if they're on?" Reynard asked, depositing his lamp across the room from mine for maximum efficiency.

"There will be a very low, very faint vibration," I told him. "You can't hear it, but you should be able to feel it."

With a nod, he moved to another box and put his hands on it. Bim stayed in the center of the room, as though reluctant to mess with things he knew nothing about.

I was reaching for the next box when suddenly Peri screamed in rage. Already on edge, I went into overdrive, spinning toward the door to confront whatever danger had alerted her.

But even then, it was too late. The metal door was already closed, and just as I slammed into it, I heard the distinct thunk of a latch clicking into place.

To save energy, I dropped out of overdrive, but that didn't stop me from pounding on the door hard enough to leave dents in the metal. From the other side I heard the muffled sound of laughter, and a speaker on the wall crackled to life.

"Temper, temper, Agent Adams. Even a Gertz GEP can't tear open solid metal."

Reynard moved up beside me on my left, Bim on the right, axe at the ready. "You won't get away with this, Strand. The Federation knows you're here. My ship even has vid of you loading sunstones. Everyone will know you're responsible for our deaths."

"Ah, but you see, I have no plans to kill you or your friends, Agent Adams. All I have to do is keep you locked away here and wait. Eventually, you'll starve to death, of course, but it's fair punishment for criminals like you. As for the Federation, I've broken none of their laws. I'm here at the invitation of the king. Your vids are worthless."

"What are you talking about? We aren't criminals." My words were interrupted by the deep vibration of huge bells tolling mournfully. The noise was muffled and faint, coming as it did through the many passages under the castle. But not even distance could stop the disturbance it caused in the ground, and I felt it all the way from the soles of my feet to the top of my head.

Instantly, Reynard stiffened, and from my other side, Bim growled.

"What is it?" I asked, alarmed by their reactions.

"Something has happened," Reynard said. "Something bad. The bells are only rung under dire circumstances."

That evil chuckle came again. "The commander is correct. I'll leave it to your imagination to wonder what it is. Now, I must go. It's almost time to put the final part of my plan into action. Good-bye, Agent Adams, and thank you for falling so readily into my little trap. It was most obliging of you."

The static coming from the speaker cut off abruptly, and I turned to Reynard. "Schite. This was a setup from the beginning, and I walked right into it. I'm sorry. They should have sent someone who knew what the frag she was doing."

He pulled me closer, wrapped his arms around me. "You had no reason to think Strand would trap us this way. Even I was expecting a face-to-face attack, not this cowardly trick. How could you know?"

"I should have. At the very least, I should have had Lillith run probabilities, gone over all of them and planned for each accordingly."

"There must be something we can do." He released me and went to examine the door. "There's no opening mechanism on this side. It looks as if it's been removed."

I joined him and checked the spot where the handle had been. Only fresh tool marks remained to mar the metal surface. "If there was something I could get a grip on, maybe I could pull it from the frame."

The commander ran his hands around the edge of the door and then shook his head. "It's smooth. I can feel the seam where it opens."

Bim stepped forward, his axe drawn back, but I put a hand on his arm before he could use it. "It would only dull your weapon," I told him. "The metal is too hard for an axe, and you may need it to be sharp later."

He looked at me, a heavy brow arched, and I grinned. "I just thought of a way to get us out of here."

"How?" Reynard asked.

"Good thing he doesn't know about my psi ability. Catch me," I told Reynard, already shuffling through the DNA I had stored. "I'm going to find Marcus."

CHAPTER 19

I landed in utter chaos. It seemed that Marcus and all his employees were confined in a small storage room at the Terpsichore. All the women except Treya were crying, and she was ranting at the top of her lungs, threatening someone on the other side of the door.

The men looked pale and grim, especially Marcus. He stood in the middle of the noise, hands clenched at his sides, head bowed.

"Marcus?"

I spoke quietly, but not quietly enough. At the sound of my voice, Treya spun to face me. "You!" she spit. "This is all your fault. I should have known you were no Bashalde."

"Shut up, Treya." Marcus's voice was so level that the noise in the room instantly stopped. "Where are you?" he asked me.

"Strand has us locked in a metal room under the castle. What happened? We heard the bells."

"The king and the four extra guards Reynard assigned him are dead. And they're saying you murdered them, that you're a spy for the Federation sent in to remove him so the ban would be lifted. The king was killed with your knife, and two of Braxus's men are swearing they saw you and the commander flee the scene."

"You know that's not true," I said.

"Of course I know it," he snapped. "But Braxus has the king's guard whipped into a frenzy. They've arrested all of us for harboring a spy, and now they're out searching for you and the commander."

"Can you get out?"

"No. They've blocked the door and left two guards in place. None of them will listen to reason. When they don't find you, I think the rest of them will be back, and it won't be pretty. They need someone to blame, and we're handy."

"Okay, don't panic. I'm going to send you some help. If you have to, block the door from this side. Don't let them in under any circumstances."

Without waiting for more conversation, I pulled out Lowden's DNA and locked it into place.

Instantly, I was in his tent. He was pacing in front of Jancen while the elderly man wrung his hands. He saw me first and gasped. Lowden spun, his mouth dropping open at my appearance.

"I'm sorry," I told them. "There's no time to explain how I got here. You know Politaus has been murdered?"

They both nodded.

"Good. I didn't do it. Whoever stole my knife did. Now Braxus is in charge of the guard, and he's sent them after Marcus Kent and Marcus's employees. Probably to keep him busy so he can't help me. I need you to take your men to the Terpsichore and free them. If you don't, the guard may very well kill them."

Lowden bowed. "As you ask, so shall it be done."

"Thank you. And please hurry."

His grin was feral. "Do not worry, Agent Adams. It won't

be the first time my people have faced the Madrean Guard. As always, we will prevail."

He was running for his tent opening, already shouting orders, when I pictured sliding back into my body.

The first thing I felt was Reynard's arms around me, and then I became aware of the cold floor under me. Dread washed through me as I thought about telling him what I'd learned.

Slowly, I opened my eyes. He was on his knees, cradling me close, leaning slightly so he could see my face. Bim was standing guard over me, and Peri was hanging upside down from a shelf, cooing at me.

When I didn't say anything, the commander's expression altered to one of grief. "Politaus?"

"I'm sorry." I lifted a hand to cradle his cheek. "He's dead along with four of the guards."

Releasing me, he pushed to his feet and then just stood there, like he didn't know what to do next. "I think I knew as soon as I heard the bells," he murmured. "But I didn't want to believe it. I should have been there to stop it."

"There was nothing you could do," I told him, scrambling up and putting a hand on his arm. "I know he was your friend as well as your king, but even if you'd stayed with him all the time, they'd still have found a way."

He took a step toward the door and then stared at it blankly. "I need to take command of the guards. They must be in disarray by now."

I moved in front of him, forced him to look at me. "Reynard, listen to me. Braxus has taken over. He's told the guards that both of us are responsible for the king's death. Two of his men are swearing they saw us leaving the scene together. That's what Strand meant when he called us criminals."

His eyes, so blue and empty a second before, suddenly

ignited with the flames of rage. "Braxus has signed his own death warrant. If it takes me the rest of my life, he will die at my hands. Did you find someone to get us out?"

"Not yet. The guards are holding Marcus and his people hostage at the Terpsichore while they search for us. When they can't find us, I'm afraid they'll go back and kill them. I've sent Lowden and the Bashalde to free them, but the situation leaves me with a dilemma. Everyone I know on Madrea is either locked up, busy fighting the guards, dead, or they're our enemy."

"There must be someone!" He paced away and then back. Without warning, he doubled his fist and slammed it into the door. "I should be fighting, defending my people from these bastards."

My mouth opened to console him, but something he said suddenly struck a chord. Something about fighting. I thought furiously.

Fighting. I'd only had one real fight since I landed on Madrea.

Durtran! He'd said he owed me after our sparring match at the king's supper.

I clutched Reynard's arm to keep him from doing more damage to his hand while excitement surged through me. "Tell me about Durtran," I urged. "Was he loyal to Politaus? Is he an honest man?"

"Yes to both," he said, catching onto my idea. "He wouldn't believe the lies told about me, either. Durtran and I know each other well."

"Where would he be at a time like this?"

Reynard didn't even hesitate. "The same place I'd be. In the guard room, taking charge of his men and trying to keep order."

"So he wouldn't be alone."

A sigh lifted his chest. "Probably not."

"It's okay." I patted his arm. "I'll just go into my dream state and watch him until he is."

"That could take hours."

I gave him a wry look. "It's not like we're going anywhere else. Besides, it may be the only chance we have to get out of here."

"You're right." He sat on the floor and leaned against a shelf. I sat in front of him, using his body as a backrest.

"I'll be able to support myself unless I jump into my ghost form. If that happens, you'll know I've found a way to get Durtran alone. Now, what does the guard room look like?"

Bim turned to face the door, standing guard as Reynard wrapped his arms around me in a loose hold. "The office is fairly small, about five meters by five meters. The walls and floor are stone, and there's a wooden desk facing the door. Weapons and shields are hung on the walls."

I'd closed my eyes as soon as he started speaking, and built a hazy image of what he'd described. Then I put Durtran at the desk, wearing the uniform of the king's guard.

Immediately, the mental picture solidified and I watched as Durtran snarled at two men standing in front of the desk. "I don't care what Chine said. He has no standing with the guard. You will spread the word that if anyone locates the commander or the woman, they will bring them to me. And they damn well better not have a scratch on them. Do you understand?"

"Yes, sir." One of the men squirmed before he spoke again. "But Braxus—"

"Just because Braxus sits in the throne room does not make him king!" Durtran roared. "The new king will be chosen by the people. Until he is, you will obey the orders of your senior officers or face treason charges. Now, remove yourself from my sight and go do your job."

The man saluted and practically ran from the room. The other one arched a brow at Durtran. "Don't you think you're being a little heavy-handed? The men are upset and confused. Remember, they lost their king tonight, too."

"They are soldiers. Their duty comes first, no matter how upset they are." He ran a hand over his face and I could see the weariness in his eyes. "There's something wrong here, Hallis. The commander was completely loyal to the king. He'd never be part of a plot to kill him, no matter how enamored he is of the woman. Braxus's men are lying."

"Walk carefully, my friend," Hallis told him. "Unless we can find proof of a conspiracy, we may all be in danger of committing treason."

Hallis didn't seem to be in a hurry to leave, so I decided to take matters into my own hands. After all, Reynard had sensed my presence the first time I'd peeked in on him. Maybe Durtran was sensitive, too.

Get rid of him, I sent. *You need to be alone.*

Durtran shook his head and then rubbed the back of his neck.

Okay, this was good. He obviously felt something. I just needed to be a bit firmer.

It's me, Echo. I'm here but I can't show myself until you're alone. Send him away and close the door.

He blinked and looked around the office, then stood abruptly. "Hallis, I need you in the field. Make sure the troops aren't running wild in Bastion City, terrorizing the people. And close the door on your way out."

The man looked puzzled, but didn't argue. Instead he gave a short bow. "As you wish."

When the door was closed, Durtran looked around again. "Have I lost my senses?" he murmured.

I gave a final push and appeared in front of him. "No, your senses are fine. So are your instincts. The commander had nothing to do with the king's murder. And neither did I. We were framed by Braxus and Losif Strand. I'll tell you the entire story later, but now we need your help."

"Is it true that you're an agent of the Federation?"

"Yes," I admitted. "But I wasn't sent here to interfere with the king or the ban. That's just another lie."

He nodded. "I suspected as much. How can I help?"

"Losif Strand has trapped me and the commander in a room under the castle. The door can only be opened from the outside, so we need you to come let us out."

"How do I get there?" he asked without hesitation.

I gave him the directions for the path we'd taken, since that was the only way in I knew. "Be careful, Durtran. There's a vidport on a tree in the clearing. If Strand has anyone watching it, they'll know what you're doing. There may also be guards at the door, although we haven't heard anyone."

Before I could slide back into my body, the office door was flung open and Hallis charged in, yelling, "Second! The Bashalde are attacking our troops!"

In the middle of his declaration, he ran right through me, then staggered to a halt and turned slowly to stare.

Well, scritch. So much for being discreet. Might as well make the best of the situation, since it was too late to vanish.

"I'm afraid that's my fault," I told them. "Braxus ordered a contingent of the guard to lock up Marcus Kent and his employees. I sent the Bashalde to free them before Braxus could call for their deaths."

"Why would he want Kent dead? The man is only a tavern keeper."

"Marcus knows too much. He knows who I am and why I'm here. He can also testify that both he and the commander were with me when my knife was stolen."

Durtran glanced at Hallis. "Order the troops to yield to

the Bashalde and allow them to free Kent. I won't have a full-scale war break out between our people on Braxus's orders. And Hallis, you will tell no one what you've seen and heard here."

"They wouldn't believe me, anyway," the man muttered as he ran back out, giving me a wide berth.

"Will he keep silent?" I asked Durtran.

"Yes. He's a good man."

"In that case, I'll see you soon." With a final nod, I slid back into my body and opened my eyes.

"He's on his way," I told Reynard, sitting up to face him. "Now all we have to do is hope he makes it in time. Braxus won't wait long before he uses the Sumantti. He's already giving orders and taking charge as if he were king."

"It took us hours to get here."

"Yes, but we weren't in a hurry, and we searched every room on the way. Durtran knows approximately where we are and will come straight to us. Meanwhile, I have one more trip to make."

Shifting my position I leaned against Reynard again, shut my eyes, and shuffled through the DNA I'd recently collected. When I found the one I wanted, I pushed.

Kiera looked up, startled, from the pool where she lounged. Dragon birds were lining the sides, squabbling over the soapsuds floating in the water and diving in and out of a waterfall on the other end.

I grimaced. "Sorry. I didn't mean to interrupt your bath."

"Don't worry about it." She climbed out of the pool and reached for a drying cloth. "What's wrong?"

"You need to tell the Limantti that I don't think it'll be much longer before the Daughter Stone is released. Things are happening really fast now. She needs to be on the alert."

Smith nodded. "Is there anything I can do to help?"

"Just be prepared. We may need you both."

"I'll go to the Mother Stone right now."

"Thanks." I slid back into my body, satisfied that I'd done everything possible to stave off the catastrophe heading in our direction.

When I sat up this time, Bim squatted next to us and opened his pouch. Pulling out a familiar cloth-wrapped bundle, he offered it to me.

"Good idea." I smiled at him, then unwrapped the food and divided it into three parts. "We should eat while we have time."

"Where did you go?" Reynard asked, taking his share.

"To alert Kiera Smith. We may need the Mother Stone to try and contain the Sumantti when she's finally released."

"Is she really as beautiful as you told Lowden she is?"

I glared at him. "Probably more so. Which is why you're never going to meet her."

"No one could be more beautiful to me than you are," he said.

"Uh-huh. You're still not meeting her."

At least my comment made him smile a little, even if it did look forced. And I also realized that somewhere along the way my resentment of Kiera had faded away to nothing. It's hard to stay upset at someone you were counting on to help save your life and the lives of millions of others.

We fell silent as we ate, and I eyed the stasis boxes lining the shelves. I knew the Sumantti wasn't there, but I really needed to check just to be sure. It would the height of irony if we were locked up with the stone the entire time and didn't know.

I popped the last bite into my mouth, dusted the crumbs off my hands and stood. When I moved to the boxes, Peri went with me, strutting along the shelves, chortling at each box I touched.

Of course, the stone wasn't there. I'd just checked the last one when Peri let out a warning squawk and faced the door.

We all spun, weapons at the ready as a muffled yell sounded, followed by the thud of a body hitting the floor. Everything went silent, and then the mechanism on the door began to turn.

With a final click, the door swung open. Durtran stood in the opening, out of breath and covered in dirt. With a short bow, he grinned at Reynard. "Commander, you do pick the damnedest places to hide. Don't you think it's time you returned to duty?"

CHAPTER 20

"Durtran!" Reynard strode forward and embraced the man, carefully avoiding the bloody sword in his hand. "I never thought I'd be so happy to see your ugly face." He stepped back, gesturing at the sword. "You had trouble getting here?"

"There were two guards at the entrance of the passage. They objected to my presence." He paused. "You know about Politaus?"

Solemnly, the commander nodded. "Echo told me. How did it happen? I assigned four men to stay with him at all times. They should have stopped any attempt on his life."

"Their bodies were found outside his room, necks broken as though they were taken by surprise. The king must have heard or sensed something, because he rose from his bed and started toward the door. His body was found just inside the entrance, dressed in his sleeping robe, Echo's knife embedded in his chest."

Reynard hung his head for a moment, fist clenched, then looked up. "Where is Braxus?"

"I'm not sure. He was in the throne room but has since vanished. We think he's in his quarters, but he isn't answering our requests for entry. He could be almost anywhere."

My body tensed at his words. "Gentlemen, I hate to interrupt, but if Braxus has sequestered himself, we're running out of time." I turned to Durtran. "How did you get down here so fast? I wasn't expecting you to make it for another forty-five minutes at least."

"Hallis. I had to leave him in charge, which required an explanation of why I was abandoning my post. Luckily, he's familiar with all the passages. His mother is one of the cooks, and he was raised with the other boys here in the castle. They looked at exploring the dark hallways as an adventure. He told me where the entrance to these lower levels is located."

"Good. That means Strand won't have any idea we're free. Let's get going." Peri jumped to my shoulder as we collected the lamps, clutching the fabric of my shirt and vibrating with anticipation as we walked out of our prison.

We went to the end of the hall and stepped over the bodies of the two guards Durtran had dispatched. From their clothing, neither were native Madreans, I noted. For a moment, I was disappointed they didn't have blasters, but for Durtran's sake, it was a good thing they didn't.

"Which way?" I asked him now.

He pointed the way we'd been heading when we stopped to check out the hall. "There. We need to stay in this main passage."

"Lead the way."

"Do we need to continue searching for the girls?" Reynard asked as we jogged down the hall, our boots echoing on the stone floor. Durtran was in front of us, Bim behind.

"No. If Braxus is preparing to use the crystal, they've been removed from the room where they were held. We'd only be wasting time. Better to concentrate on finding him and Strand."

"Wouldn't it save time if you used your ability to locate them?"

"It might, if I were familiar with every room in the castle. Or even on Madrea, for that matter, since they may have gone to another building. So, I could check on them in my dream state, but unless they are in a place I've visited, I still won't know how to find them."

"I see what you mean." He frowned. "We'll have to look in all the obvious places. Braxus isn't capable of traveling very far, so I doubt they've left the castle."

"You know Braxus. Where's the most likely place for him to be?"

"Normally, he confines himself to his living quarters or the book depository, which is just next to his rooms. Only rarely does he appear in public places."

"Then we should start there."

In front, Durtran slowed. "The stairs are just ahead. They're dirty, narrow and steep. We'll have to go single file, so watch your step. They let out on the level directly under the castle. From there, it's not far to another set of stairs that come out in a storage room near the kitchens."

Silently we went up the stairs, holding our lamps high to illuminate the treacherous steps. Durtran was right, the dirt was thick and choking here, puffing into the air with each movement we made. I drew in a relieved breath of clean oxygen as soon as we stepped out into a small room.

There was only one entrance and we followed Durtran through it, turning left when we were clear. He headed straight to another room and waited until we were all with him. "Almost there. I should warn you, if we meet any of the troops there may be trouble. Braxus has declared you both fugitives, although I now know he isn't expecting you to be captured."

"No, he isn't. They wanted us to die in that room. He just needed someone to blame so suspicion wouldn't fall on him. I imagine after some time passed and no one found us, he'd say we escaped on my ship."

I thought for a second. "Reynard, Bim, put your weapons away," I told them, sheathing my own knife. "If we run into anyone, Durtran can say he's captured us and is taking us to Braxus."

"No offense to Durtran," Reynard said. "But none of my soldiers will believe he overpowered the three of us."

I shrugged. "So we turned ourselves in after we got lost in the underground passages. I'd rather give it a shot than have to kill men who are only doing what they've been ordered to do."

The commander gave a curt nod and slid his sword back into its scabbard as Bim did the same with his axe. "As would I. Let's see if it works." He gestured and Durtran turned into the room.

Again, we followed Durtran and stepped out of a small storage room just outside the kitchen. Two weepy-eyed women gaped at the commander, then dipped in a curtsey before walking into the kitchen.

I watched them go, concerned they might sound an alarm, but both simply went to work cooking and ignored us.

"Lillith?" I subvocalized hesitantly, wondering if I would be able to contact the ship now.

"Echo! I heard what you told Marcus and was on the verge of coming to free you myself."

A wave of relief swept over me at her voice. "I handled it. But I need to know Marcus is safe."

"He is. Lowden's men freed them. They're locked inside the Terpsichore holding off the rest of the troops. And two Federation destroyers have arrived. They're in orbit around Madrea. If Strand tries to take off, they'll have him."

"Excellent. Now I have work to do. Which way to Braxus's quarters?" I asked Reynard.

"This way." Reynard took off at a fast, quiet run. "It's on the other side of the castle."

We were halfway down the carpeted expanse when I felt the first trickle of power. It slammed into me with the force of a meteor and sent me staggering to my knees. Above my head, Peri circled frantically, screaming in anger as her eyes went blood red.

"Echo!" Reynard dropped down beside me, fear lining his face, but I couldn't move, couldn't react to his concern yet.

Holy Zin! They were releasing the Sumantti. But the action was hesitant, like someone had opened the stasis box a crack and then slammed it closed again.

For freedom to be so close, only to have it wrenched away, was more than the crystal could stand. I sensed her rage growing, felt her struggling to free herself. And she was too fragging close to figuring out the stasis field. If they didn't release her, she would explode out on her own. Either way would be disastrous.

Peri darted back and forth in agitation as I clutched the commander's arm. "They're releasing the crystal. We have to hurry."

He stood and pulled me to my feet, supporting me until I found my balance, while Durtran shifted restlessly in front of us, his gaze constantly scanning the hall for danger. Bim had loosened his axe and moved up to stand on my other side, but even he looked worried.

"How much farther?" I gasped.

"If we run, not long," Reynard told me. "The end of the hall, turn right, and it's four doors down."

Peri took off, zooming down the hall so fast you could barely see her wings moving, then hovered and chattered encouragement as we chased after her.

We were almost at the end of the corridor when three soldiers stepped out of a room directly into our path. Reynard's sword was in his hand in a blur of movement, but Durtran didn't give him a chance to use it.

"To me!" he yelled.

Immediately the men came to attention, drew their weapons and fell in with our group, no questions asked. As one, we thundered around the corner.

I'd barely taken two steps when the full blast of an enraged Sumantti hit me. Grinding my teeth together, I forced myself onward even as I instinctively pulled out the Imadei and closed my fist around it.

No! I sent. *Don't do this. I'm almost there. I can help you.*

She shoved me away so hard it nearly took my head off, and I closed my eyes in reaction to the pain. Instead of slowing, Bim took my left arm on one side and Reynard took the right. Together, they hustled me toward a door that I could feel bending outward from the power filling the room. Somewhere nearby, I could hear Peri's frantic calls and they made enough of an impression that I opened my eyes again to look for her.

She hovered just this side of the door, beating the men in front of me with her wings as she tried to drive them back.

"Stop!" I screamed, catching the same thing she'd picked up on. The group ground to a halt a split second before the wooden door exploded into a million splinters.

Power poured from the opening, sweeping Strand's men into the hall ahead of it. Around us, the stone walls of the castle trembled and shook, cracks forming that looked like twisted trees.

The shouts of the men were muffled by the roar of displaced air as they engaged Strand's contingent in battle just beyond the tornadic surges of power that pounded the far wall. Peri joined them, diving to attack, and then soaring back to the ceiling, wings spread, riding the gusts of energy like they were there for her benefit.

I saw Reynard engage two men at once, his sword flashing with effortless grace. At his back, Bim wielded his axe with more power than technique. Part of me wanted to assist in the battle, but there was no time. I had to get inside that room.

Doing my best to ignore the fight, I put one foot in front of the other, leaning into the gale emitted by the Sumantti. It took all my strength to move through the surging power, and I knew I'd never make it to the enraged crystal in time to stop it from destroying the solar system.

Use the Imadei!

The voice that sounded in my mind had a doubled quality, as though two people were speaking with one voice, but it was a voice I recognized.

Kiera?

Use the Imadei! Her voice came again, transmitted by the Mother Stone. *Hurry! We'll feed you all the power we can.*

I don't know how!

There was a sudden twisting sensation inside my head as if a final link had clicked into place.

Now! Kiera's voice was so loud and frantic I could barely grasp the words. *Before it's too late!*

Pushing aside my terror, I reached for the small crystal with my mind in a way I'd never done before, and I felt a brief lull in the maelstrom. More determined now, I delved deeper into the stone, mentally pulled it around me like a cloak.

Abruptly, I could move again, even though I could see that both the storm and the battle still raged around me. It was as if I were enclosed in a thin black crystalline bubble of stillness that protected me from the Daughter Stone's power. And all throughout the crystal I could sense the DNA of psynaviats, the alien creatures that inhabited it.

Good. Kiera's voice was marginally calmer. *Go to the Daughter Stone and put your hands on her.*

Easily now, I moved forward, went through the door into Braxus's quarters, then stopped to get my bearings.

Gaia stood in the center of the room, her hands clamped bloodlessly to the Sumantti, her face a rictus of pain. She seemed to glow with an unnatural black light as her long red-gold hair whipped around her.

But I could see that her pain-glazed eyes were locked on Losif Strand. He stood across the room, one hand buried in Banca's hair to pull her head back, a knife to her exposed throat.

When he saw me, he grinned and tightened his grip, but if he spoke, I didn't hear him. I was suddenly too focused on Banca to pay attention to the man holding her.

For the first time, the child's face was showing emotion. But it wasn't the fear you'd expect. No, her face was suffused with intense pleasure. Like a child in a candy store, there was no mistaking her glee.

Paying no attention to the knife at her throat, she laughed and clapped her hands before reaching out for the Sumantti.

And slowly, the Sumantti's cataclysmic power reversed direction, seemingly against its will, the beams fluctuating wildly as its focus narrowed and aimed right at the child Strand held. And instead of disintegrating, she drank it in at an astonishing rate and reached for more.

Holy Zin. The child was some kind of psychic vampire.

I felt more than heard Gaia scream. It yanked me out of my shock, and I gathered the force of the Imadei, prepared to launch a defense against the Sumantti that would save not only the girl, but Madrea.

But before I could act, Braxus hobbled toward the crystal, his bent body mostly hidden by his loose robe. With one twisted hand he reached toward Gaia. "Heal me!" he screeched. "It is my right to rule!"

"Naw!" It was Banca who shrieked in denial, as if she had no intention of sharing the Sumantti's power. She made a slapping motion with one hand. Even though she hit nothing but air, Braxus was lifted and shaken like an empty sack before he was flung against a wall. He slid lifelessly to the floor and lay still.

But her motion had yanked the knife Strand held away from her throat and pushed him to the side. He stumbled and went down while the thin line of blood left on Banca's throat closed up and vanished as if she'd never been cut.

With a look of distaste aimed at the girl he'd held hostage, Strand scrabbled backward away from her, his knuckles white on the knife hilt he still grasped defensively.

Okay, enough was enough. I couldn't wait any longer.

As soon as I moved toward Gaia, Banca's attention refocused on me. She stood frozen in place, her face twisted with rage as she batted at me from across the room. But unlike Braxus, I was prepared for her move and I had the Imadei to protect me.

That didn't mean I didn't feel it, though. I winced at the power that leaked into my insular world, then fought it off and kept going.

She struck out harder, pounding me with the force she wielded, the power she stole from the Sumantti, and a crack opened in my shield. Ignoring everything else, I fought to close it without effect even as I continued forward.

You can do it, Kiera's voice encouraged. *Don't give up.*

With renewed determination, I pushed on. I'd almost reached Gaia when Peri darted by me, seemingly unaffected by the power fluctuating in the room. With a scream of rage, eyes blood red, she dived at Strand, digging her talons deep into his face.

Somehow, the leader of Helios One had fought his way to his feet and was pushing toward me, his knife now aimed in my direction.

Fear washed through me, breaking my concentration and giving Banca a chance to widen the crack in my shield. Fear, not for myself but for Peri as she dodged Strand's knife and swooped to attack again. How could one lone dragon bird hold off a seasoned fighter armed with a long knife?

She couldn't, and if I went to help her, Banca would win.

The thought barely went through my mind when Reynard charged by me, a feral grin on his chiseled face as he engaged Strand.

Trusting him to handle the situation, I plowed my way through Banca's resistance to Gaia, reached down and covered her hands with mine, at the same time expanding the bubble of protection so it enveloped her and the Sumantti.

Or at least I tried to cover the Sumantti. But no matter how hard I struggled to close it, Banca kept a pathway open to the stone, using the crack she'd made in my shield to drain power. We fought for dominance until I was ready to collapse from exhaustion, while the child just kept getting stronger.

Abruptly, Peri left off her attack of Strand and turned her attentions to Banca. Somehow, she cut through the flow of power like it wasn't even there and reached for the girl's face with all four feet.

It wasn't much, but it diverted Banca just enough to allow me time to begin mentally closing the breach in my shield. I'd almost succeeded when, from outside, I felt a dramatic increase in the energy flowing into me, and knew the Mother Stone was helping.

Stop this, I commanded the Sumantti. *As long as you fight, she'll continue to drain your power. You have to stop.*

She heard me. I could even feel her attempts to obey. But Banca wouldn't let the stone go, wouldn't let me completely close the crack. Swatting Peri away with one hand, she refocused on the opening in my shield, keeping it open with the power she was draining. Even as I poured my strength and the Limantti's through the Daughter Stone, the child sucked it in. The more the Sumantti struggled, the more power Banca drained from the stone.

Inside the crystal I could sense the tiny Psynaviats dying, their DNA winking from my consciousness like stars gone nova as the life force left them. Pain screamed from the rest, sending me into another panic.

And it wasn't just them. I had become a conduit to the Mother Stone on Orpheus Two. She, too, was feeling the strain as Banca drained away their energy, and still Banca drank it in and reached for more.

Help them! Kiera screamed in my mind. *She's killing them!*

I reacted without plan, without reason, without thought. Running on pure instinct, I reached into the crystal with my psi ability and made a minute change in the DNA of the alien life forms. When it was complete, I forced them out of their environment and into Gaia through her hands.

The flow of power cut off instantly as the last of the psynaviats left the stone. It was as if someone had thrown a switch and all around us went still and silent. Gaia collapsed into my arms, her eyes closed and so still I thought I'd killed her. But when I checked, she wasn't dead, just unconscious. The alien life flowed in her body, confused by its new home. And yet, already it was slowly regaining its strength.

At the same time, the Mother Stone withdrew to ponder what had just happened. Her puzzlement left a lingering after-effect in my mind. I couldn't help her, because I had no idea how I'd done what I'd done. I was simply grateful it worked.

The ringing of metal on metal drew my attention, and I turned to see Reynard parry a thrust from Strand's knife. Before I could go into overdrive, Reynard spun, slid his sword under Strand's partially raised arm, and impaled him through the chest.

Gently, I placed Gaia on the floor and then moved to stand beside Reynard as he stared down at Strand. The leader of

Helios One lay sprawled on the floor, one hand gripping the shaft of Reynard's sword where it was buried in his body. His breath came in labored puffs and hate gleamed in his eyes.

"Bitch."

The word was barely a whisper and I arched a brow, but he wasn't looking at me. He was glaring at Banca.

The crystal still sat on the table, but now it was nothing but a big piece of quartz. Over the top of the stone, Banca stared at me, her eyes blank, no expression on her face.

It was hard to believe she was the same child I'd battled a few moments before, and I wasn't sure what to do about her. She looked so damn innocent when she wasn't trying to kill you.

The sounds of battle in the hall behind me died away, and Durtran and Bim charged into the room. I held up a hand as they flanked us.

"It's over, Strand," I told him. "You lost. Any last words?"

With a shudder, Strand released his grip on the sword, blood pouring in a steady stream from the wound, his face white. "That child is a monster. You should kill her now, while you have the chance. She sucked the life force from two of my men while we were holding her. But I suppose she's the Federation's problem now." He gave one last gasp and went limp, his eyes fixed and unmoving.

Reynard leaned down and checked for a pulse on the man's neck before pulling his sword free. "He's dead."

With a sigh, I turned to Durtran. "Did you kill all his men?"

"No, some of them threw down their weapons. Those we took into custody."

"Good. They'll do nicely as witnesses against Strand's cohorts in the Federation. Lillith?"

"On my way."

"Land as close to the castle as possible. I need to get Gaia into sick bay. I have no idea what the psynaviats are doing to her."

"What about the other one?"

I glanced at Banca. She hadn't moved since I'd rendered the Daughter Stone inert. "We'll have to take her, too. She shouldn't be dangerous for a while. She fed well today. Prepare a room where she can be restrained for now," I told the ship, disgust tingeing my tone. "Maybe Dr. Shilly will know what to do with her. In the meantime, we've got some mopping up to do here on Madrea and time is wasting."

From the size of the crowd surrounding Lillith all of Bastion City and the Bashalde were present to see us off. It had been a busy few months since Strand had died and the remaining crewmembers had taken his ship and fled. Fortunately, they were successfully nabbed by the Federation before they could clear Madrea's gravitational field.

But my work here was done, and it was time to go. Madrea was now ruled by a council of six comprising equal parts Madrean and Bashalde. To my delight, Durtran was chosen as council leader. Their first act had been to lift the ban, which allowed negotiations to begin for the sunstones. As a result, Madrea's future looked bright.

The chatter of the crowd faded as I paused halfway down the ramp Lillith had extended and scanned the faces looking up at me. Of course, I'd dressed for the occasion. I was wearing my sedate royal-blue jumpsuit with the hot-pink boots and holster for my blaster, so maybe I'd stunned them into silence with my brilliance. Overhead, Peri swooped and dived in excitement, circling the throng as though sending them her own good-bye.

It was amazing how many of the people waiting were familiar to me. There were Cammi and Treya standing with Marcus, while Leddy glowered at them. Next to them were Bim and Lowden. Jancen stood with Durtran and the other council members to one side.

But the one face I wanted most to see wasn't there. Peri

picked up on my disappointment and settled to my shoulder, cooing softly from her perch as I looked over the sea of faces again.

Reynard wasn't there. He'd stayed with me on board Lillith for the entire two months except for the time he'd spent handling Politaus's funeral. Luckily, he was fascinated by the ship and it took his mind off the loss of his friend and king, but this morning he'd left before I woke and I hadn't seen him since.

Maybe he just couldn't bear saying good-bye, I thought, my heart breaking a little more at the idea of never seeing him again.

Pasting a smile on my face, I continued down the ramp and went to Marcus, giving him a quick hug. "Are you sure you want to stay here? Dr. Daniels would be happy to have you back."

"I'm sure. This is my home now." He glanced at Cammi when he said it. "But I'm going to miss you."

"I'll miss you, too."

"Have you heard any more about the girls' condition?" he asked.

Lillith had ferried both Banca and Gaia to the Federation ship, and they'd been immediately rushed to Centaurius. Dr. Shilly had been sending me updates ever since they'd arrived.

"The psi inhibitors seem to be working on Banca, although she still doesn't talk or do much of anything. Dr. Shilly doesn't think she'll ever be normal. She may not be completely human. They're still running tests. But I couldn't get a lock on her DNA even though she was well within my range several times, so it doesn't bode well for a good outcome."

A spurt of gilt went through me at the thought of the other girl, even though part of me knew there was nothing else I could have done. "Gaia stays unconscious for the most part, although when she's awake she doesn't remember who she is or what's happened to her. Dr. Shilly isn't sure she ever will. At least she's out of danger now. He's trying to find a way to get the psynaviats back into the crystal, but so far they don't seem inclined to return."

I turned to Treya. "If you ever decided to give up dancing, you could make a fortune on Centaurius doing makeup for the ladies."

"Yes?" She looked thoughtful. "Maybe someday I'll give it a try."

"Cammi." I looked at the woman and then leaned closer. "Take care of Marcus for me."

"I will, you can count on it."

"Leddy," I gave her a quick kiss on the cheek. "I'm going to miss your cooking most of all."

"Don't tell anyone," she whispered, "but I put a fifty-pound bag of coffee beans in your ship."

"You're an angel of mercy," I whispered back. "Thank you."

From there, I was passed around and hugged by more people than I could count. Even Bim took a turn, and then blushed bright red. Lowden and Jancen both informed me that since I was now an honorary Bashalde, I had to return for gatherings occasionally so my adopted family could make sure I was healthy and happy.

When I reached Durtran he bowed. "Agent Adams, we owe you more than we can ever repay. If there's anything I can do, please ask."

I paused, nearly hiccupping on the emotion choking me. "Tell Reynard I said good-bye," I said. "Tell him I'll always love him."

Surprise flitted across his face. "The commander? But I thought—"

"Please," I interrupted. No way could I get this out more than once. "Just tell him."

"Of course." He bowed again and then turned. "Commander!"

"Here!" The voice came from the rear of the crowd and was followed by clanging and the sound of pounding feet. Reynard burst through the mob, his arms loaded with swords, books, and a bulky bag that obviously contained clothing.

Durtran grinned at him. "Commander, Agent Adams wanted me to tell you that she'll always love you."

Reynard laughed. "Of course she will. We're promised."

I gaped at him, shocked down to my toes. "What are you doing?"

"You didn't expect me to move halfway across the universe without my things, did you?"

"You're going with me?"

"Well, of course I am." He frowned at me. "When Politaus died, my vow was fulfilled. There's nothing to hold me here now, and every reason to go." His voice softened. "Wherever you go, I'll follow, Echo Adams. You're my life."

"Oh, Reynard. I love you so much." He dropped his load as I launched myself into his arms, sending Peri squawking and scolding into the air. Around us, cheers erupted, but I was too busy to listen.

Nearly everything I'd ever wanted was now mine. There was only one thing left to accomplish and it would have to wait until I got back to Centaurius.

Finally, I released him and helped him retrieve his things. Together we carried them up the ramp, stopping at the top to wave good-bye. As soon as we were inside, Lillith shut the air lock doors and lifted off.

"Why didn't you tell me you were coming with me?" I asked him.

He shrugged. "I thought it was understood." Lifting my hand he gently touched the ring. "After all, we're promised."

"Yes," I said softly. "We certainly are."

EPILOGUE

The halls of the Bureau of Alien Affairs seemed strangely silent as I stopped in front of a real wooden door with a discreet gold plaque on it.

Nervously, I smoothed the lines of the bright red vegan silk suit I wore, while Peri muttered darkly on my shoulder. "If you're worried, you should have stayed with Reynard," I told her. "I'm perfectly capable of handling this myself without your protection."

Her thoughts were full of doubts as I lifted a hand and knocked.

"Come in," Dr. Daniels called.

He stood as I entered the room, his blue eyes twinkling. "Ah, Agent Adams. I've been expecting you."

"You have?" Surprised, I paused in the middle of the room.

"Please, sit." He moved to a sideboard and took a bottle of Sirius '45 from a wine bucket. "I believe this is your favorite, and we have cause for celebration."

"We do?" I parked my butt in an overstuffed chair and eyed him suspiciously as he poured two glasses.

"Yes. The people who made up Losif Strand's alliance

were found guilty on all charges this morning. They'll spend the rest of their lives on Inferno, along with the men who originally signed onto the Federation ship to steal the Sumantti."

I nodded, distracted for a moment. "That is good news. I'm glad it's over."

"As am I. How is the commander settling in?" he asked, handing over one of the glasses and taking the chair next to mine.

"He's ecstatic. We can't even go for a walk because every time he sees a new gadget, we have to stop so he can figure out how it works. When he's not here at headquarters doing his job, he's logged into the computers, studying. I think he's leaning toward an engineering degree."

"Well, he'll have a job with us as long as he wants it, no matter what field he specializes in. You were absolutely right about his abilities. There's not a martial arts instructor in the bureau who can beat him, plus he's like having a human lie detector around. We've never had such a well-behaved junior class before." He smiled. "But you aren't here to talk about the commander, are you?"

"No, I'm not." I rolled the glass between my hands while Peri shifted uncomfortably on my shoulder. "It's about my job."

He nodded. "Yes, this talk *was* a bit delayed by your mission. We both know you weren't created to be a field agent, even though things turned out fine this time. Any suggestions on what we should do with you?"

"As a matter of fact"—I took a deep breath and plunged off the precipice—"I want your job."

He threw his head back and gave a deep belly laugh. "You never disappoint, Agent Adams. Unfortunately for you, I don't plan on retiring anytime soon. On the other hand, there's a lot for you to do here at Alien Affairs, so I'm sure we can keep you busy at something. Maybe a job as my assistant?"

"Really?" Stunned, I could only stare at him.

"Really. Not only are you organized to a fault, you're supremely educated on Federation politics. And of one thing I'm sure. With you around, life will never be dull. Welcome aboard, Agent Adams. You start tomorrow."

I drained my glass, and then let out a whoop of joy as Peri did blissful loops around the room. Life was good. Yes, it was very, very good.

JOCEYLNN DRAKE'S

NEW YORK TIMES BESTSELLING
DARK DAYS NOVELS

NIGHTWALKER
978-0-06-154277-0

For centuries Mira has been a nightwalker—an unstoppable enforcer for a mysterious organization that manipulates earth-shaking events from the darkest shadows. But the foe she now faces is human: the vampire hunter called Danaus, who has already destroyed so many undead.

DAYHUNTER
978-0-06-154283-1

A master of fire, Mira is the last hope for the world. Now she and her unlikely ally Danaus have come to Venice, home of the nightwalker rulers. But there is no safety in the ancient city and Danaus, the only creature she dares trust, is something more than the man he claims to be…

DAWNBREAKER
978-0-06-154288-6

Destiny draws Mira and Danaus toward an apocalyptic confrontation with the *naturi* at Machu Picchu. Once the *naturi* are unchained, blood, chaos, and horror will reign supreme on Earth. But all is not lost as a rogue enemy princess can change the balance of power and turn the dread tide.